Novels by Louis de Wohl

THE GLORIOUS FOLLY
THE LAST CRUSADER
THE SPEAR
THE SECOND CONQUEST
THE GOLDEN THREAD
THE RESTLESS FLAME
THE QUIET LIGHT
THE LIVING WOOD

THE
GLORIOUS
FOLLY

*A novel of the time
of St. Paul*

by

LOUIS de WOHL

PHILADELPHIA AND NEW YORK

J. B. LIPPINCOTT COMPANY

For the Foolishness of God Is Wiser Than Men;
and the Weakness of God Is Stronger Than Men

—*I Corinthians 1:25.*

Author's Note

This is a novel whose central figure is St. Paul—not a "life" of the great Apostle, thus those who love him as he ought to be loved are bound to miss a great many things.

On the other hand, my book may stimulate some to re-read the Pauline Letters or The Acts, the best true adventure story ever told.

Those who know my historical novels know that I have always tried to remain true to history wherever possible and to "invent" only where history was silent. This is the case here, also, with two exceptions. I have identified the Roman Cassius Longinus with the historical Governor of Syria, A.D. 45-49, of the same name who, however, had a different background and was, at least temporarily, the brother-in-law of Caesar Gaius Caligula.

And I have identified Acte, daughter of Cassius Longinus and of Naomi, with that Acte who was Nero's first great love and whose Christian leanings are affirmed by many historians.

BOOK ONE

CHAPTER ONE

THE RIVER ORONTES was a blue, soft-flowing god, more lenient than the yellow god Tiber, less willful than the muddy god Nile. Orontes was a pleasant god, producing the most amazing fertility all along its shores and nowhere more so than around Antioch, the City of Joy.

Antioch was rich. No other city in the world could boast of running water in every house, of a main street like the Avenue of the Colonnades, paved with marble and splitting the entire city in halves, of being so well lighted by thousands of street-lamps that a man could read a book at midnight and lovers and pickpockets were ill at ease.

Antioch was, at least according to Antiochians, what Alexandria and Damascus only tried to be: the true metropolis of the East.

The ancient palace of the Seleucid kings, on a charming little island formed by the river in the north of the city, was now the residence of the Governor General of Syria, the Proconsul Lucius Vitellius. The two armored sentinels at the main gate looked like statues, but they were thinking of the ambubalae, the flute-girls, in the taverns off the colonnades.

A small ship was waiting at the palace's private jetty. On board, a number of Roman officers in russet tunics were huddled together, talking in whispers. Their chief alone had been asked to enter the palace, which was not a good sign. The younger officers had hoped for a few amusing nights—there was no city for that like Antioch —and the older ones were worried about their careers, more or less closely linked up with that of their chief.

In the anteroom of the proconsul's study the Tribune Varro was on duty. He was thinking of a girl named Fulvia, a thousand miles away in Pompeii and earnestly considering the chances that she was still faithful to him. The chances, he thought, were rather small.

Cleon, the fat little major-domo, came in, mumbling that he must see His Excellency.

"His Excellency is not free," Varro said.

Cleon smoothed the folds of his yellow robes. He looked dejected. "The list of guests for tonight's banquet," he murmured. "His Excellency always wants to sign it himself—you know that. Rank, place, everything. What am I to do?"

"Wait," Varro said stolidly. "Or come back later."

The major-domo pursed his thick lips. "The great tribune is using his official voice," he stated. "That means somebody important is with His Excellency. Which makes it worse."

"Why?" Even talking to this olive-skinned Antiochian bumblebee was better than thinking of Fulvia.

"Because important visitors stay longer, noble tribune. Besides, it might occur to His Excellency to invite the visitor for the banquet and then my list would be upset."

"Very unlikely, I should think," the young officer said dryly.

"Oh, ah, so the important visitor is not in favor, is he? Who could he be, I wonder. Not one of the Armenian nobles, surely— *they* are all to be at the banquet. It wouldn't be the great Tetrarch, by any chance?"

"Don't be an idiot, Cleon. Herod knows better than that. He wouldn't come anywhere near His Excellency, not after—well, never mind."

The major-domo delicately adjusted one of the curls which sprouted from his massive head like so many tiny, oil-black flowers.

"You never know with him," he said, leaving it open whether he meant the Tetrarch or His Excellency.

Varro wrinkled his strong, Roman nose. "Too much elegant stink on that thing you call your head," he said, "and not enough brains in it. If Herod were here, we would have the guard out, wouldn't we? And the anteroom here would be full of his retinue, jabbering away like six dozen monkeys. It's the Governor of Judaea. Now, are you satisfied?"

"Another excellency!" Cleon's eyes widened. "But then surely, surely, His Excellency will invite His Excellency for dinner. He always does. Now where do I place him? The Armenian nobles . . . all the important ladies are taken. What am I to do? If only I had known. . . ."

"Shut up." Varro frowned. "They'll hear you in there if you go on yelling. I've told you he won't stay, haven't I? Not here in the palace, anyway."

The major-domo raised his brows. "Trouble," he said softly.

"Never mind the reason." The young tribune had a vague feeling that he had said too much.

"There's always trouble in Judaea," Cleon murmured. "The Jews are a troublesome people. We should know, we Syrians. Very troublesome and obstinate. Nothing good ever came from Judaea and nothing ever will."

The sharp, clear sound of a bell came from behind the heavy double curtains. Varro turned abruptly and lifting the tasseled brocade entered the huge, oblong room the governor used as his study.

The priceless carpets from Persia and Arabia were arranged in such a way that a broad aisle of cool, naked marble was left free, leading straight to the governor's desk.

Varro saluted.

The Proconsul Lucius Vitellius nodded amiably. "I want the Legate Marcellus to come here, Varro, if you please."

"Yes, sir." Varro saluted again, received a second amiable nod, turned and vanished behind the curtains.

"One of the Varro family of Umbria," Vitellius remarked. "Father was cavalry prefect of the Twenty-sixth, the mother, let me see, she was a Licinia, a great-granddaughter of Crassus."

"Marcellus," said the Governor of Judaea, brushing Varro's ancestry aside. "Is he to be my successor?"

Vitellius looked at the pale, heavily lined face, the watery eyes with pouches under them, the sour mouth. "He's only sixty-three," he thought, "a mere fifteen years older than I am. Am I going to look like that when I'm his age? The gods forbid."

"Yes," he said quietly.

"But look here, the man's had no experience. Why, he came from Rome not much more than a year ago. . . ."

"He came with me," Vitellius said silkily, and the governor looked up in sudden dismay.

"I didn't mean . . ."

"Of course not."

"What I meant is, he has had no experience with Jews. Syria isn't Judaea."

"So you've told me, on various occasions."

The governor sat up. "I am perfectly aware that I've made some mistakes," he said. "I defy anybody not to, when he's dealing with the most incomprehensible people on earth. We never see the inside of a Jewish house, except in war, and no Jew will accept our hospitality. We are unclean. They really believe that. *We* are unclean. . . ."

"My friend Agrippa in Rome has told me a good deal about Jewish beliefs and customs," Vitellius said.

"Of course. I only mention it because it doesn't make things easier, does it? We have only official relations with them and those consist mostly of listening to complaints."

"You should be glad to be rid of the whole thing."

"I would be, Vitellius, I certainly would be, if it weren't for —for the circumstances of my retirement."

"I must report the truth to the Emperor, you know," Vitellius said, with a shrug. "Can't afford not to. And I admit the truth does not sound too good."

"Show me the report, Vitellius. . . ."

"You know perfectly well I can't do that."

"But how can I defend myself before the Emperor, if . . ."

"Friend, you have been in the service longer than I, you should know that you will have the opportunity to defend yourself—unless, of course, the Emperor decides differently. I cannot foretell what Tiberius is going to do, can I? Try and be fair."

"You are asking me to be fair." The governor's lip twitched.

"Do you think it's fair to me to be sent off to Italy on the first available ship. . . ."

"The *Thetis* is a perfectly good ship. A bit old, but still quite seaworthy."

"I know that ship, Vitellius. I came here, or rather I came to Caesarea in it eleven years ago. Eleven years among Jews."

"You hated them, didn't you?" The proconsul's beautiful, well-kept fingers began to play with the bell, such a lovely little thing, King Artabanus had given it to him; it wasn't Parthian, though, but came from Sina, from the Silk Country. So much more pleasant to use than Indian gongs. "Perhaps that is the real reason why you could never get on with them, you know. Hatred is a bad adviser. You allowed them to ruffle your feelings, to annoy you—and then you express your annoyance by some hasty action, as for instance that unfortunate Samaritan affair six weeks ago."

"I thought it would be that," the governor said bitterly. "They complained of course, the confounded rascals. I gave you the most accurate report about the whole affair. You know we always get that kind of trouble. Some person, half mad with studying old scrolls and fasting and praying himself silly, gets the idea that he must save the people—save them from what? From paying taxes of course, and from the occupation forces. From us. But it's invariably dressed up in a religious cloak, even when they rob caravans. Robbery, tax-dodging, petty personal ambitions, anything sails under the religious flag and is ultimately directed against us. That's your Jews, and your Samaritans are exactly the same. Some idiot—we don't even know his name—told them to ascend Mount Garizim with him. There he'd show them the holy vessels used by their prophet Moses. Moses is supposed to have buried them up there. A likely tale! But they believed it; they assembled, four or five thousand strong and armed, Vitellius, fully armed."

"Some of them," Vitellius interjected curtly.

The governor took no notice. "I got the report that they are moving toward Jerusalem, that they are out to kill—religious fanatics. Had I let it go, there would have been bloodshed in

13

both Samaria and Judaea and I had had trouble enough lately."

"That," Vitellius said, "is quite true. Unfortunately."

"I decided to nip this thing in the bud," the governor went on. "I managed to catch them on the march and I routed them. They had a few hundred dead. . . ."

"Eleven hundred and forty-six," Vitellius said. "Quite a lot of dead Samaritans."

"There weren't that many."

"Excuse me," Vitellius said coldly, "but there were."

"They told you a pack of lies, of course."

"Of course. They reported over two thousand killed. But I had the reports of my own agents, friend. I may not have been very long in this country, but experience can be gained elsewhere too. You did not trouble much to find out what was going on, you just squashed them. There is no love lost between Samaritans and Jews, as you know, in fact their mutual enmity is proverbial, but even in Jerusalem they didn't like what you did."

The governor gave a mirthless grin. "Caiphas told you that, of course, didn't he? No, don't tell me. I know it. I know Caiphas. And if you knew him as well as I do, you would think as I do—namely that Caiphas engineered the whole thing."

"And why," Vitellius inquired, "should the High Priest of the Jews do that?"

"To make things difficult for me, of course. He has always hated me. He's probably complained to you about me a dozen times. So he probably thought it might be a good idea if this time the Samaritans did the complaining. The man is a born intriguer, Vitellius."

"What else can one expect him to be?" the proconsul asked. "You don't expect him to love us, do you? If you knew just a little more about politics you would have learned to exclude personal feelings. People like that can be dealt with. As it is, you have managed to be on bad terms with him, with the entire Sanhedrin, with the population of Judaea and now also with the Samaritans. It's just a little too much. Can't you see, man, that the enmity between Jews and Samaritans suited us admirably? We could always play one against the other. Why, the Emperor himself taught us that, years back, when he was the head of the Staff College. Divide and rule. You have practically united them—against us. It will give me a lot of work, that wonderful victory of yours at Mount Garizim."

By now the governor had an idea of what Vitellius' report to Tiberius would be like. His hands began to tremble and to his dismay he could not stop them. "Vitellius," he said in an unsteady voice, "suggest to the Emperor, if you feel you must, that he should recall me and send out another, a younger man, or that you would like Marcellus to be my successor. But don't have me sent back as you told me you—it's . . . it's such a disgrace after all these years of service." The obstinate mouth was not made for pleading, the heavy jowl not appropriate to self-pity.

"Vitellius," said Vitellius, "would like to agree. The Proconsul Governor of Syria can't."

The Governor of Judaea closed his eyes. For one wild moment he thought of openly defying his superior. The thing had been done—though rarely, very rarely with success. And he had not enough material to use against this courteous, charming man who could smile as he pronounced a death sentence. Besides, Vitellius had a great many friends at court, his son Aulus was actually in the company of Tiberius on Capri, a very handsome boy, they said, too handsome for his own good. Even so, if one dared to take the risk . . .

Vitellius seemed to guess his thoughts. "You will consider yourself as suspended from office from this moment on," he said coldly. "I shall give you an escort of honor to the port. You can reach Seleucia tonight before sunset. I have a small ship there, the *Melita,* to take you back to Caesarea. I would have sent you to Italy straight from here, but the port facilities in Seleucia are still not good enough for the handling of large ships. That's another thing I have to see to. The *Thetis* will leave Caesarea three days after your arrival."

The governor murmured something about unseemly speed.

Vitellius smiled. He said nothing.

Varro came in and saluted. "The Legate Marcellus, sir."

"He may come in."

The legate was a large, florid man in the uniform of the Sebasthene cavalry. His sword clanked and his heavy, army sandals were noisy on the naked marble aisle. The governor winced.

"Such a useful system," Vitellius said lightly. "You always know when someone's coming. Can't have people sneaking up on me."

The legate gave a stiff salute.

"My dear Marcellus," the proconsul said amiably, "this is Pontius Pilatus, the *former* Governor of Judaea. He will embark tonight in Seleucia for Caesarea and from there on the *Thetis* for Naples. I entrust you with his . . . safety."

"I'll gladly vouch for that, sir," the legate said phlegmatically.

"Good. You will see him off at Caesarea Harbor. Has Piso given you my written instructions?"

"Yes, sir. It's all in the best of order, sir."

"That's what we like to hear. My dear Pontius, I'm afraid I must ask you to excuse me now— Next time we meet we'll probably be watching a really good show at the Circus Maximus."

Pontius Pilatus rose. "I am sorry, Marcellus, that you have to begin your new duties as my jailer. Vitellius, I ought to thank you, I suppose, that you spare me chains. I wish you luck with Caiphas. You will need it." He walked away, not without dignity and Marcellus, on a nod from his superior, followed him noisily.

Finished, Vitellius thought. There was little doubt how the man would be received by Tiberius. The Emperor had never been a paragon of patience and now, at almost seventy-nine, he was the crustiest, testiest old man between Persia and Britain. Some of young Aulus' letters did not sound too happy. If Pilatus were very lucky, he'd be exiled to some godforsaken place, Pandataria, perhaps, or some small town in Gaul or Spain. Finished. Now one could write to the High Council of the Samaritans. A little hint, perhaps, that the impulsive action of the former governor was due to the fact that he had given too much credence to certain Jewish sources, which, of course, by no means justified that action, for which he would have to defend himself before the Emperor himself. In any case the Proconsul Governor of Syria had taken extremely swift action. The dignitaries of the Samaritan High Council should be satisfied.

As for that Jewish High Priest, it might be worth while to scrutinize his dossier. Vitellius was just going to ring the bell when Varro came in. "An imperial courier, sir."

The proconsul stood stiffly to attention when the man entered. Scarlet tunic, scarlet-dyed leather bag with the imperial eagle in silver on it, this was not the ordinary state mail—it was a letter from the Emperor himself, with the big seal attached. He took it, kissed it ceremoniously and signed the receipt the courier handed him. "I'll talk to you later," he said, smiling. "In the meantime the Tribune Varro here will look after you."

"Thank you, sir."

Alone, Vitellius weighed the scroll in his hands. This could be anything. His own death warrant, though that was not likely, not after what he had heard from his friends at court. There would have been certain warning signals. Something about Aulus? Maybe. Or there had been a complaint? Nonsense, the Samaritan High Council had complained to him, not to the Emperor and if they had written to the old man as well, he could not even have their letter yet, not at this time of the year.

He loved tantalizing himself sometimes, his fleshy fingers playing with the imperial seal as his mind ran busily from one possibility to the other, nibbling at them. The announcement of fresh troops to be sent; of troops taken away from him to be used elsewhere? Such orders would come through the regular channels. Praise? Preferment? Not from Tiberius.

Yet he had done at least one very big thing for the old man since he had taken over Syria: the treaty of alliance with the King of the Parthians. Every trick in the book and a few extra had been necessary to get that two-legged eel to come to terms, but he had succeeded and they had met, fantastically, in the middle of the bridge across the Euphrates River, the frontier between Roman and Parthian territory. The Roman territory was under the limited rule of the Tetrarch, of Herod Antipas, damned fox, and of course Herod would insist on playing the host; he'd had a tent raised on the bridge, a silk tent, must have cost a pretty packet, slaves in the Herodian livery, sumptuous banquet—he'd even managed to get some ice to chill the wine and the fruit. It was Herod's big show. Vitellius had not interfered. After all, if Herod wanted to spend his good money, so much the better for the Roman administrative funds. Besides it was always good policy to negotiate a treaty after, rather than before, a banquet.

The negotiations had been a resounding success. The Parthian even went so far as to bow ceremoniously before the Emperor's statue, a thing unheard of in the relations between Parthia and Rome. Everything had been signed and sealed in a couple of hours.

Vitellius had slept soundly after that and the next day had returned to Antioch to write his report.

Some months later had come a letter, just like this one. It contained only two lines: "Everything you told me in your report about the Parthian treaty I already knew from my friend Herod." The Fox must have spent thousands to get his own report to Capri before the official one, but apparently it was worth it. Now the Emperor called him his friend and had no word of thanks for the Proconsul of Syria. Officially this was a rebuke for tardiness. But behind it lay much more, and what it was, was not difficult to guess. Herod had presented the whole affair as his own effort, he had managed everything, Lucius Vitellius had done only what Herod told him to do. . . .

Vitellius had never mentioned the matter to Herod, of course. So easy for the Fox to lie his way out. "How could I imagine that the official report would not be there at least at the same time as my own, if not before? Surely it would have been discourteous for me not to send in my report too? It was full of high praise for your diplomatic agility, your loyalty, your wisdom, rest assured of that." Damned Fox. King of All Foxes.

"One day I'll get even with you," Vitellius said aloud. His fingers tightened around the scroll. Scroll. He had not yet opened the imperial letter. Whenever he thought of Herod, he seemed to forget everything else—he, who half an hour ago had preached to old Pontius Pilatus the necessity of the exclusion of personal feelings. . . .

The thought amused him. He broke the seal, unrolled the gold-edged parchment and the first thing his eye fell on was the name of Herod. "No," he said softly. "No. No. It can't be." Then he read the letter:

"Tiberius Caesar Augustus to the Proconsul L. Vitellius, Governor of Syria, Greetings:

"My friend the Tetrarch Herod Antipas has reminded me of the wrong done to him and his realm by the Arab chieftain who calls himself King Aretas of Petra. You will seize Aretas and send him to me in chains. Failing this, you will send me his head."

Vitellius bit his lip. Far from getting his own back, he must now win Herod's war for him, that absurd war caused by Herod's own lechery. Seven or eight years ago Herod had married Aretas' daughter. But then he had fallen in love with his stepbrother's wife, Herodias, who promptly left her own perfectly good husband for the sake of the Fox. The young Arab princess found out that she was to be repudiated, decided not to wait for such a humiliation and returned to her father. Aretas, infuriated, mobilized his army. So did Herod, but he had wisely abstained from leading it himself. At the very first encounter the Herodian troops dispersed in all directions except in that of the enemy and Aretas occupied a good-sized strip of Herod's territory. And that was that.

For years nothing more happened. But now that Herod had made quite sure that he was in Tiberius' good books, he had used his credit to the full and the Proconsul Governor of Syria was just good enough to do his dirty work for him.

Varro appeared in the door and at once Vitellius relaxed.

"Yes, son, what is it?"

"The major-domo is outside, sir—has been for quite a while. He wants to see you about the list of the guests at tonight's banquet."

"Of course," Vitellius said. "Let him come in, will you? Ah, and by the way—I want the legates Priscus and Trebellius here tomorrow morning—with their staff officers. And Tribune Piso, too."

"Yes, sir," Varro said, holding aside the curtain for Cleon to enter.

The major-domo waddled in, beaming.

CHAPTER TWO

"I submit, my lord, that this is the time for action," said Saul of Tarshish.

The High Priest, Joseph Caiphas, did not answer at once, but shifted a little in his chair and put his finger-tips together. He was in his mid-sixties and there was silver both in his beautifully kept beard and in the strong eyebrows. He did not dislike firebrands. They had their uses, at the right time. But woe to him who lets a firebrand decide what the right time is. Besides, Saul of Tarshish was a young man, thirty, perhaps, thirty-two at the most, although his hair was already receding a little.

"He will be bald in ten years' time," the High Priest thought, "one of those irascible little baldheads so easily given to shouting, making up with noise what they lack in inches."

"What action?" he asked in a low, musical voice.

The answer came like an arrow released from the bowstring: "To protect the Law and the Temple."

Caiphas gave a wintry smile. "I was doing that long before you were born and I have never stopped."

"That," Saul said, "is why I have come to you, my lord."

The High Priest noted, with amusement rather than annoyance, that the young man was not easily ruffled and could turn a snub to his advantage. A useful man for a debate, then, and since Rabban Gamaliel was his teacher and had been for years, he should have the necessary knowledge as well.

"And against whom or what do you wish me to defend the Law and the Temple?" Caiphas asked placidly. He knew the answer, of course, but he wanted the young man to state his case.

20

He had asked for an audience, but it was not quite clear as yet whether he was the mouthpiece of someone else, of a group maybe, or whether he was on his own. Besides, one should always be able to listen to a man. When Annas had begun to snap at people instead of listening to them, Caiphas knew that his father-in-law had become senile.

"Against the followers of Yeshua, the Nazarene," Saul said in a cold, measured voice, with just the hint of an inflection suggesting that he suppressed adding, "Against whom else?"

"The name of Yeshua is not a rare one," the High Priest said with studied indifference. "Are you perchance referring to the Yeshua the Sanhedrin condemned for blasphemy some years ago— six, if I rightly remember the case?"

Saul would have liked to scream, "Of course I mean that one and you know it. Have done with this game of question and answer." But the forms had to be observed when talking to any man, and especially to the High Priest, Kohen Gadol, the ruler over Jewry, the anointed one, of the line of Aaron which Caiphas was—although there were those who thought his election doubtful because it was due to Roman interference at the time when Valerius Gratus was Procurator of Judaea. So he merely said: "That is the man."

For one brief moment the answer conjured up a picture of the past, a tall man in a tattered scarlet cloak with a crown of thorny twigs on his head; the man could not see because his eyes were full of blood. They had put a reed in his right hand, to look like a scepter. And Pilatus pointed to him and said something like "Here he is" or "That is the man."

"The man is dead," Caiphas said tonelessly.

"No, my lord, he is not dead."

The High Priest frowned. "I know there are some fools gabbling about his resurrection and return, but surely you do not hold with that nonsense." Those eleven men guarding the tomb should have been killed instead of being paid painfully large sums for confessing that the Nazarene's disciples had stolen the body while they were asleep. The story had got out and turned up again and again in the most unlikely places; it seemed to be as elusive as the Nazarene's body.

"The principle of the resurrection," Saul said stiffly, "is perfectly sound teaching."

"It is the teaching of the Pharisees," Caiphas corrected dryly. "Therefore it must be laid at their door that fools now talk of the resurrection of the Nazarene."

"A principle," Saul said primly, "is no less a principle because it is misunderstood by the ignorant."

Another wintry smile rewarded him. "You *are* a Pharisee," the High Priest acknowledged. "But resurrection or not, what is it you want of me?"

"Authority!" Saul exclaimed. "Authority to burn out the nest of vipers, to clean the House of Israel of a superstition as dangerous as any that made our forefathers transgress. More dangerous. For blasphemy is worse than idolatry."

"Such zeal," Caiphas said, "is most becoming, if somewhat surprising in a disciple of mild Rabban Gamaliel. Can I assume that he is in agreement with your views?"

"Every good Jew will be in agreement with them, my lord, though many may not recognize the issue clearly enough. The mind of Rabban Gamaliel is focused on the beauty and truth of the Law, not on the transgressions of the ignorant and superstitious."

"In other words, he does not agree with you," Caiphas stated.

Saul stepped nearer. "The plague has come upon us, my lord. The false teaching is spread in the very heart of the city, it is being preached in the Temple itself, in the Inner Court and the Hall of Solomon. It is taught from the pulpits of the synagogues. A number of priests follow it. . . ."

"Only some of the lower ranks," Caiphas said calmly. "Do you attach much importance to that?"

"God forbid that I should judge anyone belonging to the priesthood," Saul said, but the suppressed smile of irony on his lips belied his words. There were twenty-four requisites for the priesthood, thirty for royalty, but forty-eight for a doctor of the Law.

The chasm between Pharisees and Sadducees was wide and continually broadened by mutual enmity. Even now when Saul of Tarshish wanted to be granted authority by the High Priest, he could not, could not entirely, keep enmity and bitterness out of his pleading. "We are the guardians of the Law of Moses," he went on. "When the Law is in danger, we must cry out. But now even that is no longer sufficient. How long, my lord, will this seed of the Evil One be tolerated? It is no longer true that this teaching affects only those without learning. Two days ago a Levite of good standing, like myself a student of the Law, Joseph of Cyprus, succumbed to the poison and now calls himself Bar Naba —the Son of Consolation! And a rabbi of the Synagogue of the Hellenists mouths blasphemy from the sacred chair. . . ."

"You are referring to the Rabbi Istephan whom they call Stephanos?" the High Priest asked.

Saul's eyes widened. "You know then," he said in an exasperated voice. "You know all about it."

"Such is my duty. It is my duty also not to act on impulse but to study the problem and solve it in the best way possible. Which is not always immediate action."

"A Galilean fisherman is their leader," Saul said contemptuously, "their original leader having been executed. 'Cursed by God is the man who hangs from a tree.' But who can expect the Amha'arez to know anything about Holy Scripture. The fisherman's name was Simon bar Jonah, but that Yeshua of his gave him a new name, too: Cephas or Petros as I heard him called in three of the foreign synagogues. The Rock. Don't you see the similarity?"

"What similarity?" the High Priest asked haughtily.

"Cephas . . . Caiphas. It looks as if Yeshua wished to make clear that he had made that fisherman his High Priest, does it not?"

"This is foolishness," the High Priest said, frowning. "The meaning of Cephas is a 'stone,' a 'rock.' The meaning of my name is 'the Seeker.' "

"Ah, but Yeshua was fond of word play. Did he not call two of his disciples the Sons of Thunder? Boanerges? And does it mean nothing to you, my lord, that you are a Seeker, but the fisherman the Rock? He no longer seeks, he has found and all is settled and firm. They are undermining your authority. Is it not true that Yeshua many a time attacked the priesthood, just as he attacked the Pharisees and the Scribes and everyone else in high places?"

"I am here," Caiphas said stolidly. "And the blasphemer is dead. But do you know why he died?"

"Because such was the will of God."

"That," Caiphas said, with a thin smile, "is the answer to anything and everything. Let us be a little more specific."

"Because you and all the Sanhedrin found him guilty of blasphemy, then."

"Oh no. We could condemn him, but we had no power to have him killed. You forget that we are not the masters in our own house. The Roman procurator alone could carry out the death sentence. And what is blasphemy to him? The superstition of a strange people. No, the blasphemer was killed because we told Pilatus that he regarded himself as the King of the Jews. And I said in a loud voice: 'We have no king except Caesar.' That forced Pilatus' hand. He had to kill him. We could have accused him of high treason if he had not. Rome, Saul, Rome is the omission in your equation. What would you have me do? Drag Rabbi Stephanos from the pulpit before the Sanhedrin? Have him warned? Have him whipped? We have done just that to that fisherman you mentioned and to other disciples of the blasphemer. Has it helped? It has not. They are not afraid of warnings or of blows. They're afraid only of death and death we cannot give them because Rome has tied our hands. Do you think I have not thought of all this before you came here to remind me of my duty? Do you think we of the Sanhedrin are asleep?"

The cold fire in the High Priest's eyes would have frightened most men.

Saul remained unmoved. He said: "If the Law cannot be protected within the law, it will have to be protected without."

24

"I must warn you against that course—officially," Caiphas said. "You hate the followers of Yeshua. . . ."

"I hate them because I love the Law."

"When you grow older you will learn, perhaps, that a man who wishes to go far, should not be swayed by either hatred or love. He should remain aloof."

He rose, the sign that the audience had come to an end.

"The Law is aloof," Saul said. "That is why the servant of the Law cannot afford to be so. Aloofness excludes zeal, and without zeal on the part of the guardians of the Law the blind, the ignorant and superstitious will bring about the fall of that most glorious structure, more sacred even than the Temple." He bowed deeply and left.

Youth, Caiphas thought, believes in the existence of power only when it is constantly used. No idea of temporizing. Yet this young man might go far. Most students of Rabban Gamaliel were just aping their great teacher. This Saul had judgment of his own and he had courage, too; not the mere insolence of the young.

Behind the active part of the High Priest's mind a thought came up as from nowhere: the Tower of Babel. He let it come before the judgment seat of the intellect. The Tower of Babel? Why should he think of that? Perhaps it was because Saul had mentioned something about a glorious structure coming to a fall. There was no other reason he could think of. But there was no relation between the two things, except inasmuch as they were both structures, and he dismissed the thought with a shrug.

Cephas . . . Caiphas. The Rock and the Seeker. What next! The folly of Pharisaic teachings was the root of all trouble. If, as they taught, every man had an immortal soul, then every man was important in his own right, a being branching out into eternity. No wonder then that a priest was no longer an absolute authority —nor, for that matter, was a Pharisee rabbi. They did not understand that they were digging their own graves. And as if that were not enough, they had to stick to the idea of the King Messiah as well *and* teach it in public. Was it surprising in such circumstances that time after time some poor, misguided fool proclaimed himself to be that new Authority? It was a natural consequence and even more natural that each and every one of these fools should find a number of disciples. The Nazarene was the only one of them who had been a real danger. And he was dead and the dead did not return, whatever the babblings of sleepy guards, hysterical women and equally hysterical Galileans. Only a live Messiah was dangerous.

Cephas was not dangerous. Caiphas would see to that.

Even so, it was curious that the dead Nazarene could still make proselytes for his cause. Joseph of Cyprus was supposed to be a reasonable man. Rabbi Stephanos was a brilliant man, as brilliant as young Saul of Tarshish. . . .

Aza, the secretary, came in with a bag of dispatches. The High Priest very rarely saw his face. Aza was a submissive voice, a shadow at the door, a hand putting documents in front of him.

"Go and see Rabbi Ruben ben Joel," Kohen Gadol said. "I want him to pay an official visit to Rabban Gamaliel and to tell him to keep an eye on his student, Saul of Tarshish. He is to tell Gamaliel this: it would be a pity if a student of the Law should, for the love of the Law, become a transgressor against the Law. That is all Rabbi Ruben needs to know."

A few moments passed while Aza memorized the sentence.

"Yes, my lord."

"Next: I want two reliable agents to be present at every service of every synagogue, foreign and otherwise. The best of them will go to the foreign ones. They will take notes afterwards and they will compare what they have taken down."

Beside Kohen Gadol the secretary quoted softly: " 'Two witnesses are necessary and their testimonies must agree.' "

"You do not have to show me that you understand," Caiphas said. "All you need do is to carry out my orders."

"Yes, my lord."

"Go to the chief of the Temple guard. Tell Tubal to keep up regular patrols. He knows what I mean. No disturbances at present. He, too, can watch young Saul. That is all. Go."

CHAPTER THREE

LIFE WAS UNBEARABLE; it was unbearable because quite obviously no one knew any longer the difference between right and wrong.

Saul walked up and down the length of his room in the Street of the Weavers, the street to which he belonged by right since the weaving and making of tents was the trade he had learned, the trade that provided his livelihood, a good and a necessary thing. His father used to quote: "'A man is obliged to teach his son a trade: whoever does not teach his son a trade, teaches him to become a thief.'" And Rabban Gamaliel agreed: "The study of the Law together with a trade is a good thing; for being busy with both makes one forget sin. All study of the Law not coupled with labor is vain and an incentive to sin."

Quotations, quotations . . . yet when it came to upholding the Law against those who would destroy it, where were the wise men? They would bend sideward and backward, they would hem and haw, they would sigh and shrug and talk of caution and of the wrong moment. Kohen Gadol did . . . and Rabban Gamaliel, too, and each of them had his own reason. Kohen Gadol was afraid of Rome. Rabban Gamaliel seemed to be afraid of God. As if God could be against His own Law! "'Be a pupil of Aaron, the Peacemaker,'" he said, "'and draw men toward the Law.'" It was one of his favorite quotations, Saul had heard it more than once. Gamaliel was growing old. Old men were always for caution. They would warn, "Do not act on impulse" because they themselves had no impulses left.

Should he have chosen the School of Shammai instead of that of Gamaliel, the School of Hillel the Wise? But that was no longer an issue. He needed allies. If the School of Shammai could give them to him, he would accept them, however much they might disagree on a number of points, important points, but nothing when everything was at stake.

Kohen Gadol had forsaken the cause of Israel. But what else was to be expected from a Sadducee? "Forget about love and hatred"! A man without love or hatred was no longer a man. He was soulless. But then the Sadducees did not believe in the soul, not as immortal. Yet what else could it be, created as it was by God's own breath?

But the Pharisees, too, were shouting instead of fighting. Who, then, was to defend the cause of God attacked in the Law of God?

Could it be that it was again as in the olden times, when a young man had to lead the people? When David came to the rescue of his king he was not even a young man, but a boy.

Or was that vanity? God forbid that his mind should think of the Law and his heart of his own glory!

At once he began to pray the psalm of devotion to the divine Law, the whole psalm from *aleph* to *tau*. Swaying forward and backward he tasted the sweetness of the words that seemed to justify his every thought.

> *You are just, O Lord,*
> *and your ordinance is right.*
> *You have pronounced your decrees in justice*
> *and in perfect faithfulness.*
> *My zeal consumes me,*
> *because your foes forget your words.*
> *Your promise is very sure,*
> *and your servant loves it.*
> *I am mean and contemptible,*
> *but your precepts I have not forgotten.*
> *Your justice is everlasting justice,*
> *and your law is permanent.*
> *Though distress and anguish have come upon me,*
> *your commands are my delight. . . .*

When he came to the last words he knew what he had to do.

*   *   *

Rabbi Stephanos could not receive him at once. He was busy distributing what seemed to be an unending stream of baskets full of food to an equally unending stream of women. There was bread and fish and olive oil and fruit in each basket and the rabbi blessed it before he handed it out to eager hands stretched forth from beneath the veil. The rabbi's own hands were small and white almost like a woman's, but although he was of slight build he looked strong. There was a reddish sheen on his thick eyebrows and his beard.

"Forgive me," he said when the last of the women had departed, "but I had to serve these first. I don't think you have come for a basket of food and you don't look like a man whose questions can be solved by a simple yes or no. Your mantle says that you are a Pharisee. Who is your teacher?"

"Rabban Gamaliel. I am Saul of Tarshish."

"Gamaliel . . . did he send you to me?" There was a light of joyful expectancy in the curiously light eyes.

"No."

The light vanished. "Come into my study," Rabbi Stephanos said simply.

The study was an austere room with a single window. The yelling of hucksters and the noise of children playing in the street came through the unprotected opening.

"Sit down," Stephanos said. "You look much troubled. What can I do to help you?"

Saul stared hard at him. "You can die."

Stephanos raised his bushy brows. "Have you come to kill me?" There was no terror, not even surprise in his question. He might have asked whether Saul had come for some small favor. And he went on: "I don't think you have. You are alone and unarmed and you do not look like a madman."

"There is one other way," Saul said stolidly. "You can lead those you have led astray back to where they belong. And the first of them is Joseph of Cyprus."

"His name is Bar Naba now. You know him well?"

"He is—was—my friend. When he was, he talked like a good Jew and a sane man. Now that you have been working on his soul he is like a man under a spell. You are his demon. . . ."

"Let us leave spells and demons out of this," Stephanos said.

"How else can one account for such a change? And you do know how to weave spells. I heard you talk once in the Synagogue of the Cilicians. You are a disciple of that group following the teachings of Yeshua, the Nazarene. Will you deny it?"

"God forbid," Rabbi Stephanos said merrily. "I glory in it, and in it alone."

Saul nodded. "That is the kind of language Joseph talks now."

"It is the language of those who have recognized the Messiah."

Saul jumped to his feet. "Rabbi Stephanos, how can you believe that this Nazarene was the Messiah? It is a thing that may be told to the Amha'arez, but not to you. You have studied the Scriptures. You must know better than that."

"I believe," Stephanos said, and there was steel in his voice now, "I believe with absolute faith that Yeshua of Nazareth is the Messiah."

So many arguments came racing in Saul's mind that his face was twisted with the pain of not being able to release them all at once. They flooded his mind, struggled with each other for outlet.

"One by one," Rabbi Stephanos said quietly, as if Saul were a pupil and had to formulate an interpretation in a neat order of points.

"The Messiah," Saul said breathlessly, "cannot come from Nazareth. According to the prophet Micah he must be born in Bethlehem."

"Which is where he *was* born. He was reared in Nazareth."

"He must be of the family of David. . . ."

"He was. And according to the Prophet Zacharias he must ride into Jerusalem on an ass's colt and he did."

"The Messiah," Saul cried, "must be preceded by Elias."

"And so he was. The forerunner of the Lord appeared. He was the voice in the wilderness, crying out to prepare the way of the Lord and to straighten his path; and he was persecuted and murdered as all the prophets were persecuted and murdered."

"You are talking of Jochanaan whom they called the Baptist, not of Elias."

"Jochanaan's office was that of Elias. Yeshua Himself has told

30

us that. But Elias in person was seen as well and there are three eyewitnesses alive to confirm it."

Saul raised both hands. "Rabbi Stephanos, I pray that the Lord will give me patience to go on listening to you. The Messiah is supposed to change the world! He will bring peace everlasting. He will make the name of Israel great and will have dominion over all the nations. Has anything like that come to pass?"

"It will come to pass."

"But the Nazarene is dead and he died on the cross. Don't you know what Scripture says about the man who hangs on a gibbet? There is a curse on such a man, says the Law."

"The Messiah redeemed us from the curse of the Law. He never knew sin, but God made Him to be sin for our sake so that in Him we might be turned into the holiness of God. And the Messiah is alive, more alive than you are. He has risen from the dead."

"I must be dreaming, then," Saul sneered. "But in this dream of mine the Romans are still here and we are not masters in our own country. Kohen Gadol, strange as it may seem, has the same dream. He told me so."

"You went to see Kohen Gadol?" Stephanos asked quickly.

Saul bit his lip. "Is there anything wrong about a Jew visiting the High Priest?"

"Not in principle." Rabbi Stephanos smiled sadly. "But it was he who condemned Yeshua in an unjust trial. It was he who delivered the greatest man Israel ever brought forth into the powers of the Romans to enforce His death. The Messiah has told us to love our enemies. It is a difficult command, but never more so than when one's enemies are also His. God forgive them. Eyes do not see, ears do not hear. . . ."

"Are you calling me blind?"

"Yes, Saul. And the day will come when you will become aware of it yourself. Blind. The Messiah came, He fulfilled everything the prophets foretold and still you do not see. Read what Isaiah says about the just servant who would be led like a lamb to the slaughter, who would be bruised for our sins, yet by his bruises

31

we are healed. Read, Saul, read. As for Rome, the Messiah will conquer it."

"How?"

"Through those who believe in Him."

"Through you, then?" Saul jeered. "Are you a leader of war, Rabbi Stephanos?"

"The Messiah will not conquer through war, although blood will flow freely, as His own blood had to flow, as a ransom for you and me."

"Not for me," Saul cried. "You tell me idle dreams. Conquer Rome! You and that fisherman from Galilee and those women to whom you give bread with one hand and false doctrine with the other! They will laugh at you in Rome, as I would laugh at you now, were it not for those whom you have led astray."

But Rabbi Stephanos did not seem to listen. "Rome," he said. "I will go to Rome, when the time comes, and to Athens and to Ephesus, to all the lands between here and the Pillars of Hercules; and everywhere I will proclaim the glory that has come from our midst. . . ."

"You're mad," Saul stammered. "Mad . . ." But he could not tear his eyes away from Stephanos' face, that strong, pale face with the strangely clear eyes; for the first time he observed a striking resemblance to his own; almost it was his own face—he might have been looking at his reflection in a mirror. "He is Saul gone wrong," he thought. "God shows me Saul gone wrong."

"We are the Chosen People," Stephanos said in a firm, even voice. "Chosen to give the whole world the Shema. 'Hear, O Israel, the Lord our God is one Lord.' And chosen to give the world the Messiah so that all shall be healed by Him, if they will believe in Him and bow to His name."

Saul caught hold of himself. His eyes narrowed. "And what makes you think that you will be able to achieve what the Nazarene himself could not?"

"Did not," Stephanos corrected. "For He could do all things."

"You are blaspheming. . . ."

"Indeed I am not. The power of God can do all things and

the power of God was in Him. He did not do it Himself, because His task was to die for you and me so that we may be healed. And because He wants us to do something about it as well." Rabbi Stephanos smiled. Suddenly he looked very young, a young warrior straining for battle. "He left us a task," he said. "We are allowed to do something for His sake. To me that is vital; and vital it should be to you, too, Saul. You are a man of action, I think."

Saul took a step back. "God forbid that I should have any part of you and your errors."

"You have not heard one single word from me that a good Jew should not listen to," Stephanos said. "What I told you is the truth and Yeshua promised us that the truth would set us free."

"Free of what?" Saul snapped. "Not of the Romans, I can see that. Free of the Law, perhaps?"

"The Messiah has not come to take away the Law, He has come to fulfill it. And he has fulfilled it."

"There! You want to abrogate the Law!"

"All the Law does, Saul, is to give us full consciousness of sin. Yet all of us have sinned and have need of the glory of God. And that is why God has offered us a free gift—His Grace through the Anointed One, and in Him. The Messiah is the supreme sacrifice. . . ."

"What are you saying?"

"No human creature can become acceptable to God by observing the Law."

"You dare to say that!" Saul shouted. "I will listen to you no longer. You called me a man of action. I will act." He moved towards the door.

"Has it come to this then, that a man who wishes to defend the Law will no longer listen to Scripture?" Stephanos asked.

Saul stopped.

"It is written," Stephanos said: " 'There is not one just man . . . there is none who seeks after God. All have gone astray together; they have become worthless. There is none who does good, no, not even one. Their throat is an open sepulchre; with their tongues they have dealt deceitfully. The venom of asps is beneath their lips; their mouth is full of cursing and bitterness. Their feet are swift to shed blood; destruction and misery are in their ways. . . .' "

Saul turned again and fled. He could still hear the strong, young voice pursuing him: " 'And the path of peace they have not known. . . .' "

Then he was out of earshot.

CHAPTER FOUR

"A LETTER FROM our chief agent in Antioch," Aza reported.

The High Priest looked up. "Who was the messenger?"

"Jaqob ben Zakkai."

Kohen Gadol nodded. "Was his journey . . . eventful?"

"He was stopped once by a Roman patrol. They did not find the letter." Aza permitted himself a thin smile. "He would not tell even me where he had hidden it," he added.

The High Priest looked with distaste at the stained, crumpled little piece of parchment. "You may read it to me," he said.

Aza unfolded it with some difficulty. The writing was so small that he had to decipher the words one by one. " 'Nahum ben Ezra sends Greetings to Samuel ben Phabi,' " he read.

There was no such man, of course. It was a precaution in case the letter fell into the wrong hands.

" 'It may be of interest to your business affairs that changes are taking place here and elsewhere. Do increase your stocks, because there is likely to be much business with the army which protects us, as always when there is war at hand.' "

A war? With whom? The Parthians? The Persians?

"Go on."

" 'We are doing very well, delivering foodstuff and fodder to both legions and to some of the auxiliary contingents as well. No one, of course, knows where they will be going, except the high commanders.' "

Two legions. Not enough for a major war. That settled Parthia and Persia.

" 'They need great quantities and we are doing our best to comply. The noble proconsul himself will be in command, they say.' "

Against Herod? Most unlikely, Kohen Gadol thought. The Tetrarch was much too sly not to remain on good terms with the Emperor. Besides there was no need to send an army against him. He had scarcely any troops of his own left, after his defeat by Harethath of Petra, or Aretas as they would call him in Antioch.

" 'Some of our friends think that the war will be against Aretas of Petra. . . .' "

The High Priest raised his hand. "Wait, Aza." Aretas of Petra. The obvious solution. And yet it was strange. There had been no incidents lately, the frontier was fairly quiet. Of course, the Emperor might wish to fortify Herod's position by inflicting a defeat on the Arab King. If that was the idea, Pontius Pilatus would strongly oppose it. Pilatus and Herod had never got on well, except for a short period a few years ago. Petra. They would have to march in a southeasterly direction. . . . "Go on, Aza."

" 'We shall be busy at least another four weeks with our deliveries. . . .' "

An excellent report. It read like a sound business letter and yet conveyed almost the exact strength of the army—two legions with their auxiliaries would be about twenty-five thousand men—as well as the aim and even the probable date when the campaign would start.

"That is not all, my lord," Aza said.

"Isn't it? Go on, then."

" 'I hope you will be pleased with the new procurator. . . .' "

"What did you say?" Kohen Gadol asked sharply. "Read that again."

" 'I hope you will be pleased with the new procurator,' " Aza read. " 'The Legate Marcellus is supposed to be a fine commander who has spent all of his life in the army and is deeply devoted to the noble proconsul. When you receive my letter, he will have arrived in Caesarea and the former procurator will be on the high seas. May he have a safe journey, though as you know there are storms sometimes even at this time of the year. This is all for today. Let me know whether there is anything I can do for you.' "

"Masterly," the High Priest said. His eyes were sparkling. "A masterly report, Aza."

"Yes, my lord."

Yes, my lord. Aza was not stupid but even so it was rather doubtful whether he understood. Nahum ben Ezra was not very much interested in the safe journey of Pontius Pilatus. If he mentioned storms it was to indicate that there had been one and that it had shipwrecked Pilatus' career. Apparently the procurator had been dismissed. He was in disfavor, perhaps even in disgrace.

Kohen Gadol leaned back, exhaling noisily. At long last, the old enemy was defeated. Ten years. Eleven. Tiberius liked his men to remain in office a long time. He was old and did not want the bother of changes, he had admitted that once. But now it had happened.

Pilatus gone. One could scarcely believe it.

"After all," Caiphas said as if to encourage himself, "Nahum has always been reliable. We can trust the news, I think, Aza."

"Assuredly, my lord. And my lord will remember that one of his agents is constantly in the proconsul's place, the Major-domo Cleon."

"Yes, I remember." Kohen Gadol smiled. "No one sees, hears and smells more than a major-domo." The procurator on the high seas! And the new man, Marcellus, a man who had spent all his life in the army—in other words, a man without political experience; he was a man "deeply devoted to the proconsul"—in other words a crony who was getting his procuratorship as a reward or a bribe and not because of any particular ability for the post.

"Aza . . ."

"My lord?"

"I want that young man to come and see me at once."

"The messenger, Jaqob ben Zakkai, my lord?"

"No, you fool. Saul. Saul of Tarshish." Slowly Kohen Gadol caressed his beard, as soft as silk. "He was quite right," he said almost gaily. "It *is* the time for action—now. No, don't go, wait. What is known about his recent movements?"

Aza had the report ready. "The day before yesterday he paid a visit to Rabbi Stephanos. It lasted for almost an hour. He came out in a state of great rage."

"That is natural. Then?"

"He went to see Rabbi Jonah ben Ruben."

"The hothead of the Shammai School," Kohen Gadol remarked contentedly. "No need to ask what they were talking about. I think I know every word of their conversation."

"After a conference of two hours he departed. Next morning he received an invitation from Rabban Gamaliel."

"He went?"

"No, my lord. He excused himself."

Kohen Gadol nodded. "He does not wish to listen to peaceful arguments. He is straining at the leash. We shall unleash him. It is well. Go, and come back with him."

CHAPTER FIVE

TWENTY-FOUR HOURS later a man was dragged through the streets by half a dozen Temple guards, followed by a crowd of angry, wildly gesticulating people, most of them well dressed.

"What is going on?" a coppersmith asked. "Who is it?"

"Why, it's Rabbi Stephanos!" an old potter said, astonished.

"They're arresting Rabbi Stephanos," yelled a boy up to the window where his mother looked out.

"What on earth for?" the coppersmith asked. "He's a good man, isn't he? And a preacher, too."

"He feeds the poor every day," a woman said bitterly. "Perhaps they don't like that."

"It's the clique of the Temple," a one-eyed man sneered. "You know what they're like."

A black-robed man snapped: "Don't talk such nonsense. That man is spreading dangerous doctrine. I've heard him." But then he saw the dagger in the one-eyed fellow's belt and he turned hastily away.

"They aren't taking him to the Temple, are they?"

"No, and they wouldn't. It's not a matter for the Great Sanhedrin, but for the Small, and that means the High Priest's house."

"They're going to the High Priest's house," shrilled the boy.

The whole group followed and others joined them from street corners and shops.

When the arrested man was led into the High Priest's house a crowd of almost three hundred was there, too, arguing and debating so noisily that an officer of the Temple guard came out several times and bellowed at them. They would fall silent then, and resume their noise almost as soon as he had disappeared.

Only one small group did not join in and kept aside. One of them was a big, broad-shouldered man with a brown beard and features not unlike a lion's. He and his few companions were very simply dressed in homespun garments. They looked like men from the countryside. They looked worried, too, and to one or two of the onlookers it seemed that they were praying.

For a long, long time nothing happened. Then noise came from inside the house, inarticulate, ferocious, almost like animals howling. The people in the crowd looked at each other, aghast.

Suddenly the heavy door was flung open and a mass of men came tumbling out as if they had burst it open by sheer force of weight. There were not many of them, forty or fifty, perhaps, not more, but such was the impact of their concentrated fury that they broke through the crowd like the spearhead of an attacking column. They were through and storming on, before the crowd could take in what had happened.

"Where are they taking him?" one of the silent group asked in a whisper.

The lion-faced man gave no answer. Instead he began to walk in the same direction, neither slowly nor hurriedly, the walk of a man accustomed to hilly country. He no longer looked worried. He looked like death.

In the midst of the turbulent group Saul of Tarshish pressed forward, pale and haggard, his eyes red-lidded from sleeplessness. He had not eaten for two days.

Just ahead of him two men were escorting Rabbi Stephanos, whose robe was torn. One could see the muscles of his back moving. They would not move much longer.

In a corner of Saul's mind the Law was pleading in a thin voice that all this was not legal, that formal judgment had not been given and could not be given at a first hearing. Perhaps Kohen Gadol had said something about that at the end, but whatever it was that he had said, he could not make himself heard in the stormiest session the Sanhedrin had had in Saul's memory, ending in uproar and tumult. Yet surely the judgment that would have been given formally at a second hearing was obvious. The Law of Moses was clear and unrelenting about what must be done with a blasphemer.

No one spoke now. There was only the thudding of feet and the laborious breathing of men, many of them middle-aged, walking swiftly and eagerly toward their goal, the Field of Stoning, outside the city.

The guards at the wall tower looked on with silent indifference. They were Romans, the sun glistened on the copper of their helmets. For a few moments Saul was worried. Despite their show of disinterest, they might spring into action at any moment. But they were ordinary legionaries, there was no officer with them and they did nothing. Most likely they did not really know what was going on. There had been no stoning for a long time. "Why, I have never seen one myself," he thought, and a feeling of distaste welled up in him for the first time.

He bit his lip. The servant of the Law could not afford to shy away from the consequences of justice.

Yes, justice. Even if the procedure had not been as formally correct as one might wish, the fundamental issue was beyond all doubt. Two witnesses were sufficient to establish a case and there had been two witnesses and more than two at the Synagogue of the Cilicians where Rabbi Stephanos spoke. He had repeated most of the things he told Saul in his study and added others. Saul did not miss a single word, neither did the men chosen to be the official witnesses whom he had taken there with him. They had heard him speak of Yeshua the Nazarene as if he were Divinity; they had heard him speak of the Law as of something that had been fulfilled by the Nazarene and thus was no longer necessary! The Law no longer necessary! It was enough and more than enough, so they interrupted his mouthings and dragged him away.

And then the fool, the blaspheming fool, instead of trying to justify himself, would preach a sermon to the Sanhedrin and pretend to be the accuser instead of the accused. The members of the Sanhedrin, he said, were guilty of having betrayed and murdered the Messiah. If he wanted to ruin himself and his cause he could not have done better. But he talked as if he were one possessed and perhaps he was. In the end he looked up and cried that he could see the glory of God and Yeshua standing at God's right hand. So of course the members of the Sanhedrin put their fingers in their ears, crying out to make such blasphemies inaudible. A hundred voices shouted, "Death!—Death to the blasphemer!" and one of those voices was that of Saul of Tarshish. He could still hear himself shouting, his voice breaking with a shrill sound almost like a woman's, a thing which happened to him sometimes when he was very excited.

Then the rush had started, suddenly, inexorably like a gust of rain. . . .

The thudding of feet stopped and the group came to a halt. Before them lay the Field of Stoning, that accursed ground, with its pit. Nothing would grow here, not a single tuft of grass, all was rocky ground, covered with rubble.

One of the official witnesses came up to Saul. "Will you throw the first stone?"

Again that feeling of distaste welled up, stronger even than before and again he mastered it. He could see Rabbi Stephanos, only a few feet away from him. They had released him. His eyes were raised to the sky, his lips moving.

Saul gulped. "It is not for me," he said and to his dismay once more his voice broke. "It is for the witnesses to do so," he added, speaking slowly, reining in his voice. "You and Baruch. Such is the Law."

The man nodded. "Then you guard my mantle," he said curtly. He took it off, folded it with care and laid it at Saul's feet. The men next to him followed his example. Mantles and cloaks were laid down, flung down, six, eight, twenty. The men's arms must be free for their work. And there were people gathering at a distance, most of them rabble, shabbily dressed. Somebody had to keep watch that the garments were not stolen.

Saul remembered dully that he was here in an official capacity. He ought to have taken command; he ought to have given orders. . . . But he did not move from where he stood, the guardian now no longer of the Law and the execution of the Law, but of a heap of clothes. His breath came in long, hoarse sighs. He felt humiliated, ill and angry.

The first witness took over in his stead. At his order two men ripped the already tattered clothes off Stephanos' back. It was he who gave the frail, slim figure a push that sent it sprawling into the pit. It was he who first seized a stone, the size of a child's head, raised it high and threw it down at the white-skinned man in the pit, hitting him on the left shoulder. Blood began to flow and at that sight a dozen, two dozen men bent down and seized stones, small stones, large stones, whatever they could lay hold of. Not all their missiles hit their mark and none of them hit the man's head.

He had raised himself up and Saul could see his eyes, he could see them because they were looking at him, only at him. There was no reproach in them, no accusation, no anger. Yet they seemed to convey something, a message, an urgent message they wanted to pass on, and for one terrible moment Saul again felt that he was looking into a mirror, looking at himself down there in the merciless pit.

The feeling was so strong that when another stone hit Stephanos full in the chest, Saul staggered just as Stephanos did. He could not avert his eyes from the stricken man, now covered with blood. He saw him raise his hands feebly, he heard him cry out: "Lord

Yeshua, receive my soul!" and he shuddered at the thought that a dying man was still capable of persisting in blasphemy.

Stephanos' voice rang out one last time and though his mouth was full of blood the words came clear and loud: "Lord, do not lay this sin against them. . . ."

Three stones crashed down and he fell. He was dead, and still the stones came flying.

Somebody barked an order. There was silence, a dull, breathless, bitter silence. After a while hands came to pick up a mantle. More hands. The heap of clothes was diminishing. It was all over.

The men began to walk back slowly, not one of them said a word. Saul walked with them. They passed a group of onlookers, simple men in rough clothes, men from the countryside. One of them, a big, broad-shouldered man kept looking at Saul intently. Why at him? Saul stared back. The man had features not unlike a lion's and a brown beard, sprinkled with the first silver. So strong was this face that Saul faltered and even for a moment stopped, as though he expected the man to say something to him.

But the man said nothing, although he looked as if he were suffering.

Saul resumed his walk. After a while he felt somebody tugging at his mantle. It was the first witness and Saul freed himself, hiding a little shudder. "What is it?"

"That man who was staring at you just a moment ago . . ."

"What about him?"

"Do you know who he is?"

"No."

"It is Cephas—they call him Petros at the Cilician Synagogue. He just lost one of his best men . . . perhaps the best of the lot." The first witness gave a short chuckle.

That man . . . Cephas? The Rock? He did look like a Galilean, of course. Strange . . . there was no hatred in his face, no enmity—yet he must have seen what had been done to Stephanos.

Saul turned his head. The man was no longer there.

No hatred. No enmity. Not in the dying Stephanos either. These people were no longer human. And if that was what their teaching brought about, they were even more dangerous than he had thought.

Saul took a deep breath. "Do you know where he lives?"

"No, and it won't be easy to find out . . . harder than ever now." Another chuckle.

Saul's nerves were frayed. "Easy or not," he snapped, "we must find him."

"Only Kohen Gadol can order an arrest."

"He will order it. I shall go and see him about it. There must be many more arrests. This is not a matter of a single case. We must stamp out this movement or Israel will be torn in half."

The man looked at him sideways. "I didn't think you'd feel like that," he said, "not after . . ."

"It does not matter what I feel," Saul said vehemently. "The work must be done."

Meanwhile the big man with the lion's face and three of his companions were down in the pit, lifting up the body of Stephanos and wrapping it in a rough cloak, which after that would never again be used. Then they prayed.

And Cephas said in a deep voice: "They have spoken of the Law and they have heard witnesses. But here lies the First Witness of the Lord and as such he will be known for ever." There was deep sorrow in his eyes as he added: "He has done what I should have done . . . that night. He has confessed the Lord." And two large tears ran down his cheeks.

For a while no one spoke. They all honored their leader's burden. Then a youngish man with dark eyes and features of almost Greek regularity said in a whisper: "We must carry him off quickly or they will come for his body and take it away to the Valley of Hinnom."

Cephas nodded and bent down. As the others moved to help him he waved them aside. He lifted the frail body as if it were that of a child and began to climb up steadily from the bottom of the pit.

CHAPTER SIX

THREE WEEKS LATER, during a hot afternoon, a man rode into Jerusalem on a black horse. The horse was unmistakably an Arab, with its small head, blood-red nostrils, long mane and tail. The man himself was not so easy to place. He was dressed in the white, flowing garments worn by Arabs and Syrian travelers alike, but his features and complexion were neither Arab nor Syrian. He was still young, in his early thirties perhaps, but there were lines at the corners of his mouth and eyes and one straight furrow between his eyes which seemed to indicate that he had known suffering. Not physical suffering, however. He rode with an ease and self-assuredness that spoke of years of training.

The two legionaries at the gate let him pass without questioning him.

"What do you think he is?" one asked. "He looks like a Roman, doesn't he?"

"He is a Roman. Look at the way he rides. Cavalry school back home in Spoletum or even in the Praetorian barracks. He's an officer."

"Why's he dressed like a native then?"

The legionary grinned. "I'm not the oracle of Delphi. But if you ask me . . ."

"I *am* asking you, wise one."

"Well, then, why should a Roman officer dress up as a native? He's in Intelligence, that's what he is. Bet you half an amphora of Levi's wine against one goblet and that only half filled that he's riding straight to the Antonia."

But the legionary would have lost his bet. The rider did not go anywhere near the fortress. Instead he rode up the Street of the Silversmiths and turned into the maze of side streets near the fruit-market. In front of a large house an old man was sitting in the shade of an arcade.

The rider jumped off his horse, went up to the door and knocked. There was no answer. He knocked again.

The old man said: "The house is empty."

The rider turned to him. "Empty? Surely this is the house of Jochanaan bar Zebedee. . . ."

"It was."

"You mean he sold it?"

"No."

"I do not understand you."

The old man laughed, baring the stumps of four black teeth. "Do you belong to *them* too?" he asked.

From the shadowy entrance of the house opposite two men stepped forward. One was wearing a black robe, the other, a muscular individual, was obviously a servant of some sort.

"Who are you?" asked the man in the black robe. "A friend of the people who used to live here?"

The rider looked at him steadily. "Yes," he said. "Do you know where they have gone?"

The black-robed man said frowning: "You are not a Jew, are you?"

"Well, no, not exactly," the rider said. "It is a point that might be argued, though. What is it to you?"

Blackrobe studied him closely. "Surely you are a Roman."

"I was born in Rome, yes. What is the meaning of this examination?"

"Forgive me," Blackrobe said very politely. "It is an error. We were mistaken. But the people you are looking for are no longer here. I don't know where they have gone." He withdrew, taking his servant with him.

The old man giggled.

"Do you know anything about them?" the rider asked him.

"I know nothing," the old man said in a singsong voice. "Nothing at all."

The rider turned abruptly, mounted and clattered off. He rode across the fruit-market where yelling vendors offered him oranges and half a hundred different kinds of figs and dates, turned into the Street of the Basketmakers and came to the small square where the Synagogue of the Cilicians stood. He asked a young man where he might find Jochanaan bar Zebedee.

"I don't know him."

"He often went to this synagogue."

"I don't know him," the young man repeated sullenly.

"Then do you know where Petrus is—but perhaps you call him Cephas? The son of Jonah?"

"I don't know him," the young man said for the third time and the rider saw that his eyes were shifting from side to side. "The fellow is afraid," he thought. He said in a low voice: "Petrus baptized me. Will that suffice to convince you that I mean no harm?"

The young man lifted his arms. "I told you I don't know," he said aloud. But he added almost in a whisper: "Try the house of Philas in the Street of the Jewelers. The second house from the square on the left. Come after sunset." He made another emphatic gesture, indicating impatient regret.

"That's better," the rider said. He wanted to ask more questions but the young man turned and walked away.

"What has come over these people?" the rider thought as he, too, went on. This was not the atmosphere just before or after a riot of the kind that occurred so frequently in Jerusalem. He had dealt with a good many of them in his military past and he knew the signs. Before the riot the angry groups, the wild looks, the bulges where arms were hidden under long robes; or, more dangerous still, the sight of empty streets where the very houses seemed to look baleful and hidden eyes could be felt following one's every movement. After the riot: the sullen stares, the scurrying of people round street corners, the atmosphere of leaden depression. It was not like that now. Life was going on very much as usual. But when a man asked for Jochanaan bar Zebedee or for Petrus, they were afraid to talk. Some kind of trouble was afoot. Both Petrus and Jochanaan had been arrested, he remembered, five years ago by the Temple crowd and the leader of that crowd was still the same stony old scoundrel. But it would have to be a very recent development or he would have heard about it back in Pelusium or at least in Gaza.

That black-robed man now—he did look like a hawk waiting

for his prey. For Jewish prey. As soon as he saw that his suspect was a Roman he had let go at once. Some internal Jewish strife was on. The rider began to worry a little about Petrus and Jochanaan, but only a little. They were not easily defeated.

He decided to take a short rest, find fodder for the horse and a meal for himself. He found all of that at Iskander's inn, one of the few inns where one could get a separate room to have a meal in peace, undisturbed by the constant chatter and bickering of Greek, Syrian, Armenian, Phoenician and Arab guests. Jews did not visit this kind of inn because the cooking was not supervised for ritual purity. He ordered his meal and went to see whether his horse was being properly provided for. The quality of the fodder was not bad by Jerusalem standards. Water did not abound here as it did in Alexandria or Antioch. There was an old slave to whom he gave instructions. "When he's had his meal, give him a good rub with this brush. Here, take that rug. He must be covered at night. And this is for you."

"Thank you, great lord."

Satisfied he went back to his room and soon Iskander himself came with a tray of meat, roast on the spit, cheese, bread and fruit. He served it adroitly and lingered a little as innkeepers will. "The noble lord is on a long journey?"

"Well, yes. I've come from Alexandria."

"Oh, the wonderful city, I wish I were there. . . ."

"With your inn, you mean, I suppose."

"Ah, yes, noble lord, a man must live, even lowly men must live. Alexandria . . . what a city! You, of course, have seen still greater things in Rome. . . ."

"Rome," his guest said. "It has been many years since I've seen Rome." There was no regret in his tone and no longing. "A Roman must be able to live anywhere."

"Of course," Iskander assented, "the administration of so great an empire demands it. You are a high official, my lord, a high official or a high-ranking officer, you need not say anything, I can see it. Innkeepers must be able to see that—and many other things."

"And report them . . . to whom?" The question was asked in

a friendly tone, but Iskander blanched.

"I report to no one, my lord, I assure you, to no one. I'm a peaceful man, I never meddle in anything."

The guest said, "Your food is good. May your business prosper. I have no wish to frighten you. How are things in Jerusalem? Everything quiet and peaceful?"

"Oh yes, noble lord, quite peaceful. The last upheaval we heard of was the revolt of the Samaritans which was quelled."

"That's a long time ago," the guest said, munching. "But there is some strife between Jewish factions, I believe."

"There is always strife between Jewish factions," Iskander said with the half-ironical, half-conspiratorial expression of a Greek talking to a Roman about Jews. "They are born for quarreling. We Greeks . . ."

". . . never do anything of the sort, of course. What are they quarreling about now?"

"I don't know for sure, noble lord, but there must have been something, because quite a number of people have left the city with their families—some faction or other, I suppose. I don't know any of them. It all started with somebody being stoned to death. Now stoning is their punishment for what they call blasphemy, though what it is I don't know."

The guest frowned. "Stoned to death! In a riot?"

"It must have been some kind of judgment. The man was a preacher in a synagogue. He must have said something that displeased the Temple authorities, so they had him arrested and . . ."

"Who was he?" the guest interrupted. His face was tense.

"His name was Stephanos. I remember it because it's a Greek name. He was a Jew, though. Many of them have Greek names, nowadays."

Stephanos. The guest remembered the alert, intelligent face, the clear eyes, the combative eloquence of the brilliant young man. Petrus had great hopes for him. He once said that Stephanos had the best mind in the Faith. Stephanos stoned to death. And whole families leaving the city—fleeing from it, was probably more accurate.

"You are not eating, noble lord. I hope this Stephanos was not a personal friend of yours. . . ."

"He was," the guest said curtly. After a while, he added: "Are you sure he was judged and condemned by the Sanhedrin?"

"So I heard, noble lord, but I could not swear to it. There are so many rumors these days. . . ."

"Quite so." The guest rose.

"I will go and get a lamp for you, my lord. It is getting dark."

"No need for that. I'm going to take a walk." The guest put a few silver coins on the table. "I'll leave my horse with you," he said. "And I shall be back at midnight, or earlier. I shall need a room for the night. Will someone be up to let me in?"

"I shall let you in myself, noble lord." Iskander pocketed the coins, bowing and smiling.

"Good." The guest left. It was fast growing dark. The first stars shone in a somber sky. There was no moon.

The Street of Jewelers was not very far from the Antonia, he knew it well from the time when he had been stationed here. He had been here last five years ago. It seemed like thirty. There were moments when the time he had spent in this City of Peace seemed as unreal as a dream and others when this dream seemed to be the only reality.

He had known what memory would do to him if he came back. Some said that a murderer always felt the urge to go back to the place where he committed his crime. Perhaps murder was not the only crime to have that effect. Perhaps the weight of his action here, on that tremendous day, was heavier than murder, although he had been forgiven and even taken up into that new Body, that incorruptible Body whose Head was in eternal glory, he, of all people. . . .

"I have been forgiven," he thought, "but I have not expiated."

He had needed all his courage to come back to Jerusalem and even so he did not dare again face the sight of that terrible hill where it had happened. He had made a detour and entered the city through one of the eastern gates.

The Street of the Jewelers . . . the second house on the left, coming from the square, the house of Philas, whoever he was.

The street was empty now, the shops closed. He found the door, knocked and after a while knocked again. Perhaps the young man at the Synagogue of the Cilicians had lied to him, given him some address at random to get rid of him. If so—no, someone was moving inside. The door creaked on its hinges and an old man peered out. He was holding a small lamp. "Peace be with you," he said in an unsteady voice. "What is it you want? The shop is closed now."

"I am Cassius Longinus. I hope to find some of my friends here."

A tall shadow appeared behind the old man and a deep voice said: "Let him come in, Philas. He is a friend."

"Petrus," Cassius said joyfully. The impact of the few words spoken by that unforgettable voice caught him off balance and tears came to his eyes. A moment later he found himself embraced by strong arms and, as he had more than once before, he felt like a son coming home to his father.

"You are welcome," Petrus said, releasing him, "though I wish we could have met again in better times. How did you find this place?"

Cassius told him, as they walked into a fairly large room where there a few men were sitting.

"A brother," Petrus said simply.

They, too, embraced him and he was given a seat and offered wine and bread and fruit. To please them he ate a date and sipped the wine. Despite ten years spent in the Orient he was still too much of a Roman not to come to the point quickly.

"Is what I have heard about Stephanos true?"

Petrus nodded silently.

"The fellow who told me spoke of judgment given against him— he knew very little about it. Surely *that* can't be so!"

"It is true. They led him before the Sanhedrin."

"But they hadn't the right—" Cassius broke off. The Roman governors reserved the *ius gladii,* the right to kill, to themselves and watched jealously that this privilege was not interfered with.

But he was not speaking to Romans now.

"No, they had no right to have him killed," Petrus said. "Not according to the order of the world, for they did not deliver him to the Roman authorities as they did our Lord and not according to the order of God's justice. For he had done no wrong."

"But why did we . . . why did the procurator tolerate it then?" Cassius asked.

"I do not think he knows anything about it. The man Pilatus has been sent home. . . ."

"Yes, I heard that when I was in Gaza."

One of the men at the table leaned forward. "The new procurator has only just commenced on his duties. And Caesarea is too far away to hear the cries of a man stoned in Jerusalem."

"There is still a Roman commander in the Antonia," Cassius protested.

"The Legate Sempronius," Petrus said and Cassius waited in vain for a further explanation. He knew Sempronius, a fairly capable officer but a man who belonged to the great tribe of those whose basic rule was: "If in doubt, don't." This would apply particularly during a change in high office when he did not know what course the new man would set. Sempronius would close his eyes and ears and pretend to know nothing.

"We are Jews. Shall we complain to a Roman about what Jews have done to a Jew?" another man muttered.

"You are speaking in the presence of a Roman now," Cassius reminded him gently.

"The death of our brother Stephanos was only a beginning," Petrus said. "There have been many arrests since then, of both men and women. So many that the rest of the community began to feel that their turn, too, might come at any moment. So they left the city as quickly as they could. They have scattered in all directions, and many have left Judaea altogether and gone to Samaria or to the seaports." He gave a deep sigh. "If our Lord came today and asked me, 'Cephas, where are my sheep, where is my flock in the city I loved so much'—I would have to answer Him: 'Lord, only a few are left and even their lives are threatened.' "

There was a pause. Then Cassius said: "They have made use of the change of government. Pilatus was bad enough as a procurator but they would not have dared to act like this as long as he was in office. Even so, it seems they didn't dare arrest *you*. What about Jochanaan? And Judah, the son of Alphaeus?"

"Jochanaan is still here," Petrus said, "but in the house of his brother Jaqob and they have not dared arrest him so far, or any of his family. They seem to want to spare the apostles of our Lord, for some reason. Perhaps they hope that way to drive a wedge between us and our flock. But, of course, our turn may come at any moment. And they did arrest many of Jochanaan's friends in his house before he closed it."

"I see. And they are still watching it, as I happen to know."

"I have sent Philip to Samaria," Petrus said. "Joel here will go there tomorrow, and Thomas and Matthew will leave for Galilee."

"You should go too," Joel warned.

"I shall stay," Petrus said.

"Yet you are sending us away. . . ."

"That is different. You can do little good here at the moment. It may be that our Lord permits this to happen because He wants us to scatter and to carry His message to as many places as possible."

"Then why us? Why not you?" Joel insisted.

"Because you have not failed Him before, here in Jerusalem and I have. I will not move from here unless our Lord tells me to."

"The cause of all this is that man Caiphas again, I suppose," Cassius said bitterly. "The same man now as . . . then."

"Yes," Peter said evenly. "He and one other. A young man. One Saul of Tarshish."

"I never heard of him."

"Neither had I, until this happened. He was the one who had Stephanos arrested, and for weeks he has been breaking into the houses of our brothers and sisters and having them dragged away to prison. They say he is quite without mercy."

"If he is," Cassius said, "he must be without God."

The smile of Petrus was honor, reward and affection, all in one.

"Saul of Tarshish," Joel said, "thinks that he is God's chosen instrument to uphold the old Law. And he thinks God *is* the Law. I saw him arrest my brother's widow and her two daughters and old Josiah who is nearing eighty."

"He left the city today," Petrus said.

"That's because there is scarcely anyone here whom he can persecute," Joel said. "There are no more than a few dozen of us left in the whole of Jerusalem. He is looking for other communities."

"I could go and see Sempronius," Cassius suggested lamely.

Petrus shook his head. "The Roman commander cannot interfere with the prison sentences; only with a sentence of death."

"I very much doubt whether he will do anything about the murder of Stephanos," Cassius said. "Not at the present time anyway. I would have to see the new procurator. His name is Marcellus. Apart from that I know nothing about him. He must have come from Rome fairly recently."

"Not even the Emperor in all his glory can make our brother Stephanos live again," Petrus said. "Only our Lord can and He will, when the time comes." His broad chest heaved in another sigh. "Now you know about us here, son. What about yourself? I saw you last when I bound you and your young wife together."

"Naomi is well," Cassius said. "At least she was when I set out on my journey. I never knew how much happiness God could give us even here on earth before I married her. We are expecting a child soon. I hoped to find a letter from her at the house of Jochanaan."

"I very much fear you will never get it," Joel said. "None of our brothers has had any for several weeks. There is a net of spies watching for mail. That way they get new addresses."

Cassius flushed. "Has it gone that far?" he growled.

"You have told us nothing about yourself, except for the happiness you found in your young wife," Petrus said. "Are you still living in Tyre?"

"No, I have given up working with the merchants there. To go on would have meant participating in their tricks and ruses. I left them, very much to their surprise."

Petrus smiled. "There is nothing more baffling to such people than an honest man. They cannot make him out."

"Exactly," Cassius said. "I think they're still trying to find out who offered me a higher percentage. They cannot think of any other reason why I should have given up working with them. I am just now returning from an exploratory visit to Egypt, in connection with an exchange of goods by sea—via Gaza, Caesarea and Tyre. I'm not really cut out to be a merchant—soldiering was my profession, as you know—but I do know something about organizing."

"But you said you no longer live in Tyre?"

"No, we have gone to Damascus. There are at least six hundred of us there who share the belief in our Lord and are baptized."

"Damascus . . ." Petrus repeated. "You and your wife are living in Damascus." He and the others exchanged glances. "I sent two messengers there—one yesterday and one this morning. To the elder there, Ananias."

"I am devoted to him," Cassius said warmly. "He comes to our house often. But why do you look so worried? Is he ill?"

"I had to give him evil news," Petrus said, "and now I must tell you also. The man Saul of Tarshish left the city this morning. . . ."

"You told me that."

"With him he has documents signed by the High Priest himself, authorizing him to arrest and imprison all those who call upon the name of Yeshua. And he is going to Damascus first."

CHAPTER SEVEN

As a very young man Cassius had done service in one of the many German campaigns. The spear of a Chatt warrior, a heavy *framea,* had hit his shield full square. The muscular power behind the throw had run through his whole body from head to foot, shaking it and making every nerve tingle.

That was exactly what he felt now, and, as then, his speech was breathless and halting. "Going to . . . Damascus?"

"Yes. He left this morning at the third hour."

"To arrest . . . and imprison . . . men and *women?*"

"Many women were arrested and beaten here in Jerusalem," Joel said. He pointed to a tall man who had so far been silent. "This is Bar Naba. Before he became Bar Naba his name was Joseph and he hails from the island of Cyprus. Saul of Tarshish was his friend. They studied together under the same teacher. Bar Naba has been away from the city these last weeks, and returned this morning to find that the man who was his friend had become his enemy and the enemy of all those who believe in the name of Yeshua. Two cousins and a niece of his were beaten by the Temple guards, when Saul had them arrested in their house, the house where he had been an honored guest many a time."

Bar Naba hung his head. "It is true," he murmured, "and he would have done the same to me. But he thinks he is serving God's Law. He is misguided."

"Will you pray for him?" Petrus asked quietly.

"I will."

"Without feelings of hatred?"

"Without feelings of hatred."

"It is well."

By now Cassius had recovered. He asked sharply: "How many men have gone with this Saul?"

"A number of Temple guards are with him," Joel told him. "We do not know how many. It is a small caravan."

"Do you know the way they've taken?" Without realizing it Cassius had adopted the ways and the tone of a Roman officer. His Aramaic, after ten years in the country, was good and fluent, but now a strong Latin accent suddenly broke through.

"There is only one road up to the Sea of Genesareth, which they now call Tiberias," Petrus said. "My messengers are going round the lake on the west side, passing Magdala, and across the Jordan. I don't know which way the caravan is going to take."

"The other way is shorter," Cassius said. "The eastern way across the desert. They will have camels and asses to carry water. That fellow Saul seems to have little patience. They'll take the short route. Your messengers may arrive too late." He rose. "But I won't," he added. "A horse is quicker than camels."

"You can't get through the desert alone!" Joel warned.

Cassius gave a mirthless smile. "Leave that to me," he said.

Petrus stretched out both his hands to him. "Your wife is a Jewess," he said, "but you are a Roman. Even Saul with all his zeal would think twice before harming her."

Cassius held the Apostle's hands reverently, but his voice was hard as he said: "I shall see to that."

Petrus looked at him very gravely. "Remember who your Lord is," he said.

Cassius gently withdrew his hands. "You once explained to me that marriage is a holy thing," he said.

"Yes. I was present when our Lord blessed it at Cana."

"Then I think He wants me to protect my wife. Forgive me, my father—and you, brothers—but I must go at once." He bowed deeply to Petrus and left.

As the door closed behind him Bar Naba asked, "What is he going to do?"

Joel shrugged his shoulders. "Perhaps he will ask the Roman commander for help. He would do nothing about a Jewess. But if she happens to be a Roman's wife . . ."

"He will go straight to Damascus, I think," Bar Naba said. "He said so, did he not? He will warn the community. And perhaps he will ask the Roman commander *there* for help. They have one too, haven't they?"

"I don't know of any place where there is no Roman commander."

Petrus did not seem to hear them. For a long while he was silent. When at last he spoke, his voice sounded deeply worried.

"This is the first time that Cassius has left me without asking for my blessing."

*   *   *

Cassius ran. He ran all the way back to the inn. When he found the door closed he thundered against it, first with his fist, then with his foot. A man opened, lamp in hand. It was Iskander.

56

"I want the stable opened at once," Cassius said. "My plans are changed. I must leave now."

"Now, noble lord, in the middle of the night?"

"You heard what I said."

Iskander obeyed. There was no slave in the stable at this time and the innkeeper held up his lamp to enable his guest to get his horse ready. It did not take long, and the quick, deft movements convinced Iskander that his guest was a cavalryman, a cavalry officer, of course. A cavalry officer, dressed like a Syrian or Arab instead of wearing uniform, and without so much as a single slave to cater for his needs. And now this hasty departure . . .

"Here," Cassius said, "take this for the room I won't need."

"Thank you, noble lord."

The little Arab gave a low, contented whinny when he felt the fresh night air and Cassius caressed the beautiful, proud neck before he mounted.

Iskander saw rider and horse mingle with the shadows of the unlit street and then vanish. He wondered whether he should tell Chief Secretary Aza about the mysterious Roman, or Mirus who was the agent of Herod Antipas. Herod's man usually paid much better than the tight-fisted Temple, but the Temple had more power here and one could not afford to neglect it. He decided to tell them both.

* * *

Cassius was riding toward the eastern gate, not far from the Temple. So immersed was he in calculations of speed and distance that he pulled up only just in time when he found the gate closed.

"Who are you and where are you going?" barked a voice in shockingly bad Aramaic.

He turned toward it. From the murk three legionaries came forward. Before any of them could say anything further, Cassius pushed back the hood of his long cloak and said in clipped Latin: "Who is in charge here?"

"I am," a sturdy man replied, now also in Latin. "You an officer, sir?"

"Open that gate for me, quick," Cassius rasped. "I'm in a hurry."

The language was unmistakable and it would not have done a simple guard-leader any good to ask an officer for the password, or worse still, his credentials. Yet he had to cover himself.

"Open the gate," the man said. As the other two obeyed, he went on: "In case you should return tonight, just remember Vitellius."

"Vitellius?" Cassius asked.

"That's right, sir, the same password, sir, *just as you gave it to me now.*"

The man grinned and Cassius grinned back. "Your name and rank?" he asked, as the huge wings of the gate creaked back.

"Aulus Turnus, patrol-leader, second cohort, third centuria."

Cassius gave him a friendly nod and rode on. There was something to be said for the army. A lot of brutish idiocy, absurd marches, even more absurd periods of waiting, constantly renewed attempts to make a fighting machine out of a mass of sweaty, leering, wine-bibbing, women-greedy ex-peasants and ex-laborers—but with all that a sense of humor as salty and biting as the spray of the sea; a comradeship that would make one man risk his life a dozen times for another and yet turn into fierce enmity all of a sudden over a worthless bit of femininity picked up at random in one of the thirty-odd countries where they were garrisoned or where they went to conquer. That man Aulus was typical, as typical as the fact that the Legate Sempronius had made the name of the Governor of Syria the password. All passwords were inscribed in the legion's log-book. Yesterday's was, perhaps, "Great Governor" and tomorrow's would be "Proconsul" or "The Emperor's friend" —such nice reading one day for the great man in Antioch, such proof of his legate's admiration and devotion. . . .

As he rode on he remembered with a shiver that a hillock would be visible a little farther to the left, shadowy and formless, rather flat on top. The place where it happened, the place where he . . .

He forced himself to think of Sempronius. One might have rushed to the Antonia and asked to see him. They would have waked him up perhaps, or more likely called him away from the dice. In the first case, he would have been in a temper. In the second, he would have been drunk. But even if he were neither he

58

would have done nothing. He had done nothing about the death of Stephanos—almost surely he knew about it—and in that case there had been a definite breach of Roman law. He would certainly do nothing in a matter where the High Priest was within his formal rights. It was a pity, of course. Twenty men on horseback, bah, ten—and the caravan of Temple guards with that fanatical fellow in their midst would never reach Damascus.

The road would be fairly good at least all the way to Tiberias. The speed of a mixed caravan of camels and donkeys. . . . It was a pity. The more so as he could not take his own men with him. The less they knew the better. And here was Gibeah, right ahead, these few white houses, shimmery in the starlight.

A minute later he halted in front of the tiny inn. This time there was no need to knock at the door. Two of his slaves were sitting, or rather crouching, in front of it and jumped to their feet.

Cassius dismounted. "No need to wake the others," he said curtly. "We must separate here. Syrus, you know the way home, the western way across Phoenicia, you have done it often enough. You will guide the others. Atair, you are responsible for the goods. We shall meet again in Damascus. I must return quickly, so I'll take the way across the desert."

"Alone, master?" Syrus dared to inquire.

"Yes, it can't be helped. You wouldn't be able to keep pace with me."

"The desert is dangerous, master . . ."

"I know that. Get me my sword, Atair, and a dagger too, the Spanish one. And one of those small knapsacks."

"Better take a spear too, master," Syrus suggested.

"No!" Cassius turned away. "No spear," he repeated.

"But bedding, master—and you'll need at least one other horse to carry water and food."

"I haven't got another horse here and I have no time to wait. I'll get what I need in Galilee, in Tiberias perhaps—or in Hippos."

Atair came back with sword, dagger and knapsack. He gave Cassius the arms and fastened the knapsack with leather thongs to the back of the saddle.

59

Cassius mounted again. "See you in Damascus," he said and rode off.

"What's come over him?" Atair asked, wide-eyed.

"Dunno. Never seen him like this before. And he plans to go through the desert alone!"

"Why didn't he take your spear? He looked quite upset when you offered it to him."

"When I come to think of it," Syrus said thoughtfully, "I've never seen him touch one. I wonder why. . . ."

Atair shrugged his shoulders. "What does it matter? All I hope is that you really know the way home."

"I do. But there's another thing I wonder about . . ."

"What?"

"Whether the master will get through."

Atair looked in the direction where Cassius had disappeared.

"I wouldn't like to be the one who tries to stop him."

*   *   *

A man on horseback is not an unhappy man. Even if his thoughts are riding him as hard as he is riding his horse, he is suspended above the earth and very near to flying.

The road to Galilee was an army road at least as far as the lake. Herod had seen to that, letting thousands of men sweat their lives out to please the Emperor he fawned upon, the old specter still huddling on his throne in faraway Capri. It was to gain favor with him that Herod had changed the name of the lake from Genesareth to the Sea of Tiberias.

Cassius galloped along, sparks flying from the Arab's hooves, and for the first time he felt almost cheerful. The shadows of Jerusalem and of that terrible hillock with the flat top lay far behind and far behind also lay the worried face of Petrus. Perhaps Petrus had guessed what his plan was—as much as could be called a plan, for most of it was still cloudy and nebulous. Let him guess it then. Cassius was a soldier once more, he had to be and as a soldier he felt that grim, biting joy that is born of fighting anger and cold steel.

From time to time he let the Arab rest a bit, slowing down, but never stopping, so that the horse would not get stiff. But it was when he was riding fast that his brain, in tune with the speed, was at its most fertile.

If that man Saul arrived in Damascus, he would do there what he had done in Jerusalem. If the High Priest's agents intercepted the mail going to the addresses of men known to be followers of the Nazarene, they would have intercepted the letter to him which Naomi had sent to the house of Jochanaan bar Zebedee. So they would know about her. They would have compiled a list and her name would be on it.

The commander of the garrison in Damascus, Quintus Fuscus, would not be much help. Most of the time he was in his cups, a dirty old rascal, fond of bawdy stories, but shrewd and in his own way as diplomatic as Sempronius of Jerusalem. He had the same code as all the other Roman administrators: never to interfere with the internal squabbles of the colonials, unless he had to. The High Priest had jurisdiction over the Jews in all matters pertaining to religion. To interfere with that could cost Fuscus his post. Cassius could just hear him: "My good Cassius, I cannot possibly stop this kind of thing. And if you ask *me,* you should have known better than to marry a Jewess." And, of course, Fuscus would not lift a finger to protect Ananias or any other member of the community.

Something had to be done *before* the caravan arrived in Damascus.

They could not tell him how many men this Saul had taken with him. There would be no less than twenty or thirty and there might well be more. The Temple guard consisted of a little over three hundred men all told. If Saul wanted to make mass arrests and take the prisoners back to Jerusalem, he might have fifty men with him, including slaves to guard the tents, the bedding, the foodstuff and the water. They would have a number of camels and more donkeys.

Too much for one man, even a man aided by surprise.

But of all those people only one man mattered, the man Saul. If he did not arrive in Damascus, the rest would be impotent. He was the driving force, he alone had the documents lending him the authority of the High Priest himself. He probably had a few scribes with him, secretaries and one or two officers of the Temple guards, but these people were arms, hands, fingers, they could do nothing without the head; they would not dare take any action on their own. Thus the struggle was between only two men, Saul of Tarsus or Tarshish as they called it, and Cassius Longinus.

As the shadows of the first houses of Be-era flew past Cassius decided that Saul of Tarsus would have to die.

CHAPTER EIGHT

THE PURSUIT WENT ON. Cassius spent one night at a very dirty inn at Bethel. "Has a caravan from Jerusalem passed by here?"

"Yes, lord, ten hours ago."

"How many men?"

"Forty, lord, perhaps a few more."

"How many Temple guards?"

"Perhaps half of them, lord. Those would be the men on the camels."

Twenty-five at the most. The slaves did not count. But they had ten hours' start. It was terrible that one had to sleep, to become a dead thing, instead of diminishing the distance, but sleep he must and even more important the horse must rest.

There was another night at Sichem.

"Yes, lord, a caravan passed by, about eight hours ago."

Two hours won, only two hours. This Saul was driving them on like a demon, himself driven by the demon of his zeal, the zeal for what he thought was God.

Even in his sleep Cassius heard the rhythmic drumbeat of the Arab's hooves.

The nearer he came to Galilee—and to the caravan—the more imperious became the matter of having some kind of force of his own. Not for a moment did he repent having left his slaves behind and not only because they had no horses. He could have bought horses for them, though they would not have been as good as his Arab. But it was better, much better to keep them out of this. They were loyal enough, all six of them, he had picked them carefully for the journey to Egypt. Syrus even believed in the Name. But they must not know how Saul came to an end. It would be best if no one knew who killed Saul. The desert was full of bandits, assassins, holy and unholy robbers. One of them might deal with the zealous upholder of the Law and vanish into the desert, never to be seen again.

He did not need a caravan of his own, only a few rough, well-armed fellows who could ride and fight like demons; men to whom the authority of a Jewish high priest meant little or nothing, Arabs, preferably, from Basan, from Nabataea, or from the Trachonitis. A dozen, no more and perhaps fewer, just enough to succeed in a surprise attack.

Again and again he plunged into these problems, trying to ward off the thought of what would happen if he failed . . . and the other thought, that had made him rush away so quickly from the room in the house of Philas and from the presence of Petrus. Was it a hint when Petrus said: "Remember who your Lord is"? And another when that good fool, Syrus, innocently suggested that he should take his spear with him?

He had never used *any* weapon since that day on the terrible hill, not in five, no, in six years.

The thought would not budge. "Better face it, get it out and over with. We must not kill, Lord. I know you have said so, we must not kill, we must love one another, we must turn the other cheek. But I am not fighting this man Saul because of what he has done to me or will do to me, but for what he has done and will do to others, to good men and women, Your servants, who believe in Your holy name and first and foremost among them my wife, the wife You gave me, Lord, and for whom I am responsible to You. So I am going to stop him. You don't want cowards for servants, do You, Lord? You could kill that man Saul Yourself with a wink of Your eyelash. But You do make use of men. Here I am then, to be so used."

Now then. It was out. But somehow it was not over. He wondered a little what Petrus would have said to his prayer—if it was a prayer—and the thought did not make things easier.

But it could not be helped. This thing had to be done. There was nothing else to do.

Meanwhile the Arab was thundering away again, the third day, up the Jordan Valley to the lake, where the Lord used to teach before He went to Jerusalem and death and where He had been seen after His death by Petrus and the son of Zebedee and the others. Perhaps you had to be a man like Petrus and those others to see Him as He was now. To them He would show Himself in His love. Ordinary men had to content themselves with doing their best as they saw it, though of course Petrus might not think that this was the way . . . he *must* get rid of such thoughts, they were laming him.

The *soldier* Cassius was needed now.

When he reached the lake he was no more than two hours behind the caravan and he had no difficulty in reckoning that they had gone eastward round the lake. They were taking the short route, just as he had thought.

*   *   *

He found the men he needed, after some search, in Hippos, the frontier town, with the desert already in sight, a reddish barrenness that seemed to stretch out and up into infinity.

Hippos was the place where nomads drove their herds to sell them for the kind of goods they needed yet could not make themselves, especially arms, cooking utensils and garments.

In one of the places where Arabs could change their money into cheap wine Cassius met Ashab. Ashab was a burly individual who had lost one eye in a brawl. He seemed to be good at losing things of value for he had managed to get rid of most of his money by playing dice with a Syrian whom he described as the Father of Luck and the Grandfather of Treachery. His men, seven in number, were giving him ugly looks. They had been unfortunate enough to back his luck.

Ashab was perfectly willing to enter the service of this stranger who told him that he had a blood feud and needed their daggers.

"A holy task," Ashab said, drinking Cassius' wine, "and most pleasing to the gods. How much will you pay us?"

Pressed for time as he was, Cassius had experience enough to know that he would lose Ashab's esteem from the very start if he did not bargain with him, so bargain he did and after an hour the price was fixed.

"That son of a mangy dog whose blood you want is not traveling alone, surely?"

"No, he has some soldiers of the Jewish Temple with him. They will fight, but badly. He has got a number of slaves, too, and they won't fight at all."

"How many soldiers?"

"Twenty and a few," Cassius said.

Ashab spat. "Too many for us. We are only nine. We better do it at night. These Jews are not accustomed to the desert as we are. My men move without noise and the man will be found in the morning with his throat cut, without anybody knowing how it happened."

Cassius frowned. To kill one's enemy in the middle of his guards was one thing; to have him murdered in his sleep was quite another. This no longer had anything to do with soldiering. Even slaves were better than this brand of hired assassin. "You forget two things, Ashab," he said. "One is that I am the avenger and the man must be killed by my steel. The other is: how could your men recognize him at night? They might easily kill the wrong man."

"That is true," Ashab admitted. He scratched his head. "Nine against twenty-five and in daylight," he said doubtfully.

"Leave the planning to me," Cassius told him coldly.

"Gladly," Ashab replied. "But if we lose horses in the fight, you must pay us for them. Men are cheap, but good horses are not."

"Every loss will be replaced. There are good horses on the market of Damascus. Is it agreed?"

65

"It is."

"Call your men for the handshake. We must leave."

Ashab obeyed and Cassius shook hands with every member of his troop, desert Arabs all of them, hook-nosed, with straggly beards and shifty eyes and smelling of sweat, wine, sheep wool and dung. They were armed with curved daggers, lances and small, round shields. Two of them had bow and arrows as well. Their horses were good, most of them mares of a breed Cassius knew very well.

The troop left Hippos at the ninth hour. The caravan had regained five hours' start.

Cassius could not help grinning wryly at the thought of the reasons he had given Ashab for the necessity of an attack in daytime. He would have to find ways and means to discover what that man Saul looked like, before he could attack at all. Then and only then could he think of making a plan. He had never taken this route before. Much depended upon the kind of terrain he would find. He asked Ashab about it.

"Sand, nothing but sand, Avenger of the Blood. A little later rubble which the demons carried down there from the slopes of the Hermon Mountain. We shall pass that mountain later, it will be on our left. There are many caves there where a caravan can rest in the shade. From there on it's straight riding. But when you see the city from afar it'll be another two hours or so before you reach it. It's a green city, with many gardens and fields surrounding it. . . ."

"I know the city."

On the first day they did not make much progress. The terrain was indeed sand, as Ashab had said, sand and rubble, but the rubble itself was an obstacle and the way led upward all the time. There was a difference of several thousand feet between the level of the Lake of Tiberias—a level lower than that of the Mediterranean Sea—and the high plateau of Basan. To deal with such ground the camels and asses of the Jerusalem caravan were better equipped than the best horses and thus there was the danger that the start it had would increase rather than diminish.

66

Cassius comforted himself with the thought that an attack on such terrain was out of the question. His only hope was the kind of hit-and-run tactics in which Arab riders excelled and that was quite impossible here.

They camped in a cave, first carefully searching it for snakes and other pests. One of Ashab's men found and killed an asp—the snake that was said to have killed Cleopatra—and a small scorpion. The night was surprisingly cold.

On the second day they reached the high plateau after a last bit of steep and difficult ascent and then for the first time they could give the horses full rein. They thundered across the reddish surface in a broad front, with a hundred and more yards between each rider. Ashab insisted on that and he was right. Soon one of his men gave a long-drawn, high-pitched cry and they all converged on him. Triumphantly he pointed to a bit of ass's dung. "The caravan has passed here," Ashab told Cassius. "This is the only way we can be sure about it. There will be tracks later, but only when we have diminished the distance. The wind covers them with sand in a few hours' time."

They found both asses' and camels' dung several times that day and the last bit was fairly fresh, despite the glaring heat.

"Three hours old, no more," Ashab declared. "Tomorrow morning we shall first see their tracks and then it won't be long before we see them."

It was evening then, but Cassius insisted on riding on for one more hour, until dark set in. When they camped again, Mount Hermon, huge, massive and over nine thousand feet high, was already behind them.

"They can't escape us now," Ashab said. "We shall reach them long before noon, when they still have several hours' ride to the city." He grinned as he saw Cassius' eyes flashing. " 'Vengeance is the food of the brave,' " he quoted.

Cassius gave no answer. Once more they carefully searched the camping place with torches and again found a scorpion, this time a large one, under a rock. The Arab who killed it left the squashed brown body where it was.

"Vengeance is the food of the brave." Cassius thought of what Petrus had taught him, years ago: vengeance was the Lord's. "The vengeance is mine, saith the Lord. I will repay." But this was not a matter of vengeance. He must stop this man from going on with his merciless work of destruction. "The Christ did not die for scorpions," he thought grimly.

Once more the night was cold, so that he wrapped himself in his cloak and covered his horse too, to the silent amusement of the Arabs. For a long time he could not sleep, and as soon as the stars paled in the first gray shimmer of the dawn he was up and awakened the others. A drink of water mixed with wine, a few dates and off they went again.

Half an hour later it was warm, an hour later it was hot and soon the sun shone down with naked brutality.

"There," Ashab exclaimed suddenly, and he pointed with his lance. "There they are."

"I don't see anything," Cassius said.

"It looks like a small cloud, but it's dust. There isn't much of it, but it's only a small caravan."

The man was right.

"At last," Cassius said.

"What about your plan?" Ashab asked.

"We must get nearer first," Cassius told him.

They rode on. After a while the cloud of dust changed into a kind of caterpillar winding its many-footed way across the dunes, humping up and stretching out again as it passed over the soft slopes. The spears of the Temple guards and their helmets and armor sparkled in the sunlight.

"Nearer," Cassius said hoarsely. "Still nearer. Draw your men together, Ashab."

The Arab obeyed and the little troop rode on as a compact mass.

"That's enough," Cassius said. "Keep that distance for a while. I shall be back in a few minutes." He spurred his horse and soon rode parallel with the caravan.

The guards saw him, of course, and one of the two officers turning back, saw the troop too, following at a few hundred yards' distance. Cassius saw that the man hesitated and he smiled coldly. He knew what was going on in the officer's head. Should he disregard the presence of so small a troop or order his men to take up formation, fronting against a potential band of robbers? But there was little danger of an ambush here in the open country and so near the city and by itself the little troop was powerless. The officer was craning his neck, looking all about him. There was no other troop in sight. He gave no order.

From under the hood of his wide, white cloak Cassius stared hard at the caravan. Ten guards on camels were the vanguard; then four men on donkeys, well dressed, bearded, with intelligent faces. Scribes or clerks of the Temple, most likely. Then one man alone, also on a donkey's back, but that animal was one of the swift-footed, beautiful little asses they were breeding in Arabia. The man was young, about Cassius' own age. Behind him, at some distance, came the two officers, then six guards, then a train of heavily laden donkeys, ridden by slaves. Eight more guards brought up the rear.

There was only one man here who could be Saul of Tarsus. Cassius looked at him again. Thirtyish. A small man, sensitive, thin-boned, pale; very pale. Eyes downcast, deep in thought. Dressed in black, in the fringed black dress of the Pharisees. That was Saul. That was the quarry.

Cassius could not tear his eyes away from the hated sight, the haughty face. The complete self-assurance of the man could be felt even at this distance. Saul of Tarsus, the judge. Saul of Tarsus, the executor of divine justice, as inexorable as death.

A cry went up from the head of the caravan. One of the guards there was waving and pointing with his spear.

The officer in charge raised his hand to shadow his eyes. Smiling, he gave a sign and the caravan came to a halt. Beckoning down from the towering height of his camel to the lonely rider on the white donkey he explained something. Saul of Tarsus, too, peered toward the horizon.

There, like a mirage, a city rose in the faraway plain, white and pearl-gray, with wall and towers and surrounded by a garland of green freshness as with a necklace of emeralds—Damascus.

Saul of Tarsus gave a nod and rode on. So, at a sign of the officer, did the whole caravan.

Cassius turned his horse and rode back to his troop. The Arabs had kept the same distance. He looked at Ashab. "When I give the sign," he said in a cold voice, "we shall swoop down on them from the left. There is a rider in a black robe, the only man in such a robe. He is riding a very good donkey, a white one. That is my man. I shall go for him directly. You, Ashab, will keep at my side. Three of your men will guard our left flank, the four others the right. Let the horses rear to create confusion. As soon as I have killed my man I shall ride on in the same direction and you and your men will follow. Don't kill anybody else if you can avoid it, just brandish your weapons and ward off their blows, if there are any. The whole thing should be over before they can act. Repeat to me what I just told you so that I can be sure that there is no misunderstanding."

"When you give the sign," Ashab said, "we attack from the left flank. I shall be at your side, three of my men on the left and four on the right of us. We let the horses rear and show fight. We do not kill unless we must. As soon as you have killed your man we ride on in the same direction."

"It is well," Cassius said. "We must wait a little longer until they have passed those dunes ahead. A quarter of an hour perhaps, or a little more. We need flat terrain, and there should be some a little farther on. Ride behind me and wait for my sign."

*   *   *

The caravan was moving a little faster now, despite the heat. Not only the men, the animals too felt that they were coming to the end of the long journey.

Saul alone remained unmoved. In front of him was not a city shimmering in the splendor of the sun's rays, not the end of a journey and the beginning of rest but the place where he would kill vipers and adders, where there was an ulcer he would lay open with his knife.

There was no country in the world where they did not kill a murderer. But a murderer killed only the body of his victim. What then should be done to one who poisoned and killed another man's soul? That was the crime of those who would set up as the Messiah a man who had hung on a gibbet. How would Stephanos have answered that?

Saul frowned. Again and again he asked himself what Stephanos would say. But Stephanos' brain was rotting away and his blasphemous mouth was closed forever. And thus would die every man and every woman who led others down that path, the path towards the abrogation of the Law and thereby not to its fulfillment as they liked to think—if one could call it thinking—but to lawlessness and the destruction of the chosen instrument and the Chosen People of the Lord.

"You would not believe me, Stephanos, when I told you that. To your last breath you went on mouthing your blasphemies, to your last moment you thought—if one could call it thinking—that it was you who held the keys to the truth. Now where are you, Stephanos? Did the Lord turn your soul into stone in the place of perdition? I will not dwell on such thoughts. God forbid, that you should make me think things that are not pleasing to the Lord whose Law I uphold.

"You cannot be right, Stephanos. It is impossible that you should be right. The Messiah cannot hang on a gibbet. The Messiah cannot suffer. The Messiah will come, please God it will be in my lifetime, he will come in glory, the Prince of Everlasting Peace, preceded by Elias. Elias who traveled this very road in his time, at the behest of the Lord. 'Go,' the Lord said to him, 'and return on thy way through the desert to Damascus.' And like Elias I can say: 'With zeal have I been zealous for the Lord God of hosts, for the children of Israel have forsaken thy covenant!' Not all of them, no, it is not as bad as it was when only seven thousand were left who would not bow their knees before Baal. And I will see to it that it will not become as bad as that again. Only a fraction of the people have fallen before the false Messiah. There is no need for an Elias. Saul will do. I will cleanse the cities and towns one by one, I will purge the countryside, and ripen the minds of the sons of Israel for the true Messiah to come in glory, the liberator of Thy people, whose countenance would be more terrifying for his enemies than any man could imagine—did not Enoch say so in so many words? And did not Esdras say that whomever he looked upon trembled before his gaze and wherever his voice reached, things melted as wax before the sun?

"How could such a Messiah suffer? How could he die and die the most shameful death on the cross? They felt it themselves, the benighted souls, and that was why they talked of the Nazarene's resurrection. But the Nazarene was dead, dead, as dead as Stephanos, and the Law of God alone was permanent, the Law which killed Stephanos who tried to escape from it.

"The Nazarene was dead. But how could you die with his name on your lips, Stephanos, you, a rabbi, how could you? Tell me that, dead man, if you can!

"How could you transform those men and women into what they are now, unrepentant even under the lash, never recanting their terrible error? What have you done to them that they should become like warriors for the sake of a falsehood, and as ready to shed their blood as you were? Your eyes looked at me from their faces, the faces of old men and boys, of young girls and mature women, of sick people and strong men in their prime. It is you whom I must crush in everyone of them as I crushed your master in you.

"Even to me you did a terrible thing, Stephanos, before you died; and by dying you did it. Something of myself died in that moment. You prayed for me, Stephanos. I could forgive a curse—but how can I forgive a prayer? In your very last moment you were thinking not of yourself but of those who killed you and thus set yourself up as the one who would plead for them. And by so setting yourself up you upset the order of all things. You made the accused to be the judge, the victim to be the victor. Is that what you meant by the fulfillment of the Law? Is everything to be the opposite of what it was? Is weakness strength, and strength weakness? Is folly wisdom and wisdom folly? Is life death and death life? But you cannot give me the answer, for you are dead, as dead as your master. . . ."

Always the same thoughts, recurring like the wooden moaning, the wordless moaning of the wells around which sightless oxen drew their circles, hour after hour, day after day, hopeless, with no escape, and in vain trying to kick when the silent watcher pricked them with his goad, holding them to their appointed task. . . .

Would the thoughts ever stop? They went on moaning through sleep and waking. The heat of the sun could not stop them, nor the cold of the night.

Of a sudden there was silence—but such a silence as there had never been. The animals stopped in their tracks, camels and donkeys alike and in the minds of some of the men the mysterious pointer of memory came, for the fraction of a moment, to rest, trembling, on the thought that there would be an earthquake.

But there was no earthquake. There was only stillness, a stillness so intense that it lamed their minds and made their bodies incapable of moving. Their very heartbeats seemed to have stopped. In one tremendous moment of presentiment men and beasts were immobilized. It was as if the whole of creation stood still, sun and moon and the stars in their courses.

Light flashed up, but it was not light, it was a ball of fire outshining the sun, and such was its impact that not one of the men could keep in the saddle. They tumbled and fell and shielded their eyes as best they could.

Saul was engulfed, he was caught in a world of painless fire. There was no desert and no city, there was no sun and no sky, he was hanging in space as if space were a gibbet, he was suspended over the uttermost edge of creation and the fire consumed him. He did not feel anything. There was no terror or fear where he was.

But he could hear.

"Sha-ul," said a Voice. "Sha-ul—why dost thou persecute Me?"

Hebrew. Not Aramaic. The ancient tongue of the prophets and patriarchs, spoken only when Sacred Scripture was read. Hebrew.

The Voice had to be answered. But, like Moses on Sinai, Saul had to ask a question. To ask it was the greatest effort he ever made.

"Who art Thou, Lord?"

Out of the light came the answer. *"I am Yeshua. . . ."*

And now Saul saw. He saw a man, the face of a man who was taken up in the glory of God and his mind was filled with it and yet could not contain it.

In a flash he knew what Beauty was and what Goodness was and Purity and Truth and Peace and he could not at once grasp what the Voice was saying: *". . . whom thou art persecuting."*

When the words reached him it was like being exiled, another Adam, from the Garden of God's friendship. Persecute . . . *Him?* A man might kill his father and mother, he might destroy his own children but he could not hate Love and Honor and yet be a man.

"It is hard for thee to kick against the goad," the Voice said.

Compassion. Compassion for him, instead of curses and punishment. Stephanos had wounded him with his compassion. Yeshua had killed him. He was dead. Saul was dead. Not Yeshua.

Trembling, shaking, Saul submitted to death—and was reborn in that instant. He heard his own voice say:

"Lord, what wilt Thou have me do?"

"Arise and go into the city, and it will be told thee what thou must do."

The light paled and was gone. All light was gone. It was suddenly night and there were no stars.

Groping about him in the sand Saul tried to raise himself in obedience to the Voice. He managed to get to his knees.

There was a hubbub of voices all around him, all muttering and whispering. Somebody asked him shakily: "What was it?" And another: "Could you see anyone? Someone was talking to you, surely. I could hear, but I did not understand. What did he say?"

Saul could not answer. Unseen hands helped him to stand.

CHAPTER NINE

THE LITTLE TROOP of riders at the distance of a stone's throw from the caravan had also come to a halt.

Cassius did not stir. In him the pointer of memory rested upon a moment in his life when the curtain of high heaven was split from top to bottom and the earth moaned. Now lightning would pour down in streams and the stone before the tomb would move. . . .

The thought was fulfilled and yet not fulfilled. Light poured down, but it was not lightning; it was a solid bowl of light, hovering over the caravan, engulfing it, and there was sound, but not of thunder. The sound was like a thousand bells and yet like a voice, though he could not distinguish any words. Then it ceased and the light was gone and it was all over.

Someone tugged at his elbow.

"Look," Ashab whispered.

The caravan was in complete disorder. Everywhere men and beasts were struggling to their feet. A cluster of guards were shouting at each other.

The white donkey stood riderless.

"No need to let our horses rear," Ashab murmured. "We'll just pass through them."

The man was right, of course. There could not be a better moment. Cassius felt for his sword. His arm was numb. He rode on and the men followed him. They were bewildered and uneasy, but they came.

He drew the blade from the scabbard and hid it under the folds of his mantle.

No one paid the slightest attention to him and his men. As he reached the milling, excitedly gesticulating crowd he saw Saul.

They had just got him to his feet. He was swaying a little. His face was ashen.

Cassius stopped his horse. He saw Saul's eyes and knew at once that the man did not see him.

"Lead me," Saul said feebly. "I am blind."

To Ashab's stupefaction Cassius put his sword back into the scabbard and rode on. He followed and with him his men. Now they were riding away from the caravan on the other side.

"It was a good opportunity," Ashab muttered.

Cassius looked at him as if he were seeing him for the first time. "Am I to kill a blind man?" he said in a stricken voice.

Ashab shook his head. A blood feud was a blood feud. It would have been a simple matter to end it. And a blind man was not a dead man. Besides he might only be blinded for a short while, by that ball of fire. Sometimes people recovered. . . .

"I *have* recovered," Cassius said hoarsely.

"You? I do not understand."

"I was blind up to this moment. Man, don't you understand that there was a greater hunter about than I? That man is His quarry, not mine."

The Arab looked at him, bewildered.

"Never mind, Ashab." Cassius turned in the saddle. The caravan was out of sight. He stopped his horse and the others halted also.

"Here," Cassius said. "Take the money I promised you. The hunt is over."

With a shrug Ashab took the leather purse, emptied it and divided it at once among his men. Then they touched their foreheads with spear or dagger and sped off, their wide garments fluttering in the wind like wings.

A flight of evil thoughts, Cassius felt. My own thoughts . . .

Soon they had disappeared in the haze of the sun.

He felt giddy and empty, a vessel whose content had been poured away. His whole body was numb and he could not think coherently.

The hunt was over. But it had not been his hunt at all. All the thinking and planning, all the effort of these last days had been for nothing. No wonder then that nothingness filled his mind— except for the vague and unsettling feeling that he had trespassed on the hunting grounds of Another and that this might not go unpunished.

The Lord Himself had struck . . . had struck His enemy blind. Cassius Longinus had had no part in the hunt. The man who came to slay the slayer had slunk through the caravan like a stray dog no one bothered about.

He felt no shame—a man does not feel shame because the King is greater than he—but he felt small, as small as a child who has blundered into a room where adults perform acts entirely beyond its comprehension. And there was that vague fear. . . .

After a while he began to ride on in the direction of the city. The desert receded. The green belt stretched out and grew into thickly wooded groves with oranges and lemons shining like jewels in the rich, glossy foliage. The air was scented and full of freshness. The rivers Barada and Pharpar were curved, silvery swords guarding a world of lush splendor and fertility.

Cassius felt the numbness leave his limbs. This was Damascus. Here was home. Here was Naomi. He spurred his horse and it fell into a joyful gallop.

Soon he saw the caravan again, a little further on the left and proceeding very slowly. He paid no attention to it. The city drew him and he galloped toward it with increasing speed.

He had to slow up at the gate where traffic was constantly pouring in and out. Fortunately it was not far to his house, a small house at the edge of the Roman colony.

But when it came in sight he suddenly reined in his horse. The feeling of uneasiness was back and this time it was no longer vague, but sharp as a dagger. He had trespassed. He had incurred punishment. Ancient thoughts welled up, half buried in his childhood when he prayed to the gods, the many-faced gods of Rome, severe gods and vindictive. He tried to tell himself that the Lord was different, that He loved with a love so much greater than human love that there was no way of comparing the two.

But the Lord had struck down His enemy and blinded him. What would he do to Cassius whom He had forgiven once before in the past? Cassius who had set out to kill . . .

What if He took Naomi from him?

With a groan Cassius forced his horse forward. The slave at the gate, Firmus, looked worried, did he not? Cassius could not make himself stop and ask, he gave Firmus a nod, rode on to the portal and dismounted.

Margul, the Ethiopian, opened, grinning sheepishly and again Cassius could not ask.

"Master back," Margul said, "ah, ah, master back. . . ."

The figure of a thin old woman appared in the hall.

"Abigail," Cassius shouted. "Where is . . . how is . . . my wife?"

Abigail laid a bony finger on her lips and Cassius' heart stood still. But she beckoned him on and as he approached, trembling, she took his arm with the familiarity of an old retainer and led him to the door of his wife's room. "You must be very quiet," she said gravely.

"She is ill. . . ." he whispered.

Abigail nodded and opened the door.

Naomi was asleep. She looked thin and waxen and there were deep blue shadows circling her eyes. Yet illness seemed to increase rather than lessen her frail loveliness. She looked almost preternaturally beautiful. In her arm. . . .

"Six weeks too early," Abigail said in a low voice. "She's weak, but she will be all right and the child too."

"Did the physician say so?" Cassius breathed.

"I know more about that than a physician. But he had sense enough to say so too."

"When . . . was it?"

"This morning. The physician left only an hour ago."

This morning. This very morning.

"It's only a girl," Abigail said defiantly.

Cassius stared at her. Then he laughed outright. He could not help it and he broke off with difficulty as Abigail glared. When he turned back he saw that Naomi's eyes were open. She was looking at him, a little incredulously; then her face, not much larger than a child's, became radiant with her love.

* * *

Cassius did not leave the house that day or the day after and most of the time he was at Naomi's bedside. But he sent a hastily written message to Ananias, warning him of the arrival of the caravan from Jerusalem. "Their leader, Saul of Tarsus, may be incapacitated, but even so it will be better to take all possible precautions. Let me know at once if I can help in any way. I can always hide a number of people in my house, if necessary."

"What are you writing, Cassius?" Naomi's voice was drowsy.

"Just a note to our old friend Ananias."

"Dear old Ananias . . . what are you writing him about?"

"Giving him a message from Petrus. I saw Petrus in Jerusalem."

"Oh . . . you must tell me all about it. Did he send us his blessing?"

Cassius looked away. "No one can think of you without blessing you," he said.

The slave he sent to Ananias came back an hour later. Cassius met him in the hall. "Any answer?"

"The old lord he says he thanks you very much, master, but he knew about it."

"Good. Nothing else?"

"No, master."

Apparently at least one of Petrus' messengers had arrived before him. What could he do now? From here the entire issue looked different. Of course, Saul, blind or not blind, could still send his henchmen to the Jewish quarters and have the people dragged away. But the idea that he would send Temple guards here, to the house of a Roman, appeared almost ludicrous. It might have been very different if Naomi had gone to the synagogue when Ananias was preaching as he sometimes did. She could have been arrested there and then.

Even so Cassius had the male slaves in the house armed.

A blind man could still be a dangerous man; he might regard his blindness as of demonic origin; it might even make him more fanatical than before. Or perhaps he would delegate his powers to somebody else.

It was impossible to say whether the danger to the community was over or not.

The physician came daily and was very well satisfied with Naomi's progress.

Cassius told her about his voyage by ship to Alexandria, the wonders of the great city, the business talks with a number of firms there. He told her that Petrus was well. It was too early to tell her about Stephanos and the persecution the community had undergone in Jerusalem.

"But where are the slaves you had with you? Abigail says you came alone."

"They'll arrive in a few days. They travel more slowly. I was in a hurry to be back."

She would not have been a woman if she had not asked why.

He grinned at her. "Guess. I give you seven guesses."

"Then it must be very difficult to find the reason. It can't be the baby, because she came too early."

"It was not because of the baby. Have you thought of a name for her?"

"Oh, Cassius, we've talked about that so often."

"We almost quarreled about it, too."

"That's right, but then we didn't know whether it was going to be a boy or a girl. Are you disappointed? I mean, aren't you, just a little?"

"About having another Naomi? How could I be! She is exactly like you!"

"I hope not," Naomi said firmly. "It would mean that my ears are six times larger than my nose and my nose the size of the smallest copper coin. It would mean . . ."

"She has your eyes, like polished onyx, and your long eye-lashes. . . ."

"And a large tummy and fat little legs and arms. But I am glad you aren't disappointed. I should be, but I'm not. And as she is a girl we can eliminate lots of names we thought of: Petrus and Stephanos and Jochanaan. . . ."

"And Caius and Lucius and Cornelius."

"But I still want her to be called Miriam."

"After your friend Miriam of Migdal, I know. I would have preferred to call her Naomi because that reminds me of someone I know, but it would lead to sad confusion later, I'm afraid."

"Exactly. Miriam is much better. It was the name of our Lord's mother, too."

The hill outside of the walls of Jerusalem, the terrible hill with the flat top. A woman had seen everything that happened there, everything. Cassius had not seen her face. She was veiled. Or was it that he did not dare look at her?

Naomi's hand touching his own brought him back and he managed to smile. "There can be no more perfect name for a woman," he said. "But don't you think I ought to be allowed a voice in this too?"

She nodded solemnly. "You are thinking of your own mother, I know. I wish I had met her. She must have been very beautiful."

"She was."

"And she was half Roman and half Greek, you told me."

"Her father was Roman, her mother Greek, from Corinth, and she was given her mother's name: Acte—the Shore. It's a happy name don't you think? She was a happy woman too, as soldiers' wives often are in spite of many hardships. Everybody loved her. It was the first great blow of my life when she died."

"Acte," Naomi said thoughtfully.

"Why not Acte *and* Miriam?" Cassius asked. "We often give a child several names in Rome. It is an honor we accord to our relatives and it puts them under the obligation to do something for the child—remember it in their will usually," he ended dryly.

"The Romans are not the only ones to think of such things," Naomi told him, with a smile.

"I suppose not. But don't you think two names are a good idea? Later, when she has grown up, she may choose which she would like to be called. If she should marry a Roman or a Greek she might prefer Acte and if her husband is Jewish she could be Miriam."

"She will probably always be both," Naomi said gravely. "And I pray to the Lord that it be a good thing."

Next morning she was so much better that Cassius felt he could leave the house for a while. He went to the Jewish quarters to find Ananias. The old man was out. One of his nephews told Cassius that he had gone to an inn in Straight Street and that they did not know when he would be back.

Cassius knew the inn. It belonged to a man called Judah and was one of the hostelries for Jewish travelers, where food was prepared in the ritual way Jews insisted on. The idea came to him that this might well be the place the caravan from Jerusalem had chosen for its headquarters. But why should Ananias go straight into the lion's den?

He decided to have a look. He was dressed in Roman clothes now, a white tunic and the short, light mantle that had come to replace the solemn toga, except at official functions, so if members of the caravan were about they would probably not recognize him. Besides, what if they did? It would be different if he had done what he had set out to do. . . .

Straight Street was very presentable, with a fine Corinthian colonnade, and Judah's inn was one of its best and largest houses.

Cassius knew better than to try and enter it. He would only have caused embarrassment. Even before he married Naomi he knew about the severity of the Jewish law which forbade taking Gentiles into the house or entering their houses. There had been a great deal of talk about such matters before he was allowed to marry Naomi and even when he did her people were still uneasy about a great number of points.

Petrus himself at the time solved the problem, quoting another Naomi in Sacred Scripture who had welcomed a girl called Ruth as her daughter-in-law, although Ruth was not a Jewess.

The stables of the inn were behind it. Cassius sauntered over and saw a number of camels and donkeys guarded by a couple of men who might well belong to the Temple guard. He could not be sure as they were not in uniform.

Returning to the street he lingered a little, pretending to be interested in the goods of an ivory merchant, displayed in a shop adjacent to the inn. The owner promptly tried to make him enter the shop—that apparently did not defile it—but he remained outside, where he could keep the entrance of the inn under observation.

After a while a youngish man came out and Cassius recognized young Levi, another of Ananias' nephews. He put down the ivory tusk carved adroitly by Indian workmen into the shape of a whole caravan of elephants and had taken a step toward Levi when two other men appeared. One was Ananias himself, his beautiful white hair flowing out from under his turban, the other a small man, leaning on Ananias' arm and dressed in a simple robe with a hood covering his head.

The two walked away, and Levi was about to follow them when with a few quick steps, Cassius caught up with him and touched his arm. As Levi turned Cassius saw that the young man had been crying.

"Greetings, Levi," he said. "What has happened?"

Levi tried to speak and could not. He looked after Ananias, and the smaller man and then back to Cassius. "Come with us," he murmured, "I will tell you, if I can . . . if I can. No, we mustn't go nearer them . . . I daren't. . . ."

It took quite a while before he recovered from what must have been a violent emotional upheaval. By then they had left Straight Street and were walking toward one of the gates.

"My uncle woke me up this morning," Levi said, and his speech was still a little halting. "He asked me to come with him to Judah's inn. He wouldn't say why, at first, but I was afraid because I knew —we knew—that the men from Jerusalem were staying there. So he told me that the Lord Himself had commanded him to go there. The Lord had appeared to him in his dream and asked him to inquire at the inn about a man called Saul of Tarshish. . . ."

Cassius paled a little. "Your uncle knew that Saul had arrived," he said. "I told him so myself in a message and there was a messenger from Petrus too, I believe—from Cephas as you would call him."

"Yes, I know. And the Lord told him that Saul was now at his prayers and just at this moment had a vision of a man called Ananias coming in and laying hands on him to cure him of his blindness."

"Go on," Cassius said in an uneasy voice.

"My uncle says he told the Lord that he had heard about that man and all the hurt he had done to the saints in Jerusalem and that he had come here with the authority of the High Priest to imprison all those who called upon the Lord's name. But the Lord told him to go nevertheless and that He had chosen this man to be His instrument to bring His name before the heathen and their rulers and before Israel too."

"This man Saul? The man who killed Stephanos? The man who . . ."

"Yes."

They were passing through the gate now.

"Then the man with your uncle now is . . . Saul?"

"Yes." Levi gulped. "He is no longer blind," he added with some difficulty.

"What?" Cassius shivered. "I saw his eyes," he said. "The man was not simply blinded by the sun. He was really blind. And you say he sees now?"

"I know he does. My uncle told me; and then he—Saul—himself came down the stairs from the upper room and I saw him."

"How did it happen?"

"They prayed together and my uncle laid his hands on Saul's head."

"And he saw. . . ."

"He saw at once."

They were approaching the Barata River now. At some distance a small boat was sailing downstream and on the other side a few men were fishing.

Ananias and Saul had reached the riverbank. There they stopped and Cassius saw from the way they stood, motionless and with bowed heads that they were praying. Young Levi beside him joined in.

Then Saul took off his mantle; he shed his robe, too, and stood naked but for the loincloth. The terrible persecutor was a frail, forlorn figure. He looked very young and very humble.

Only when he started wading into the river did Cassius realize that Ananias was about to baptize him in the name of the One whom he had hated so much.

"He was blind and now he sees," Cassius thought. "But this is the still greater miracle."

Now only did he begin to realize to what extent his rashness might have interfered with the will of God; man's only sin and sorry privilege. But he realized also the act of divine courtesy that revealed the truth to him with that mute eloquence speaking directly to the heart. He remembered how Petrus once told him that if the offender was contrite the vengeance of the Lord consisted in drawing him closer to Himself and he felt the upsurge of such joy that his eyes filled with tears. He did not know that this, too, was prayer.

CHAPTER TEN

A FEW DAYS LATER the aged Ananias came to see Cassius, still shaken by the turn that events had taken. "A new man is born," Ananias said, "and our Lord alone knows how far he will go. There is no other man I know of who was called to accept our Lord the way Saul was called. That by itself points to something unheard of."

"The worst enemy," Cassius mused, "might become the best ally—though I don't know whether there is evidence for that theory in history."

Ananias smiled a little ruefully. "He is not exactly the best ally yet, but I don't think that is his fault." He told Cassius how Saul had insisted on being allowed to preach in the principal synagogue on the very next Sabbath. "That was yesterday. He would not listen to my warnings. He has a will of iron—it takes the Lord Himself to make him change his mind. So we went to see the head of the synagogue and he, of course, complied at once—he thought, very naturally, that Saul was here as the representative of the High Priest, although Saul did not present his documents. Nevertheless the head was not too pleased. Our colony here in Damascus is a happy one and he was very much afraid that Saul would incite the members to controversy and perhaps to worse. . . ."

Cassius nodded. "He had heard about what happened in Jerusalem, no doubt."

"He certainly had—I told him about it myself. Mass arrests, men and women flogged by the Temple guards, the terrible death of Rabbi Stephanos—he knew all about it, and he knew also that Saul had brought Temple guards with him. He was very worried, very worried indeed."

"But he gave in?"

"He had to. There was no way of denying Saul the right to speak. Also the head probably felt that it would be a direct insult to the High Priest."

Cassius could not help smiling. "Then what happened?"

"There was much apprehension among the congregation, too," Ananias told him. "Ah well—Saul spoke. And he did tell them about the mission on which he had embarked, and then about the event that made him see everything in an entirely different light. He told them that Yeshua of Nazareth was not only the Messiah, but the Son of God and that He was the Law from now onward. That all those who were baptized in His name partook of His nature so that the Messiah, the Son of God, had His dwelling in many They could not believe their ears. . . ."

"They acclaimed him?"

"No . . . no. They were most embarrassed. No one before had dared to put it all so boldly. And you see, they weren't at all sure that he was not setting a trap for them, trying to find out which of them believed in Yeshua as the Messiah. They did not dispute or argue with him or interrupt him. They just sat, in stony, incredulous silence. There are some who now fear him even more than before. The head himself did not know what to say."

"Saul must have been disappointed," Cassius said.

"Perhaps he was," Ananias replied thoughtfully. "I do not know what is going on in that big, hard skull of his. But I do know that he very carefully destroyed the documents, the powers of authority the High Priest gave him, before he left."

"Saul has left Damascus?"

"This morning."

"With his men?"

"No, alone. He said: 'I will hold no further consultation with any human creature. I will go where I am alone with my Lord.'"

"He has gone into the desert?"

"Yes."

Cassius turned away. There was a time when he himself had done that. It seemed to have been a thousand years ago, but he still knew how it felt. "What about his men?" he asked after a while.

"They are still here," Ananias replied, with a shrug. "They are powerless, I think, without him and without the documents. But another man may be sent from Jerusalem, when word arrives of what happened. Saul was the most zealous man in the fight against those who believe in the name of Yeshua, but he could never have done so much alone. He was the tool of the High Priest and Kohen Gadol is not a man to be thwarted easily."

Cassius nodded. "The danger is not over," he said, "but at least we have gained time. Now I know what I have to do."

"You?"

"Yes, Ananias. I would have stopped Saul's caravan from getting here, if I had had time to reach a responsible Roman commander. The High Priest has violated the *ius gladii*. The execution of Stephanos was illegal, from the Roman point of view."

"The Roman point of view . . ." Ananias repeated doubtfully.

"Yes, I know, it's another world. Petrus, too, felt that and the others with him in Jerusalem. One of them said that Jews could not complain to Romans about what Jews had done to a Jew. I could have answered him that unfortunately there was a very terrible case of precedence for just that, but it would have been very wrong for me to do so."

"Why?" Ananias asked softly.

"Because I was in the presence of Petrus. And because the Jews are not only the people who condemned our Lord to death but also the people which gave birth to Him, among whom He was reared and out of which came His first believers. The more the belief in our Lord spreads, the more the world may forget that. Perhaps this Saul will remind them of it when the time comes."

Ananias pressed his hand. "It is good to see a Roman who is just."

"Oh well, perhaps we're not quite as bad as we seem," Cassius said lightly. "Anyway, if Petrus and the others cannot or will not complain to the Roman authorities—I have no such scruples. As a Roman it is even my duty to report this flagrant case of breach of law to the authorities. The High Priest probably thought he could make use of change of office and a brand-new procurator of Judaea who could hardly know what was going on. As soon as Naomi is well again I shall leave for Caesarea and ask to be received by the Legate Marcellus. By now he is no longer so new. And if he is not co-operative, I shall go to Vitellius himself. After all, Rome can't afford to have its laws flouted."

Ananias said nothing, but Cassius knew what he was thinking and the pain of it made him wince. "I know," he said, almost vehemently, "there is precedence for that as well, and it's exactly the same sort of case. Pilatus gave in because he was a coward and Roman justice had the blackest day of its history. One cannot be proud of the good deeds of one's people unless one is ready to be ashamed of the bad ones. I can only hope that Marcellus won't be another Pilatus. We have lost Stephanos. . . ."

"And gained Saul," Ananias interposed surprisingly.

"I suppose he is a gain. He must be, as the Lord has chosen him. But let's do whatever we can do, so that there will be no more stonings, be it in Jerusalem or anywhere else."

*　　*　　*

That evening Cassius' slaves arrived at last, safe and sound.

"You must have walked all the way to be so late," Cassius told them, frowning. "I almost gave you up."

"It's not our fault, master," Syrus defended himself. "We are lucky to be here now. The Roman army is on the march and there was one officer who wanted to take our donkeys away. We had to

88

plead before a tribune that the owner was a noble Roman and in the end he let us go. But we've been under arrest for three days, all of us."

"The Roman army on the march?" Cassius repeated incredulously. "Where to?"

"They didn't tell us, master, but it's a big army. Two full legions and auxiliaries. They were going east, across Galilee. . . ."

"Not east," Atair corrected, "southeast."

Cassius shook his head. Southeast of Galilee? It was not an expedition against the Samaritans then. The Decapolis? Not at all likely. Perea?

"Who's in command, do you know?"

"The great governor himself, they say, master, but he wasn't with his troops at the time."

More and more mysterious—unless, of course, it was an expedition against some Arab rulers. Petra, most likely. The King there was a ruler of considerable importance who at one time had even claimed Damascus as part of his realm.

"Thank you, Syrus," Cassius said. "Thank you, Atair—you have done well and you will be rewarded."

"Ah, master, ah."

"Now leave me. I must think."

Alone, Cassius began to pace up and down the room. War. If Vitellius himself was in command, Marcellus would certainly remain in Caesarea and there was no need to alter his plans. . . .

Suddenly he remembered that the time of the Passah Feast was near. That probably was the reason why Vitellius was not with his troops. He was paying a visit to Jerusalem. And in those circumstances Marcellus was likely to be there too. Therefore a journey to Caesarea was entirely futile. On the other hand, it was dangerous to wait until things quieted down. He would have to go back to Jerusalem.

It was hard to leave Naomi so soon—and the child; harder still to tell her about it.

She did cry. But she said: "You must go. A day without you is not really a day at all; it's a day lost. I shall lose three weeks out of my life again; but you must go. Now there are two of us waiting for your return. Come back safely."

"I love you," Cassius said.

* * *

He saw the Roman troops on his way back. An endless column of rusty red tunics and bluish armor, with small groups of officers at the head of each cohort. The centurions with their vine staves. The covered carts with foodstuff. The siege engines, drawn by a dozen mules each. A group of high-ranking officers with a pack of young aides around them. The eagle of the legion, more sacred to them than all the temples of Rome, carried by the *aquilifer,* the best soldier of the legion with half a dozen decorations for bravery on his chest. The cavalry with their swaying vexilla.

He had marched with them through German forests and he had served with them in Judaea. He knew them well. He knew what made them laugh and what made them angry; what they could do and the little they could not do. They went tramping across the Jordan Valley into the desert, with the same long-suffering obedience that made them cross Alpine passes, the glowing sands of North Africa and the misty wilderness of the British Isles. They were the seal of Rome, impressed time and again on dozens of nations, on hundreds of tribes all over the known world; they were the arms of the Emperor, the Senate and the people of Rome. There was nothing like them in the world and they knew it.

Once or twice he felt the urge to ride up to them and see whether he knew any of the officers. But he resisted. The past was the past, even though a gracious memory was apt to remind one only of the good moments. There were things he still had in common with them and always would have. But there were others, too. . . .

They *were* marching southeast. Against Petra for sure. King Aretas' head was no longer safe.

CHAPTER ELEVEN

"They are coming, my lord," Aza reported as he slipped into the High Priest's study. "They will reach the New Gate in an hour."

Caiphas looked at him expectantly. "The Governor of Syria?"

"Yes, my lord, and King Herod and his wife."

Caiphas smiled ironically. "When the lion is hunting the jackal is never far away," he murmured.

"I did not quite understand, my lord?"

"Never mind. How many soldiers are with them?"

"Only about six hundred. And no eagles and no vexilla."

This time Caiphas' smile was triumphant. "We have taught them something after all," he said. "The new men seem to be more pliable. You're sure there are no other troops coming?"

"Yes, my lord. I left a net of reliable men to report anything within twenty miles' distance. I think we can take it for granted that our deputation was successful and that the bulk of the army with all the statues and pictures have bypassed the city."

"Excellent. Tell Mordecai to get my state robes ready. What else have you got there?"

"A report from Damascus, my lord. I'm afraid it's rather confused."

"In that case it's likely to come from the head of the synagogue there. I can't imagine Saul of Tarshish making a confused report."

"It is *about* Saul of Tarshish," Aza said. "But it is written by Elieser bar Zadoc."

The High Priest frowned. "Do you mean to tell me that young Saul dares to report to me through a clerk of my office instead of doing so directly?"

"Saul has left Damascus, my lord. There has been some kind of incident and he was . . . he seems to have been . . . I really do not understand at all what happened, my lord."

"You are confused yourself now, Aza," Caiphas jeered. "What kind of incident are you talking about?"

"If I may read the letter to you, my lord . . ."

"By all means, if you cannot manage to be coherent. But be quick. I must put on the state robes."

"'Elieser bar Zadoc to Kohen Gadol, Respect and Reverence: It is with regret and consternation that I must report to Your Lordship the quite unforeseen and unaccountable defection of Your Lordship's emissary plenipotentiary Saul of Tarshish. . . .'"

"What? No, you fool, don't start over again, go on."

"'A week ago,'" Aza read, "'shortly before our arrival in Damascus some kind of phenomenon took place over which we had no control and on whose origin I cannot dare to venture an opinion. In any case it resulted in the momentary panic of our caravan and Saul gave us to understand that he was no longer able to see. He was ill for three days and refused food and drink. But after the arrival of a man who must have been a physician and who arrived uncalled for he regained his sight. There was no doubt, however, that the incident had affected him gravely. On the following Sabbath he spoke in the principal synagogue and to the utter surprise and embarrassment of everyone present he denounced his own former activities and declared that he now was quite certain that the Nazarene Yeshua was the Messiah and even what he called the Son of God.'"

Caiphas threw back his head and gave a strange, toneless laugh. "Saul," he exclaimed. "Saul the Firebrand. Saul the Upholder of the Law. Saul the Pharisee." He collected himself. "Read on, Aza."

"'The next day he left our quarters early in the morning and has not appeared again. My colleagues and myself do not know what Your Lordship wishes us to do in the circumstances; the less so, as the documents of authorization Your Lordship entrusted to Saul cannot be found. We are awaiting Your Lordship's decision.'"

"Sunstroke," Caiphas said coldly. "Neither Elieser bar Zadoc nor his colleagues are fit to carry out the purging of the colony in Damascus. I shall decide about this matter in a day or two. There is no hurry. And I wish you had known better than to plague me with this twaddle at a moment when we have more important things to think of. The robes, Aza, and let them be quick about it."

*　　*　　*

"This is quite a delightful situation," said Herod Antipas. "Or rather it would be if this seventy times cursed camel of mine didn't make me feel sick."

Queen Herodias laughed. She was being carried alongside her husband, also on camelback, but in a litter of rosewood, inlaid with ivory and gold. She was dressed in a robe of Chinese silk, yellow, with magnificent purple embroideries, and wore a purple veil which left her face exposed. "It's a very good camel," she stated, "but you're not a very good rider; and that after having been married to a Bedouin princess. She ought to have given you lessons."

"She did," Herod said wryly. "But not in camel riding."

Herodias raised her penciled brows. "Ah? And what did she teach you?"

"Not to wage war against anyone with your own money."

"She's been good for something, then," Herodias said. But she was no longer amused. It was true that some years ago Herod had made war against Aretas of Petra on her instigation, instead of negotiating like a merchant with his irate former father-in-law. And in that war Aretas had won a victory which had been cheap for him but very expensive for Herod. But why bring that up now that everything was changed?

She almost forgot to smile graciously at the people bordering the streets and shouting their welcome. It would have been an unforgivable failure. How they yelled and clapped!

"We seem to be more popular in Jerusalem than I thought," she said with some surprise.

"Nonsense, my dear," Herod replied, "we're not and we never will be. You know why. Besides, Jerusalemites never think in terms of loving or liking anybody. They have no sympathies, only antipathies, but these antipathies differ enormously. They dislike us— they hate the priest-crowd; and they loathe the Romans."

"Even the rich who are protected by the Roman government?"

"Certainly. A large and irascible dog who snaps at all intruders is a useful animal, no doubt, but does that mean that you have to take the brute on your lap and caress him? He'd only snap at you too."

"But then why this wild acclamation?"

"Partly it's paid for—there are funds for that sort of thing, you know. Partly it is because Vitellius agreed not to bring 'pictures' with him into the city—the eagles and so on. There are a number of good men here whose task it is to whisper into as many ears as possible that Vitellius agreed to that because I insisted on it."

"Oh, I see." Herodias smiled again. Her husband's foxiness never failed to amuse her. Besides, it gave her a feeling of security. The man would never be caught, he would always know a way out. She had had that feeling from the first day they met and it was one of the reasons why she had left her former husband to marry him. She knew as well as he did the reason for their unpopularity: her divorce by itself was bad enough, but she had married her husband's stepbrother and that was against the Law. All their troubles stemmed from that accursed Law. As if it were the concern of this rabble whom she chose to marry. That was the real reason. That and one other thing, a thing she refused even to think about. . . .

She went on regaling the clapping people with dazzling smiles. "You might have left me some illusions about my popularity," she said.

"I'm a realist, my love."

"That's what all men say when they wish to be nasty."

"Not at all." Herod laughed. "Take Vitellius, for example. Because he's a realist he's absolutely charming to you and even to me. He's almost as good at flattery as your esteemed brother, Agrippa. But how happy he would be if he could have our throats cut. Mine at least."

Instinctively Herodias fingered her own throat. No wrinkles, nothing sagging, still a young woman's throat. Not at all bad for her age. And the heavy amethyst necklace set off her skin well. Most women could not wear them.

"Do you really think he still hasn't forgotten that your letter to the Emperor arrived before his official report? To me it doesn't seem to make much difference."

"I have never known a woman who thought that a few days more or less could make a difference," Herod said philosophically. "Unless she was in love, of course. You will have to take my word for it. Cleon tells me that I'm Vitellius' pet enemy and that he was absolutely beside himself when he received the Emperor's order to fight my war for me."

"Who is Cleon?"

"My best agent in Vitellius' palace in Antioch, Vitellius' own major-domo. Forget his name as quickly as you can."

"Are you sure no one can overhear what we are saying?"

"Your question comes a little late." Herod grinned. "But set your mind at rest. That's one thing to be said for camels. *And* for public acclamation."

The procession entered the Temple square.

"Look," Herod said, "the entire garrison is assembled in front of the Antonia—there's Sempronius, the Legate. He licks Vitellius' spittle as eagerly as Vitellius that of Tiberius. One wouldn't think so by looking at him, would one? The god of war personified."

The clipped tones of a Roman command came loud across the square. Fifteen hundred spears crashed against fifteen hundred quadrangular shields. The tubas blared.

Sempronius rode forward to greet, first, Vitellius, then Marcellus who in turn introduced him to the royal couple whom the legate had never met before, although he had been in Jerusalem for the better part of two years.

"It's a shame, really, that we are here so seldom," Herod said with a winning smile. "Judging from the warmth of our welcome we have many more friends here than we thought."

Vitellius' smile was just as winning. "How could it be otherwise," he said, "especially when your gracious queen is with you. I hope you will both grace our table at the Antonia tonight, my lord King."

"Thank you, thank you, we shall be only too pleased. But I think there is someone else here to greet us. . . ." Herod's smile contained more than a trace of sarcasm.

Following his glance Vitellius turned his horse.

There was the gigantic structure of the Temple, white marble, bronze and gold, with curtains fluttering gently in the wind, clear blue and dark blue, brown and red, symbolizing air and water, earth and fire. There was no building like it in the whole world. It seemed to be the father and mother of all the styles known to men, combining them all in a strange, weird harmony of its own. Walls and towers and courts and courts again, rows of pillars and columns and gateways and arcades.

And in front of it, on the massive staircase was assembled the entire priesthood, flanked by crowds of Levites and strong detachments of Temple guards. In the middle of the whole array the solitary figure of a man could be seen, in flowing robes and with a high headdress that made him appear even taller than he was.

"Our friend Caiphas has come to greet us in person," Herod said amiably. "I hope he is in the best of health—he certainly appears to be."

"There will be a special reception for him tomorrow afternoon," Vitellius said. He raised his arm in a stiff salute and immediately Marcellus, Sempronius and the group of officers behind them followed his example.

The answer they received was a dignified nod, no more.

Herod saw Vitellius' eyes narrow. He smiled.

*   *   *

"I wish to speak to the centurion on duty."

The sentry at the main gate of the Antonia gave the visitor an appraising look and called out for his superior. The centurion on duty appeared.

"I am Cassius Longinus," the visitor said. He added in a low voice, "Who's head of Intelligence now?"

"Tribune Vindex . . . sir."

Cassius laughed. "Is he still at it? After all these years! I must speak to him at once."

It was strange to be led into the same old building, up the same staircase, along the endless corridors with their unmistakable atmosphere of Roman soldiery—leather was in it and steel and maleness and mustiness. They had given Vindex new offices, though.

And here he was in person, a little grayer but otherwise unchanged.

"By Jove, you're Cassius Longinus," he said. "I thought you were dead."

"Not yet, tribune."

"Well, what do you want of me? I'm up to my eyes in work, what with all the visitors we have. No, don't tell me. You want an invitation for tonight's banquet. I suppose I can squeeze you in."

"No need for that, tribune."

"No? What do you want then? Re-enter the army, perhaps?"

"No, tribune."

Vindex nodded. "I should have known better. You look prosperous. Army jobs don't pay much. Well then, what's on your mind?"

"I want an audience with the procurator, tribune."

"You can't have it," Vindex told him. "The Governor of Syria is here *and* His Majesty King Fox with his vixen. There's a reception for the High Priest. There's . . ."

"When is the reception for the High Priest?" The question cracked like a whip.

"By the Furies below," Vindex said. "You seem to be interested in the old Temple tiger."

"I am."

"Do you mean to say the audience you want has anything to do with him?"

"Exactly."

Vindex narrowed his eyes. "Let's have this as clear as possible, shall we? You want to talk to the procurator about the High Priest?"

"I thought I'd made that quite clear," Cassius snapped.

"Meaning that you know something about him you want the head of the administration to know—something you feel he doesn't know yet?"

"I don't know. I doubt that he does."

"Then why not tell *me* what it is? I'm still the head of Intelligence."

"It's not a military matter," Cassius said cautiously.

Vindex grinned. "It's political, isn't it?"

"It is. Legal, really."

"You don't want to complain to the procurator because old Caiphas has picked your pockets, do you?"

"I wouldn't bother the procurator with such a minor offense," Cassius said coldly.

"Oh, oh . . . so it's a major one. Look—I may be able to help you. In fact I'm almost sure I can; but you must tell me what it's all about."

"Caiphas and the Sanhedrin condemned a man to death and the man was stoned."

Vindex whistled through his teeth. "Not a Roman citizen, was he?" he asked hopefully.

"I don't know. I don't think so. He was a Jewish rabbi."

"And the man was definitely not surrendered to us? They just went and stoned him? To death?"

"That's right. And he was one of the finest men I ever met."

"That's beside the point," Vindex said. "I don't care whether he was as virtuous as my oldest aunt or as blackguardly as Cerberus. What matters is that they didn't have the right to have him executed. Where did it happen?"

"Here in Jerusalem."

"What? When?"

"About two months ago. Perhaps three."

Vindex' face fell. Cassius knew what he was thinking: that as head of Intelligence he should have known all about it. To come up with this issue so late could cost him his promotion. It was precisely for that reason that Cassius had hesitated to give him the whole story. But there was no other way to reach the procurator.

"Look, Vindex," he said. "Date and place are minor issues. You can't know everything that's going on. The very fact that they managed to conceal it from you speaks for their guilt."

"I don't know," Vindex said. Suddenly he made up his mind. "Wait here," he snapped. He strode out of the room, leaving Cassius with very mixed feelings. If Vindex was going to talk to the Legate Sempronius about it instead of going straight to the procurator, the legate might want to hush it up. Sempronius' fears would be exactly the same as Vindex'. The legate was responsible for all his departments.

All he could do now was to wait. From the door of the office he looked out to the Lithostrotos, and the sight of the large square evoked terrible memories of Roman justice. There it was the Lord stood on the day when puny men thought they could sit in judgment over the Supreme Judge Himself. It was the same feast too, the Passah Feast. Seven years ago, only seven years ago . . .

Hurried steps clanked in the corridor and Vindex came back, looking very excited. "Come with me at once," he said. "Out here—this way."

"Where are we going?"

"Procurator's office. Hurry up. They're all there."

"What do you mean, all?"

"In here," Vindex said, opening a door. "Cassius Longinus, formerly an officer in the army," he announced curtly.

Cassius saw a whole group of high-ranking officers standing around a tall middle-aged man with shrewd eyes, in a resplendent uniform with the insignia of a proconsul.

"Cassius Longinus?" the man asked. "Not a son of General Longinus?"

"Yes, sir," Cassius said.

"I served under him for a short while," Vitellius said. "What are you doing out here?"

"A bit of trading, sir. I am living in Damascus."

Vitellius nodded. "I seem to remember that your father had trade interests too, when he was retired."

"Yes, sir, but he wasn't very fortunate with them."

"Wasn't he? That's regrettable. You doing well?"

"Moderately so, sir."

"That's what all merchants say when they're making millions," Vitellius stated and the group of officers around him laughed dutifully.

"Now about this complaint of yours," Vitellius went on. "Vindex here tells me that you know of a case where the Jewish High Priest condemned a man to death—who was the man?"

"Rabbi Stephanos, sir, a preacher of the Cilician Synagogue and a very fine man indeed."

"What was he accused of?"

"Blasphemy, sir."

Vitellius nodded. "They tell me that stoning is the ancient punishment for that offense."

"That's right, sir. Stephanos was stoned to death."

"And the reigning High Priest, Joseph Caiphas, presided over the Sanhedrin meeting at which the man was condemned?"

"He did, sir."

"Did he order the execution?"

"I don't know about that, sir, but if he had obstructed it, Stephanos would still be alive."

Vitellius nodded again. "Thank you, Longinus. Vindex, we shall need a number of witnesses. You'll know where to get them, I'm sure."

"Yes, sir. When do you want them?"

"At once, of course. Go and get them."

Vindex saluted and clanked away.

"I don't think I shall have to talk this over with my esteemed friend, King Herod," Vitellius said. "Longinus, you have rendered me a service."

"Have I, sir?"

"Yes. I did want to get rid of that infernal fellow Caiphas, you know. Old Pilatus told me the man was a born intriguer, so I read his dossier with great care. Pilatus wasn't always right . . ."

"No, sir."

". . . but he was this time. Lots of material, but nothing you could really lay your hands on. This bit is just what I needed. Much obliged to you. What can I do for you?"

Cassius grinned. "Nothing, sir."

"Don't be absurd. There is no such thing as a man with no wishes—except for Diogenes; and even he wanted Alexander to move aside, so that he could enjoy the sun."

"I don't want you to move, sir," Cassius said. "I'm very glad you're here."

Vitellius laughed. "I think it's wrong that you're not in the service of the empire. A member of the Longinus family playing the merchant in Damascus! It's ridiculous, really. Come with me on our little war with Aretas and later on I'll give you first a cohort and then a legion."

So it was Aretas. "I've left the army for good, sir."

"What about a post in the administration then? You seem to be good at finding out things. Vindex tried to give us the impression that he had you up his sleeve all the time, but I think that's non-sense. He knew nothing about this stoning before you came, did he?"

"Vindex is a good Intelligence officer, sir," Cassius said a little stiffly. "I'd hate to do his work, though. I really am quite happy as I am, sir."

Vitellius closed one eye. "Married?"

"Yes, sir."

"Not a Roman lady, I suppose?"

"No, sir, my wife is a Jewess."

"I see. Well, let me know if you want to change your mind about entering empire service again, will you?"

"I will, sir."

Vitellius' attitude was a little more remote now. Many Romans, both military and civilian, married women of the countries where they were stationed; very often they adopted the customs and habits of their wives' countries and were no longer empire-minded. "You haven't become a Jew yourself, have you?" he asked casually.

"Not exactly, no, sir."

"What do you mean, not exactly? I know they're proselytizing a good deal, even in Rome they have made a number of addicts . . . of believers, I should say."

"I have not become a Jew formally, sir," Cassius said. "And I certainly do not regard the Jewish High Priest as a spiritual authority of any kind. But I do hold the same beliefs as the Rabbi Stephanos. We both believe . . ."

"Don't tell me any more," Vitellius interrupted quickly. "It might weaken your case. I take it your information was true to the best of your knowledge?"

"Yes, sir."

"Very well, that will do. Thank you very much."

The audience had ended.

CHAPTER TWELVE

"We are definitely a success," Herod said cheerfully. "But I wouldn't choose the peacock-blue dress for today's reception, my dear."

The slaves had hurried out of the room as soon as he came in.

Herodias was looking at herself in the mirror of polished silver. "Why not? It's lovely, I think."

"It is much too lovely, my dove. Jerusalemites are austere, orthodox people."

"There won't be any at the reception. I've seen the list of the guests. They can't have orthodox Jews. The defilement nonsense, of course."

"Yes, I know, but there is that earlier one—call it a conference or meeting or whatever you wish—in the open hall of the praetorium, and there the High Priest himself will be present and many other orthodox people. I don't want any trouble with my starchier subjects just when things are going so well."

"Oh, well," Herodias conceded, "perhaps I'll wear something less elegant for that, and then change for the main reception and the banquet."

"If there is time, my dear, and I very much doubt whether there will be. There is nothing worse, believe me, than keeping Romans from their dinner. Hungry Romans are extremely dangerous. And they can't start without us."

"I shall only need half an hour."

"Yes, I know," Herod said, "but five or six of them. You are doing very well without so much preparation, my dove. Why, even Vitellius is making sheep's eyes at you."

"You told me only yesterday that he is charming to us only because he is a realist."

"True enough," Herod admitted. "But you are very real, my little peacock, even if there is henna and gold dust in your hair and Phoenician purple on your lips and . . ."

"You're worse than Vitellius."

"I have a right to be. I'm your husband—which cost me the major part of my army. Now don't be angry with me. It may be all for the best. It's a great thing for our prestige that the Emperor is sending his own army to avenge us—with very categorical instructions, too, I heard."

"From Cleon again?"

"I told you to forget that name. No, from one of my military friends. He works in the clerical department in the Antioch palace which gives him the opportunity to see most of the documents. It's always good to have more than one—er—friend at places of interest. They must never know about each other, of course."

"I see."

"Now get ready, my love. And really, a simpler dress will be much better. I regret it myself, believe me. I am proud of you, of your beauty—you know that. I often wish I had less . . . austere subjects. However much we may try to adapt ourselves, and we have to, unfortunately—we are not Jews. Our ancestors hail from Edom and Arabia. We are Edomites with Arab blood and the Jews are alien to us and we to them. Our great ancestor, the first King Herod, would never have become King without his friend Marcus Antonius—who had a great deal of trouble establishing him as Tetrarch—and later without Augustus. We need Tiberius just as much."

"I know, I know, you're always preaching that to me."

"Because it's vital, my dear. Without Rome we are nothing. Not yet, anyway. I am working on that issue, but it's too early to talk about it even to you. I don't like to admit our nothingness, naturally, but I'm not stupid enough to close my eyes to the fact. And Rome means: the Emperor. Not Vitellius or Marcellus or anybody else. By the way, Vitellius . . ."

"I don't think Tiberius in Capri bothers much about the color and cut of my dress."

"By the way, Vitellius seems to be very busy. He has been seeing a good many Jews, Sadducees, Pharisees and even a number of rather tough individuals. I wonder what he is up to and . . ."

"I shall be late for the reception if I don't get dressed now."

"Heaven forbid. I'm going."

*   *   *

The meeting with the High Priest in the court of the praetorium was strictly official. It would have been unthinkable for Kohen Gadol to enter the house of a Gentile. Practically the entire Sadducee priest clan was present and a great number of Pharisee rabbis.

King Herod and his queen arrived almost on time and Vitellius received them with exquisite courtesy. Despite the solemnity of the occasion he found time to whisper to the Queen: "What a delightful dress, a most unusual blue. . . ."

"Peacock-blue, my lord governor." Herodias smiled.

"I must ask you never to appear like this in Egypt," Vitellius said gravely. "The Egyptians would think that Cleopatra had come to life again and Rome's worries about that province would start afresh."

"She had a good figure before she had four children," Herodias said, smoothing her dress. "But I'm told her nose was formed like a beak."

Vitellius grinned admiringly. "We are lucky she did not look exactly like you, or Octavianus would have succumbed to her, too, and the entire history of Rome would have taken a different course."

He turned away and gave a salute as the High Priest stepped forward. After a brief exchange of greetings Caiphas declared that he would like to use the opportunity of standing face to face with the highest Roman authority outside of Italy to ask for a favor.

"Speak," Vitellius said laconically.

Caiphas told him that ever since the times of the High Priest Hyrcanus the ceremonial robes of the High Priest, worn only in the Temple, had been kept in a certain tower. When Herod the First was King he had had the tower enlarged to a fortress which he named the Antonia, after his friend Marcus Antonius. For reasons of his own he continued to keep the robes in the tower and so at first did his son and successor Archelaus. After the Roman occupation of the country the Roman authorities carried on the custom and ever since the commander of the fortress daily lighted a candle in front of the stone chest where the robes were being kept under the High Priest's seal. Seven days before every feast in which the robes were used the commander gave them to the priests who then purified them so that the High Priest could use them. The day after the feast they had to be given back to the Roman authorities. Thus it was on the three great feasts of the year and on the Day of Fasting. Could not the lord governor do away with this procedure? Now, at the time of the Passah Feast the robes were in the Temple, where they belonged. Could they not remain there altogether?"

"My lord governor," King Herod said quickly, "permit me and my wife to join in with this plea of Kohen Gadol."

Vitellius thought for a moment. "Why do you believe, my lord High Priest, that King Herod the First wanted to keep the robes in the tower?"

"He probably thought it would render his position more secure," Caiphas had to admit. "He had many enemies—or thought so."

Vitellius smiled. "Rome has no need to use sacred vestments as hostages," he said aloud. "I am willing to alter the custom forthwith. The robes will remain in the Temple."

The Jewish delegations were vociferous in their gratitude.

Out of the corner of his mouth Vitellius said to the Legate Marcellus beside him: "It'll save us a candle a day." Then he stepped forward again. "I regret that I must now mention a very unfortunate matter," he said. "My lord High Priest, I am told by a number of witnesses that at the time when the former procurator, Pontius Pilatus, had just left the country, a certain Stephanos was condemned to death under your jurisdiction. Is that true?"

Caiphas bit his lip. "There was such a case, yes," he said after a while.

"Where is the condemned man?" Vitellius asked politely.

"He is dead," Caiphas replied fretfully.

"Dead," Vitellius repeated. "And what did he die of, my lord High Priest? A fever? Consumption?"

Caiphas remained silent.

"Well, if you choose not to answer, I will supply the answer myself." Vitellius' tone was sharp now. "He was stoned to death. You had him executed."

"I could not stop it," Caiphas said sullenly. "There are crimes that arouse the blood of our people. I am afraid it is difficult for a Roman to understand that."

"Rome has granted you the right of keeping a Temple guard," Vitellius said icily. "If they are not capable of protecting a prisoner in their power, they must be replaced by Roman soldiers."

Caiphas drew himself up. "No Roman soldier can enter the Temple or its precincts," he protested. "The Emperor himself has granted us that privilege."

"In that case you, too, should fulfill your obligations," Vitellius replied. "And one of them is: no man can be put to death in Judaea except when judgment of death is given by the Roman authorities. There has been a gross violation of the *ius gladii*. You, the High Priest, are responsible for that. In the circumstances I regret that you can no longer remain in charge of your high office. The ceremonial robes, whose possession I have granted to the Temple, will be worn by someone else."

Caiphas took a step back. When he began to speak, Vitellius cut him short at once.

"As the representative of the Emperor," he roared, "I declare you deposed. As your successor I nominate another member of the Sanhedrin, Lord Jonathas bar Ananus."

A thick-set man with an almost blue-black beard stepped forward so quickly and eagerly that the onlookers realized he had been forewarned.

106

"The nomination of a high priest . . ." began Caiphas, but Vitellius cut him short.

". . . is a matter for the Governor of Syria or his immediate subordinate, the Procurator of Judaea. You yourself were nominated by the Procurator Valerius Gratus, predecessor of the Procurator Pontius Pilatus. My lord High Priest Jonathas bar Ananus!"

"My lord governor?" the eager-faced man said.

"You will assume your office forthwith and I expect a more harmonious collaboration with the Roman authorities than has been the case, unfortunately, under the reign of your predecessor. You have my best wishes."

A very slight bow indicated the end of the meeting.

"Can't say it doesn't serve him right," Herod whispered to his queen. "Never liked the old Temple-monger. But I doubt whether the new one will be any better."

Jonathas bar Ananus was still bowing to Vitellius, Marcellus and the royal pair as Caiphas stalked away, ashen-faced but erect.

"At least he's got dignity," Vindex whispered to Cassius who was standing next to him.

Cassius gave no reply. He could not help thinking of the verdict another Roman judge had given in this place. The downfall of Caiphas was no vindication, not even the beginning of it. The two events did not bear comparison.

The Sadducees and Pharisees left in complete silence.

"I congratulate you, my lord governor," Herod said. "You have brought about something well-nigh miraculous."

"What's that?"

"You have made Pharisee rabbis speechless. Believe me, there are not many who can say that about themselves. Old Caiphas was not very popular, but all the same . . . I can only hope you won't have any trouble with the dear rabble."

"We are quite prepared for that," said the Legate Sempronius contemptuously.

Vitellius gave him an oblique look. He and Marcellus exchanged glances. "I don't think there'll be much danger, my lord King," he said nonchalantly. "Besides I have given orders to inform the inhabitants of the city that I have abolished the tax on market fruit for all time."

Herod nodded admiringly. "You need no one's advice, my lord governor."

"I'm a mere tyro compared with you," Vitellius said cheerfully. "How wise of you to support the former High Priest's claim for those vestments so quickly. The people will love you for it. Well, I shall see you at the banquet tonight, you and your delightful queen. If you will graciously excuse me now. . . ."

*   *   *

The news arrived early on the fourth day of the Governor of Syria's sojourn in Jerusalem.

A small detachment of cavalry escorting a state courier came riding like the whirlwind to the main gate of the Antonia.

The courier had to wait a few minutes in the anteroom of Vitellius' suite, because they had to get the governor out of bed. He was still half asleep and rather scantily dressed when he made his appearance.

The courier gave him a fairly bulky document. Vitellius took it, saw the imperial seal, kissed it, and signed for it.

"Are you from Capri?" he asked, breaking the seal.

"No, excellency. From Rome."

Vitellius looked up in surprise. "Is the Emperor in Rome then?" It was an open secret that Thrasyllus, Tiberius' astrologer, had advised him years ago never to enter the capital again.

"The Emperor Gaius is in Rome, yes, excellency," the courier said gravely.

Vitellius stiffened. There was no need to read the documents now. So many thoughts, so many feelings assailed him that he needed a full moment before he could ask his first questions.

"When did it happen? Where? How?"

"The former Emperor died on the sixteenth of March," the courier reported, "on the third day of the fifth month of the twenty-third year of his reign. He had been ill for some time. Before he died he gave his signet ring to Prince Gaius."

Not likely. Not at all likely. The old man had hated Gaius, he used to say, "Gaius has remained alive to my misfortune and to that of everyone else," and "I have reared an adder in him." Gemellus would have been a much likelier choice. This was an official version, no more; but also no less. And this courier would report back to Gaius, to Emperor Gaius, twenty-four, no, twenty-five years old. The rule of a boy after the rule of an old dotard. Vitellius remembered a gawky youth with a crowing voice. He nodded. "Thank you," he said courteously. "I shall commend the speed of your journey to the Emperor."

When the man had gone Vitellius read the documents. Accession to the throne. The Senate's proclamation. Funeral speech for Tiberius, delivered by the new Emperor. Order to all governors to swear in the population of their provinces to him. That was all.

No, it wasn't. There was a tiny strip of parchment attached to the last document and covered with writing. Block letters. No signature, except for the crude drawing of a bird, which told Vitellius who the sender was—his best-paid friend in the Senate, Aulus Tricetius. "A pillow smothered the old one so that the young one should reign. Macro did it. Many things will change."

So it was murder. Macro was the Prefect of the Praetorian Guards. That meant that Gaius had the guards on his side, which in turn meant that his throne was safe . . . for the time being. He had always been popular with soldiers, even as a child, when he used to travel with his father, Germanicus, from one military camp on the Rhine to another, always dressed as a soldier, down to the tiny soldiers' boots made specially for him, of which he was so proud that he screamed when they wanted him to wear anything else. *"Caligula,"* "Little Boots," the soldiers used to call him.

Vitellius sat down, rested his aching head between his hands and began to think about the new situation. Suddenly he giggled. He laughed. He roared with laughter, so loud that Varro, another aide and the door-slave came rushing in, thinking that he was shouting for help.

"Wine," Vitellius ordered. "The morning wine." The slave ran to fetch it and Vitellius laughed again. "Oh Fox," he said. "Oh, King of Foxes . . ."

The aides looked at each other, speechless.

Vitellius glared at them. "Write out an order, Varro. To the High Priest Jonathas bar Ananus. The Sanhedrin will assemble at the praetorium this afternoon at the ninth hour to swear allegiance to the new Emperor." Both aides tried hard not to show their surprise. Vitellius went on: "Same message to the learned bodies, the magistrates, the civic functionary bodies and the Temple guards. Next: message to King Herod. He is expected here at my office at noon."

"You are supposed to be at the King's palace at that hour, sir," Varro dared to interpose. "He invited you for the midday meal and . . ."

"At my office at noon," Vitellius repeated sharply. "My regrets for not being able to attend. Unforeseen circumstances. Most urgent business. You know how to formulate the cursed thing, what are you my aide for?"

"Yes, sir."

"Next: message to the Legate Calvius Priscus, Subcommander of the Expeditionary Force on the way to Petra. This must be sent by special courier under a sufficient escort, Varro. Ausonius will tell you the route to be taken. I want top speed. Text of the message: 'Emperor Tiberius has died. Senate and people of Rome have confirmed the ascent of Prince Gaius to the throne. You will at once order the troops under your command to swear allegiance to Emperor Gaius.' Got that? Then say, 'After that you will—'" He broke off. Once more he was shaken with ferocious, uncontrollable laughter.

*   *   *

"Well, what did he want of you?" Heridias asked. But at the sight of her husband's face she paled and jumped up. "What's happened?"

"Tiberius is dead," Herod said tonelessly. "Prince Gaius is Emperor. And the war is called off."

"No!"

"Vitellius told me so, in so many words. You should have seen his face. He was positively gloating."

"But . . . how dare he do such a thing? Surely the new Emperor . . ."

"The expedition against King Aretas of Petra was ordered by the late Emperor," Herod said, mimicking Vitellius' tenor voice. " 'I have no idea whether Emperor Gaius wishes me to go on with it. Naturally I must wait for what orders he will see fit to give me in that respect.' "

"That Arab wife of yours is very lucky," Herodias snapped.

"That's one way of putting it, my gentle dove," Herod replied. "Another would be that perhaps you do not bring me much luck."

"Oh, it's my fault now, is it?" Herodias' voice was shrill with anger.

"If it weren't for you," he said, "there would never have been war with Petra. There would be an alliance instead."

"Then why don't you go back to her?" she jeered. "Perhaps she'll receive you with open arms."

"Be quiet, my jewel," Herod said. "I have no time now for such nonsense. I must try and think what we can do. Vitellius has assembled the Sanhedrin, the learned bodies and everybody else. They'll swear allegiance. So will the rabble. The Jews never liked Tiberius much, not after he expelled them from Rome by the thousands and let them perish in Sardinia. Now they'll hope that Gaius will give them better treatment. Maybe he will, I don't know. But what am I to do?" He tore off his heavy headdress and threw it on the floor. "Tiberius was the cornerstone of my edifice," he said, "I relied on him completely. I knew I had won him when I named the Lake of Genesareth after him and the town as well. And now this. Shall I change Tiberias into Gaiapolis? Or Caligulapolis?" He gave a bitter laugh. "I don't even know the imperial brat. There, do you hear that? They're singing in the streets and screaming in his honor."

"We still have money and money begets power," Herodias said defiantly.

"How much money do you think one needs to make up for the loss of an emperor? And you didn't see Vitellius' face just now."

"His own position may no longer be secure."

"That's possible. But it doesn't help. The war is called off. Don't you realize what that means? Never mind your own little bit of feminine spite. They'll jeer at us now, not only in Petra but everywhere. All the dear neighbors. Nothing is so successful as success. The Roman Emperor was for us. Now he may be against us. Young men always like to reverse the decisions of their predecessors. We are isolated. We are utterly alone!"

"Don't shout at me. It makes me quite ill."

"Alone, alone, alone. A thousand plans are spoiled. I tell you, my precious one, there is a curse on us."

"Oh no," she cried, "not that song again, I beg of you. . . ."

"A curse," he repeated dully. "That man Jochanaan must have cursed us before his head fell—to please you and that bitch of a daughter of yours."

"He insulted my honor! And I won't have you talk like that about my child."

"Very well." He grinned without mirth. "I'll put it this way: she is exactly the kind of daughter you would have."

"Will you be still?"

His voice sank to a half-whisper, but he had to go on. "I know we're under a curse, Herodias. I know it because I dream of him. His head fell when the moon was full and each time when the moon is full I dream of him. And as if that weren't enough . . . there is the other. . . ."

Herodias was trembling. "Another?" she asked. "You never told me about that. Who is the other?"

"That man Pilatus crucified six or seven years ago," Herod whispered. "A Galilean. From Nazareth."

"Oh, that one."

"Yes, brainless one . . . that one. Pilatus sent him to me. I was curious. They'd told me so much about the miracles he could perform. I wanted him to perform one for me . . . just one . . . but he said nothing, he did nothing, he did not even look at me. One of the priests present asked whether he regarded himself as the King of the Jews. He still said nothing. I was angry with the priest, so I pretended to fall in with his joke and had the Nazarene dressed in a purple cloak, an old one, full of holes. And I sent him back to Pilatus."

"Well, what was wrong with that?"

"Everything," Herod shouted. "You don't understand. You can't understand. You never saw the man. It was like . . . like spitting at the sun. It soiled *me*. And I sent him back and Pilatus had him crucified because Caiphas and his stinking crowd demanded it. I could have let him go, couldn't I? I could have let Jochanaan go too, but I didn't. And ever since then I have been unlucky in everything."

"Superstitious rubbish," Herodias fumed.

Herod swayed forward and backward. "Perhaps it is," he said, "I hope it is. But I'm afraid . . . I'm afraid. . . ."

"What are you afraid of?" she asked angrily.

"That I prepared my own fate," he said in a shaken voice. "That one day I also shall have nothing left but a tattered purple cloak."

*   *   *

Cassius went to take his leave from Vindex.

"I'm afraid you've been a fool," Vindex told him.

"Why do you say that?"

"Somebody told me you spoke up nicely for me when I had left the presence, so I suppose I ought to be grateful to you."

"You know that?"

"Somebody always tells me things," Vindex said.

"All right—but why does that make me a fool?"

"It doesn't. But you declined all the offers Vitellius made you."

"That's right."

"He was awfully keen on getting rid of Caiphas and you gave him the legal grounds. You could have got anything from him. Why did you refuse?"

"I told him why. I'm a happy man. I have a lovely wife and she has just given me a little girl. I'm going home now."

"A wife and a child—that rarely stops a man's ambition."

"It isn't an easy thing to explain, Vindex. There was a time in my life when all I wanted was vengeance. My father was murdered by one of Sejanus' friends. But the man is dead and so is Sejanus. Now my only ambition is to serve God."

"Which god?"

"There is only one."

"That's what the Jews believe. You *are* a Jew, then?"

"I believe in one God."

"I talked to a number of people while getting my witnesses together," Vindex said. "Some of them told me about that Nazarene whom we crucified just about the time when Sejanus fell, remember?"

"Yes, Vindex. I remember. They called Him Yeshua. We would say Jesus."

Vindex nodded. "Just as they say Haretath and we Aretas. Vitellius called that new High Priest the Son of Ananus, the Jews say Hanan or Hanaan or something like that. Well this Jesus then—do you believe in him?"

"Yes, Vindex."

"So that's the real reason you came here! To avenge the death of Stephanos who believed in him too."

"No. To save others from sharing Stephanos' fate."

Vindex rubbed his chin. "Do you mean to say you believe that this Jesus was divine?"

"Yes, Vindex."

"A man who was executed!"

"He rose from the dead."

"So they tell me. But surely you don't believe *that?*"

"I witnessed it, Vindex."

"You're mad," Vindex said. "I've thought so ever since you said you were a happy man."

Cassius laughed and for some reason it made Vindex downright angry. "You're mad," he repeated sharply.

"It does sound like folly," Cassius admitted. "But it's not *my* folly."

"Whose is it then?"

"God's. It's a glorious folly. A divine folly. And as it is divine it is true."

BOOK TWO

CHAPTER THIRTEEN

THE MAN who walked toward the city gate was as brown as a tree trunk. The midday sun was broiling hot but he did not seem to feel it. He was wearing a loincloth and the tattered remnants of a coat. An old kerchief only half covered his matted hair, but it shaded his eyes—large, strangely luminous eyes, deep set.

When he arrived at the gate he was stopped. Half a dozen men surrounded him, white-robed, with leather shields and curved swords. He stood still as they searched him perfunctorily.

"Not a coin on him," one of the men shouted over his shoulder to a silent figure in the shadow of the arch.

"Nor a weapon," added another.

"A beggar, that's all he is." They spoke the guttural Arabic of the stony desert.

The man in the shadow stepped forward. He was dressed like the others except for an armband of heavy silver. "Who are you and where do you hail from?" he asked, first in Arabic, then in Aramaic.

"I am Saul. I was born in Tarshish."

"Tarshish is far from here. And it's Roman."

"I am a Roman citizen by birth."

The Whiterobes laughed and their leader said, "Rome must be very proud of you. But this city is no longer Roman."

"It was when I left it, three years ago."

"Oh, so you've been here before. Very well. Take note, then, that the Roman Caesar has given the city back to its rightful owner, King Haretath, Ruler of Petra, Lion of the Desert, Son and Grandson of the Stars, to whom may the gods give a thousand years. What is your profession?"

"I am a scholar, a weaver and a tentmaker."

"Three kinds of work and none of them good enough to provide you with a coat. Look at these rags! Now you listen to me and get this clear: the King's ethnarch, Orybas, likes people who work and pay taxes. He doesn't like beggars. Understand? Right. You may enter."

They stepped back and Saul walked on calmly, as if he had only been waiting for a door to be opened for him.

When he was out of earshot the leader of the guard said: "Mabrith —follow that man and see where he takes lodgings. He may be a Roman spy."

*   *   *

Ananias did not recognize his visitor at first. Even when the brown man with the straggly beard said humbly: "You baptized me," the old man shook his head. "I haven't baptized so many that I wouldn't know you."

"You healed my blindness," the visitor said.

Ananias gaped at him. Saul . . . Where was the pale face, the haughty mouth, the frail body he remembered? This man was cut out of hard, brown wood and his eyes, no longer hard, were those of a dreamer.

"I know I have changed," Saul said softly. "Although there was no mirror where I have been and not enough water to see the reflection of my face."

"Saul, where *have* you been? But come in first, come in, you look hungry and thirsty. . . ."

"A little water is all I need. I had some dates given me this morning when I approached the city."

"I'll get some wine. . . ."

"No, water will be better. I have lost the habit of anything stronger."

But Ananias did not rest until his guest had eaten a little bread and some figs and he insisted on lacing the water with wine. "You have been in the desert, of course, I can see that. Three years in the desert! You didn't mind the terrible loneliness of it?"

"I was never lonely. And I have learned much because I learned how to listen."

Ananias eyed him a little nervously. The sun of the desert had destroyed many a good mind. And those eyes . . .

"I am not ill," Saul said gently. "But I learned that the Lord can teach us better when we are quiet and listen. I should have learned it long ago, from Sacred Scripture. Now I know what I must do, and the beginning is here, in Damascus, where I was given back my sight."

The aged Ananias shifted on his chair. "Much has changed in these three years," he warned, "and little has become better. There is another High Priest in Jerusalem—no, there have been two since you left. First Jonathas bar Hanan and then Theophilus, only a few months later."

"How did they become high priests?" Saul asked.

"The same way as Caiphas did before them. The Romans nominated them; that is, the Governor of Syria did, Vitellius. He deposed Caiphas for having authorized or at least tolerated the stoning of Rabbi Stephanos."

Saul nodded. "It was an infringement of the Roman law," he said. "So Caiphas was deposed by the Romans; and I was raised by the Lord. Yet it was I who suggested the attack on Stephanos. I, too, shall suffer, though in a different way."

"You know that?" Ananias stared at him. "You were told, perhaps?"

"I was told."

Ananias thought of his dream—if it was a dream—when the Christ told him to go and visit Saul in Judah's inn and to heal his blindness. "Go, for this man is a chosen vessel to Me to carry my name among nations and kings and the children of Israel. For I will show him how much he must suffer for My name." Ananias had never repeated these words to Saul. If the Lord Himself was going to tell him, He would do so in His own good time and it would not have been right to interfere.

He nodded slowly. "You are a chosen vessel," he said. "And as you are that you must be careful to remain whole in the Lord's service. There is danger for you in this city."

"There is danger for me in all cities from now on," Saul said. "There always will be, until I die."

"The men who came with you from Jerusalem have returned there a long time ago," Ananias said. "But there is no longer a *ius gladii* here. Arab law is not Roman law. The King's ethnarch, Orybas, does just what he likes and calls it law. And there are members of the Jewish colony who stand well with him. They have ways and means to get anything they want. There was much evil talk about what you said in the synagogue before you left and there will be some who remember it, I am sure of that."

Saul nodded. "I shall remind the others."

Ananias threw up his hands. "You won't . . . you don't want to speak again, Saul, surely? The mood of the congregation has changed too. Even I do not speak there any more, but only in private assemblies of the congregation of the faithful. Now if you would like to address *them* . . ."

"No. I will attend, of course. But if they are faithful to our Lord, they have no need of me. They are your flock and your responsibility. My task is to speak to those who still have to learn who our Lord is. I must tell them what I learned on Sinai."

"On . . . Sinai?"

"I come from there." Saul took a deep breath. "I visited Stephanos very shortly before his death," he said in a dark voice. "He told me many things; and everyone of them was true. He was killed through my fault, my most grievous fault. I must take up where he left off. I must do the work I prevented him from doing. It is the murderer's duty to look after the kin of him whom he has murdered. Stephanos' kin is all the world, Jews and Gentiles alike." The words fell slowly, evenly, like so many drops of water. It was the proclamation of a program, a life program.

Saul rose to his feet. "We are the children of the promise," he said. "We are the sons of Sarah, the free woman, not of Hagar, the slave. Such is the freedom that the Christ has won for us."

"It is a new conception," Ananias stammered. "They won't grasp it, I fear. They . . ."

"To prove it," Saul went on relentlessly, "God has sent the Spirit of His own Son into our hearts and it is crying out in us: 'Father!' We are sons, and ours is the inheritance. All of us who have been baptized in Christ's name have put on the person of Christ. How then can there be any more Jew or Gentile, slave or freeman? We are all one person in the Christ. And thus we are indeed Abraham's children."

"It is unheard-of boldness." Ananias was swept away against his will. "Just that is one of the marks that the Lord is speaking through you." But what will they say in the synagogue? . . ."

"They will hear me. What they will do then they must decide for themselves. The Lord does not enforce His truth on man; not yet. He will do so only when He returns and then it will be too late for us to do what we can still do now: to make our own decision, for Him or against Him."

* * *

The door-slave announced two visitors and Cassius frowned at him.

"Who are they and what do they want?"

"They would not give their names, master. They are dressed in long burnouses, with the hoods up, so I could not see their faces. One of them is an old man, master, I could see his white beard. He was the one who spoke, master, and he said it was most urgent and that you knew him well."

Cassius shook his head. The door-slave was a new man and did not yet know his way about. Roman households did not feel secure since the garrison had left and that infernal Arab had taken over. Many Romans had deserted the city altogether and he himself was arranging for a transfer of all his business affairs to Antioch. The Arabs were demanding new taxes, they were utterly unreliable, and crimes had multiplied in the city. He would have gone by now but for the negotiations still pending about the sale of his house.

123

The two visitors could mean anything, including a sudden dagger thrust after which the widow Naomi would be forced to sell the house at a cheaper price.

"My sword," Cassius ordered. "Tell Syrus and Atair to arm themselves and come with me."

"Yes, master."

When Cassius and his slaves entered the hall the two men in their burnouses made no motion to disclose their identity. But there was something vaguely familiar about the older man. Cassius approached him closely, smiled and ordered the slaves to leave. Then he said: "Why this mummery, my dear old friend? And who is your companion?"

"Not here," Ananias replied. "Allow us to go where we cannot be overheard."

"Come into my study then."

In the study Ananias dropped the hood of his burnous. "You know my companion too," he said. "But I am not so sure whether you are going to recognize him. I didn't, at first." He pulled the other man's hood back as well.

There was a pause. "Saul of Tarsus," Cassius said slowly.

Ananias smiled. "Your eyes are younger than mine."

"It is not that. But I met him in circumstances that made it impossible to forget his face, however much it has changed."

"I have brought him here," Ananias said, "because you once told me you were willing to take any man of our congregation into your house if his life was threatened."

"I did say that." Cassius nodded. "Though when I said it, it was this man who was threatening the lives of our brothers."

Saul said nothing.

"He has spent three years in the desert," Ananias said. "Then he came back and four days ago he spoke once more in the principal synagogue."

"Embarrassed them again, has he?" Cassius asked lightly.

"Never have I seen such an upheaval. After a few minutes they began to interrupt and a little later they tried to assault him. Yet he spoke for our Lord all the time. In the end they called him an apostate and they would have killed him in the very Temple if a few of us had not helped him to escape."

"Some men seem born to make trouble wherever they go," Cassius said and was promptly angry with himself for saying it.

Still Saul remained silent. But Ananias came to his aid. "The same was said about our Lord when He walked on earth," he said reprovingly. "And I told you, Saul spoke for our Lord."

Cassius nodded. "I know, I'm wrong. I take it back."

"Some of the members of the synagogue did not content themselves with having driven him from the Temple," Ananias went on. "They wanted to take his life, as they said he had blasphemed. My nephew Levi told me about it and that they were resolved to disturb the peace of my house to lay hands on Saul. So we hid him in Ruben bar Japhet's house in the little street behind the well called Birlah. But they found out and he had to flee in the middle of the night. Next day we heard that some of his enemies had gone to the ethnarch and complained to him about Saul."

"Does the Arab care about what Jews call blasphemy?"

"As little as the Romans," Ananias retorted. "But the ethnarch cares a great deal about money and he was well paid to order his soldiers to keep a close watch at all the gates of the city, day and night, and to arrest Saul at sight."

Cassius grinned at Saul. "That sermon of yours in the synagogue must have been a good one," he said. "They seem to have paid a lot for it." He turned to Ananias. "I begin to understand. You've brought him here in this disguise because he's not likely to be looked for in the house of a Roman. But if his enemies have made some kind of formal accusation against him—a trumped-up accusation of theft or something—the ethnarch may send soldiers here too."

"I didn't think of that," Ananias said, crestfallen.

"I'm leaving for Antioch shortly," Cassius told him, "and I'm selling this house to a wealthy Arab, a friend of Orybas. If that man should find out that I am harboring a man looked for by the ethnarch's soldiers, he might regard it as a very convenient opportunity to get my house for nothing. You see what I mean, don't you?"

Suddenly Saul spoke up. "I must not endanger your friend," he said to Ananias. "So far I have let you protect me, but now that the commander of this city is set against me too, I must not let you take any further risks for my sake. I will go. The Lord will see to it that I escape from my enemies."

Again Cassius grinned. "Well spoken. But even the Cassius Longinus of old would not have refused anybody asylum just because it was a bit dangerous. However little you and I may have in common otherwise, we have our Lord in common and that is more than if we had been born of the same parents."

"It is right for you to offer me asylum and I thank you," Saul said. "But it would not be right for me to accept it. Ananias did not mention the ethnarch to me before or I would not have come here with him."

Before Cassius could answer a door opened and a tiny girl appeared. She was about three years old.

"Acte," Cassius exclaimed, half angry, half amused. "What are you doing here? Your father has visitors."

The little girl listened gravely. Then she looked at the visitors. " 'Nias," she said delightedly and ran up to the old man who opened his arms to her. But a short way off she stopped. She had seen Saul. Slowly she turned toward him, looking at him intently. Then she walked straight up to him. "Who are you?" she asked peremptorily.

"I am Saul," Saul said.

"Sha-ul," Acte repeated. "You have him." And she gave him her doll, a half-squashed little something of rags and wood.

Bending down to her he accepted the royal present. A smile of extraordinary gentleness lit up his brown face and his long, sensitive fingers caressed the child's head.

"Good Sha-ul," Acte said, happily. "Must look well after him, good Sha-ul." Then only she turned to Ananias. "Good day, Uncle 'Nias," she said with great dignity.

"And a blessed day to you, child," the old man said, beaming. "You like Uncle Saul, do you?"

"Ye-es," Acte said emphatically.

"Why?" Cassius asked lightly.

"I like him," Acte insisted. "He's like Isha."

"Like who?" Ananias asked, perplexed.

"That's her own way of pronouncing the Name." Cassius' smile was a little strained. "Naomi calls him Yeshua and the Roman way would be Jesus."

As Saul, deeply moved, turned aside, Naomi appeared in the door. She greeted Ananias with a smile and a slight bow, then looked at Saul.

"I hope the child has not disturbed you too much," she said.

"This is Saul of Tarsus," Cassius said, quietly.

Naomi looked at the man who had been the cause of Stephanos' death; the man whom her husband had set out to kill in order to protect her; the man who had become a follower of the name he had so utterly hated in the past and whose slim fingers were gently caressing Acte's curls. She smiled. "You are welcome," she said and once more she bowed.

"Thank you, gracious lady," Saul replied. "But I was just bidding your husband farewell. I must not endanger him and his house. Now less than ever." He looked down at Acte.

Naomi's graceful head turned toward her husband. "If he's in danger, surely we ought to . . ."

Cassius took over. "Saul, what would you do, if you were free to act as you please; if there were no obstacles of any kind in your way, no angry Jews from the synagogue, no ethnarch, no soldiers?"

"I would go to Jerusalem," was the instantaneous answer.

"To Jerusalem?"

"Yes. I must meet Cephas—you would call him Petrus. I must meet the other apostles too. I must work to undo the evil I have done."

Cassius nodded. "Then the thing to do is not just to try to hide you, but to get you out of the city and on the road."

"They're watching the gates," Ananias reminded him.

127

"I know, you told me that. Tell me, does anyone of your flock live in the Street of the Towers? A reliable man, I mean."

"I know of several such men," Ananias said. "There's Daniel bar Thomas—but his wife is not yet one of us; there's Alexander bar Gideon . . . he would be better, I think. He is a widower and has no close relatives, so he would not object to a little risk. And what you have in mind is likely to be risky, isn't it?"

"It could be. As I said, we want a really reliable man. This Alexander may fit the part. I suppose he has the usual kind of apartment—with a window or two toward the outside?"

"Yes . . . oh, I think I begin to understand."

"Of course you do." Cassius grinned. "It's a custom in quite a number of cities and towns out here—they use the outer houses as part of the fortifications, of the city wall itself. It's not very good for the inhabitants in wartime, of course, when their bedrooms are manned with archers, shooting through the windows. The windows are fairly small. It is fortunate that our friend here is not a very big man. He'll get through."

But Ananias shook his head. "There is a drop of thirty feet," he said. "He could never get down alive."

"Not if he jumps." Cassius laughed. "But we could let him down the wall on a rope, or better still, in a basket with a rope attached to it."

"There are moments, I believe, when there is nothing so useful as a Roman brain." Ananias was downright enthusiastic now. "I don't know how to thank you."

"Thank me? I've done nothing. I think I'd better come with you to see that all goes well. There are a few points that worry me. Now go and inform your most reliable friend in the Street of the Towers. Let him get the basket and the rope. I'll keep Saul here in the meantime. Tonight, two hours after sunset, arrange for a cart to come here, the most ordinary kind, drawn by a donkey. There should be a few bags of vegetables or fruit in the cart and some sackcloth. The driver will deliver the stuff to my house. Nothing surprising about that. But when he leaves, Saul will be in the cart, covered with the sackcloth and I shall go with the driver, or follow him at some distance. We'll go to your friend's house, unload our goods there—and with a bit of luck Saul will be on the road to Jerusalem by midnight at the latest."

There was a moment of silence. "A perfect plan," Ananias said admiringly. Saul nodded.

"Good Sha-ul," little Acte sang. "Like Isha."

Naomi looked at Saul sharply. There was little or no likeness. Yeshua was tall and . . . there just was no comparison at all. And yet there was something indefinable, a blending of gentleness and diamond hardness, of purity and fire that made her feel that her child was right, if only as right as one would be who said that a lamp was like the sun. . . .

*   *   *

At the beginning all went smoothly. Cassius sent his slaves to bed early and then put on an old cloak, carefully made dirty with some earth from the garden.

"Do you think it is likely to be dangerous?" Naomi asked him uneasily.

"Not at all. Don't worry. But I must be there to make sure that they don't bungle it. None of them is a soldier."

The cart arrived at the appointed time and with a sturdy man named Baruch. "I'm Alexander bar Gideon's brother," he said and Cassius became immediately suspicious, as he remembered Ananias saying that Bar Gideon had no close relatives. But Naomi asked: "Of the same parents?" and the man shook his head. "My father and his mother were brother and sister."

"There's only one word for 'brother' and 'cousin' in Aramaic," Naomi explained to her husband in Greek. "Don't you remember when they spoke of our Lord's brothers and sisters? I didn't know myself at the time that He was an only child and that they were His cousins."

"Call Saul then. We'll go at once."

Damascus was not Antioch. The streets were badly lit. No one bothered about the cart. Twice they saw one of the ethnarch's patrols, but the first one was marching off to change the guard at one of the gates and the second seemed to have made a close examination of one or more of the many inns. The men were drunk to the point of staggering.

"It would have been more difficult when your people were still around." Baruch grinned.

"I should hope so."

Then they reached the Street of the Towers, whose houses formed a long stretch of the city wall. When the cart halted, Cassius saw that one of his fears had been realized: the house was very close to one of the smaller towers. These towers were always manned. In Roman times there had been two men on each and five on the larger ones. Now one never knew how many there might be up there. The Arab guards often had women with them to make the hours pass more agreeably. Only last week the ethnarch had one of his men hanged because he had got drunk and thrown a woman from the tower. Archers they were, as a rule.

Cassius said nothing until he had got Saul out from under the heap of sackcloth, into the house and up the stairs to Alexander bar Gideon's poorly furnished apartment. The owner was there, an intelligent-looking youngish man, and with him two friends.

"That tower," Cassius said bluntly. "Do they use their torches these days?"

"They do sometimes," Alexander answered. "Not often, though."

Cassius went to the window and looked out. The tower, far more massive than the house, protruded beyond the wall. The guards could overlook the window; and if they did when Saul was being let down, the game was up. There would be the sound of a horn and a few minutes later a troop of Arab cavalry would be out and sure to catch the fugitive before he had a chance to find a hiding place.

As if in confirmation of his anxiety a reddish glow became visible outside, at the top of the tower.

"They're burning a torch now," Cassius said. "We must let it burn itself out before we can risk it and even then—wait, I've got it. How long do these torches last?"

"A quarter of an hour, perhaps a little more."

"Right. Wait till it's out. Then wait another quarter of an hour. Then and then only get our friend here over the wall. And mark my words: get him over the wall, whatever noise may be coming from the tower. Can I be sure that you will do it that way?"

Alexander nodded. "I'll see to it."

Saul looked hard at Cassius. "You are not going to take any undue risks, are you?"

"No," Cassius said cheerfully. "No undue risks. Just risks. Don't forget that we must both serve our Lord, each of us in the way for which he is fitted. Farewell."

Saul pressed his hand and Cassius, with a nod for Alexander and his friends, left the apartment. Outside the house he waited in the shadow of the door until the glow of the torch dimmed and vanished. He waited a few more moments and then sauntered over to the tower entrance. It was unlocked. Perhaps they were expecting women again. He smiled grimly. Old Fuscus, the last Roman commander here, had not been a first-rate man by any standard, but he used to keep at least some kind of discipline. Silently he began to ascend the stairs.

After a while he could hear the soldiers talking. Their Arabic was so close to Aramaic that he could understand most of what they said. They were talking about women.

He climbed up the last stairs and appeared on the platform. Two soldiers only. Good.

"Blessed be your night," he said in a thick voice.

The soldiers stared at him as if he were a ghost. They were archers. One of them had a face disfigured by pockmarks, the other, a broad-shouldered fellow, had an eye missing.

"Who are you?" snapped the man with the pockmarks. "What do you mean by coming up here?"

Cassius drew himself up. "I'm a citizen," he declared proudly. "Been living here long before you fellows came. I've got my rights, haven't I?" He began to sway a little. "Beshides I'm sorry for you," he went on. "Musht get awf'ly bored alone up here."

The big archer grinned. "He's had one too many," he said.

"Nonshensh," Cassius told him with great dignity, again drawing himself up. "N-never drink too mush."

"But you can't come up here," the pockmarked one reprimanded. "This is a military post."

"Musht come up," Cassius contradicted. "Mush shee whesher you keep good wash. I pay my tacshes. Mush see whesher the town is well guarded."

But now the big archer seemed to have lost his sense of humor too. He took a step forward. "Go down at once," he ordered. "Or I'll throw you down."

Cassius closed one eye. "Throw me down?" he asked in baffled surprise. "You? Me? That'sh funny. I'd like to shee that."

"So you will, man, unless you go down at once."

Cassius began to laugh. "Tell you what," he said. "Here, take this." He produced a number of silver coins and shoved them into the hands of the smaller man. "You're the umpire. If thish big lout can get me on my back, the money's hish and you mush give it to him. If I get him, you can keep it for yourshelf. Ish it a deal?"

The pockmarked man laughed. "Go for him, Khadish. Find out whether there's more silver on him."

"By the moon and the stars, you may be right, Surash. We'll search him a little, shall we?"

"Not together," Cassius protested. "That'sh not a fair fight. One after the osher."

"I can deal with you alone, don't worry," the big Arab jeered. As he rushed forward, Cassius stepped aside. His right fist shot out and connected with the archer's jaw. The man grunted, shook himself and attacked again. Cassius seized him round the middle, took half a step back, swung his body round and threw the Arab across the narrow platform right at the pockmarked fellow. The two Arabs went down in a heap. Cassius jumped, tore the horn from the big man's belt and threw it off the tower. He had only just time to parry the dagger thrust of the smaller man. "Shame," he said. "Two against one and then you need a dagger?" He no longer pretended to be drunk. A kick of his right foot sent the little man sprawling. The big one was trying to get up. Cassius hit him twice, three times, four times on the jaw and he crumpled again.

132

The smaller man was winded. It was not difficult to send him into unconsciousness. A single blow sufficed. The fight was over.

Cassius peered across to Alexander bar Gideon's house. There was a rope hanging from the window; it was moving; and there was a dark round something farther down. The basket. Down it went. Now it stopped. The shadowy form of a man separated from it and ran into the darkness and disappeared. The basket began to move upward.

Carefully Cassius examined the two Arabs. They would be out for a few more minutes. He threw a dozen more silver pieces all over the floor. It would keep them from coming down too quickly if they came to before he was out of reach and it would compensate them for their bruises. Then he raced down the stairs. When he reached the door of the tower he gave a good look right and left. No patrol. He hurried across the street and dived into the maze of crooked alleyways that was the Jewish district.

After a while he slowed down. A walk of about half an hour and he would be home. His left shoulder hurt. So the big fellow must have hit him after all. He had not noticed it before.

He began to think of Naomi and of Acte. "Like Isha," she had said about that man Saul. Whatever made her say such a thing? It seemed to amaze Naomi too, and after all, she had seen Him—and seen Him alive. Yet he, too, felt that Saul reminded him of somebody. Not at their first meeting, out in the desert, but now. There was some resemblance to—to Stephanos, of course. Strange that he should resemble the man whose death he had caused. And he was going to Jerusalem to meet Petrus and—how did he put it?—to undo some of the evil he had done in the past. He could not undo Stephanos' death. Could he replace him? Stephanos had had a brilliant mind. This Saul did not seem to be very successful so far.

Yet when little Acte had said that he was like "Isha," Cassius had made up his mind that he was going to help him beyond giving him shelter for a few days. And it had come off.

He grinned a little ruefully. "I haven't paid off much yet, Lord," he thought. "Just a bit. But there may be more to come. Even a soldier can be useful at times. Just wait, Lord."

CHAPTER FOURTEEN

KING HEROD ANTIPAS and his queen were being visited by another Herod: Herod Agrippa who was Antipas' uncle and Herodias' brother and who came almost directly from Rome.

The visit was taking place at Antipas' summer residence in Galilee, in the little town of Tiberias on the lake shore. After a sumptuous banquet the royal personages retired to the palace roof for the *commissatio,* the after-dinner snacks, consisting mainly of special titbits whose purpose was to stimulate the palate sufficiently for a number of very rare wines. The *commissatio* was a Roman custom, but Herodias had insisted that it was a good idea. "My brother is likely to be more Roman than the Romans. Let's show him that we know as much about Roman customs as he does."

If Agrippa was impressed, he did not show it. There was no doubt, however, that he appreciated the wines and the food.

"After all those official toasts," King Herod Antipas said, "let's have a sincere one for once."

"You shouldn't have said that, you know." Agrippa smiled. "When a man proclaims that he's going to be sincere and frank he is sure to produce a thunderous lie—or he wants to be rude. It's like a merchant who writes across his shop window 'Here you will be served honestly.' If you hadn't known the fellow was a cheat, that would tell you." He was a man of forty-five or forty-seven, a few years older than his sister whom in a masculine way he resembled. The same ivory complexion, the same almond-shaped eyes with thick lashes, the same sensual mouth.

Herod Antipas rubbed his pointed chin and raised his goblet. "All I want to say is: Here is to the black sheep of the family who has succeeded after all!"

"Well, it's not exactly a lie, I suppose," Agrippa said, "but it's rude all right. After all, all the members of our family are black sheep, so why pick on me?"

"I don't know of any other," King Herod countered, "who has

spent most of his life contracting debts as fast as he could and having to flee from one place to another, from one country to another, to escape his creditors."

Agrippa nodded. "A man may wage foolish wars and lose his army and a good portion of his country, he may lop off the heads of a number of inconvenient people, he may lie and cheat and betray as much as he likes. But he mustn't be poor. For that's the only unforgivable sin. I know your philosophy, dear uncle. You preached it to me often enough when I was your guest before, here in Tiberias."

"I made you Chief Administrator of Tiberias when you didn't have a copper piece to your name," Herod Antipas told him acidly.

"So you did. Nice of you to remind me of it."

"I could remind you also of the deficit the municipal books showed in no time at all."

"Let's not bring that up again," Herodias interposed. "As you say, my brother has been successful since then—very much so, if one can believe the reports. Is it true that the Caesar has given you *all* Philip's lands?"

"Certainly, my dear. *And* those of Lysanias. *And* the title of King."

"Too bad for Philip's widow—my only daughter," Herodias said with a wry smile.

"Oh, don't worry about pretty Salome. I let her have the revenues from salt and copper. That's more than even she can spend."

"You have always had a generous nature," Herodias conceded stiffly.

"As long as the money belonged to someone else," her husband added.

"Of course a girl's best friends ought to be her parents," Agrippa said amiably. "Her mother and her stepfather, in the present case."

Herod said nothing.

"To me money no longer matters much," Agrippa went on. "It did when I didn't have any, naturally. Now I shall have a great deal of work to do, co-ordinating my newly created kingdom. That is what I call interesting work."

"I wish I really knew how you've done it," Herodias said enviously. "It's amazing."

"Luck, sweet sister," Agrippa told her. "Luck and perhaps a little ingenuity." He leaned back luxuriously and, goblet in hand, surveyed the surroundings with an air of indulgent benevolence. "Nice little place you have here. These flat roofs do lend themselves well to roof gardens. A bit narrow, of course, for real receptions. But just right for a cordial family meeting." He took a sip.

"Thank you. I know there is no comparison with your palace in Caesarea Philippi," Herod said.

"You look as charming as ever, sister mine," Agrippa went on. "But if I were you I'd ask my husband for a bigger clothes allowance. Peacock-blue, my dear! It's been out of fashion in Rome for years. They're wearing green now, all shades of green, shot with gold, and dove-gray, shot with silver. And most of the really good dresses are set with jewels. The wives of senators, even of simple knights, my dear. Luxury is no longer illegal as it used to be in the bad old times. But perhaps you haven't heard about that yet."

"We are living in a remote corner of the world," Herodias said modestly. "I hope you will bear with us despite our backward ways."

Agrippa knew that she could cheerfully have strangled him and she knew that her brother knew. It was never easy for the descendants of Herod the Great to hide their feelings from each other, which, however, never prevented them from trying.

"Tiberias is a place that has become very dear to me and to my husband," Herodias went on. "One grows so tired of living in fortresses, trumpet calls at the most inconvenient moments and everybody going about heavily armed as if war were imminent. We love this peace, though you may call it a rustic peace."

"There is no lack of soldiers here," Agrippa pointed out. "I saw quite a number when I arrived."

Herod smiled. "Surely, the least we could do was to match your escort. And you arrived with three hundred men."

"Something like that, yes," Agrippa agreed. "One has to, you know. I'm not much of a stickler for etiquette myself, but my new subjects are."

"King of the Trachonitis *and* of Abilene," Herodias said. "You *must* tell us how you did it. It can't have been all luck."

"I admitted that there was a little ingenuity as well," her brother reminded her. "But the main reason is that Caesar Gaius is an immensely generous man. I almost had to stop him from making me still further presents."

"Nevertheless it's bound to be a miraculous story," Herod Antipas said. "The last thing we heard about you, you were in jail."

"So I was, dear uncle, so I was." Agrippa helped himself to a hot truffle. "As you probably know I went to Italy, or to put it more exactly, to Capri a couple of years ago. . . ."

"Yes, just before they could arrest you for your debts in Alexandria."

"Not in Alexandria—" Agrippa corrected, "in Anthedon. I managed to escape to Alexandria, where the Alabarch Alexander lent me part of the money to pay those debts. Not much, only two hundred thousand sesterces."

Herod Antipas looked up as if to enlist the sympathy of the heavens.

"Don't worry, uncle mine," Agrippa delicately dissected a stuffed thrush. "It's all repaid now. However, I went to Capri where Emperor Tiberius received me graciously enough. But that rascal of a Herennius Capito, the commander of Jamnia, informed him that I had not repaid an earlier loan of three hundred thousand sesterces and I promptly fell into imperial disfavor. Tiberius was *not* generous."

"He was a great, great friend of mine," Herod Antipas said with some sharpness.

"Naturally." Agrippa nodded. "However, he wouldn't have put me in jail for such a trifle. The trouble was that I told Prince Gaius how glad I would be when he ascended the throne, as no doubt he soon would. We were having a nice drive in the gardens near Puteoli and my freedman Eutychus, who was driving us, heard

137

it and went and reported it to the Emperor's police chief. That's how I got into jail."

"Naturally," Herod Antipas imitated Agrippa's silky voice. "But then Tiberius very conveniently died and Gaius became Emperor and had you released at once."

"That's right. And what is more, the new Emperor found himself swimming in money and power and in his exuberance was ready to share with those whom he regarded as his true friends because they had shown affection and loyalty to him before he became Lord of the World."

"Of course, of course." Herod emptied his goblet and had it refilled at once. "And so you gobbled up a kingdom that fell from the Emperor's dinner table. You are right—it was luck. Well, I hope it'll hold."

"Caesar Gaius," Agrippa said placidly, "is a very young man. Not yet twenty-seven. I shall go back to Rome next year to report to him about Eastern matters. At his request."

"How interesting," Herodias interjected. "I hope you won't tell him about my peacock-blue dress."

"I hope you won't have to be wearing it still," her brother replied.

"And what will your policy be while you're here?" Herod Antipas asked casually.

"To get on well with everybody." Agrippa grinned. "I have already prepared my first big speech to that effect. How wonderfully useful platitudes are. And there are so many of them! A ruler could spend a whole lifetime without uttering anything else. Ah well." He popped half a peahen's egg into his mouth.

"The Trachonitis and Abilene," Herod mused. "Why, you'll be as powerful as I am."

Agrippa began to laugh. "That's not exactly world-shaking, is it? I mean no disrespect, my dear uncle, but after all, there are considerably greater powers out here. The Armenians for one—to say nothing of the Parthians and Persians."

"My relations with Armenia are excellent," Herod said coldly. "As for the Parthians, your Intelligence service cannot be very good if you don't know that King Artabanes is a close personal friend of mine."

Agrippa wrinkled his nose. "Parthians are notoriously stingy people. I believe you, willingly. But I don't think you'll get much advantage from that friendship."

"Won't I?" Herod pushed back his chair. His face was flushed from wine. "You may think that you know everything about what's going on here, but I assure you, you don't." He emptied his cup and had it filled again.

"In fact I know very little," Agrippa replied. "And I haven't got an Intelligence service yet. That, like many other things, will come later. I'm brand new, don't forget. But simple common sense tells me that a man in King Artabanes' position will see to it that his allies are strong in *some* way. Now your food and your wine is excellent, dear uncle, but the fortifications of, say, Machaerus, are not exactly modern, are they? And your army—what's left of it after the debacle of your war with Aretas. . . ."

Herod Antipas rose. "You come with me, nephew. I'll show you one or two things that you haven't seen in all your life."

"Money bags, I suppose," Agrippa jeered. "I know you've got many of those. You always have had. They call you the King of Foxes. They ought to call you King of Taxes instead."

"Come with me," Herod repeated fiercely.

Shrugging, Agrippa obeyed. They went down the stairs to the great hall and further down to the cellar.

A guard of twelve men under an officer rose to salute them.

"My, my," Agrippa said. "Do you need soldiers to guard your wine?"

"This is not the wine cellar, nephew. See for yourself."

Armed men opened a number of heavy doors. Every one of them was guarded. The last one led to what seemed to be almost a subterranean city. There were workshops, smithies, and huge stacks of weapons and armor of all kinds.

For the first time the self-assured royal visitor was visibly shaken. "But this is *big*," he exclaimed incredulously. "Looks as if you could arm twenty thousand men here at any given moment."

Herod Antipas laughed. "You've seen only part of it. And I have two more such places. According to this month's figures I have complete armor and equipment for seventy thousand men. Now repeat, if you can, what you said about the Parthians only being interested in a strong ally."

Agrippa looked contrite. "I'm afraid I have underrated you, uncle. I didn't know you were out to make history."

"Oh, I wouldn't say that," Herod Antipas replied quickly. "But not so long ago Vitelliuˢ stopped the war against Aretas because Tiberius died and on my own I wasn't powerful enough even to defend my lands against an attacker—let alone wage war. I had become too dependent, and frankly, it humiliated me. So this is my answer—to myself."

"One would have to find the soldiers for all this, of course," Agrippa murmured a little dubiously.

"When you've got money, you can get men as easily as equipment," Herod told him.

"Well, I wouldn't like to be Aretas of Petra—not after what I've just seen."

"Oh, never mind him." Herod shrugged his shoulders. "I shan't make any moves against him; not as long as he is in favor with Rome, or rather with the present Emperor. And he is, isn't he? I wonder why."

"I wonder about it myself," Agrippa admitted. "But then I'm afraid the Emperor's mind is not readable to ordinary men." There was a trace of mockery in the cultured voice.

"He must be in favor," Herod Antipas insisted. "Why else should the Emperor have given him Damascus?"

"The Emperor did not ask for my advice in that matter," Agrippa said nonchalantly. "However, I'm on fairly good terms with him and that is just as well. Such a very solid protection against any danger a bellicose neighbor might create."

"I entirely agree," Herod assented just a little too emphatically. "As for me, I would never try to go against the greatest power on earth in any way. I'm not such a fool."

"Of course you aren't." Agrippa turned away. "I shall need

more of your excellent wine after this, uncle. Your sudden disclosure of hidden power has come as a shock to me."

Herod laughed and slapped Agrippa's shoulder.

They grinned at each other like schoolboys.

"Let us go," Herod said. "Herodias isn't the kind of woman one can leave alone for long. If one does, she'll make up her mind about something and when she does it's not easy to make her change it again."

*　　*　　*

Herodias had made up her mind but she did not disclose the result as long as her brother remained in Tiberias. Agrippa departed after three days and the dust thrown up by the feet of his camels and horses was still visible on the horizon when she had her husband summoned to her favorite room. When he entered she sent all the slaves away.

"We must act at once."

"What do you mean, my dove?"

"Isn't it obvious?"

"It seems to be to you; it isn't to me."

"We must go to Rome."

"To Rome?" Herod was taken aback. "Why? What for?"

"Oh, how can you be so slow-witted! And they call you the Fox! Are we going to let that brother of mine get everything he wants from the Emperor in exchange for a bit of flattery? Can't we flatter, too? Can't we do better than that?"

"We might," Herod assented. "But I wouldn't like to leave here for a lengthy journey just when your noble brother is installing himself in my immediate neighborhood. He needs a bit of supervision."

Herodias' graceful hands flew up in despair. "What fools foxes can be! Don't you see that this is our opportunity? My brother made only one mistake in these three days, but it was a bad one. He told us he would not go back to Rome before next year. That's why we must act now. Do you think he's going to let us share his good fortune when he is back? Not he. I've known him all my life and he's generous only when it suits his ends. We must go at once, without so much as breathing a word to anyone where we are going. He'll find out, of course, but by then I hope it'll be too late. Besides he *must* stay and organize his new kingdom. Why, it's bigger than ours. And all for a bit of flattery! I have studied that new Caesar in the light of what he told us. Twenty-six. Generous. Easily influenced. Above all: *new*. All we need is a ship. And presents, unusual presents for that young fool in Rome. Something really spectacular. A dozen dwarfs or giants or girls . . ."

"There's nothing unusual about girls, surely." Herod smiled. "Except you, of course, and I won't part with you, not if the Caesar offered me all the countries east of Italy up to the frontier of the Silk Land."

"The girls will have to be unusual," Herodias insisted. "We could have them impregnated with some green substance and say they're from a rare tribe in the desert. They will have to be pretty, of course, but that's easy enough."

"Oh come now, jewels would be much better."

"We would never be able to match what he's already got. Our gifts must be something he has never seen before. He'll be furious with my brother for never having told him about that rare tribe. But never mind the details. We must go, that's the main thing."

"I loathe sea voyages," he husband said plaintively.

She flared up. "If I didn't know better I'd say you're growing old. You are the son of Herod the Great. Are you going to tolerate this no-good brother of mine establishing himself as a monarch, with the pomp and glory of a king of Persia, at your very frontier? Are you going to content yourself with being his poor little neighbor? Didn't you see how he was gloating? Now that we have lost those lands your precious ex-father-in-law stole from us we're little better than landed gentry. What would your father have done in the circumstances, tell me that!"

"There's something in what you say, my dove, but . . ."

"You have given my brother food and shelter when he was penniless. He's been living on what we gave him. And now he dares to look down on us, the half-baked King!"

142

"That's a woman's argument. Why do you hate your brother so much? You didn't seem to be so pleased when I threw him out, five years ago, for being insolent to me."

"What's strange about that? He's my brother, so of course I wasn't pleased when you humiliated him. But now *he* is humiliating *us*—do you expect me to be pleased about that?"

Herod shook his head. "And then they say women aren't logical," he muttered.

But she was in no mood for levity. "I know what you have been preparing all these years. You have shown him some of it. Perhaps that was a mistake and perhaps it wasn't. But do tell me this: Are you far enough ahead to enter a grand alliance against Rome?"

"N-no. Not yet. It'll take several more years. Two or three at the least."

"Very well. Then this is the time to go to Rome on a loyalty visit. Let's look around and see whether the Romans still are what they used to be. And let's undermine my dear brother's position a little. I want to have a look at this young Caesar."

"I'll think it over," Herod suggested.

"I *have* thought it over," Herodias said.

CHAPTER FIFTEEN

"They don't believe you." Bar Naba's voice was low and compassionate.

Saul gave him one of his rare smiles. "It is not surprising, is it? Why should they believe me? How can I explain to them what has happened to me? Even you must have found it difficult to give credit to such a story."

"I did, at first," Bar Naba admitted. "Not for long. But then I have known you many years, Saul. Yours is a difficult character, you're impetuous, irascible, impatient and you can be very disagreeable in an argument. But to my knowledge you never told a lie, if only because you despised lying as a coward's weapon. You told me that much one day, when we were pupils of Rabban Gamaliel."

"Gamaliel . . ." Saul looked out of the tiny window in his friend's room. There was the same life as ever in the streets of Jerusalem. There was the same seller of oranges and lemons at the street corner, drawing attention to his goods with shrill exclamations and wild gestures. Not only buildings but men, too, could go on unchanging in a changing world. "When I was here last, I did not go to Gamaliel because I knew that he would not understand me. And now I cannot go to him either and for exactly the same reason, although I have changed completely."

"He is static, you are dynamic."

"That's only part of it. He is Judaism, Bar Naba. Judaism at its most noble and venerable. He cannot understand violent, barbarous action. All he wants is wisdom and the peace it creates. But for the same reason he is incapable of grasping that his era has passed away and that he, too, will wither and pass away if he cannot open himself to the new age. I am only half his age and I used to be his pupil. I can do nothing about him. I doubt whether he would receive me. Most people don't, as you know, and I cannot even blame them. I am the man with blood on his hands."

"There are some who think it is all a trap of yours," Bar Naba said, with downcast eyes.

"Of course, of course. I can scarcely expect anything else. Still, I hoped that the apostles would hear me, or some of them—one of them—as you did. Thank the Lord for you, Bar Naba. You are doing honor to your new name, you really are the Son of Consolation to me. Three days in this city, and every door closed in my face." He sighed. "There will be many more such days." He seemed to be talking to himself now. "There is a cross of pain and one of violence and one of betrayal. There is also a cross of frustration and of waiting. But nothing is in vain, however much it may seem to be. Nothing."

"You have changed a great deal," Bar Naba said.

"I feel I am no longer I at all, but moved by Someone Else. The Saul you knew is dead, Bar Naba. He died in the desert, an hour's ride from Damascus. His shell was given a new life. So now I am a child again in this new life and like a child, my joys and pains and disappointments are total. And they are still mine though I am no longer I. I shall have to grow up."

Bar Naba cleared his throat. "I will go now. I don't know what to say to you."

"Don't say anything then. Pray for me instead."

*　　*　　*

Bar Naba came back in the afternoon, looking elated and grave at the same time. "I have news for you, Saul."

"What is it?"

"Cephas will see you."

Saul rose at once. With his eyes closed he thanked God in a swift prayer. Then he turned to Bar Naba. "You are a true friend. . . ."

"Don't give me too much praise," Bar Naba interrupted. "Cephas still does not believe in you. But he says: 'The Lord was always approachable. We are supposed to follow his example.' He said it like a man going into battle."

"The Lord has honored him beyond all others," Saul said, "and I am the least of all those He called. He called me, as one might say, as an afterthought. I am not going to fight Cephas; I am already his prisoner."

Bar Naba gave him a doubtful look, but said nothing.

They went out and to his surprise Saul found that they did not have far to go. Cephas was staying at a house no more than five minutes' walk from Bar Naba's abode. It belonged to Miriam, a relative of Bar Naba's. She was absent, but in her stead her son welcomed them.

"He's my nephew," Bar Naba said. "His name is Mark."

The young man spoke polite words of welcome, but his young, eager eyes were searching the strange guest who only a few years ago had been the most dreaded figure to all the followers of the Messiah in the city. "Cephas is expecting you," he said, opening the door to another room.

Behind a rough table a tall man rose. His face was not unlike that of a lion.

145

With a sudden shock Saul remembered that he had seen Cephas before—on his way back from the Field of Stoning. The first witness had pointed him out and he had thought of having him arrested. And Cephas, too, remembered. Saul could see that. The lion's face was very grave.

"You have not changed, Cephas," Saul said almost shyly. "So it is not surprising that I should remember you. But I have changed in many ways; so much that the people I knew in Damascus did not at first recognize me. Yet you did. Your eyes are sharp and I am glad of it. For now I have hope that you may be able also to look into my heart."

"You always were a good speaker, I am told," Cephas said slowly. "I cannot read the hearts of men as our Lord could, but no doubt He will show me the truth about you in His own good time."

Bar Naba and Mark withdrew silently. But for a long time not a word was spoken in the room as the two men stood looking at each other. They were different, utterly so, in everything. One big and towering, the other small and almost frail. One as simple as a peasant, the other erudite; one trained for three years in the company of Yeshua, the other trained for three years in the solitude of Mount Sinai. Different as they were, they were looking, searching for what they had in common. And they found it.

"I have come to work for our Lord," Saul heard himself say. "For He has called me."

"I am working for Him because He called me," Cephas said.

"I killed Stephanos and persecuted the faithful," Saul said, "yet He deigned to reveal Himself to me. What can I say before such a mystery?"

"You did not know Him when you killed and persecuted," Cephas said. "I have been His constant companion. I knew Him in His glory on Mount Thabor. I knew He alone had the words of eternal life. Yet I betrayed Him three times in one night and the last words He heard me say before He went to His death were blasphemy and treachery. His mother was there while He hung from the cross, and so was Jochanaan. Not I. I was sitting here, in this house, in the very room where we are now, trembling for my life. My guilt is heavier than yours, Saul, and I have more to atone for than you."

"So we are guilty," Saul said. "Everyone is. Perhaps we could not help others, being mere men, if we did not know what guilt is. It is clear to me that He always knew that you would betray him. . . ."

"He told me so before I did, but I couldn't believe it. . . ."

"He knew it when He chose you, just as He knew of my guilt when He chose me. Guilt of the past or of the future—it is all one to Him who comes from infinity, who was before time and will be when time has ceased to be. But we, whom He chose despite our guilt, what else can we do but love Him?"

"I do not know for certain what you mean about time," Cephas said slowly. "But I do love Him. And I believe you love Him too."

Saul stifled a sob. He took a step forward and so, at the same instant, did Cephas. And they embraced.

"Stay here," Cephas said. "Don't go back to where you live. Somebody will go and fetch your things. . . ."

"There is nothing to be fetched." Saul was smiling under his tears.

"So much the better." They beamed at each other.

"Let's go walking together," Cephas said. "There is much I must show you. . . ."

"And tell me!"

"Where we were together . . ."

"And what He said!"

"Yes. If only I could convey to you how He said it. His voice . . ."

"He spoke to me too."

"I forgot that. Bar Naba told me. It was on the way to Damascus."

"And later again—on Sinai. That's where I learned about His eternal legacy to us, His Body and His Blood. If it weren't for my guilt I would be the happiest man on earth."

Cephas pressed his hand. "You know that you will suffer, don't you?"

"Yes. He told me."

"Are you worried?"

"Only that I might not be able to pay my debt to Him."

Cephas smiled. "No one can—not in full. Ours are token gifts, no more. All the rest is made up by His love."

Saul nodded. "He makes all things new."

"He said so Himself. He has begotten us anew."

"Only three years ago I would have called it folly, Cephas—no, I did call it folly."

"It *is* folly," Cephas said. "But this folly comes from Heaven. It makes unheard-of things possible. The most evil deeds are changed into good."

"How so?" Saul's face was tense.

"You persecuted the faithful, Saul. . . ."

"Yes, and I cannot help wondering why the Lord tolerated it for a moment!"

"You drove them out of Jerusalem," Cephas went on imperturbably. "They fled from you as men will flee from a sandstorm to some place where they can find shelter. They settled down in Caesarea, in Tyre, in Antioch. Many even crossed the sea for faraway countries. But wherever they went, they took our Lord with them and wherever they stayed, they won new believers. By driving them out you have made them spread the belief in our Lord."

Saul's eyes shone. "The foolishness of God is wiser than men; and the weakness of God is stronger than men."

Cephas smiled at him. "I believe," he said, "if our Lord were to speak to you now He would say: 'You are not very far from the kingdom of Heaven.'"

*   *   *

Saul went to Golgotha. He spent a whole night on the terrible hillock and another in front of the cave where the body of Yeshua had rested for a while.

He never tired of asking questions about those days. Who saw the risen Lord first? What was the message to the apostles in the

148

Upper Room? Why didn't they believe it? Was it true that the risen Lord sat down to *eat* with them? How many people had seen that? Was there anything different about the risen body? Was it true that it could go through closed doors? How many people had seen the Lord after His resurrection? Did they talk to Him? Touch Him? Did He tell anybody when He would return? What was the official report of the Temple guards who had been watching the tomb?

He went to the fountain of Siloe. He went to the court where Yeshua used to teach, to the synagogue where He had preached. He went to the Mount of Olives, to the Garden of Gethsemane, to the Upper Room, the Cenacle, where the Last Supper had taken place.

He met Jaqob, not the son of Zebedee and brother of Jochanaan, but the other apostle of the same name, the very cousin of the Lord.

"There is some kinship of the flesh," Cephas told him, "but no outward resemblance whatever."

Jaqob was a frail man, ascetic-looking, with premature gray hair, deep-set eyes and the forehead of a thinker. Unlike Cephas he was rather stiff and aloof, neither trustful nor suspicious. It was impossible to know what he was thinking. But the purity of his life and his great piety made him deeply respected even beyond the congregation of the faithful.

The Upper Room was the only place to which Saul returned several times, once with Cephas who broke bread and gave him a piece, speaking the same words the Lord had spoken on that last evening before His death; and once with Bar Naba to pray in memory of that other great event, when the Holy Spirit came down on the apostles and on Miriam, the Lord's mother.

Mark showed him the place in the Garden of Gethsemane where the Lord had been taken prisoner. "I was there myself at the time," the young man said. "Our Lord told the soldiers to take Him alone and to let us go, but they tried to get hold of us too. One of them seized me and in my fear I tore myself loose so wildly that he was left with my linen shirt in his hand and I escaped naked."

Within two weeks Saul took in a thousand details and for the first time he was again glad that his was a trained mind and that he could sort out and classify and store up all he was told.

"It may be difficult for some to take it all in at once," Mark said one day. "I was present—I knew Him—to you He revealed Himself. But all those who never met Him and never had an experience like yours . . ."

But Saul shook his head. "The Old Law came to us through angels, yet it was valid and retribution would come to him who refused to listen to it. Just retribution. What excuse shall men have if they do not pay heed to the new message, given to them by the Lord Himself and guaranteed by those who heard it from His own lips?"

Mark was a young man. "Stephanos told you about it, yet you did not listen to him."

"And I have no excuse," Saul replied quietly. "All I can do is to praise God all my life for His mercy."

The next day he appeared in the Synagogue of the Cilicians, where Stephanos used to preach; and he spoke. The effect was very much the same as in Damascus. There were some who recognized him after a while and would not believe their ears, others who shouted, "Blasphemer," and closed their ears with their fingers, and still others who debated with him hotly and angrily.

A rumor began to race through the city that Stephanos had come back from the dead in the guise of him who killed him and voices were heard who swore that in that case he would be stoned to death a second time.

Nor were these empty threats. When Saul spoke a second time, he was set upon and only just escaped from the synagogue. The same evening Mark warned him that he must not go out, as three men were waiting for him at one corner of the street with two more holding watch at the other.

Saul left the house only in the morning when the street was full of people. He went to the Temple. In the court where Yeshua used to teach he lay down, with his arms stretched out and prayed. "Lord, Thou knowest that I will not fail Thee by cowardice as in the past I have failed Thee by pride. Thou has told me Thy holy will on the road to Damascus. Tell me what it is now."

It happened once again. There was that stillness so unlike any other, so utterly complete that even the beating of his own heart was gone. He no longer felt the stone pavement of the court supporting his body. Again he was suspended over the uttermost edge of creation. There was no light this time. But the Voice he heard was the unforgettable Voice of the desert on the road to Damascus and as he heard it he saw again what he had seen before, although his eyes remained closed.

"Make haste and go quickly out of Jerusalem, for they will not receive thy testimony concerning Me."

He heard himself plead.

But the Voice rose above his weak murmuring. "Go. For to the Gentiles far away I will send thee. . . ."

When he came home, he found Cephas waiting for him and with him Bar Naba.

"There is danger for you here, Saul," the lion-faced man told him. "Two of the High Priest's scribes have been seen, taking notes of what you said yesterday in the Synagogue of the Cilicians."

Saul bowed his head. "I will go."

Cephas took him by his shoulders. "Thank you for making it easy for me," he said with disarming honesty. "We shall fight separately for the same cause. But we shall meet again." And he gave him the kiss of peace.

"Shall I come with you?" Bar Naba asked warmly.

"Not now," Saul told him. "But we shall meet again, please God." And they embraced.

Within the hour Saul left for Caesarea, out of the High Priest's jurisdiction. From there he went to Tarsus.

CHAPTER SIXTEEN

BAIAE, not far from the slopes of Vesuvius, was without any doubt the most elegant little resort of the Roman Empire. To have a villa here was the ambition of all those who wanted to "belong." A square yard of ground here was worth almost its weight in gold.

For the sake of a villa in Baiae hundreds and hundreds of slaves died in the tin, lead and quicksilver mines of their masters; last wills were forged or secretly burned; old relatives put out of the way; provinces were sucked dry, cities looted. Marcus Silvanus denounced his brother as a conspirator against the Emperor; Tullia Vettia had her miser of a husband poisoned.

For Baiae was not only a most charming spot, where no eye would be offended by the dirt and misery of poor districts; it was the favorite resort of the young Emperor and therefore of the court. And it was impossible to "belong," unless one was a member of the imperial court.

Rome was jubilant about having a young man as a ruler. Year after year, decade after decade one had suffered under the tyranny of the despot of Capri, the typical tyranny of an aging man who trusted no one and seemed to regard generosity as a vice, in fact as the only vice to abstain from. Old Tiberius' avarice was surpassed only by his cruelty.

What a change then, when Caesar Gaius began to flood all those whom he liked with presents and gifts! His was the natural generosity of a young man who has been kept short for years and now at long last has all the money he wants. It was only natural, too, that in the over-brimming enthusiasm of his youth he overdid it a little sometimes, and there were those—there are always those —who wagged their heads and spoke of impending bankruptcy and ruin, as if the empire were not the inexhaustible reservoir of riches it was.

Pedants, pessimists, men with a chip on their shoulder. But even they had to admit that Caesar Gaius, despite his temperament, did not engage Rome in costly wars. It was stupid and ungrateful to begrudge him his fun. What if he did have all the ships of the Western fleet assembled to form a bridge across the Baiae bay to Puteoli, and then rode over it, forward and back, again and again, for two whole days? It was rumored that Tiberius' trusted astrologer, Thrasyllus, had predicted that it was as likely for Gaius to become Emperor as to ride on horseback across the bay between Baiae and Puteoli. So he was showing the astrologer that he could achieve both these things—or rather, showing his ghost, for Thrasyllus had had sense enough to die just a little while before Tiberius.

Perhaps the young Caesar was too generous toward foreigners— he had given some oriental rulers huge amounts of money and land, especially to the King of Commagene who received a hundred million sesterces, as well as getting his kingship. And perhaps he was overgenerous to his bosom friend, King Herod Agrippa who was one of those Jewish rulers—there were so many of them and most of them were called Herod Something-or-other, although this one was at least pro-Roman at heart, as was evidenced by the second name he had adopted.

But on the whole these costly presents made for peace, and be- sides, foreigners were not the only ones to receive them. The young Caesar had a heart for his people. He gave brilliant shows in the circus, not only in Rome, but in dozens of places in the provinces, shows lasting from early morning till late at night. At one of them all the charioteers in the main race were of senatorial rank! It was perfectly ridiculous that some people muttered about "loss of senatorial dignity." The old boys performed astonishingly well, much better than they did in the Senate.

And how pious the Caesar was! He had the temple of the Divine Augustus completed—Tiberius had always hedged about the neces- sary funds—and the ancient temples of all the gods in Syracuse restored. No wonder the gods loved him.

Affairs? Of course he had affairs with women. He was a virile young man, wasn't he? That some of the women were married was perfectly natural and even inevitable. Beautiful women usually married early. Could one expect the young Caesar to content him- self with the plain ones, whom no one else wanted?

Some of his relatives seemed to acquire the habit of dying rather suddenly, mostly by suicide; and invariably their wills mentioned the Emperor as their heir. Well, they could not have left their ill- gotten wealth to a worthier man.

The Caesar himself was a good family man, there was no doubt about that. Why, he practically adored his three sisters and nothing was too good for them. Some people would use even that for all kinds of sinister assumptions and the most horrible gossip. It just went to show that to some people nothing was sacred.

And his sense of humor! Once he gave a feast in the circus and all the gladiators were over sixty years of age! Some of them were in their seventies and two were over eighty and, as was only fair, they had to fight each other. Besides most of the old fellows came from good families, which added a very special note to the occasion.

Then there was a fight between a hunchback and a huge, fat Negress, so funny that all Rome laughed about it for weeks afterwards. The hunchback tried to hit the black monster on the head, but cut off her left ear instead and the infuriated Negress, howling with pain, tore the sword from him and split his back just where it was twisted. The young Emperor almost choked with laughter. And the amusing pranks he played on his uncle Claudius who, as everybody knew, was a half-wit, or as near as made no difference, and had a habit of falling asleep at the dinner table. Surely a ruler of greater severity would have regarded such behavior as an offense against the dignity of the Emperor and have punished it accordingly. Yet all Caesar Gaius did was to have the old fool undressed so that when he woke up, he found himself stark naked, or else his head was thickly covered with fruit juice and cream. There was such a delightful, playful child in the young ruler of the world! Such a relief after so many years of grim seriousness. Also the death warrants were almost invariably reserved for rich and powerful people, serve them right. Even so, there were not really very many of them, not in the first two years of Caesar Gaius' rule. Later they became more frequent, and that, too, was quite understandable, really.

At first the young Caesar wanted to be everybody's friend. If after a while some people showed themselves to be ungrateful, it was only human for him to react, perhaps a little vehemently. The terrible thing was that every execution seemed to rouse more people to fresh conspiracies and thus the cases began to multiply.

They multiplied so much that the young Caesar, in his justified exasperation, cried out one day what a pity it was that all those people did not have one single neck so that they could be executed with one single blow. There were some who said that he had uttered that exclamation at the circus because the people had favored a faction of charioteers for which he had a dislike. He loved racing and horses. His fastest horse, Incitatus, was provided with an ivory-covered stable and a manger of pure gold.

For the Senate, that bunch of lickspittles, turncoats and speechifiers, he had the contempt they deserved and what was more, he had the courage to show it. What a glorious joke, to have his horse Incitatus nominated Consul of the year! What a joke on the Senate and above all on the inevitable second consul, worthy old Maximinus whom everybody asked whether he, too, was training for the next race, and whether he did not need fresh shoes to make up for the constant strain on his feet, as unfortunately, he only had two!

What a shame the Caesar had to make the terrible discovery that his own sisters had conspired against him! His sisters, whom he loved so much, and yet all three of them conspiring to put Aemilius Lepidus on the throne. Even then the Caesar was lenient: Lepidus alone was executed, the three imperial sisters were merely sent into exile. And surely it was only compassionate of him to forbid his sister Agrippina to take her little son with her. After all it was an open secret that the climate on those isles where she and her sisters went was deadly. The little boy would not have survived six months there.

*　　*　　*

To Baiae came a charming young man with the charming name of Fortunatus. He was a freedman of a ruler whose generosity, on a smaller scale, resembled that of the Emperor: the newly appointed King Herod Agrippa of Abilene and the Trachonitis.

A few weeks earlier he had been summoned to Agrippa's palace in Caesarea Philippi. He found his former master in buoyant spirits.

"Fortunatus, it has come off! We have out-foxed the King of Foxes."

"I never doubted for a moment that you could do that, my lord King."

"Thank you. I managed to create the impression in my esteemed uncle that Caesar Gaius is a fountain of gold and power, ready to flow for just anyone. My noble sister Herodias became greedy, too —I know her. She is a greedy girl, Fortunatus; she always was. It's a family trait, I'm sorry to admit. Few Herods have been without it. I'm free of it myself, thank God or the stars or whoever's merit it may be. Herodias is one of the worst of us when it comes to greed. I wouldn't be surprised if it was she who made up the Fox's mind for him. I certainly did everything I could to bring it about. So now they're going to Italy with marvelous presents for the Emperor. They expect wonders from him and something tells me that wonders is what they will get. My uncle is out for more territory. He'll want Petra, of course, and Damascus. He may even try to persuade the Caesar that my territory is too large and that he could do with a slice of it. They'll sail next week on the *Agamemnon*. That's a good boat, I'm told, though not too fast. But fast or not, you must find a faster one, my Fortunatus. For it is vital that you should arrive just a little before they do."

"I hope and trust that can be done, my lord King."

For a brief moment the elegant Epicurean was gone. The full-lipped mouth became a thin, blood-red line, the chin jutted out and there was a glint of fury in the dark eyes. "It *must* be done," Herod Agrippa snapped.

"The *Agamemnon* will sail from Tyre, I believe," Fortunatus said. "She's a comfortable boat. No doubt she was chosen for that reason. King Herod Antipas is not a very good sailor. But comfortable boats are not very fast. Too bulky. I shall go to Ptolemais. To the naval authorities there. I may spend some money on this, my lord King?"

"Anything you need."

Fortunatus grinned. "Some Roman warships are leaving Ptolemais a week from today. I shall pass as your courier and ask for a cabin on board one of them. That's against the regulations, but with a little gold. . . ."

"You can go as my ambassador! Then they can't refuse you."

"No, my lord King. An ambassador means official visits, a guard of honor, all that kind of thing. And within a couple of days King Herod Antipas will have a report about it. You do want my visit to be secret, don't you, my lord King?"

"Definitely."

"Then let me go as your courier."

"Very well. The first thing you'll do when you arrive is to go and see Lucius Vitellius."

"The former Governor of Syria?"

"Exactly. He's in Baiae now, like everybody else, and very close to the Emperor."

"I didn't know he was a friend of yours, my lord King."

"He isn't. But he will be. What matters is that he hates my dear uncle. That's much more valuable than if he were merely a friend of mine. You will give this letter to Vitellius. He will then introduce you to the Emperor."

"And when I stand before the Ruler of the World—what do I say?"

Agrippa told him.

*　　*　　*

The resourceful Fortunatus arrived in Baiae safely and delivered his master's letter to Vitellius. He observed that it contained an extra strip of parchment which Vitellius, after a short glance and a little grunt, shoved among the many papers on his desk. Fortunatus did not raise an eyebrow. He knew what it was: an order from King Herod Agrippa to Sebulun bar Obed, the richest of all the Jews in Rome, to pay Vitellius the pretty sum of three million sesterces.

"What a pity," Vitellius drawled, "that during my proconsulship out east I had to deal with Herod the Fox. It would have been so much more amusing to have done business with your master instead."

"No doubt it would have been more advantageous." Fortunatus smiled.

Vitellius gave another little grunt. "I daresay the Caesar would have received you without my help," he said. "I know, of course, that he regards your master as a personal friend. But it so happens that I see him every day and therefore I can fit you in at the most opportune moment, which is not quite unimportant, especially lately. There have been certain changes. . . ."

Fortunatus looked at him questioningly. "Changes, excellency?"

"Yes, you see, the Caesar has become a god. That's no joke, my dear fellow, no joke at all. He told us about it himself. It came to him quite suddenly. The papers here on my desk are the plans for his first temple."

Fortunatus gulped. "I have heard, of course, that the rulers of the World sometimes become gods," he said in an uncertain voice, "but I thought that could happen only after . . . only under their successors."

"Ah yes," Vitellius said blandly, "that's how we used to handle the matter. But Caesar Gaius decided he wouldn't wait that long. His divinity, incidentally, encompasses all other gods. Now you, as a foreigner who has only just arrived here, you have never heard of that. But you might discover it, as soon as you are in the presence, and . . . er . . . act accordingly. I daresay it would make a very favorable impression."

"No doubt it would," Fortunatus affirmed, a little breathlessly.

"You will understand, naturally, that a god must be addressed only in the spirit of the most profound humility," Vitellius went on. "Above all a god must never be contradicted."

"Of course," Fortunatus said, "or rather, of course not."

"Ah well, we understand each other." Vitellius remained serious. "Now when the King of Foxes lands he will probably avoid meeting me. He'll ask for an audience directly. That means the Magister palatii and that's old Tertullius. He'll make him a handsome present, I suppose. But I think Tertullius will forget to open Herod's eyes to the fact that our Emperor has become divine and that will be all to the good, though not for Herod. I think I shall see the Caesar this afternoon. When you have your audience, Fortunatus, do remember that the Fox was once a very close friend of Sejanus, will you? In Sejanus' conspiracy the then Prince Gaius was at the head of the list of those to be eliminated—I mean proscribed. He still hates the very name of the man."

"My lord Vitellius," Fortunatus said enthusiastically, "how right my master was to tell me that you are the wisest of all Romans!"

Vitellius grinned. "He said nothing of the sort. Admit it at once."

"If he didn't," Fortunatus said politely, "he should have."

* * *

King Herod Antipas and Queen Herodias arrived on the *Agamemnon* a few days later. They had brought half a shipload of presents, including two Sudanese Negroes almost eight feet tall and a number of rare animals.

At the appointed time they were led into a large hall of the palace and made to wait. With them was the Magister palatii, Tertullius, fat and perspiring and behind them twenty Praetorian Guards, fully armed.

After a few minutes the situation became slightly uncomfortable. When Herodias started to ask a question, Tertullius' eyes widened with horror and he laid a fat finger to his lips. Herod looked about, but there was not even a chair in the room, except for a thronelike seat, obviously destined for the Caesar. Had something gone wrong? The reception so far had been formal, but quite correct. A guard of honor, litters put at their disposal, sumptuous quarters given to them in one of the palace wings. But they had not been allowed to take their presents with them into the audience, their retinue had to remain outside and now they were made to wait like ordinary petitioners.

A quarter of an hour passed. Herod could see that Herodias was seething with rage. She was biting her underlip.

Suddenly a trumpet sounded so loud that it startled them both. The huge middle door crashed open and more Praetorian Guards marched in to take positions all along the walls. They were followed by a number of high-ranking officers and palace officials. Then came a large group of senators and knights, among them a familiar figure: Lucius Vitellius, former Consul, former Governor of Syria. Like all the others he gave a stiff, formal salute. He did not approach them.

There was another trumpet signal and to the utter surprise of the royal pair all those present, except the soldiers, went down on their knees.

The tall, awkward figure of a young man appeared. He was wearing a purple tunic and a long-flowing mantle of the same color, forbidden to everyone else in the entire empire. His hair was waved artificially; it looked like a wig. Perhaps it was a wig. Enormous jewels glittered on his golden sandals and all along the hem of his mantle. But the strangest thing about him was that he had a small golden beard affixed to his chin; it was not made of hair but of metal, of gold. In his hand he carried a golden instrument not unlike a long arrow, except that it was not straight. Neither Herod nor Herodias were familiar enough with the ever-changing religious customs of Rome to realize that the Caesar had adopted the ceremonial beard and lightning of the greatest of gods, Jupiter.

The Caesar walked straight to the throne chair, sat down and asked in a surly voice: "Who is that standing before us?"

Tertullius raised his bald head from the floor. "Divinity, they are King Herod Antipas and Queen Herodias who have craved an audience from the Ruler of the Earth and the Heavens."

"They do not seem to know who I am," the Caesar said. "But never mind that. They soon will. King Herod! You have in that little Galilee of yours a number of arsenals, containing the equipment for seventy thousand men. Why?"

Herod became deathly pale. "Agrippa," he thought. "Agrippa and Vitellius." But he was not called the King of Foxes for nothing.

"To be worthy of being an ally as well as a vassal of the greatest Emperor ever," he said. "All I have is entirely at your disposal."

"Of course it is," the Caesar said. "And I shall dispose of it. No little king is in need of such quantities of arms. Not when he is a vassal of Rome. Rome protects those dependent upon her. You know that just as well as any other of the thousand kings who serve me. Therefore you had other things in mind, and what they are is easy to see. You are conspiring against me and the empire. No, say nothing, if you value your life! Now I know for certain that the other accusation made against you is true as well: you have been a close friend of the monster Sejanus. You knew of his conspiracy to overthrow my august predecessor Tiberius. Not a word! Your guilt is written all over your face. You have ceased to be the ruler of Galilee and the rest of your tetrarchy. Rome can give, but Rome can also take away. Your lands will be given into worthier and, above all, more loyal hands. And the only comfort I can give you is that these hands belong to a relative of yours: King Herod Agrippa. Tribune Chaerea!"

A graying soldier stepped forward. "My Emperor?"

"The former King Herod Antipas will be taken by ship to Lugdunum. That's in Gaul, in case you don't know."

"My lord Emperor," Herodias cried, "please, hear me!"

"Noble Queen," the Caesar said courteously. "Believe me I am most sorry to see you ruined by the machinations of this wretched husband of yours. For the sake of your brother Agrippa I will leave you in possession of your personal revenues and put you under your brother's protection."

Herodias drew herself up. "The Emperor is most kind," she said in a voice trembling with rage. "Indeed, your words are worthy of your high rank. But I will not accept your mercy. I love my husband. I have shared his good days—I will not leave him now in his misfortune."

"You said no to me, I believe," the Caesar said incredulously. "You must be mad. My offer is withdrawn. Your revenues will be given to your brother and you will go to Lugdunum with that husband of yours." He began to laugh. It was a weird, guttural laughter. "You will find congenial company at your place of exile," he jeered. "A few years ago a man was sent there whom you know very well. If he's still alive, that is. The climate there is rather damp, I'm told. He's a former Procurator of Judea: Pontius Pilatus. Take them away, Tribune."

Chaerea stepped up to Herod, but hesitated.

The King of Foxes was swaying on his feet, his face drained of blood; he seemed near fainting. "There is a curse upon me," he said. "There has been for a long time. Now it's there for everyone to see."

"Be quiet," Herodias whispered to him. "You will only make it worse for us."

He did not even hear her. "I had a man killed once," he said. "Just one stroke of the sword and his head fell. Now seventy thousand helmets will not protect me against his vengeance."

"What is the man jabbering about?" The Caesar asked no one in particular.

"I mocked a man once," Herod said in a strangely high-pitched tone. "I had him dressed in the rags of an old purple cloak. And ever since I have known that a tattered purple cloak would be all that would be left to me in the end. Pontius Pilatus had that man crucified. The same day, too. And where is he now? He and I, we are under the same curse. No wonder we shall meet in exile. We are brothers."

Herodias gave a half-stifled groan.

"They are both mad," the Caesar shouted shrilly.

Herod laughed. "No man ever thought I was mad when I was lying," he said. "Oh, the many lies, the juicy lies, the double and triple lies. But now when I speak the truth, I am declared mad."

"Tribune Chaerea," the Caesar rasped, "I gave you the order to take these two away. Are you frightened of them because they're mad, you old woman? Away with them—out of my sight. And I never want to see them again."

CHAPTER SEVENTEEN

LOOKING UP from his loom Saul saw a tall man in a wide, white mantle, smiling at him. His hands dropped. "Bar Naba," he said incredulously. "Is it really you?"

"I thought I'd find you here in the Street of the Tentmakers," Bar Naba said, beaming, and he stretched out his arms.

Saul jumped up and leapt forward. "Four years," he stammered as he and his friend embraced. "Four years . . ."

"And much has happened." Bar Naba nodded. "Or else I wouldn't be here even now."

"I've often thought you'd never come at all," Saul told him, "and that the Lord wanted me to wait longer, much longer. He told me to wait, you know."

"Have you forgotten Jeremiah?" Bar Naba asked.

"Jeremiah?"

"Yes. 'It is good to wait with silence for the salvation of God.'"

Saul smiled. "It comes easier to some than to others, but I have learned. Later, perhaps, I shall tell you how. At this moment I am indulging in happiness. I will ask no question and give no answer. Bar Naba with me in Tarsus! This is a feast day."

And feast they did, on the roof of the rickety old house, on bread and thin slices of roast lamb and on figs and drank the rough, red wine of Cilicia.

"This is a beautiful city," Bar Naba said. "It reminds me a little of my own town, Nicosia, but it's bigger and the mountains are wild here and look like rebels."

"Tarsus is more Greek than anything else," Saul agreed, "except in its beliefs. What a multitude of gods they have here! There is Baal from Phoenicia and Isis from Egypt as well as Zeus, Aphrodite and a local demon of the name of Santan, who is supposed to be Baal's friend and messenger. Every year they parade his statue and that of Baal through the streets and then burn them solemnly. But in the spring he comes to life again and there is a wild feast with the most abominable rites. . . ."

"I wonder," Bar Naba said thoughtfully, "whether there isn't some dim kind of presentiment in this, some first, nebulous divining of a truth still hidden from them. In fact I often wondered whether the Gentiles, too, were not being prepared in some way for the coming of the Lord. . . ."

"What good could that be?" Saul asked cautiously. "If it were not His will that they, too, should know the full truth and partake of it, when the time comes?"

"Questions and answers have begun at last." Bar Naba smiled.

163

"Once more you have changed, Saul. In former days you couldn't have waited that long."

"I told you I had learned," Saul replied, "though not from Jeremiah."

"From whom then?"

"From the example of our Lord. What is any man's mission compared to His? Yet for thirty years He waited in Nazareth, working with His hands, until His time had come. So when you arrived after only four years, I knew He had had compassion on me once more."

"You knew I didn't just come for a friendly visit?"

"You are a worker in His vineyard, Bar Naba. You have no time to waste, not even on friendship."

"Much has happened," Bar Naba admitted.

"You have come from Jerusalem? From Cephas?"

"I came from Antioch. Cephas and the brothers sent me there to see what was happening. We had reports that the Church was growing daily."

"Are there so many Jews in Antioch, then?"

"A good many, but . . ." Bar Naba paused. "Not only Jews are looking for the Truth," he said after a while.

Saul's eyes began to flash. "I knew it," he murmured. "It had to come. But Cephas? Jaqob? How did they face the problem?"

Bar Naba said very slowly: "Cephas has had a vision."

Saul had to exert himself not to show his excitement. "Are you allowed to tell me about it?"

"It is no secret. He told the other apostles. He told me."

"What has . . . no. Tell me everything in your own way."

"We had gone to Lydda. There the Lord gave Cephas the power to cure a man of palsy. Two messengers came from Joppa to ask for his presence in their town, where a girl named Dorcas had died. Everyone loved and respected her, for she had done a great deal of good. We were sitting at table when they came. Cephas and I went with them at once."

"And?"

"He raised the girl from the dead."

"The name of the Lord be praised," Saul said.

Bar Naba smiled, for he could hear only happiness in his friend's tone and not the slightest trace of spiritual envy. "We stayed on in Joppa after that," he went on. "Many people learned to believe. One day, at noon, Cephas went up to the roof alone to pray. He was hungry and waiting for a meal they were preparing in the kitchen. Then he fell into a trance. He saw Heaven opening— What is it?"

"Nothing," Saul said quietly. "Go on, please."

"Something like a great sheet came down," Bar Naba went on, "It was held by its four corners, though he could not see by whom, and on it were all kinds of animals and birds and creeping things. And a Voice told Cephas to eat. But he said: 'It cannot be, Lord, never in my life have I eaten anything profane, anything unclean.' But the Voice said: 'It is not for thee to call anything profane which God has made clean.'"

"Yes," Saul said. "And that is the full answer; the complete justification." He was so full of joy, so radiant, that for a moment Bar Naba thought that he was being lifted up in a trance too. But Saul said eagerly: "Go on, I beg of you."

Bar Naba obeyed. "Three times this happened before the bundle or sheet was withdrawn and Cephas came to. He was still wondering and searching in his mind for the meaning of his vision when three messengers arrived, this time from Caesarea. A Roman officer had sent them, a centurion of the name of Cornelius."

"A Gentile," Saul said, nodding.

"Yes, They asked Cephas to come to Caesarea, to the officer's house. Two of the men were slaves, but the third was a soldier, and Cephas liked him because he had a kind face and because, like his master, he worshiped the true God, as some Romans will when they have been stationed for some time in our country. The soldier told him that God had revealed to his master Cornelius where Cephas was and had told him to send for Cephas and to listen to what he had to say to him. So Cephas welcomed the three men and had them put up for the night. The next day they traveled together to Caesarea. There the Centurion Cornelius was waiting for them at the door of his house. He gave one look at Cephas and fell at his feet. Cephas raised him. 'Stand up,' he said, 'I am a man like thyself.' He wondered about that later on—about what made him say 'like thyself.' For were not Jews to be a nation set apart and not like other men?"

"This is a great tale," Saul said. "Go on, go on."

"They entered the house then," Bar Naba said, "and there was the Roman's family, and all his closest friends were assembled too. Cephas stopped for a moment and almost took a step back. Almost! He smiled instead and said: 'You know well enough that a Jew is contaminated if he consorts with one of another race or visits him, but God has been showing me that we should not speak of any man as profane or unclean.' So Cornelius told him once more why he had sent for him and Cephas listened carefully. Then he said: 'Now I really understand that God is not a respecter of persons, but in every nation he who fears Him and does what is right, is acceptable to Him.' And he told them all the story of our Lord. He was still speaking when the Holy Spirit came over the assembly and they broke into Hebrew and Aramaic. You know how awkward the Romans are about either; yet they spoke each one as if it were their own language."

"There is only one language in our Lord's world," Saul said in a strange voice. "He has undone the curse of Adam; he has undone the curse of death; and he has undone the curse of Babel."

"Cephas had them all baptized after that," Bar Naba said. "But when we came back to Jerusalem, the faithful found fault with him for what he had done."

Saul nodded understandingly. "And Cephas? He did not give in, I hope?"

"Not Cephas. He said: 'If God has made them'—the Gentiles—'the same free gift which He made to us, when faith in the Lord Yeshua has gone before it, who was I, what power had I, to stay God's hand?'"

"That is fine," Saul said, his eyes shining. "But he might have added: If the Lord sat down with us when He was walking on earth—shall we not sit down with the Gentiles? What is greater: the difference between the Lord and us, or that between us and the Gentiles, even after the most severe reckoning of that Law from which we were freed? This is a blessed day for me, Bar Naba."

"Now when I came to Antioch and saw that the Gentiles were as hungry for the Truth as our own people, I knew whom I needed to help me in the work there." Bar Naba took Saul's hands. "And that's why I am here," he concluded. His voice broke with joy.

"In Jerusalem the Lord told me that He was sending me to the Gentiles," Saul said. "So I went. When I came here, He told me to wait. So I waited. For my will counts as nothing before His will." He rose. "Come, Bar Naba."

"Where to?"

"To Antioch, of course. There is no time to be lost."

CHAPTER EIGHTEEN

CASSIUS LONGINUS arrived at the governor's palace in Antioch a few minutes before the third hour. He was mildly amused at his own punctuality, a remnant of his military past. He could never rid himself of it, at least not when he had an appointment with a Roman, whether an official or not. It was a little silly, really. After all, he was independent in every sense. He was wealthy, too, though that had come only within the last few years. Business in Antioch was flourishing. There was nothing he wanted from Rome, certainly nothing that official Rome would be able to grant. And on top of all that the Governor of Syria, Vibius Marsus, was a personal friend, though the governor was very considerably his senior. He was thirty-eight now—Marsus was nearing sixty.

They had met shortly after Marsus' arrival in Syria, two years ago, and had liked each other at once. Marsus had known Cassius' father well and was a first cousin of old Decimus Cinna, the commander of the Twenty-first Legion, under whom Cassius had served in Germany. So many names had come up from the past, joyful, sad or humorous.

Since then they had met fairly frequently. He had been invited to some official occasions to the palace. He had invited the governor to his house, and Marsus had come, benevolently owlish, with his staff and security police, for an official dinner. Thus he met Naomi. He knew about her, of course, and seemed quite taken with her. He had the nice, rather old-fashioned manners of the well-bred bachelor who has never become a cynic. Yet there had been events in his life which would have made cynics out of many men.

He had been out here before, back in the times when Prince Germanicus was in command, the nephew of Tiberius and father of Prince Gaius—the late Caesar Gaius—and when all those wild young women who were Gaius' sisters had been conspicuous. Marsus was here when Germanicus was poisoned by the monster, Piso, and he had taken Germanicus' widow, Agrippina, back to Italy, where that great lady was treated with so much hatred and contempt by Tiberius—who probably instigated the poisoning of her husband—that she ended her own life.

Later Marsus had been drawn into a sensational lawsuit, together with several other men in high position, including Arruntius, and, of all people, Vitellius, but, though all the others had lost their reputations and fortunes, Vitellius and Marsus had come out of it almost unscathed, the former because he was the father of all eels and the latter because he was decent enough to be innocent and adroit enough to be able to prove it.

"The noble Cassius Longinus to see His Excellency."

Cassius marched into the enormous study, the same Vitellius had once occupied. But Marsus was not the man to await his visitor behind a desk. He came forward with his quick little steps, a quick little man with big, round eyes, that seemed to look startled even in repose.

"Welcome, welcome, do sit down, friend, have some wine—no? Of course, I forgot, it's only the third hour."

"Yes," Cassius said, sitting down on the chair where Pilatus had sat, eight years ago, on his day of humiliation. "And I don't mind telling you that I'm wondering a little why you should wish to see me so early."

"You are a late sleeper? I gave up sleeping years ago. Can't afford losing a third of my time, not as governor of this accursed part of the world."

"What's wrong with Syria?"

"I don't mean Syria so much as Judaea."

"What's wrong with Judaea, then?"

"Everything. And it's getting worse. Friend, there are times when I can't help thinking that a fool is more dangerous than a madman."

Cassius laughed. "You do love talking in riddles."

"Nonsense. Never do anything of the kind. Caesar Gaius was mad. No wonder Chaerea and his friends stabbed him to death. Only surprising thing is that they didn't do it sooner."

"I agree—so far," Cassius said.

"And our dearly beloved Emperor Claudius is a fool," Marsus went on blandly. "Oh, shut up, Cassius, I know I shouldn't say it and I know that it is your sacred duty to protest formally and to denounce me to the authorities. Fortunately I am the authorities. The man's a fool, Cassius, he's never been anything else and never will be. In the past at least he couldn't do much harm. Now it's different. And what is really annoying is that his good qualities rather than his faults or vices are creating the worst trouble."

"Riddles again," Cassius said cheerfully. "But I'm glad you've discovered that he has good qualities as well as—others."

"He has a sense of gratitude. Rare thing, too. In an emperor almost unique. Unfortunately he has a way of extending it to the wrong people."

Cassius shook his head, laughing. "What else do you expect from a man whom you regard as a fool?"

"Nothing. Mind you, when I say the wrong people I don't mean that he isn't able to recognize to whom he owes gratitude—except in my case. He is grateful to some people who really did help him. But it so happens that they—that at least one of them is extremely dangerous."

"I see. And that man is out here and he's King Herod Agrippa, your pet aversion. What has he done this time? And why did you ask me to come here on a pleasant morning to tell me about it?"

"The trouble with you, Cassius, is that you are a happy man. You have a good, beautiful wife, a delightful daughter. . . ."

"I concede both points."

"You are rich. . . ."

"That's not necessarily a source of happiness. Especially not with your tax-collectors sniffing at my books all the time."

". . . and all the responsibility you have is towards your family. My agents tell me that you are the member of some religious sect, built around a rather mysterious personage called the Anointed One, the Christ. . . ."

Cassius raised his brows. "Why not ask me directly, Vibius? I'll tell you about it with pleasure. You're wasting the taxpayers' money."

"You can't do without agents in my position, friend. And as you see, I am perfectly frank with you about it. I shall ask you directly, too, don't worry. There are one or two points . . . but let's leave that for a little later. You mentioned my pet aversion and you are right. I don't like Herod Agrippa and I know he doesn't like me. It isn't often that I dislike people at first sight, Cassius, but when I do, soonor or later I invariably find very good reasons for it. He'd be an extremely dangerous proposition for any governor of Syria at any time. What makes it quite intolerable is that he and our dearly beloved Caesar Claudius are bosom friends."

"I know that, but I could never quite understand why. The two couldn't be more different."

"I can tell you all about that," Marsus said. "First of all they were brought up together. Young Herod Agrippa was a hostage in Rome and you know how we deal with those foreign princelings— let them grow up in the company of our own nobility, Romanize them as much as we can, the idea being that later when—and if—they ascend the throne, they will have Roman sympathies. Creating allies by education. It's asinine, of course."

"Is it? Why?"

"Because instead of becoming impressed by our power, they invariably get far too clear a picture of our weaknesses. Besides there will always be some young whippersnappers around who look down their noses at them for being orientals or barbarians or whatever they may be. The result is a smoldering hatred, well concealed, of course. That German fellow Arminius was a good example. We educated him—why, the seven-foot swine even went through a complete course at Staff College, strategy, tactics, everything. He learned the very best tricks of treachery as well. Cost us three of our best legions, as you know, and almost broke poor old Augustus' heart. That happened in the case of a German, you understand, a simple-minded, straight-forward Cheruscan whose early environment was filled with dumb, bullnecked German numskulls. Now what can we expect when the pupil is a crafty young oriental with a mind as slippery as the body of a wrestler? And a Herod to boot, my dear Cassius, a Herod! I don't know how well versed you are in the history of that somewhat terrifying family, where murder has always been regarded as the natural way of settling an argument and treachery as a virtue."

"I thought the man was just a spendthrift with an inordinate portion of sheer good luck."

"He is that, but it's only part of him. As Sylla said about the Divine Julius: there is more in him than just a Marius."

"Caesar was a very young man at that time. Herod Agrippa must be fifty-odd years old, and most of his life he was no more than . . . well, as I said, a spendthrift, a maker of debts and everything else that goes with that type of man. Can a man change much at fifty?"

"Yes, Cassius, he can, if his life is changed for him. Caesar Gaius in his madness, put him in a position of very real power and Caesar Claudius in his foolishness increased it still further. Can't you see the cunning of the man who managed to be the devoted friend of both young Gaius and old Claudius? Power is what he was out for. And power is the headiest wine of all, unless you have a scientific or philosophical mind."

"Like yours."

"Like mine, for instance," Marsus admitted without any false modesty. "My desire for power has been amply fulfilled, indeed I have a surfeit of it. I have held all the great offices in the empire, except the throne and if the gods existed, they would know and give witness that I wouldn't like the purple. It isn't a healthy color, my Cassius. And despite my age I happen to be rather fond of living. I wouldn't change places with Emperor Claudius for anything. Do you believe me?"

"I do," Cassius replied. "Perhaps it isn't even difficult for me to believe it. I feel about the same way myself. Or . . . almost."

"Right. But let's go back to what you call my pet hate. He's shown remarkable diplomatic abilities. First he managed to influence Caesar Gaius against his uncle, the Fox, in such a way that the Fox was not only stripped of his kingdom, but that he himself was given it in addition to everything he had before. Then he won Claudius' confidence to such an extent that he was given even more lands and now he rules over the Trachonitis, Iturea, Gilead, Galilee, Basan, Samaria and Abilene, the lands of three Herodians, Antipas, Philip and Lysanias. And, on top of it, Claudius gave him Judaea."

"Perhaps it is better that Judaea is no longer a Roman province," Cassius said thoughtfully.

"Well, I admit it has always been a source of trouble. But it has not ceased to be that. On the contrary: it worries me more than ever."

"I wonder why. And I wonder, too, how Herod won so much influence over Caesar Claudius."

"Don't you know that? Strange that we never discussed it before."

"Not so strange, really," Cassius said. "You had no particular reason to talk about it. You have one now. You must have."

"That's right. You know, of course, how Gaius was murdered by the Tribune Chaerea and the other conspirators as he was leaving the circus."

"That's about all I know. We poor benighted provincials aren't told much, are we?"

"Just as well. You poor, benighted provincials might lose the rest of your respect for Rome and things Roman. Anyhow: Chaerea was on duty that day and he went up to the Emperor to ask for the official password. Gaius always liked to make fun of Chaerea who had a rather squeaky, high-pitched voice. He liked to call him an old woman and to make all kinds of disparaging remarks about him in front of everybody. Naturally, Chaerea resented it. This time Gaius gave as the password, 'Jupiter Optimus Maximus,' but in a high voice like Chaerea's. The tribune squeaked back: 'Take then what he sends you,' and thrust his sword in the Emperor's face. . . . Then the other conspirators joined in and Gaius fell, in a kind of grotesque parody of the great Julius' death in the Senate. Then they went to the palace and killed Gaius' wife and daughter, whereupon the Praetorian Guards a little belatedly remembered that it was their duty to protect the imperial family and started killing off the conspirators and everybody else in sight. In the meantime that venerable bunch of toadies, the Senate, convened to debate the situation. For the first time they could feel important. There was no Emperor to say yes to. Inflated with their own importance they quite seriously thought of reintroducing the republic! Back to the good old times. No Emperor, no dictator, only the Senate and, if necessary, the people."

"Not a bad idea, come to think of it."

'Possibly. But you need the right people for that kind of system and we haven't got them any more, my Cassius. Men accustomed to bow and to say yes to anything, *anything* a mad emperor demands of them cannot be turned, overnight, into so many Catos, Brutuses, Cincinnatuses and Scipios. Well, at the palace the Praetorian Guards had murdered everybody who could have been connected with the conspiracy and a few more and now they were looking for a new emperor to pay them. They had no idea whom to choose. Then one old soldier saw a pair of feet behind a curtain. He drew back the curtain and discovered dear old Claudius, the pride of the Julian family, Caesar Gaius' uncle, whom the nephew had left alive only because he was such a convenient butt at the dinner table. Claudius, of course, thought the man had come to murder him and promptly fell to his knees, begging for mercy."

"You're joking."

"I'm not. This is exactly what happened. The soldier told him to get up and to accept the purple. Claudius thought it was another joke being played on him and did neither. Other soldiers came. They liked the idea—if Claudius would give every guardsman a nice, tidy sum. To this he agreed at once—perhaps only to get rid of them. But they hoisted him on their shoulders and carried him away to the Praetorian barracks. He looked so worried that everybody who met him during that weird procession thought he was going to be executed."

Cassius could not help laughing. "What a story," he said, "considering that all we were told here was a solemn proclamation: that after the assassination of Emperor Gaius his uncle, Tiberius Claudius Drusus Caesar had assumed the purple."

"No use telling our dear provincials the whole truth, is there? But the most dangerous man not only knew about it, but actually helped to bring it about. Herod Agrippa was in Rome at the time. . . ."

"You don't mean to say that he . . ."

"Just listen and decide for yourself. The Praetorian Guards had chosen Claudius as their Emperor. The Senate insisted on the republic and mobilized the municipal guards who occupied the Forum, the Capitol and other strategic places. Rome was on the brink of civil war. Poor old Claudius himself was only too willing to resign, I'll say that for him. But the guards wouldn't let him! And then his old friend Herod Agrippa appeared in the guards' camp and talked courage into him. Remember that, Cassius! A little Jewish potentate talking about courage to a Roman, a Roman of the noblest blood and lineage. Then he went back to the senators who by now were in such a dither that they asked him to come in and address them!"

"Unheard of," Cassius said.

"He made quite a speech too," Marsus said grimly. "Didn't forget to point out to them the strength of the forces at Claudius' command and that the municipal troops had little fighting value. All quite true, incidentally. Keeps his eyes open, that man. Then he suggested that he—he, mark you—should lead a deputation to Claudius and entreat him, in the name of the Senate, to resign. He was a friend of Rome, he said, and therefore ready to risk his life to save the city from civil war. The idiots fell for it, and he set out with half a dozen of the biggest blockheads in the assembly. Back in Claudius' camp he first made his speech and poor old Claudius didn't know what to make of it. Then Herod took him aside and virtually told him what he ought to reply. And that reply was brilliant; just the right mixture of promises and threats. And now Herod gave his friend the final piece of advice: to promise a still larger sum of gold to all Praetorian officers and men and to have them all sworn in. Claudius did what he was told. In the meantime Herod informed the Senate of Claudius' answer—his own answer— and the Senate was just as frightened as Herod knew it would be, and after some delay Claudius was accepted and there you are. Our beloved Emperor was chosen by a few soldiers—most of them German mercenaries, the Praetorian Guards are full of 'em—and put into the saddle by a Jewish ruler. Can you be surprised that Herod Agrippa can do no wrong in the Emperor's eyes?"

"What a strange thing the empire has become," Cassius said. "I'm glad my father did not live to see it. But tell me—apart from a very understandable feeling of indignation that Agrippa dared to meddle in the most important affairs of Rome—what is it that makes you dislike him so much?"

Vibius Marsus began to pace up and down the study. "I am hurt," he said, "that this cunning little Herodian could practically *make* a Roman emperor. But how do you expect Agrippa must feel about it? He has made another man, a man he has known all his life and whom he must despise, the Lord of the World. Is it not inevitable that he must think: 'This I could do for the poor fool, Claudius. Why should I do less for Herod Agrippa, who is anything but a fool? Claudius has complete confidence in me. If any ruler ever had the chance to build up all the power he wants free from Roman interference, it is I. And I would be a greater fool than Claudius, if I didn't do it.'"

Cassius listened intently. "Are there any signs that he is planning anything of the kind?" he asked.

"Yes."

"Can you tell me what they are?"

"There are some of the usual indications: a steady increase in his armed forces. Increase of equipment, too, with forges and smithies working day and night. And yet we know that he found huge supplies in his new province of Galilee, when he took over there. He is building up an excellent Intelligence service too. He's hand in glove with the priesthood in Jerusalem, and the present High Priest is not a very nice man—we've had a fairly nasty crop of them lately, Caiphas, Jonathas, Theophilus and now Simon Cantheras. . . ."

"One Sadducee seems to be very much like another."

"So you see, he's managed to get the—er—spiritual forces on his side as well."

"Is that all?" Cassius asked innocently.

Vibius Marsus abruptly halted his nervous prowling. "No, it isn't. By all the Furies, I wish it were. I could cope with it then and I would, even if Caesar Claudius had me recalled for it. There are two more points. He is heightening the walls of Jerusalem and building new fortifications. Curse it, Cassius, our Emperors seem to have the idea, nowadays, that the best way to start a new reign is to give away cities and even entire provinces of the empire to their very dubious friends. I should be happy, perhaps, that I needn't worry about another Procurator of Judaea, as my predecessors had to. Pilatus was weak and Marcellus a clumsy ox. But I'm *not* happy to have Agrippa there instead, lording it over a realm as big as that of the first Herod. What does he mean by heightening the walls? He's not doing it for us, that you can be quite sure of. If he is allowed to go on Jerusalem will be impregnable. And there is the other thing. . . ." He began walking up and down again. "I can't fathom it," he said. "I can't lay my hands on it. But there is something else going on. He's had a number of visits from other rulers— all right, that's natural enough. But they all had to come to him. He never repaid their visits. Is it because his is the largest realm? That could be, but I doubt that it's the whole story. There is something else and what it is eludes me." He stopped again in front of

Cassius. "Believe it or not," he said, "but that's the main reason why I wanted you here this morning."

"What do you mean?"

"I have many agents," Marsus said, "I must have them. Many of them are quite reliable, some are entirely reliable. But none of them is any good with this. They tell me all kinds of unbelievable stories about what is supposed to be going on in Agrippa's mind. Harebrained stories, absolutely idiotic. Now I want a Roman to go there and have a look. Agrippa is bound to find out about this Roman, but he will think he is coming to inspect his fortifications. There's no need for that. I already have the plans of the whole thing, neatly copied by one of my men. Agrippa will never get the idea that I am sending a Roman there to find out about this other thing. He doesn't know your background as I do. You have a Jewish wife. You have Jewish friends. There aren't many Romans who can say that. What is more, you are yourself a member of a Jewish sect. You are, aren't you?"

"You might put it that way, though many non-Jewish people belong to our Faith."

"Tell me this, friend," Vibius Marsus said, looking at Cassius sharply. "Has this sect or group or movement of yours political ends of any kind?"

"Certainly not."

"You would be ready to swear an oath on that, to the gods?"

Cassius smiled. "I could swear an oath, but not to the gods."

Marsus pondered over that. "One more question," he snapped. "Could this . . . thing of yours be misused, say by a fool or a cunning criminal, for political ends?"

Cassius frowned. "I can't imagine it," he said, "but I suppose there isn't any issue, however pure and clear, that could not be misused. It wouldn't be by the leaders we have, though. Of that I am quite certain."

Marsus nodded. "You know these leaders then? Personally?"

"I do."

"Including the Anointed One? You see, I have heard about it."

Cassius looked past Marsus into the void. "No," he said. "I only saw Him once; and then He was dead."

"Oh." For a brief moment Marsus looked a little embarrassed. "What about his successor then?"

"I know him well, and the other apostles also."

"Apostles, eh? And who is he?"

"His name is Petrus. The Greeks call him Cephas."

"And Agrippa is not one of the leaders?"

Cassius burst into laughter. "Decidedly not."

Marsus took a deep breath. "Very well. Will you go to Jerusalem for me?"

"Frankly," Cassius said, "I'm not anxious to leave Antioch. . . ."

"Neither would I be, if I were married to your wife," Marsus said, with a courteous smile. "Let me be equally frank. It is not right that a man of your abilities should stand aside when the empire needs him. We may have had a few bad emperors. But surely the word 'Rome' still has meaning for you! This is not a question, Cassius, or if it is, I take the answer for granted. If Agrippa is as ambitious as I think he is—as I am sure he is—he will set the entire East aflame."

"He might," Cassius pondered. "But . . ."

"I know what you're thinking," Marsus interposed. "An agent, that's nothing. I have better uses for you. Come back with news about this matter and you'll be my chief administrator forthwith. I know you can organize, and I know you have business sense enough. Don't say no, friend. Rome needs you and so do I."

Cassius had some difficulty in concealing his surprise. The post of chief administrator was practically the highest after that of the governor himself and according to all the rules Marsus should have written to Rome for permission to nominate a new man. Only in an emergency could a governor do so on his own. This more than anything else showed how grave a view Marsus took of the situation.

But should he accept? What if this was just a temptation, to lure him back into the field of ambition? But that was nonsense. Even

178

if he rose to a consulship with all its honors, the greatest of which was that they would name the year after him and his colleague in that office, it could no longer thrill him. He knew of a better way to secure immortality.

His business affairs? They ran themselves by now, or almost. Agreements and contracts with a number of big merchants needed a certain amount of supervision, but apart from that there was nothing that his trusted clerks, Secundus and Babrut could not deal with.

Naomi? He was not sure what she would think, but she liked old Marsus, she had said so in her quiet way.

And he was curious about Herod Agrippa's alleged secret aims. How could Marsus get the idea of that man being one of the leaders of the Faith in the Messiah? It was out of the question, of course. To judge from certain remarks of both Saul and Bar Naba it looked as if the faithful in Jerusalem were worried about Agrippa; there was a rumor of a few arrests having taken place, though they were probably made on the instigation of the High Priest. . . .

"Well," Vibius Marsus asked tersely. "What's your answer?"

Cassius looked up. "I'll do it," he said.

CHAPTER NINETEEN

THE HOUSE to which Cassius returned was very different from the one in Damascus. Six years in the teeming City of Lights, where East and West exchanged their goods, had borne fruit. There was no comparison with the palatial buildings of the Greek and Phoenician merchant princes who owned wharves, shipping lines and mines and held the harvests of districts and provinces in pawn, but the house was large enough, beautifully furnished, and staffed with about a hundred slaves and freedmen, many of whom had adopted the Faith of their master.

Cassius made certain that those who did not were treated as well as the others, as an assurance that any embracing the Faith did so from true conviction only and not for material advantage. Every slave who had served him for more than five years received his manumission; but nearly all of them preferred to stay on as freedmen.

He found Naomi in her favorite room, next to her bedroom; she was sitting on a low divan under a little canopy of blue silk, embroidering a dress for Acte.

He sat down beside her and told her about his long audience with the governor.

When he had ended, her little face was grave, but she said nothing.

"Perhaps you don't quite realize what this means," he said. "If I succeed in my mission, I shall be the highest official in the land after the governor himself. It's almost unheard of. Better men than I have had to serve the empire for twenty years and more to get a post like that."

She nodded in silence.

"Well, then, why be sad about it?" he asked with a touch of impatience.

"Rome," she said in a strangled voice. "I . . . I'm afraid of Rome."

He shook his head. "We're not going there. And even if we should, some day—what is there to be afraid of? It is really quite an honor, you know. Strictly speaking Marsus should have obtained imperial permission before nominating a man for such an important post, but every governor has special powers in an emergency and there seems to be one now."

"You don't understand," she said miserably. "I . . . I don't know how to put it. You have told me about Rome and what they did to your poor father and how glad you were that you had nothing to do with them any longer; and now you want to go back into that world full of intrigues and lies and danger."

He rubbed his chin. "You're right in a way, but it's different when a man is in a position of high command."

"It is worse," Naomi said tonelessly. "The lightning always hits the highest point."

He laughed. "That would be Marsus—not me."

"Why did you accept?" she asked. "Aren't you happy as you are?"

"I am. You know I am. But I didn't want to shirk the responsibility. I refused point-blank when Vitellius tried to draw me back into service, remember? But Marsus is not Vitellius and . . . there is the possibility, this time, that I may do some good. That is my only ambition, Naomi."

"You think it is," she said with a sigh. "I knew this would come one day. . . ."

He was taken aback. "How could you possibly know?"

"You have that longing in you all the time . . . for Rome and things Roman. It is natural. You are a Roman. You often speak of it . . . in your dreams."

He looked a little sheepish. "I had no idea that I talk in my sleep."

He was glad to see her smile more cheerfully.

"Perhaps I am only being selfish," she said. "Don't take any notice of what I said. And I am glad that the governor thinks so highly of you and that he likes and respects you, although you married a Jewish woman."

"Naomi!"

She smiled, again without a trace of sadness. "It is natural for a Roman to be married to a Roman woman. And those who marry foreign women are in a class by themselves."

"The things you think of . . ."

She laughed outright. "Don't tell me that Roman women think only of superficial things."

"Most of them do, I'm afraid."

"You must have met the wrong ones, then," she said lightly.

"Just as well. Or we might not be married now."

She traced the proud line of his eyebrow with a slim finger. "I'm so glad we are. I thank the Lord for it every day. He—and you— and Acte. What more can I want?"

"In that sequence?"

"Yes. Nothing would be as it is without Him. Not even our love and the fruit of our love."

"Saul should hear you; he'd be pleased."

"When Saul is here I don't dare to gabble away like this; I just sit and listen."

"And so does Acte."

"Yes, I know. The child is fond enough of Bar Naba, but Saul . . ."

"What does go on in the head of a little girl of eight, I wonder."

"A great deal, sometimes. He is very fond of her, too. Touchingly so."

"He's certainly very patient with her. To me he is a very difficult man to understand."

Naomi frowned. "I suppose he is that to many," she said. "Has it occurred to you that he may be a very great man?"

He thought for a moment. "Perhaps," he said. "I don't know. What exactly is the measure of greatness?"

"The impact a man leaves on others," Naomi said, surprisingly. "If it's a lasting one, that is. Not like the impact of a clever orator."

"But that's just where he excels, as an orator! Remember how he spoke to the assembly at Eleazar's house in Singon Street? And over a hundred people came forward to be instructed in the Faith?"

"Oh, yes—but do you think he could as easily have persuaded people to worship Isis? Or to join the army?"

"N-no, perhaps not."

"Then there must be something in him or about him that is not merely he, not merely his own personality and forcefulness."

"You're right. But he's not the kind of man for whom I feel as I feel toward Petrus."

"I know what you mean. Petrus goes straight to the heart. Saul appeals to the mind, to the intellect. But he is not cold."

"I've wondered about that."

"He isn't, Cassius. I've seen him more often than you have, since he came to Antioch. He and Niger and Lucius of Cyrene often come to the house of Manahen and his wife and so does that young Greek physician. . . ."

"Lukas? There's a young fellow I like. A good physician, too,

I'm told. I wouldn't mind having him if any one of us should be in need of medical help."

"Lukas said something I shall never forget."

"What was it?"

"He said: 'Our Lord is the Mediator between God and man. Saul is the mediator between Jews and Gentiles, in our Lord.'"

"There might be something in that."

"I feel there is. And that may be the reason why he's so fond of Acte . . . the daughter of a Gentile and a Jewess."

"Careful now," Cassius said in a low voice. "I think I hear her."

Acte came in.

"By all that's good," Cassius ejaculated. "What get-up is this, child?"

Acte advanced ceremoniusly. She was wearing a simple white tunic with a prettily embroidered hem. On her almost blue-black hair perched a little crown, cut out of stiff parchment.

"Are you taking part in a play?" Cassius wondered. "If so, what are you? The queen of a great and wild country?"

"I could be," Acte said, doubtfully. "I don't know for sure, father. I am a queen, I think, but I don't know about the country."

"How do you know you are a queen, darling?" Naomi asked.

"I must be. I'm an anointed one."

Her parents looked at each other.

"What do you mean by that?" Cassius asked, a little more sharply.

"You ought to have a crown too, father," Acte said quickly. "And mother. And Abigail. We're all anointed ones, aren't we?"

"What *is* she talking about?" Cassius muttered.

Naomi drew the child to her. "Who told you that, darling?"

"Oh, everybody knows it. I was out with Abigail and we met the children of the fat Greek man. . . ."

"Whose children?" Cassius enquired.

"Oh, you know him, father, the one who's got a wart on his chin and smells of flowers."

"Seems to be Agesander of Tyre," Cassius murmured, keeping a straight face. "He has three children, all boys."

"Yes, father, and they made faces at us and shouted: 'Here

come the anointed ones, the Christianoi,' and Abigail looked very cross and told them to mind their manners, but they went on shouting until we were too far away to hear. They're brats, father."

"What language, Acte," Naomi said reproachfully.

"Why, mother, Abigail told them they were! It's all quite true, mother, they are brats and we are anointed ones, Christianoi." Acte gave the little crown on her head a push forward. "It *is* true, isn't it? But it's funny, I never thought of it before. We believe in the Messiah. And when you talk Greek you say it in Greek and it's Christos and when you talk Latin as you did the other day to old Posthumus, you say Christus, but it's all the same, isn't it?"

"Yes, darling, it is all the same Lord," Naomi said quietly.

"And it all means the Anointed One," Acte went on triumphantly. "And we belong to him, don't we, mother? Don't we, father? So we are the anointed people."

"You do talk a lot, child," her father said, frowning.

"But you asked me, father, didn't you?" Acte was nonplussed. "Or was it you, mother? King David was anointed, wasn't he? And Saul, too, I don't mean *our* Saul, but the one in scrip . . . scrip . . ."

"Scripture," Naomi said.

"Scrip-ture. Yes, him. *And* Solomon. They were all kings, 'cause only kings are anointed. So I made myself this."

"Take that foolish thing off at once," Naomi said, so sternly that Acte, startled, obeyed instantly.

"But why, mother?"

Naomi hesitated. Before she could answer, Dikos, the little majordomo, announced the arrival of two visitors, Saul of Tarsus and Bar Naba of Cyprus.

"Just at the right moment," Cassius said. "We shall let them deal with the argument."

The two grave men listened, smiling, to his story, with Acte jumping up and down excitedly at his side.

"Christianoi," Bar Naba said, pensively. "I've heard people call us that, once or twice."

"So have I." Saul nodded. "Sometimes in derision, sometimes

simply for lack of another name for those of the Faith. As for the crown, Acte, your mother is quite right. Our Lord was the Anointed One, the Christ, and the last and most glorious King of Israel. He also was and is the King of Kings and the Ruler of All the Worlds."

"Yes." Acte's black-cherry eyes were shining. "And kings have crowns and . . ."

Saul's slender hand, raised, hushed her into silence. "The only crown our Lord wore on earth was a crown of thorns," he said. "Can you expect better treatment than your King, Acte?"

She flushed violently. "N-no, I suppose not."

"Then you'd better throw that toy away, don't you think?" He patted her head gently as he had done when she was a little girl of three, and turned to Cassius. "We shall have to go to Jerusalem soon," he said.

Cassius' eyes widened. "You too?" he asked. "I'm going there myself. When are you leaving?"

"We don't know yet," Bar Naba joined in. "One of the brothers forewarned us that there will be a scarcity of food in Jerusalem."

"He said: 'a famine,'" Saul corrected calmly. "We shall have to collect food and transport it to our brothers there."

"I saw the governor today," Cassius said. "Strange that he mentioned nothing about the food shortage—we were talking of Judaea. Surely he would know. . . ."

"There is no scarcity yet," Saul told him, "but there will be. Agabus told us about it and he has the gift of prophecy."

Cassius felt a little ill at ease. He did not disbelieve in prophecy— few Romans did, though most of them would treat the matter with a kind of forced lightheartedness. But prophecies, as much as and perhaps even more than miracles of curing were upsetting when they came close to one's ordinary life. Just because they were real, they had a knack of making ordinary life seem unreal. Besides, he knew Agabus, but he had had no idea that the quiet, unassuming old man with the hairless skull and the high-pitched voice had the gift of prophecy. No doubt he did have it—neither Saul nor Bar Naba were credulous people and they both seemed to have decided to act on what the old man said.

"What a strange Intelligence service!" Cassius thought, wincing a little. "Well, we won't be able to travel together in that case," he said aloud. "I must leave tomorrow morning. But I shall help you with the foodstuff when the time comes, that goes without saying. Is there anything I can do for you in Jerusalem?"

Saul nodded. "Tell the brothers we'll be coming in six or seven weeks' time and give them our love." He turned to Acte who was playing sadly with her discarded crown. "You should not worry when people try to be insulting," he said gently. "Especially not when it's for our Lord's sake."

Acte looked up. "But what shall I do if they call me that again?"

Saul laughed outright. The stern, dignified little man looked happy, so happy that everyone else broke into smiles. "They may *think* it's insulting," he said, "but it isn't, you know. You felt that yourself. You thought it was really an honor and that's why you made yourself that crown. Well, there's no need for a crown—as yet. But you were right in one thing. It is an honor to be called one of the Christianoi, one of the Christians, the followers of the Anointed One. Taken rightly it is the only true honor there is. So be happy about it—happy, I said, not proud! Who knows, maybe all the world will call us that some day."

CHAPTER TWENTY

The executioner slowly raised his sword. He was a giant Negro, dressed only in a red loincloth. The dull, bluish blade seemed to threaten the very sky. He let it come down, swishing, in a tremendous, semi-circular blow and the head of the kneeling prisoner rolled crazily over the sand, followed by a fountain-like spurt of blood.

The Negro walked over to the head, seized it by the hair and with a ceremonial gesture lifted it up toward the palace window.

King Herod Agrippa acknowledged it with a nod and stepped back into the room where Fortunatus was trying in vain to force a smile.

"Wine," Agrippa said roughly.

Fortunatus stepped over to the low table of citrus wood and seized the decanter and a cup. His hands were shaking badly.

"Don't spoil my table," Agrippa said. "What's the matter with you? *You* couldn't see it, not from where you were standing. Man, you're quite green in the face!" He took the silver cup from the freedman's fingers and coolly savored the aroma of the wine before he drank. "*My* hand isn't shaking, is it?" he asked. When there was no answer he repeated, harshly: "Is it?"

"N-no, my lord King."

"Yet it's the first time I've had an enemy executed," Agrippa said, just a little too loudly. "And now we shall see. You understand, don't you, Fortunatus?"

"N-not quite, my lord King."

"Then you're a fool." Agrippa sat down heavily.

"He has put on weight," Fortunatus thought. He said: "I don't even know who the man is . . . was," he corrected himself hastily.

Agrippa laughed. "I forgot that you've been away for a while. The man was Jaqob bar Zebedee. Quite a good-looking man. Not yet forty. Intelligent, too, in his own way, I gather. Not in my way, though, and that was a little unfortunate for him. That is why he had to die. He believed in a King of Israel. But in the wrong one."

"High treason . . . ?"

Agrippa laughed again. "You might call it that, I suppose. In any case: I am the only legitimate King of Israel and like the God of Israel I will have no other beside me."

Fortunatus looked over his shoulder, terrified. "My lord King, if one of the priests should hear you saying that . . ."

"This is the royal palace, not the Temple. And the priests have every reason to be grateful to me. I saved their Temple for them when Caesar Gaius wanted to have a statue of himself set up in it, don't you remember?"

"I was not with you at the time, my lord King."

"That's right, you weren't. It was some time after the downfall of my poor uncle Antipas. I went to Rome to render my thanks to the madman who had given me my uncle's tetrachy and my noble sister's revenues to boot." He sipped his wine contentedly.

"Who would have thought that the Queen would refuse the Caesar's mercy and follow her husband into exile," Fortunatus murmured.

"She didn't do it because she loved him." Agrippa grinned. "Don't you believe that for a moment. She did it because she hated me. She would have had to live under my protection and that was more than she could stomach. We are good haters, we Herodians." He drained the cup and set it down leisurely. "Caesar Gaius was not an easy man to influence," he said pensively. "You never know what to expect when you're dealing with a lunatic. He really was a lunatic, you know, and there were moments when he knew it himself. But I succeeded in dissuading him from his idea of that confounded statue and the priests have been for me ever since, although they will go on pestering me about keeping those beastly laws. Got to do it, too, at least when there's somebody around to watch, and what a nuisance it is. My uncle Antipas never used to bother much about that kind of thing—I had some delicious prawns at his house in Tiberias; but then he wasn't King of Judaea and I am. Fill my cup again. And you'd better have some wine too, you're still a little green around the gills."

"If I may inquire, my lord King, is it true . . ." Fortunatus broke off.

"Is what true? Come on, man, don't be afraid! I won't have *you* made a head shorter. You've done fairly well for me in Persia and Armenia lately and I still need your head where it is. Speak up!"

"Is it true that you had that wretched man executed without a trial?"

Agrippa smiled disagreeably. "Does that bother you, my Fortunatus?"

The freedman raised both hands. "Who am I to judge my King's reasons," he stammered.

"I agree with you, my Fortunatus. But as I permitted you to ask your question, I'll give you the answer. At a public trial the wretch would have aired his insane beliefs. I'm not a madman like Gaius. I don't have people killed because I enjoy it. But I will not have them preach about a mystic king who died for them and will come back one day to rule over them. Come back, did you hear that? A plague on those fools." He refilled his cup before Fortunatus could serve him.

"The Romans used to insist on a trial," the freedmen dared to say. "They even tried that very Yeshua who . . ."

"Be quiet," Agrippa ordered. "I won't have that name mentioned in my presence. He's the cause of the trouble. As for your legal niceties, I'll give you the answer to that. As long as Judaea was a Roman province, no Jewish authority could condemn a man to death and have him executed. The Romans alone could do that. That was their famous *ius gladii*. But my friend the Emperor Claudius has given Judaea to me, with all the rights of kingship. The *ius gladii* is mine now and I made use of it today. If the Romans are fools enough to insist on public trials, do I have to ape them? Yes, fools, I say. It was utter foolishness to put that . . . that man on trial. It would have been much better if they'd done it my way." He rose and walked to the window.

The courtyard was quite empty, except for a few slaves with pails and brooms, cleaning the sand of bloodstains.

"I wish I had got hold of his brother too," Agrippa said grimly. "He's the better speaker of the two, they tell me. He must have left the city or my men would have found him by now."

Fortunatus shook his head. He could afford to do so, as the King had not turned round again. "I used to pride myself that I always understood the trend of your mind, my lord King," he said. "But this time I seem to fail. Why should you worry about these people, these followers of . . . who you know whom? After all, the man is dead. Is it not better if these . . . malcontents believe in a ghost than in someone who might turn up and really become their leader?"

Turning, Agrippa stared at the freedman contemptuously. "Life in the big cities has made you lose contact with the people," he said. "In the cities the attention of the masses is constantly occupied. There is always something new. And just as long as they have news, food and amusement all is well with them. But in the country people sit and think and when they can't think they brood. Where has most of the trouble in Judaea come from? Where is the home of the dagger-men, of the Freedom Party men, of the mystic movements? In Galilee. In the countryside. That's where the leaders of the Messianists come from. Country yokels, all of 'em. But they really believe in their nonsense, Fortunatus, and that's something alien to a man like you. They're wholehearted. And a wholehearted man is the most dangerous man there is."

"I never heard you talk like this before, my lord King."

"Things not only look different, when seen from a throne," Agrippa said slowly. "They *are* different. This Jaqob had to die."

"Yet you thought it was a mistake, my lord King, when King Herod Antipas had that man killed whom they used to call the Baptist."

"True," Agrippa replied. "And what's more I still think so." He smiled strangely. "Herod Antipas had no right to kill the Baptist, because he was Herod Antipas. I have the right to kill Jaqob because I am who I am."

Fortunatus said nothing. This was not the Herod Agrippa he knew, the generous, life-loving Epicurean, the royal spendthrift, the cunning spinner of intrigues. Some strange, tremendous change had taken place deep inside the man and the freedman could not fathom it.

"You're a good servant," Agrippa said, still smiling. "You have done well. But you do not know your master. Tell me—do you believe in anything?"

"Well, I . . . I . . ."

The King nodded. "That's the kind of answer one gets when one asks a man of your ilk a simple question. You don't know. You stammer. There was a time, I grant you that, when my own reaction might have been similar, though a little more coherent. I didn't stammer. But I, too, didn't know. Religion, to me, was a solace for the weak. And the gods? I was brought up in Rome, as you know. The gods and goddesses of the Romans were absurd, of course. Just overgrown Romans. The priests of Isis were playing tricks on credulous matrons until old Tiberius, quite rightly, banished them.

The god of the Jews—that was a different proposition. But even he doesn't make much sense, does he? If he were an almighty god, as he claims to be, why should he content himself with ruling over that particular small nation? I know I don't! So my ambition seems to be greater than his. My intelligent friends in the West believe in various brands of philosophy, each one according to his temperament. The Epicureans know how to live, or think they do. The Stoics know how to die; and there are half a dozen schools in between and all around the two. But none of them accounts for certain experiences. . . ."

"What experiences, my lord King?"

Agrippa looked past the freedman out of the palace window. The tops of the palm trees in the royal gardens beyond the courtyard were stirring a little. "When a man reaches the top of all human possibilities," he said, "in other words, when he is a king, he finds himself in a position of great loneliness. There is no one he can trust—no, not completely, my Fortunatus. And don't try to make a loyalty speech now, my good ass, I am talking of issues far too big for that. There is no one to share a king's innermost thoughts. Other kings are only enemies, rivals, whether they are allies or not. In such a situation a man will think—and sometimes he will listen; listen to voices that are not human."

That enigmatic smile again.

"There *are* such voices," the King went on, almost in a whisper. Angrily he added: "Don't say there aren't, you pitiful little monkey. I *know*."

"There are, if you say so, my lord King. There must be."

"No, no," Agrippa said, suddenly quite lenient and gentle, "you mustn't be afraid of me. Why, you're trembling, poor man. Calm down and listen. Then judge for yourself. When Tiberius had me thrown into prison I almost despaired of life. We prisoners were allowed to spend an hour every day in the prison courtyard; and there I was, leaning against a tree and full of black thoughts. Suddenly an owl came and settled down on a branch just over my head. At that sight one of the other prisoners, a German, became quite excited. I saw him turn to the guard to whom he was chained and talk to him. He inquired who I was and the soldier told him. Then the German asked for permission to talk to me and the guard, out of curiosity, gave it and himself served as interpreter. The German told me that in his country he was known as a seer and that he could give me the meaning of the omen. The owl was a royal bird, apparently, and very rarely seen in daytime. The Godhead was sending me a sign that I should be released in the near future, and then would rise to the greatest power. And that power I should never lose in my lifetime. Only when I saw the owl again in daytime, that would be a sure sign that I would be dead in five days."

"Extraordinary," Fortunatus muttered.

"I didn't think so at the time," Agrippa said. "I laughed at it. Yet deep down in my heart I felt a little warmth all the same, the warmth of a new hope. I, too, was chained to a guard—a big, smelly fellow he was—but now my chains seemed just a little lighter. A few weeks later I was free. And what happened afterwards you know—or some of it. That, Fortunatus, was the first time I heard that voice—through the mouth of a grinning interpreter who was told what to say by a dirty old German prisoner, who in turn was told by . . . whom? 'The Godhead,' he said. He didn't give it a name and perhaps it needs no name. But the message was true and that was enough for me."

Fortunatus nodded silently.

"It is clear that the Godhead does not speak to everyone, isn't it?" Agrippa went on. "This was the first real proof I had that I was different from other people." The enigmatic smile returned. "There were more proofs later on. How do you account for it that whatever happened in Rome, I only rose higher and higher? That I won the confidence of two men as different as Caesar Gaius and Caesar Claudius? I could do what I pleased with either of them. Claudius even owes me his throne. Do you understand what that means, Fortunatus? Never before in the history of Rome has a Roman ruler owed his throne to an oriental prince. So Claudius regards me as his best and most reliable friend. No wonder poor old Vibius

Marsus eats his heart out in Antioch, when his spies report to him about the walls of Jerusalem growing higher and higher. He cannot stop my rising power and he knows it. Claudius just laughs at his earnest submissions and fears and sends me copies of his letters!"

"It is the most amazing chain of luck," Fortunatus admitted, touching the wood of his chair. All wood was sacred to Jupiter and whenever a man proclaimed his or someone else's good fortune, he would touch Jupiter's wood as a sign of humility toward the god and to avert his displeasure. Fortunatus did not believe in Jupiter but he preferred to comply.

"Yes, luck," Agrippa agreed. "But where does luck come from? Who sends it? Is it measurable in purely human terms? It is a thing of the divine realm, Fortunatus, of the Godhead who let me know that I would rise to the highest power and would lose it only when I die. Now why should the Godhead shower this rain of luck on me? Obviously because the divine element wishes to influence the affairs of men through me. I am the instrument of Divinity."

"Y-yes," Fortunatus said, trying hard to hide his fear. "Yes, I suppose so. Yes."

"I *know* it," Agrippa said sharply. "Now what shall I say, what shall I do, when stupid, ignorant men try to deflect the attention of the people to some mysterious figure, some fantastic leader of their own, whatever his name may be. I must deter them from such a course by every means in my power. Do you see now why I have a right to do what for a mere Herod Antipas was wrong? *I am the elect.*"

Stiff with fright, Fortunatus stared at him.

"Divinity has a purpose for everything," Agrippa said. "And Divinity, through Claudius, has added to all my other lands this realm of Judaea and the city of Jerusalem."

"Yes, my lord King . . . yes . . ."

"There are signs and wonders everywhere, and for all to see," Agrippa stated solemnly. "The walls of Jerusalem are rising. All the kings of the Orient come to me to do homage. The Roman Caesar owes his throne to me. The Roman governor is powerless before me, despite all his legions. The Jewish prophets have predicted that the Saviour will come from Judaea, the Anointed One, the Messiah."

"My lord King . . ."

"The Messiah," Agrippa repeated, his eyes flashing. "Not some poor, benighted impostor, but a king, a great king. No, don't say anything, I know according to some part of Jewish Scripture the Messiah must be of the family of David, must be born in Bethlehem of all places and so on and so forth. Legends like that will always turn up and be written down by eager scribes. What matters is the favor of Divinity and that I have, I am filled with it to the brim. The moment will come when I shall proclaim my true status. It may come soon, Fortunatus. But first I must do two things. I must win Phoenicia, Sidon and Tyre, especially Tyre. And I must stamp out that absurd movement of the Galileans. There will be no need to kill them all. I shall pick up their leaders, one by one. Remember I said, 'Now we shall see,' and you didn't understand what I meant? I have had one of their leaders executed. Now we shall see the reaction of the people in Jerusalem. We shall see how popular these Galileans are, and their beliefs. There may be a revolt or mass demonstrations. I am holding troops in readiness for that eventuality. But if the movement is not strong enough for that I shall go further immediately."

"More arrests? And executions?"

"Yes. And first and foremost that of the biggest man they have. He used to be a fisherman. His name is Cephas."

"I see."

"All this is very secret, Fortunatus." The King's voice was quiet and gentle. "I daresay a number of people may *feel* something about my real position. I can see it in their eyes. I can see a great many things in a man's eyes. But only two people *know* about it: you and Blastus. And you two are like my own two hands. Blastus is the right hand, you are the left. You see how much confidence I place in you, Fortunatus." He rose. "You won't disappoint me, will you?"

"Oh no, my lord King, no . . ."

"It is well," Herod Agrippa said. "You may go now."

For an almost imperceptible moment Fortunatus hesitated. Then he bowed very deeply and left the presence.

His litter was waiting for him at the palace gate and he felt relieved when he sank down on the silk cushions inside. "Home," he said weakly, and the four sturdy Cappadocian slaves began to move. But he tried in vain to get some order into his thoughts. They were flying like shooting stars, flashing up and vanishing before he could catch hold of them.

"Home" was an elegant little villa with a pretty garden attached, much smaller than that of Blastus, the chamberlain, but like his, in the best district of the city.

He had himself undressed and took a bath. The horror of the execution was still about him in a physical way, there was a feeling of clamminess all over him. Soaking in the hot water he began to think coherently. What had happened to the King? To the most cunning and adroit of all minds? Fortunatus used to admire him as he admired no other man. Herod Agrippa had his own qualities in the superlative. And now he was talking like . . . like Caesar Gaius, like Caligula, the madman who imagined himself to be a god.

To pose as a great mysterious figure, the darling of Divinity, could be supreme cleverness, the ruse of all ruses, to create a nimbus, to make people believe in him blindly. But the King believed it himself! The world's finest brain had gone queer. The result was bound to be a catastrophe.

Fortunatus had gone to see the King about Blastus. The chamberlain was in charge of royal expenditures and he knew how to fill his own pockets to capacity. With that and the huge double program of building and of armament there was little left for other things. The harvest had been bad. There were the first signs of unrest all over Judaea because of the scarcity of food. And there would not be enough money for a substantial importation of wheat from Egypt.

But the King had given him no opportunity to talk about all this. First he was made to witness that horrible execution and then the King had done all the talking. Besides, his last words about Blastus being his right hand and knowing the King's secret made it impossible to come out with what amounted to a downright accusation. Nets would have to be laid very carefully and evidence collected more accurately before Blastus could be attacked.

What if Blastus had forestalled him? There might have been a subtle threat in the King's last words. "You won't disappoint me, will you?" Perhaps he should have fallen at his feet, and adored him, as he had done at his audience with Caesar Gaius?

The freedman grinned angrily. It was no longer safe to work for the King. The time had come to look for a back door, a safe way out.

He decided to get hold of a man whom he had so far very carefully avoided; a well-to-do Phoenician merchant of the name of Mago. He had ships—and one might need a ship rather urgently one of these days: but above all he was a man of great connections. . . .

He could not go and see him at once, of course. Feelers had to be stretched out, contacts made. Mad or not, the King was not an easy man to deceive. He would have to be extremely cautious.

CHAPTER TWENTY-ONE

EVERYONE inside the house of Miriam stiffened when there was a knock at the door. "Don't go, Mark," she said in a trembling voice, when her son moved toward the door. "Let Rhoda do it. Please, I beg of you."

Mark frowned, but before he could say anything little Rhoda had slipped out.

The men and women in the room huddled around the one who was in the greatest danger, a man with a quiet, thoughtful face and beautiful black eyes, Judah bar Alphaeus, the Apostle.

"Don't be afraid," he said calmly. "Pray instead."

"They'll take you away, too," a woman sobbed. "They'll take us all away."

"Not unless it is God's will," the Apostle replied. "And I don't think it is. Listen."

A conversation seemed to be going on between Rhoda and who-ever it was who had knocked, but the words could not be heard.

Mark shook his head. "Not soldiers," he said. "They'd be up here by now. I'll have a look."

He found Rhoda talking to a tall, well-dressed Roman in his late thirties who spoke Aramaic fluently. The Roman looked up. "This young woman seems to be a little disturbed about my visit," he said. "I am Cassius Longinus and I've come from Antioch to bring the greetings of my good friend, Bar Naba."

"He is my uncle," Mark said. "But how is it that you know him by this name?"

"We share the same Faith," Cassius said simply.

"Cassius!" The Apostle came down the rickety stairs and the two men embraced, with a shout of joy.

"It's all of thirteen years since we met last," Judah said, "but you recognized me at once, didn't you?"

"That's not surprising, Judah; it was you who put me on the road when everything looked hopeless."

"It never is, though."

"That's what you told me then. Where have you been all these years? I'm living in Antioch now."

"I know," the Apostle said. "I have been in Syria myself."

"And you never came to see me!"

"At that time you were in Damascus. I have been there too, but you had left. Bishop Ananias told me about you and your dear wife. You helped our brother Saul to escape from there. You see, I am well informed."

"I still wish you had come to visit us . . ."

The Apostle smiled. "You had no need of me. I must be with those who have."

Cassius looked at him, hard. "Is that why you are here now?"

"Yes," Judah said. "You know what has happened, don't you?"

"I only arrived an hour ago, left my things at the inn and had a meal. I know nothing."

"Jaqob was killed a week ago—no, not my brother, Jochanaan's brother; the son of Zebedee. . . ."

"Killed! By whom? You needn't tell me—the Temple crowd again."

"No, not this time. He was executed in the court of the royal palace. There was no trial."

"The King?"

"Yes. We managed to get word through to Jochanaan—he's in Galilee—to stay away from the city and if possible out of the King's jurisdiction altogether, though that won't be easy as his realm is now very large."

"Killed without a trial. It's barbarous."

"Not all trials are just," Judah said softly and Cassius hung his head.

"And now," the Apostle went on, "they have arrested Cephas."

Cassius recoiled as if he had been hit. "Cephas! They wouldn't dare. . . ."

Judah nodded sadly. "The community here in Jerusalem has been at peace for many years. It all happened quite suddenly and there is no explanation for it—none that we know of."

"When you knocked at the door," Mark interposed, "we feared that the King's soldiers were coming again, perhaps for Judah. First Jaqob, then Cephas—they seem to want to destroy our leaders."

"So that's why the young servant seemed frightened."

"Cephas is still alive," Judah said in answer to Cassius' worried look. "There has been no other execution and there can't be until the feast is over. The King is very careful to respect Jewish customs."

"Nice of him." Cassius was in a towering rage. "What did you do? Didn't you try to get an explanation?"

Judah shook his head. "No deputation gets past Blastus, the Royal Chamberlain."

"And all *he* has to say," Mark added, "is that the King is just and knows how to deal with evildoers. We asked him what evil Jaqob had done and he just turned away. Our next deputation, after Cephas' arrest, was not allowed into the palace. Two written petitions we sent were not answered."

"But we are praying," Judah said. "We assemble in small groups

198

only, to avoid mass arrests. The city is dotted with such groups and a stream of prayers is going up continually on Cephas' behalf. One group is assembled here in this house, at this moment. Come and join us."

* * *

After two hours of praying with the group under Judah's guidance Cassius left. He could bear it no longer. His whole being was filled with energy; he was straining for action, the kind of action that could not be expected from Judah and his friends and which they might not even approve of. The action of a soldier. Quite seriously he thought of liberating Cephas by force.

He had traveled with a dozen armed slaves. Marsus had given him a list of the Roman agents in the city—he had learned their names by heart and then burned the list. There were twenty-three names and each of those people should be able to get a few fighting men together. A raid on the prison with, say, a hundred armed men, might come off. He would free Cephas and get him away from the city, from Judaea. He'd be safe enough in Antioch. Marsus would be furious if he did, and the whole thing might lead to an open break between Rome and that unspeakable brute of a king, but what if it did? Cephas had to be saved, that was all that mattered. Cassius Longinus would never become chief administrator and Naomi would be glad.

He went back to his inn and set to work. A number of slaves had to visit a number of addresses with short notes. Visitors came, one by one—a wool merchant, a jeweler, a horse-trader, Cassius had been careful to drop a hint to the innkeeper that he was here to do business for several large firms in Antioch, so there was nothing surprising about the conferences that went on. Two of his slaves kept watch outside to make sure that they were not overheard.

As soon as it was dark he went out to pay a visit himself. Rome's number one agent in Jerusalem was not the kind of man one could ask to come to an inn. For Mago of Tyre was a multi-millionaire whose ships with the double green stripe were known in every port of the Mediterranean. Besides, he was over seventy.

The old Phoenician received him with great courtesy. He was a frail, hook-nosed man with a patriarchal white beard, braided with pearls. His gnarled little hands shimmered with jeweled rings and he was dressed in dark green silk. The beautifully fashioned furniture, inlaid with semi-precious stones, and the carpets of the huge study were worth a king's ransom. He seemed a little hurt when Cassius took only a small sip of the wine offered in a goblet of exquisite workmanship and he winced when against all custom, the Roman came straight to the point.

"You have been informed about my arrival, of course."

"Certainly, noble Cassius, and, unnecessary to say, I am entirely at your disposal. But there was no need to come at night. It is natural for a well-known merchant like you to pay a visit to another man of business." Mago smiled craftily.

"I think you will change your opinion about that," Cassius told him dryly. "I may have to leave the city rather suddenly and I don't wish to jeopardize your position here."

Mago raised his well-kept white brows. He said politely: "My position is fairly secure, noble Cassius."

"Oh, I know you're a power in the land. You have to be. Even so . . . but we'll see."

"I would like to assist you in your search for what our mutual friend in Antioch calls the King's secret," Mago said silkily. "If it exists at all, that is. But even if it does, I don't know whether it will mean anything to our friend. Roman thinking is very different from ours. You, of course, would understand that."

"You think so?"

"Surely. You've been living in the East for thirteen years since you left the army. You know Damascus. You know Egypt. You are married to a Jewess. All that should help."

"You are well informed."

The old Phoenician shrugged his shoulders. "That is like saying that the sea is very full of water," he said. "I have some news for you, incidentally, though I'm not sure as yet whether or not there is any connection between it and the . . . secret, if indeed there is a secret. One of the King's closest friends and servants has been in touch with me—not directly, of course, he has used all kinds of devious ways. I think he is trying to sell information on the highest level. It will take some time. At present he is asking for an enormous sum, as a loan. They always call it a loan. I don't know yet whether it's worth quite that much."

"Who is he?"

"His name is Fortunatus. He's only a freedman, but next to Blastus he is probably the King's best man for . . . extraordinary affairs. When he was the King's emissary in Italy, four years ago, he brought about the downfall of Herod Antipas."

"Well, you'll know how to handle him," Cassius said. "In the meantime I need action on something quite different. There's a man in the King's prison. Name of Cephas or Petrus. They may have registered him under the name of Simon bar Jonah, though. I want him freed."

Mago frowned. "He's a Galilean, I think," he said, "and the leader of a religious group or sect, rather an irregular one. His arrest is probably due to some complaint on the part of the High Priest or his set, so this won't be an easy thing to handle. The King is not exactly devout, but he takes great pains not to antagonize the Temple."

"If it were an easy matter I wouldn't have to talk to you about it. I must have that man free at whatever cost."

Mago shook his head. "The group has no connections with political organizations. If it had, I'd know about it. Why is he so important to you?"

Cassius stared at him coldly. "That does not matter," he said slowly. "You know, I'm sure, that I hold special authority. I want that man freed."

For the first time Mago looked uneasy. "I'm afraid you're underrating the difficulties," he murmured.

Cassius leaned forward. "I have given orders for a number of men to be hired for the purpose. Within a day or two I shall have a hundred men together."

"You're not by any chance thinking of using force?" Mago asked, horrified.

"Of course."

The old Phoenician controlled himself with difficulty. "How many of these men have knowledge of your plan?"

"None, naturally. What do you take me for!"

"For a man who does not know the true position here in Judaea," Mago said testily. "Things have changed since the time when you were an officer of the Roman occupational forces. The King is all powerful. He has the confidence of the Roman Caesar. He is the official ally of Rome. And he has fifteen thousand troops in the city. By the sword of Nergal! It is madness to think of force."

"I have no intention of giving battle to the King's troops," Cassius replied. "Only of carrying out a raid."

Mago gave an angry laugh. "The prison is in the center of the city. At the first alarm all gates will be closed, those of the prison and those of the entire city. Your raid is bound to fail and it will create a political incident. The consequences might be very grave. Some of your men will be captured, you can be sure! And they'll be made to talk. The King would soon know who was behind it. A strong complaint would go to Rome and the position of our friend in Antioch would be endangered—to say nothing of my own."

"I warned you of that possibility," Cassius told him.

"So you did. But I could scarcely expect anything like this—idea of yours."

"If you don't like it, find a better one," Cassius said curtly.

The old Phoenician gave a deep sigh. "I'll try. Perhaps something can be done in a different way. But if you value your life and that of that man Cephas, don't let these men of yours go to work. Promise me you won't."

Cassius rose. "I'll promise nothing," he said slowly. "But I'll let you have the first chance. I give you twenty-four hours, no more."

*　　*　　*

Like many men past their prime Fortunatus did not like to admit that there was anything wrong with him. He was fifty-three, but he could eat and drink with the best of them. It was the cook's fault

—that spiced meat had been too fat. He decided to have the slave punished and gave his major-domo the order to fetch him. The man took an absurdly long time. When he came back he looked pale and frightened. "The cook was Calabi, master."

"Well, what of it? Why didn't you bring him?"

"He . . . he has gone, master."

Fortunatus stared at him. "Gone? *Gone?* Do you mean the dog has run away?"

"Yes, master." The major-domo was trembling. "It's never happened to me before, master," he stammered. "There was no indication of any kind. It's not my fault, master. . . . Master, master, what is it?"

Fortunatus screamed. It was a long, drawn, unnaturally high-pitched scream, ending in a moan. He pressed both his hands against his stomach. His face was ashen. "A physician," he ejaculated. "Quick, man, quick . . . a physician . . . I'm dying. . . ."

The major-domo ran.

Fortunatus began to vomit, painfully and with little success. He managed to drag himself to a low divan, but collapsed at the foot of it. He was howling like an animal.

A small man came in, bald-headed, with quick, intelligent eyes. He was wearing a robe of somber hue.

Fortunatus could see him only through a mist. "Good physician," he wailed, "a hundred pieces of . . . gold . . . if you can help me. I'm . . . burning . . . burning. . . ."

The man, with surprising strength, picked him up bodily and laid him on the divan; he looked at the patient's eyes, slipped one hand under his tunic and felt his heartbeat. He said in a low voice: "You must have a very powerful enemy."

There was another spasm of unsuccessful vomiting. When it was over Fortunatus could speak only in a whisper. "It is . . . poison . . . isn't it?"

The physician nodded silently.

"C-curse the King," Fortunatus gasped. "Curse . . . Blastus. They . . . were . . . too quick for me. . . ."

The physician bent down. "There is no antidote," he said. "You only have a few more minutes. Enough for vengeance. Is there anything you want me to tell Mago of Tyre?"

Fortunatus' eyes widened. The whites were speckled with blood. "Y-yes," he whispered. "Yes. Tell him . . . the King . . . is mad. He believes . . . the Godhead speaks to him . . . through an owl. . . ."

The physician stared at the dying man, nonplussed.

"I mean it. . . ." Hatred of his murderer gave Fortunatus the strength to go on for several more minutes. Then his voice gave out and his breath became stertorous.

The physician slipped away.

*   *   *

At the ninth hour Cassius received the first message from Mago.

"Your man is not in an ordinary jail, but in the prison of the palace. A guard of sixteen men is in charge of him alone. They work in shifts of four. He is chained to two soldiers and has to sleep between them. Two more guard the door of his cell. The palace guard is five hundred strong. More troops are being held in readiness near by, in case of riots. Your man is in good health, but has refused food, except for a little bread and wine. Trying to get more information on a high level and if possible perform an act of mercy. I entreat you not to do anything foolish."

Cassius bit his lip. To try and storm the palace was insanity, of course. With half a cohort of Roman legionaries he might have had some chance of success, but not with a hundred hired ruffians, most of whom would desert him as soon as they heard what he had in mind.

At least Mago seemed to be trying. Was it possible that he could reach the King himself? That sentence about a possible act of mercy seemed to point to it. The Phoenician had all the connections in the world. If anyone could succeed, he could. Besides, he was quite obviously worried about his own position, in case he failed and the wild Roman attempted his raid after all. He would do his utmost. So there was still hope.

The next message arrived shortly before dusk. It contained the one word, "Come."

Less than a quarter of an hour later Cassius walked into Mago's study again. The old Phoenician's face was very grave. "I have been living in this country for over thirty years," he said, "and I have seen much. Rome, to me, means a great deal. The empire stands for order and security in the world and no one appreciates that more than a man who has much to lose. That is why I have been working for Rome; and in that kind of work, too, I didn't think I could be taught anything. . . . Now I know differently."

"What are you driving at?" Cassius interrupted him impatiently. "I have come to hear about Cephas."

"Exactly. I could not understand why you should be so interested in the fate of that man. I could see no connection between him and your mission." The old man smiled thinly. "I confess to you quite frankly that I thought for some time there was no connection at all and that you wanted the man freed for private reasons—either because he was a personal friend of yours, or a relative of your wife —or that you were a member of the curious sect to which he belongs. And that you were so eager to save him you were ready to forget all about your mission. I should have known better."

"What do you mean?" Cassius asked hoarsely.

Mago gave a ceremonious bow. "I mean that I understand now and that I have the most profound respect for your judgment. You saw what I could not see and I may say in all modesty that I rarely have to make such an admission."

"Never mind my judgment," Cassius snapped. "What's happened?"

"I will tell you everything," the Phoenician said, "and in the sequence in which it happened. You will understand that I could not expose myself. So I had a very reliable friend of mine obtain an audience with Blastus, the King's Chamberlain and most trusted adviser. My friend made it understood that the freedom of a man at present in jail would be worth a tidy sum to him, and Blastus at first seemed quite willing to fall in with the suggestion. But as soon as the name of the prisoner was mentioned, the audience was all over. All my friend could get out of Blastus was that your man was arrested on the direct order of the King himself."

"Bad news," Cassius said tersely. "Very bad news."

Mago nodded. "Almost at the same time I received another report," he went on. "I told you about Fortunatus and his apparent willingness to sell us some highly secret material. I have had him and his house under close surveillance ever since. The King had him poisoned. One of my men, posing as a physician, managed to make him talk before he died. The King seems to believe that he is divinely guided and has the intention of proclaiming himself as the Messiah of the Jews."

Cassius closed his eyes. So that was the explanation for the sudden enmity shown to the followers of Christ. That was why Jaqob had to die and Cephas. . . .

"You must have guessed the truth somehow," Mago went on. "I wish I knew how. No one except Fortunatus and Blastus knew about it and I know you haven't been in touch with either of them. Yet you found out the King's secret. Perhaps you never intended to get that man Cephas free. You just wanted to find out how important he was to the King. Well, now you know."

Cassius knew that kind of language. These Intelligence people, military or otherwise, had to think in so many directions that they could no longer think straight. There always had to be a reason behind the reason; nothing could be as it seemed to be. It was like a special brand of lunacy.

"I still want Cephas freed," he said.

"You're not serious," the Phoenician said. "You can't be. By Nergal and Marduk, you should be satisfied. For weeks and months we've been trying to find out what our friend in Antioch wanted to know and couldn't. You only have to arrive in Jerusalem and already you have the right theory. One day later I am able to confirm it and substantiate it beyond any doubt. What more can you want?"

"I want Cephas."

"Oh, I quite understand that he is important to you as the leader of the counter-movement. Political ideas with a religious cloak are difficult things to fight and the best thing to do is to split them. But is that man Cephas irreplaceable? Surely you can find another leader for the group. You'll have to. Cephas is as good as dead. I have made inquiries at the palace. There'll be no trial at all. He will be executed tomorrow morning."

*   *   *

To return to the inn meant to return to loneliness, a void, with only bitter, painful thoughts to fill it. There was only one other thing he could do: to find Judah and tell him that all the prayers of the community had been in vain. That too was painful; and there was a kind of grim feeling of rebelliousness about it. But he was longing for Judah, for the face of a friend, for the mind and soul of a friend who would understand his pain and share it. If only he had thought of asking him where he was staying. Now the only hope was to find him again at Miriam's house.

The way from Mago's sumptuous home to the little house near the fruit-market was not really a long one. Today it seemed to stretch into an eternity of anguish. Every step was weighted with lead. Cephas doomed. It was as bad as his own father's death, it was worse.

Once more the little servant girl opened the door for him. He inquired about Judah bar Alphaeus and she told him that he was upstairs.

"Are they praying again?"

"We never stopped," the girl said innocently.

Cassius shook his head. "I have news," he murmured. "I'd better go up and tell him."

He climbed the rickety stairs. In the upper room he found the same people assembled as before: Miriam, the owner of the house, her son Mark, old Joel bar David, Philas, two other men, three elderly women and a few young girls. And Judah. All of them were joined in silent prayer; and all of them looked dreadfully tired and weary.

"Whatever hope they may have left," Cassius thought, "I have come to destroy." He sighed and Judah looked up. Their eyes met and the Apostle came over to him. He was pale, and deep bluish rings circled his dark eyes.

"I tried everything I could think of," Cassius told him. "I failed. They're going to kill him tomorrow morning."

He had spoken in a low voice, but they had heard him and a groan went up.

Judah looked at him. He said nothing.

"I know it for certain," Cassius said with deep bitterness. "The King himself believes or pretends to be the Messiah. That is why Cephas must die. I was thinking of raiding the jail, but they've taken him to the palace prison and that is too strongly guarded. All I could get together is about a hundred men. They haven't got a chance against the palace guard. There's no hope."

"There is hope," Judah said. "There always is. Much more than a hundred, much more than a thousand men and women all over the city are storming high Heaven with their prayers. You're a soldier, Cassius. Don't give in. Fight with us." He turned away without a further word. A moment later he was praying again with the others.

Cassius glared at them.

He did not disbelieve in prayer. No one could and be one of the Christ's men. But this was absurd, a handful of people begging for the life of Cephas and calling it "storming Heaven," as if they could force their own will upon the will of God. They had been in here for twenty-four hours at least and probably longer. They were utterly exhausted and just went on mumbling.

Poor old Joel was dribbling into his beard and one of the girls looked as if she might faint at any moment. A strange crew to storm the throne of God.

If the Lord had decided to keep Cephas alive, why should He let him be imprisoned at all? What did Judah, gentle, intelligent Judah, expect of the Lord anyway? That He would slay the King in his palace or make him change his mind, as He had made Saul change his mind by appearing to him and talking to him on the road to Damascus?

He did interfere when he wanted to, but not because some poor, bedraggled, sweating creatures begged Him to do *their* will.

"Up with your hearts," Judah said. "Up with your love of God! Up with your trust in God! You are His servants, but you are His holy people too. He can keep you clear of fault, and make you able to stand in the presence of His glory, triumphant. Remember the love our Lord has for us. I was present when He said to us: 'Ask and ye shall receive . . .'"

The weary faces lit up again.

"He's a commander all right," Cassius thought reluctantly. It was like getting soldiers up for another five hours' forced march when they had had only half an hour's break.

"'Ask and ye shall receive.' I didn't ask, Lord, I just went and tried to do it myself: I got my hundred ruffians together, I frightened wily old Mago into action and I got nowhere. I'm not such an ass as to think that I can storm the King's palace with those rascals of mine. I can't do it. I'm not good enough. But please, Lord, don't let old lion-face go down like this and don't let these poor, miserable, holy idiots be disappointed, don't let *us* poor idiots be disappointed. . . ."

"Let us pray as our Lord taught us," Judah said. "Our Father who art in Heaven. . . ."

The light of the small lamp painted strange shadows on the wall. Huge ghosts raised their hands in prayer.

"Thy will be done," Cassius prayed. "But this one time, Lord, let ours be done, though I certainly wouldn't know how."

Then terror struck. There was a knock at the outside door.

"The soldiers," old Joel gasped.

"They're coming for us, too."

One of the older women started to scream, but the girl next to her clapped her hand over her mouth and she burst into tears instead. Cassius' fingers were playing with his sword-hilt. With a bitter smile he looked at Judah.

The Apostle stood erect and calm. "There is someone at the door," he said in an even voice. "We must let him in."

From downstairs came the shriek of a woman's voice, followed by hurried steps.

Rhoda burst into the room, beside herself with excitement. "It's Cephas!" she shouted.

"You're mad," Cassius snapped.

"She's overexcited," one of the women said.

"Cephas," Rhoda screamed. "Cephas, Cephas . . ."

"She's hysterical. . . ."

The knock at the door came again.

"It is Cephas," Rhoda cried. "Why won't you believe me! I've seen him."

"She may have seen Cephas' angel—his guardian angel," a girl said, trembling.

Downstairs, the knocking was repeated, stronger than before.

"Whoever it is, he's getting pretty impatient," Cassius murmured. "Look here, girl, if it's Cephas why didn't you open the door? I don't believe a word of this mad story."

Rhoda gaped at him.

But Judah moved toward the door and suddenly they all moved, incredulous, fearful, hesitant, out of the room and down the stairs.

The knocking ceased.

"I'll do it," Cassius said and he threw back the wooden bolt. "Now then." He opened the door.

A ragged cry went up from half a dozen voices.

Cephas stepped in.

Wide-eyed, shivering, Cassius closed the door behind him.

The big, broad-shouldered, lion-faced man raised his hand and immediately all voices were hushed.

"It is Cephas," Cassius thought. "There isn't the slightest doubt that it is Cephas. And yet . . ."

"The Lord," came Cephas' deep voice, "has delivered me from prison. I was sleeping, chained with two chains, between two soldiers, when the Lord's angel struck me on the side and woke me.

He told me to get up. I obeyed and the chains dropped from my hands. The angel told me to gird myself and put on my shoes. I did. He told me to wrap my cloak about me and to follow him. I thought I was having a vision."

They all stood in utter silence, drinking in his words. None of them could think about what he said, analyze it or react to it. They could only accept it. He was filling them like cups.

"We passed one party of guards," Cephas went on, "and then another. We reached the iron gate that leads into the city. It swung open of its own accord. We came out and went up one street. Then the angel left me. I came to myself and I knew for certain that this was not a vision but that it had happened in real life."

Still they were silent. There was no room yet for comprehension, for words, for joy. They stood like statues.

Cephas looked at Judah. "Tell this to your brother Jaqob and the others," he said, turned, opened the door, stepped out and was gone.

With two steps Cassius stood in front of Judah. Before he could say anything, the Apostle nodded and somehow Cassius knew that Judah understood and approved his idea. He embraced him hastily and rushed out of the house.

There, already at some distance, Cephas was stalking up the street, his gigantic shadow trailing after him in the starlight.

Cassius ran and caught up with him. "Cephas," he stammered, "my father—a favor!"

"What is it, son?"

How could he put it? It was vital that Cephas leave the city, that he leave Judaea and the entire realm of the mad King. Perhaps this moment his escape was being discovered; it was bound to be discovered in the morning and then all hell would be loose. But how could one put that to a man who had just been saved by a miracle? How could one persuade him to come to Antioch? Horses, armed slaves were ready for the journey.

"I am going to Antioch," Cephas said. "Do you want to come with me, son?"

CHAPTER TWENTY-TWO

Vibius Marsus could not sit still while Cassius was making his official report. He walked up and down the study with his quick little steps, grunting, grinning and unbearingly cheerful. "Amazing," he said in the end. "I never heard anything like it."

"That I can well believe," Cassius said dryly. "Miracles are rare."

"Oh, I don't mean that. Or, if I do . . . never mind."

"You're talking in riddles again."

The governor burst into laughter. "You are the man to accuse me of talking in riddles," he said. "Your entire report is one long series of riddles. Fortunately old Mago has sent me his report too, so I'm able to fill in the missing parts. You have achieved the impossible. An outstanding victory, and of enormous importance."

This time Cassius could not help laughing. "As far as my work is concerned," he said, "it was a resounding defeat; of no importance at all."

"You're quite mad," Marsus stated. "But it's a strangely productive kind of madness. It gets results and that's all I care for. Now I will tell *you* what you've done. First of all, you had the right idea about the King's secret. You linked it up with the execution of that man Jaqob and with the arrest of that Cephas of yours. I have had some tentative reports before that the secret was in some way linked up with religion, but I didn't believe a word of it. Herod Agrippa has no religion. He has to pose as a good Jew, for obvious reasons, but he is neither good nor is he a Jew, so that was no more than nonsense. This Messiah idea is an entirely different thing, of course. It means power. It means an aura of Divinity. It's exactly the kind of thing Agrippa needed for his plan. Can you imagine his Jews daring to tackle Rome? Not in your life. But when they get a leader who can claim—successfully claim, mind you—that he is sent by their Divinity, that he himself is semi-divine or all-divine or whatever the case may be, then they may dare anything. That's what impressed old Mago so much: that you could conceive that idea from the very start. He's a wily old bird, you know, and it's just as well that he needs us as much as he does. We're keeping the Mediterranean free of pirates and that means that he can commit his own brand of piracy which he calls trade, the old cutpurse."

"All I wanted was . . ."

"To free Cephas, I know. You told Mago often enough. So often that at long last he understood that Cephas meant a great deal to Agrippa—a dead Cephas, I mean. He stretched out his feelers and found the idea amply confirmed. Then he had his bit of luck with Fortunatus. Nice work on his part and I shall tell him so. To get his man in under the guise of a physician before the real quack arrived was masterly. Incidentally, I thought for a while that Mago had bribed Fortunatus' cook to give him the poison, but it seems that it really was Agrippa. Just as well Fortunatus was able to talk before he died! Now we know that Agrippa won't act before he has got hold of Phoenicia and has proclaimed himself as the Messiah or god or whatever it is. His relations with Phoenicia are pretty tense at the moment. But now comes the most amazing part of all. Mago told me that you seriously considered a raid on the prison, the palace prison. That he tried his best to dissuade you and thought he had succeeded. Wait . . . I'll read you what he says."

The governor stepped over to his desk, took up a sheet of very thin parchment and began to read: "To the best of my knowledge your emissary arrived here with no more than twelve armed slaves. Yet he must have been able to find a very great number of men of supreme skill. On the very morning after my last talk to your emissary, the King had all the gates of the city closed and extensive searches were made everywhere. I soon found out that the prisoner Cephas was missing; that the King had his guards first interrogated and then killed, sixteen in number and all protesting their innocence. Later several detachments of cavalry left the city in various directions. I certainly hope they are not going to catch the man. Even if he never turns up again in the city, the very fact of his existence will be a thorn in the flesh of the King. If he has allies powerful enough to get him safely out of the palace prison, the city and Judaea, he certainly is a man to be reckoned with." Marsus looked up. "You got him here safely. Did you see anything of the King's troops?"

"Yes," Cassius admitted. "Twice. But they didn't seem to see us."

"Magnificent," Marsus said. "I never had a report like this from Mago, I may tell you. He's deeply impressed; so am I, frankly. But now do tell me what really happened, Cassius."

"What do you mean?"

"How—did—Cephas—get free?"

"But I told you. He woke up and . . ."

"Yes, yes, I know," Marsus said. "The angel. But how did you do it?"

"I didn't do anything."

Marsus cocked his head sideways. "No?" he asked softly. "Either you did it or that religious group of yours has powers at its disposal that I never dreamed of—and I mean superhuman help, messengers of the gods or god. Which is it?"

"I told you exactly what Cephas told us," Cassius said. "And if Cephas can lie, then there's no honest man in the world."

"Maybe there isn't," Marsus said thoughtfully. "Most likely there isn't."

"You can talk to Cephas himself, if you wish," Cassius suggested. "He's still here."

"And hear the same story again, with you as interpreter? My Aramaic is lamentable. No, there's not much sense in that. Tell me one thing, Cassius! You are an intelligent man, well educated, a man who has seen a great deal and is widely traveled. Do you seriously believe the angel story?"

"Yes," Cassius said.

Marsus swore, loudly and at great length, and Cassius began to laugh.

"What's funny?" Marsus inquired testily.

"Forgive me, but . . . you don't believe in a god or in gods, do you?"

"Most certainly not," the governor barked. "With the exception

214

of the Divinity of the Emperor that is," he added with mock solemnity.

"Right. But in that case what does it mean when you say: 'Curse that man to the nethermost Hades'? Hades is the god of the underworld. You don't believe in any gods. You don't believe in the underworld and you don't believe in curses. After all, cursing means to condemn a man to be punished by the gods. When a man doesn't believe in anything divine, he can't curse anybody or anything. For that matter, he can't give a blessing either. So all you did was to utter a string of words meaning nothing."

Marsus jumped up. "By Cerberus . . ."

"He doesn't exist either," Cassius said gravely.

Marsus blinked. "Come to think of it, you're quite right. If I could believe in Cerberus, I could believe in Cephas' angel too—or in Agrippa's owl."

"Agrippa's owl?"

"Yes, didn't Mago tell you about that? According to Fortunatus—rather an unfortunate name for the man, don't you think?—Agrippa believes in an owl. He saw one in Italy just over his head and some seer told him that was the sign that he'd attain the highest power and would keep it until he saw the bird again. He'd die then in a few days. The things some people think of!"

"Strange story."

"For once I agree with you. Mind you, Agrippa is lucky, as usual. There aren't any owls in Judaea or anywhere near it, so he's safe enough."

"He hasn't been so lucky lately, has he?" Cassius said grimly.

"No, he hasn't—thanks to you and Mago—and the angel, of course, never forget the angel. But angel or not, Cassius, you've done extremely well and I'm grateful. You've been good enough to accept my offer to make you chief administrator of the province. Can you start at once? You can? Excellent. My clerk will write out the document of nomination. A copy must go to Rome for signature, but that won't create any difficulty, the Emperor is only too happy if he doesn't have to bother about nominations of his own.

This afternoon I shall have the men lined up who will work directly under you. I'm glad to have you. I can do with a man who's able to get King Herod Agrippa's prize prisoner away from right under his royal nose."

*　　*　　*

The young physician closed the door to the sickroom behind him. "There's no need to worry," he said, smiling. "She'll be up and jumping about in a day or two. The fruit she's been eating wasn't poisonous—just unripe."

Naomi sighed with relief. "Oh, Lukas, I'm so grateful—to God and to you."

"The lesser half of your gratitude is quite unmerited," Lukas told her. "If I hadn't come she would have gotten well, though perhaps a few days later. I told Abigail about the diet I want the girl to follow for the time being."

"You are quite sure there is no danger?"

Lukas laughed outright. "None, noble lady. We know very little, but very little knowledge is necessary to be reasonably sure of this case."

"I'll just go to her for a moment," Naomi said. "I'll be back. You'll wait for me, won't you? Or are you in a hurry?"

"I must be in Singon Street in an hour's time, but that's not far, as you know."

"Good." Naomi slipped back into the sickroom, where old Abigail was sitting grimly and bolt upright beside Acte's bed. "How is the pain, little one?"

The girl made a wry face. "It's a silly pain, mother. Too much to feel good and too little to feel bad. I'll never eat Persian apples again."

"It's all the apples' fault, of course," Abigail said, sniffing.

"No, it's not, Abigail. But they didn't like being eaten. They said so. They still do inside me."

"They didn't like it because they weren't ready for it," Naomi said. "They told you they weren't, too, by being green. There is a time for everything, says the Book. You upset the time of the apples and now your own time is upset and you can't drive out with father and me this afternoon. But you'll be all right again soon," she added quickly when she saw Acte's little mouth tighten. She gave her the all-is-well smile and a nod and left.

"I believe you're right," she told Lukas. "If you hadn't come in time I would have sent for my husband, I was so worried. I should have known better, really, but everything is so vehement with a child. . . ."

"And with a mother," Lukas said. "I'm glad you didn't disturb the Chief Administrator of Syria in his work."

"He is working too hard, I fear," she said with a little sigh. "He never worked like this for himself."

"He is doing a great deal of good, from all I hear," Lukas said. "At the beginning some of our dear Antiochenes just couldn't believe it when they heard about Velleius, Corvinus and Labeo being sent home for such a natural thing as having taken bribes. They thought . . ."

". . . that it must be because my husband didn't want to share what they call their commission with his subordinates."

"That's right. But now they talk differently."

"He hates corruption in any form," Naomi said. "But there are many who hate him for that. I often fear . . . never mind. He must do what is right. I . . . I knew this would happen."

"No doubt he will have enemies, noble lady. The best men always have. Our Lord had enemies. Saul has enemies."

"Has he?"

"Oh, many. And he always will have, I think. His will is overwhelming and people do not always like to be overwhelmed, particularly when they are wrong. And it's very difficult to be right when one disagrees with Saul."

"You haven't quarreled with him, have you?"

"Not I." Lukas laughed. "But then I don't disagree with him."

"You mean . . . you always give in?"

"I don't have to. He is right and God has given me the sense to see it."

"Yours is a fortunate nature, Lukas," she said.

"I'm a Greek, noble lady—that's perhaps saying the same thing in other words. As a Greek, I enjoy life, I enjoy living. And now that I know about our Lord, that joy of life has multiplied beyond anything I could have imagined, although I never had anything like the personal experience of Him that Saul had—and still has."

"Still has?"

"Yes, there are moments—" He broke off. "He is the born teacher," he went on, a little hastily. "I never get tired listening to him, watching him. He's so . . . so mobile, so quick in understanding, his answers come at once, as if they'd been waiting impatiently for a release. He could be a Greek himself."

"Never," Naomi contradicted. "He is a Jew of Jews, the pupil of our great teachers."

"And proud of it," Lukas admitted. "No, not proud . . . glad of it. There seems to be nothing a Jew can't do, once he has got rid of the shackles of the Law *and* found our Lord. Sometimes I feel Saul, too, is doing too much. He sleeps only a few hours and all the rest is work. And how he works! The intensity of it! He will argue with everybody and anybody. He'll blaze away at obstinate people, but for the stupid he has the patience of a mother. I often wish I could write down everything he says, so much gets lost because there is always so much more—he is inexhaustible."

"Why don't you?" Naomi asked.

"Perhaps I will. I think I will. You asked me a little while ago whether I was in a hurry and I told you I wasn't. You know, that's only due to the fact that Saul isn't here at present."

"Still in Jerusalem? I do so hope he and Bar Naba will return safely. Jerusalem is dangerous again. You know what happened to Cephas and . . ."

"Nothing will happen to them," Lukas interposed cheerfully. "Cephas was in danger because everybody knows that he is the head of the Christians. . . ."

"So you're using that word, too, now," she said, smiling.

"Oh, everybody does. They're startled at first and then they like it. It's a name that could only have been born here in Antioch, don't you think?"

"Why?"

"Well, it's a Greek word; it's got a Latin ending—the same as 'Pompeians' or 'Octavians'; but the meaning is Jewish. That's Antioch all over, isn't it?"

"On the cross," Naomi said, "there was a strip of parchment affixed just above our Lord's head and it said on it that He was the King of the Jews—in Latin and in Greek and in Hebrew."

Lukas nodded. "Pilatus himself wrote that," he said, "and he probably meant it as a sort of cruel jest. I daresay the Antiochians mean it in the same way when they call us Christians. But our Lord *was* the King and we *are* Christians. What made you think of the inscription on the cross, I wonder?"

"I don't know. I just thought of it."

Again he nodded. "Written in all the languages," he said. "Proclaimed in all tongues, for everybody to hear. And we would get our name here in Antioch, where all the world meets. And the community is growing so fast! Within the last six months it has doubled and it is still growing."

"Saul?"

"Yes, to a great part. And recently there is another reason: many of our brothers have left Jerusalem because of the danger there, just as some did when Saul himself *was* the danger, nine years ago."

"You feel it's natural that Antioch should become the . . . the center of the Faith," Naomi said. "To me it's very strange. This is such a lighthearted city. . . ."

"What of it, noble lady? Oh, I see. . . ." Lukas smiled. "I forget that lightheartedness is frowned upon in the Jewish mind. But must a human heart be heavy to be acceptable to God?"

"Without suffering," Naomi said in a halting voice, "we are not likely to turn to Him."

"That is true for many," he admitted. "But not for all. A physician after all knows something about suffering; other people's suffering, mostly. But he wouldn't be much good if it left him unmoved. Can you imagine what it must mean to a physician when he hears that our Lord helped the sick wherever he went? And beyond that, far beyond it, that through the Christ suffering has received meaning, dignity and nobility? Helping to pay off the debt, Saul calls it, for the sake of our Lord's Body—which is the Church he founded."

"He *is* a great man," Naomi said thoughtfully. "I've always thought he was."

"He is the greatest man I've ever known," Lukas replied firmly. "There is no one like him for answering the inquiring mind, but that, much as it is, is only part of him. He is like a great river, but a river which hasn't found its course and its bed yet, a river in the making. One day he'll break forth, irresistibly, and there's no knowing how many lands he will fertilize."

"If only he were back safely with Bar Naba," Naomi said.

"He should be, soon," Lukas told her. "He only went to distribute the food and money we collected for the brothers who remain in Jerusalem."

"The mad King may have him arrested."

"If so, the Lord will save him as he saved Cephas," Lukas said. "But I don't think there is much danger at the moment. From what I heard yesterday, the King has left Jerusalem and is now in Caesarea."

CHAPTER TWENTY-THREE

KING HEROD AGRIPPA had left Jerusalem and was in Caesarea. He spent the first day there in complete seclusion. All callers, including the embassies sent from Tyre and Sidon, were told that the King was in deep meditation and would see no one. He was staying at the palace formerly used by the Roman procurators of Judaea and now more than double its original size.

"The King is so fond of building," Blastus told Farduk, the leader of the embassy from Tyre. "In Berytus we have built an amphitheatre, a theatre, colonnades and baths. The amphitheatre is larger than the one the Romans built here in Caesarea, and we had a battle staged between two armies of criminals, seven hundred on each side, and the greater part of them was killed."

"Such an excellent way of getting rid of criminals," the Phoenician agreed. "Noble Blastus, may I say once more how happy we are, we and our brothers from Sidon, that the King now looks upon us with favor and that there is no trace left of the clouds that gave us such great sorrow in the past."

"Not a trace," Blastus affirmed. "And the first caravans will resume their weekly transports next month."

Farduk sighed. It was difficult to say whether he did so because he was relieved that Tyre was at last getting the supplies that only Herod Agrippa's realm could provide for them and which the King's disfavor had withheld for several months, or whether it was a sigh of regret for the seven hundred and fifty thousand drachmes he had paid Blastus earlier in the day. The only consolation was that Bulgal of Sidon had had to pay exactly the same amount. This Blastus was a barrel without a bottom.

"You may set your mind completely at rest," the royal chamberlain said affably. "But of course I must rely on you and the other members of your embassy to render homage to the King in the terms we discussed, when you meet him tomorrow in the theatre. That is essential and even I would not be able to keep my promise unless that . . . formality is strictly observed."

"This we will certainly do," the Phoenician said hastily. "I swear it to you by all the gods . . . which includes, of course, the new one." His flashing smile vanished very quickly when he saw that Blastus remained stonily serious.

*   *   *

The entry of King Herod Agrippa, ruler of Iturea, Gilead and the Trachonitis, Lord of Judaea, Galilee, Samaria, Basan and Abilene, into the theatre of Caesarea was triumphal. Five hundred horse-guards in armor preceded his golden chariot; another five hundred life-guards followed it on foot. The palace staff, led by the chamberlain, the prefect and the notables of the city and many other dignitaries bowed to him at the entrance.

Inside the huge building fifty trumpeters in scarlet coats gave the royal fanfare and everybody rose.

A long-drawn sigh of admiration and awe arose from the multitude. What they saw they would never forget.

The ruler was dressed in silver from head to foot. It was not armor, nor was it what could be called a royal robe. It was a veritable cascade of silver, shining like a cluster of stars in human shape in the light of the early sun. It was blinding, overwhelming. The heavy silver crown on his head scintillated with precious stones and the royal staff in his right hand was topped by a ruby as large as a pigeon's egg.

Slowly he sat down on the throne under the purple canopy and now at long last the people roared their welcome to the magnificent apparition. The King did not acknowledge their plaudits. He sat immobile, a silver statue, his face a mask.

The prefect, the notables and dignitaries of the city and the members of the embassies from Phoenicia arranged themselves in a semi-circle before the canopy and repeated their act of obeisance.

Then the ruler himself spoke and his first words came almost as a shock to the assembly, and especially to those standing near him. The statue had suddenly come to life.

The King spoke slowly, stiffly, in short, sharp sentences. He had come to his good city of Caesarea because its citizens had expressed through their council that they were longing for his presence.

Roar of assent and thunderous applause, quickly stopped when the King raised his staff a little.

He went on. The King was like the sun. Wherever he came he brought grace, warmth and blessing. The city of Caesarea would be given new public baths; larger and far more beautiful than those built by the Romans. Every citizen would receive wheat from Egypt and wine from the royal cellars free of charge on seven consecutive days.

This time the applause was deafening. Once more the King stopped it with a movement of his staff. He was here also to receive with favor the embassies of Tyre and of Sidon. Phoenicia, too, would grow more fertile in the light of the royal sun.

Farduk of Tyre threw up his arms. "It is no man that speaks, but a god," he cried aloud.

There was a moment of utter silence.

Bulgal of Sidon prostrated himself. "We acknowledge you as a god," he shouted. "Have mercy on us, Divinity."

Ten, fifty, a hundred, and more voices took up the shout. Many of the dignitaries of the city, not to be outdone in loyalty by the Phoenicians, prostrated themselves. Most of the Jews present were horrified beyond belief and had difficulty not to show it, but large portions of the assembly succumbed to the lure of the moment and some of the Greeks present broke into a hymn they used to sing in honor of the god Apollon.

Blastus, beaming all over his face, made a sweeping gesture as if to indicate that the people had spontaneously recognized the true status of their ruler.

The King rose.

"He will repudiate it," a young Jew murmured to an old man beside him. "Surely he will—he can't listen to such blasphemy. He will . . ."

"Quiet, Ruben, or they'll kill us."

Herod Agrippa smiled. He stretched out his hands in the unmistakable gesture of a blessing.

"Bless us, immortal god," howled Farduk of Tyre, and the members of both embassies and many other people took up the cry.

Turning slowly, the new god blessed his people. But suddenly he stopped.

On one of the gilded cords upholding the canopy an owl was sitting, staring at him from unblinking, yellow eyes.

The King staggered back, as if an invisible hand had struck him on the chest. He spun around, his silvery robes whirling through the air, and fell crashing to the ground.

*   *   *

"The people were thunderstruck, of course," Vibius Marsus said cheerfully. "The theatre emptied itself as if it had burst into flames. That fellow Blastus had him carried back to the palace and they peeled that silver stuff off him. It was made of thousands of little silver plates and at least some of them must have been sharp-edged

223

—he was bleeding in dozens of places, they say. He wouldn't allow a physician near him. He wouldn't have his wounds attended to. You've been in the army, Cassius, you know how it is with open wounds in a hot climate. First the flies, then the maggots. On the fourth day he was riddled with them. On the fifth he died."

"Did he repent?" Cassius asked in a low voice.

"Strange that you should ask that. He did, apparently. Made quite a little speech about it."

Cassius nodded. "So the prophecy was fulfilled after all. Doesn't that shake you a little?"

The governor leaned forward, beaming. "If I tell you what really happened—will you tell me how you got that Cephas of yours out of jail?"

Cassius gaped at him. "If you tell me . . . what do you mean? Do you mean . . ."

"Gods and owls and owls and gods," Marsus said gleefully.

"You're my superior now," Cassius said, "and I should really call you by your official title. But unless you tell me what happened, I shall first resign and then tell you what I think of you."

"It's much too good a story not to be told." Marsus grinned. "Especially as you're almost the only person I can tell it to—at present."

"I think I know what you mean," Cassius said. "The owl didn't get there by itself, is that it?"

"By itself?" Marsus almost shrieked. "I should say not. Cost me eight thousand sesterces to get the confounded bird there. There aren't any anywhere near Caesarea. There aren't any in the whole of Syria, except somewhere up in the Hauran Mountains and that's where I got it, after much coaxing. Eight thousand sesterces for that vermin-infested brute and the fellow who carried it to Caesarea. Another three thousand to bribe a minor official into giving my agent a place near the newly hatched god's canopy. I thought it would do something to him if the bird turned up at a particularly solemn occasion, but even I didn't hope for such a development. Do you realize what I did? That man would have gone to war against us within a few years, a war that would have cost Rome fifty million sesterces and maybe double that money. And I settled the whole thing for eight thousand. Just my luck that I can't tell our beloved Emperor about it. He'd never forgive me. And what about you, friend? Won't you tell me now what *you* did about Cephas?"

"I told you everything I know about that," Cassius said, frowning.

"Cassius, you can't keep up the story of the angel! Look what happened with Herod. You fell for that story, there's no use denying it. You really believed that there was some supernatural influence about, that a genuine prophecy had come true. And now you know what really happened. Doesn't that shake *you* a little?"

"What shakes me," Cassius said, "is the intense belief you have in your unbelief. Just because your owl was a fake, all stories involving the supernatural must be faked too. What kind of logic is that? Besides, you don't realize in the least what you've done. . . ."

"Don't I? Well, what have I done, my Cassius?"

"You have fulfilled the will of God."

"What?"

"Come now, Marsus. If the owl had appeared of its own accord, even you would have wagged your head and thought that there might be something in prophecy and the supernatural. Why? Because God made use of an owl. Now why should that be more miraculous than that He has made use of you?"

"Use of . . . me?"

"Certainly. He even made use of your mentality, so apt to try to prove there is no such thing as the supernatural. Herod Agrippa blasphemed when he allowed himself to be adored as a god. So God or an angel of God struck him—through you and that absurd bird you paid eight thousand sesterces for."

Marsus broke into a stream of expletives.

"As your chief administrator," Cassius said blandly, "how do you wish me to book those eight thousand? Under 'Intelligence Service,' 'Beasts for Military Purposes' or simply as poultry?"

"Book them as 'Religious Expenses,'" Marsus snapped.

*   *   *

Several months later Cassius was inspecting new fortifications at a ford across the Orontes River when an urgent message arrived from the governor, asking him to return to Antioch at once. He broke off the inspection and hurried back.

He found Marsus in his study. The little man looked stern and hard. "I have been recalled," he said curtly. He raised his hand, to stop Cassius from speaking. "Herod Agrippa was a truly dangerous enemy," he went on. "He managed to be dangerous to me even after his death. The Emperor is mourning the sudden death of his great and faithful friend. His own words, Cassius. 'Great and faithful friend.' His first intention was to nominate Agrippa's son as King of the entire realm of his father. The young viper is only seventeen. Well, Pallas and the other freedmen who are now ruling the Emperor and the empire managed to dissuade him from that supreme act of foolishness. So Judaea has again been declared a Roman province and Cuspius Fadus will arrive shortly to take over the entire Herodian realm. That alone would have been enough to force me to tender my resignation. But I am recalled from Syria without a word of explanation. The usual good friends have been in a hurry to give me the explanation anyway. I am recalled as a gesture of honor on the part of the Emperor for his dead friend King Herod Agrippa who regarded me as his personal enemy. So now Claudius sees to it that his dead friend's personal enemy shall not stay on longer than he did himself."

"A strange way to honor a dead friend," Cassius remarked. "I regret this very much, for your sake, for Rome's sake and for my own sake—to say nothing of Syria. I think you've been the best Governor the province ever had. I will resign now, of course."

"You'll do nothing of the kind," Marsus bellowed. "There must be at least one honest man in Syria when I'm gone. And you're honest. I know it, because I tested you. The fellow who offered you a hundred thousand if he got the government order for the new buildings in the Epiphania district was an agent of mine and I had to give him fifty gold pieces to soothe his feelings."

"I did kick him rather hard," Cassius admitted calmly.

"You may be honest by nature," Marsus continued, "or by

226

principle; or because you believe that your own brand of Divinity is going to kick *you,* if you aren't: personally, I don't care which it is. So I'm going to let you take my place as soon as I've gone."

Cassius shook his head. "You can't do that. Only the Emperor has the power to nominate your successor."

"Only the Emperor has the power to nominate a chief administrator, yet that's what you've been for some considerable time without either confirmation or interference from Rome. I shall inform Rome, naturally, that I leave you here in charge of affairs."

"Surely they're going to send out a new man of their own choice. The post of a governor of Syria . . ."

"They probably will, in due course. There may be some wrangling going on about it at this moment, and they may still be wrangling when I arrive in Rome. Pallas will have his own man and so will Narcissus and maybe Posides and Felix and Harpocras, freedmen all of them and the real rulers of the empire. But Claudius will have to give his signature to the final choice, and he may do so today or in six months or six years or not at all. You never know with a fool, do you? In the meantime Syria must be administered and somebody must be in charge. That's you."

*   *   *

A month later former Governor Vibius Marsus left Syria from the port of Seleucia and temporary Governor Cassius Longinus saw him off. He liked the crusty little man and he worried more than a little about what kind of reception he would have in Rome. Marsus really had been a good administrator. But the Emperor seemed to regard him only as the personal enemy of his late friend Herod Agrippa and there was no telling what he might do. Certainly, if ever Claudius found out about that owl story, Marsus would be in serious trouble.

He told Naomi so. What he did not tell her was that he himself might be in a certain amount of danger as well. For Claudius and the wealthy freedmen around him, he was simply Marsus' right-hand man. Besides, he had been out east for almost twenty years. He had no friends in Rome. And Velleius, Corvinus and Labeo, whom he had packed off for the corrupt scoundrels they were, might well use the opportunity to work against him, when they found that Marsus had left him in charge as governor.

The trouble was that he had allowed himself to be roped in again. He had lost his independence. Perhaps Naomi was right when she felt uneasy about his appointment as chief administrator. He had thought of it as a purely temporary affair; and now he found himself in charge of an entire province.

Bah, the Emperor was sure to send out one of Pallas' or Narcissus' men and then he could return to ordinary life.

He decided to go on living in his own house, instead of taking up residence in the palace. He would go to the palace only to work. That way he would make it clear to everybody that he did not regard his appointment as permanent. And Naomi was sure to prefer it so. Certain changes, of course, were inevitable. There would be sentries in front of his house; a guardroom had to be established. There would be a constant coming and going of dispatch-riders, messengers, officials and visitors of all kinds. He would have little peace. And at some official functions not only he but Naomi also would have to be present. She was now the governor's wife and just as he represented the power and majesty of the Emperor, she had to represent the dignity of the Empress. The dignity of Messalina—everybody knew she was one of the world's worst women. Everybody except her husband.

Cassius gritted his teeth. People in Syria would bow to him and to Naomi, as the representatives of a fool and a wanton. What an honor!

Naomi's intuition had been right. He should never have accepted in the first place.

There was only one hope: that having accepted, he could help the cause of the Christ, and better than before.

But was it possible to serve both the Christ and the Empire? Cephas—Petrus—once told him that Jesus said: "A man cannot serve two masters."

He spoke his thought to Bar Naba.

228

Bar Naba smiled. "Our Lord also said: 'Render unto Caesar what is Caesar's, and unto God what is God's.' "

Cassius nodded. "That may solve the problem. But the two sayings seem to contradict each other."

"They seem to, because they are taken out of context. When our Lord said that no man can serve two masters, He spoke out against those who worshiped Mammon and tried to worship God at the same time. But worship belongs to God alone. In that sense God alone can be our Master. The second saying originated when our Lord was asked whether people should pay taxes to Caesar. It was not a matter of worship at all, but of earthly duties."

"Thank you. I'm glad you explained it to me."

"That's what we elders are for," Bar Naba said cheerfully. "There are many cases where people are in doubt about what our Lord meant when He said this or that. Sometimes it's clear enough, but not always. And when we are in doubt ourselves, we hold council and invoke the Holy Spirit. We'll do that tonight."

"Tonight?"

"Yes, at our assembly house in Singon Street. It's the first council we have held since Saul and I came back from Jerusalem. Young Mark is with us, too."

"And Cephas? Will he be there?"

"No, he has gone to Caesarea. He'll be back in Jerusalem soon, I think."

"What is the council about?"

"The spreading of the Tidings in other countries."

*　　*　　*

For weeks on end Saul had been restless and impatient, so much so that it was difficult not to reveal it to others. Work here in Antioch had become shepherd's work, guarding the community against evil, looking after its spiritual welfare. It was still growing. It was of supreme importance. But it was not the task the Lord had set him. He fretted. "Straining at the Lord's leash," Bar Naba called it and young Lukas looked at him from worried eyes.

229

He had fasted for three days and so had all the elders and word went out to the community to join in and then to assemble in Singon Street to partake of the Lord's Body and Blood and to help in the decision to be taken about the spreading of the Tidings.

For many bitter hours Saul had wrestled with the tremendous desire to be chosen for that task. He wanted it so much that he could see it filling a place in his soul that belonged to God alone and not to anything else, however good by itself.

There could be no question of seeking glory. Glory could be only in something exceeding duty and to preach the Good Tidings was duty—and woe to him if he did not fulfill it. But his desire to be chosen was that of the horse that would carry the King into battle; yet the King had many horses in his stable and it was up to Him to choose which of them He would ride.

Thus Saul emptied himself of everything, even of his holy desire to serve; and it was like dying.

*　　*　　*

Acte went exploring. She had been in the large, old house before when her mother and Abigail took her there with many parcels and bags for the elders who would then distribute them to the poor. Sometimes Saul would be here and sometimes Bar Naba or Lukas the physician who loved to laugh or Simon whom they called Niger and who came from Cyrene like Lucius. There was always time for a chat, until Abigail had finished supervising the slaves who carried in the parcels and bags. But this time the house seemed to be deserted.

There was no one in the corridor, no one in the room where they prayed or talked to each other and mustn't-be-disturbed.

This was the room where Lukas was writing when she had last come. She had asked him what he was writing and he said, "Just making notes, little one."

"What about?"

"Things that happened. It was your mother's idea, when I come to think of it."

She had clean forgotten to ask her mother what that idea was.

She must do that someday. Meanwhile, here was another room and that was empty, too. No, it was not.

There was a man kneeling in a corner. He was a blind man—his eyes were all white and had no holes through which he could see. But he did not seem to be sorry about being blind. He was smiling. Perhaps he was praying. But his lips did not move and his mouth was open and the jaw hanging a little. He was wearing a brown kerchief on his head, just like the one Saul always wore.

Suddenly she knew that he *was* Saul. He looked quite different, but he was Saul. No, he was not praying. His hands were hanging down, just like his jaw. Perhaps he was asleep. But who would go to sleep kneeling? And yet he was asleep. Perhaps he had been very tired and fallen asleep while saying his prayers, as she had done the day before yesterday. But what had happened to his eyes?

Abigail once said something about having had to close her mother's eyes when she was dead.

"Are you dead?" Acte asked politely.

There was no answer, but Acte knew immediately that Saul was not dead. When people were dead all their families and friends were sad. But it was not possible to be sad about Saul. He looked so happy. She could see it clearly, now that she had come nearer.

Not much nearer, though; only two very small steps, then she stopped. She did not exactly know why. It was not because she was afraid of his white eyes. She wasn't.

She realized why just a little later. He was so busy being happy that she must not disturb him. But she could not think of that at the moment. She could not really think at all, because his happiness was so great.

It came to her that she must pray.

When she raised her head again, Saul was looking at her.

He had his eyes back and he was smiling, but only a little and very sadly.

She gave a little sob and ran out of the room.

*　　*　　*

The assembly hall was packed with people.

Acte, flanked by her mother and Abigail, was trying in vain to take it all in. She had never before been allowed to come here and much of what was going on she did not understand. But there was Lukas, giving her a friendly nod, and Bar Naba, too, and in one corner she could see Saul, all by himself and looking very small and quiet.

"Look, Acte," Naomi whispered to her. "Do you see the man with the dark skin over there?"

"Yes, mother."

"That is Simon—they call him Niger, the Dark One. He comes from Cyrene. When our Lord broke down under the heavy cross, the soldiers let Simon carry it for a while."

Lukas, passing by, heard her say it and turned back. "There's the proof of what Saul is teaching," he said. "That we all owe our Lord a debt of honor, and happy is he who is allowed to help to pay it off."

"What does he mean, mother?"

But Naomi did not answer and Acte saw that like everyone else she was looking at the two sturdy men who were carrying a large urn into the hall and placing it on a table.

Simon of Cyrene raised his hand and as all fell silent, he began to speak. They would be given little pieces of parchment, he said, and everyone should write the name of the man whom they considered the right one to go forth and win new lands for the Lord by teaching the people to believe in Him. Those who could not write, should ask one who could to put down the name they chose. But first they should all join him in a prayer to the Holy Spirit, to come down on them and let them make the right choice.

Then they all fell down just where they stood. They did not kneel or bend one knee, they lay down flat on the floor, Saul and Simon and Lukas and mother, too, as if there had been an earthquake, or as if they expected one; and perhaps they did.

For a moment Acte, out of sheer surprise, remained standing, but her mother's hand was tugging at the hem of her tunic and down she went as well, into a flat world smelling of earth and leather and solemnity. All around her people were breathing audibly and from afar the deep, booming voice of dark Simon was invoking the Holy Spirit and then fell silent. And the silence seemed to grow and grow all over the room; it seemed as though people were not even breathing any longer. Acte was frightened.

Naomi, lying beside her, turned her head toward her for a brief smile.

Suddenly another voice was heard, high-pitched, creaky, an old man's voice: "Set apart for me Bar Naba and Saul unto the work to which I have called them."

"Who said that? Who?" came an eager young voice.

"It's Agabus."

"Agabus . . ."

"He has the gift of prophecy."

"Bar Naba and Saul for the work. . . ."

"Bar Naba and Saul!"

The cry was taken up by a dozen, by a hundred voices. All the people were rising to their feet.

There was a cluster of men around Agabus, two of them had to support him, the old man was very near fainting.

"Bar Naba and Saul! Bar Naba and Saul!"

Simon of Cyrene looked about him. "Bar Naba and Saul," he repeated and his deep voice had the ring of finality.

"No need for an election now," Lukas said triumphantly. "I'm so glad it's Saul."

"Why?" Acte piped up, reproachfully. "I thought you liked him and now you're glad he's going away!"

Lukas laughed merrily, patted her on the arm and made his way across the hall toward Saul and Bar Naba who were embracing each other.

"Why is he glad?" Acte repeated indignantly.

"Hush, darling—he is glad because Saul is glad. Look at him!"

Saul was happy. He was beaming. He was going away and he was glad. Acte's eyes filled with tears.

Saul was embracing Simon of Cyrene who was tall, and with

233

Bar Naba on his other side, who was taller still, he looked very small, small and surprisingly young, despite his beard and his receding hair.

"At once," he said, "we'll leave at once."

Simon threw back his head, laughing. "This has made a new man of you," he said in his rumbling voice.

Saul tapped Simon on the chest. "So it has. So it has. I shall have a new name, too, a very old new name. When my father had me inscribed on the list of Roman citizens, the Decurion gave me one look—so!—and put me down as 'The Small One'—Paulus. Just the right name for me when I come to the Gentiles. Not Saulus . . . Paulus."

Bar Naba nodded, smiling. "Small, yes; like the grain of mustard seed. 'No seed is so little . . .' the Lord said, 'but . . . it shoots up and grows taller than any garden herb, putting out great branches, so that all the birds can come and settle under its shade.'"

Saul—Paul—clapped him on the shoulder in high good humor, took his arm and drew him away; and such was the impetus of his movement that everyone near him followed.

Lukas looked back at Naomi. "The river has found its course," he said. "Now he'll break forth. . . ."

"Yes," she replied. "Irresistibly."

BOOK THREE

CHAPTER TWENTY-FOUR

THE LORD of the World sniffed noisily. Balancing precariously on his gilded chair he looked like an ancient, somewhat ill-tempered monkey in purple robes.

"The Empress," he said. "Somebody go and tell her I want to talk to her. *And* Seneca. Together. Hate the idea but it can't be helped. You don't have to tell her *that*," he added hastily. "Just tell her to come. Take her an hour, I suppose. . . ."

"Quite possible, Caesar." Long, lean Narcissus scribbled down the order and gave the tablet to a servant who sped away. "The noble Senator Seneca may have to be fetched from his home."

"Take her an hour in any case," the Emperor said sullenly. "Mind you, she's better than Messalina used to be; three hours, four, anything. Poor Messalina. Miss her sometimes."

Private Secretary Narcissus cleared his throat. There were six guards in the room—the minimum—as well as four under-secretaries and a number of slaves. Someone among them was bound to be in Agrippina's pay. He had warned Claudius about that a dozen times, but nothing would stop him from making such remarks.

"Soft little kitten," Caesar went on drearily. "Not icy, not uppish, domineering, ambition-ridden . . ."

Narcissus had a fit of coughing.

"Something wrong with your throat," the Emperor told him. "I'll send you Xenophon. Only good physician I ever had. Make a note of it. Who's next on the list?"

"The noble Vatinius . . ."

"Nothing noble about him," Claudius said. "Except that his father was a shoemaker. Don't feel like seeing his face. Next."

"Marcus Ulpianus, the architect, Caesar."

"With his canal scheme?" Claudius shuddered. "Figures again, length, breadth, radius, diameter, so-and-so many working hours, so-and-so many millions. I had to listen to Pallas for three solid hours this morning, and all *he* could talk about was figures. Let Ulpianus come tomorrow, no, make it next week or something."

Narcissus scribbled and dispatched another messenger. "The next on the list," he said, "is the noble Cassius Longinus."

"Who's he?"

"A former governor of Syria, Caesar. Or rather: a former vice-governor."

"When did I nominate him?"

"You didn't, Caesar. He was left in charge of affairs, when you recalled Vibius Marsus, nine years ago."

"Marsus. I remember *him*. Enemy of my old friend Herod. I miss him too. Real friend. What did I do about Marsus when he came back? Have him killed? No? Banished? No? What did I do then?"

"Nothing, Caesar."

Claudius sniffed. "Where is he now?"

"In Sinuessa, Caesar, taking the baths for his gout."

"Gout?" Claudius grinned toothily. "Needn't do anything about him then. Gout. He's punished enough. Herod couldn't stand him, poor old Herod. But how can he be here, when you say he's in Sinuessa?"

"He is not here, Caesar," Narcissus explained patiently. "His successor is, the noble Cassius Longinus."

"That's right. No, it isn't. How's it possible that he was Governor of Syria, when I never nominated him? Be quiet. I know. That was the time when . . . no, it wasn't. I must have forgotten all about it. Never mind. Who *is* this fellow Longinus?"

Narcissus was prepared for this kind of thing. "I have his dossier here," he said. Taking up the document he began to read.

" 'Only son of General Marcus Cassius Longinus . . .' "

"We hope," Claudius said acidly.

" '. . . and of Marcia Acte Vinidia. Born in the year seven hundred and fifty-eight of the foundation of the City. . . .' "

"That makes him forty-eight now," Claudius said.

" 'Served as tribune in the Twenty-first Legion, under Cinna.' " Narcissus read on, " 'When his father got into debt, he sold himself to his father's principal creditor, Marcus Balbus, who had him trained as a gladiator. As such he won his freedom by defeating one Baculus at the Plebeian Games. . . .' "

"I remember that," Claudius crowed. "Baculus! Cost me forty gold pieces. Idiot, got himself speared like a salmon! And then they say I'm forgetful. Go on."

" 'Took service with the army as an ordinary legionary,' " Narcissus read. " 'Served under Procurator Pontius Pilatus in Judaea, discharged honorably after five years of service. Reason: health. Final rank: Second centurion, first cohort.' Then there is a gap of thirteen years before he re-entered the service of the state, this time in a civilian capacity. He was nominated chief administrator by the Governor of Syria, Vibius Marsus . . ."

"Gout," Claudius said with feeling.

". . . and it is fairly clear that he must have done some high-level Intelligence work in between," Narcissus went on. "Otherwise it would be incomprehensible that Marsus made him chief administrator since the man had never been a civil servant, and that he put him in charge when he left. Longinus sent in his reports regularly from then on, of course, but unfortunately Antonius Felix, who was in charge of Eastern Affairs at the time, is now Procurator of Judaea. . . ."

"And why shouldn't he be?" Claudius asked testily. "He isn't as intelligent as his brother Pallas, but he's good enough, Pallas says. I've got fat posts for five nephews of yours, haven't I? Relatives, relatives. All the troubles of my life come from relatives, my own and other people's."

"The appointment of Antonius Felix was no doubt an act of great wisdom," Narcissus said softly. "What I referred to as unfortunate is that he is not here to tell us more about this somewhat unusual case. All I have here is . . ."

"Don't go on boring me with details," the Emperor said. "Let's have him in and be done with it. Wait! What's he want of me?"

Narcissus looked at the audience list. "Permission to return to Antioch as a private person," he read out. "He has asked for that before, but we had to refuse."

"Ah. Why?"

"Just the general rule, Caesar. The presence of a former governor is often a source of embarrassment to his successor. He is now making the appeal to Caesar himself."

"One of Marsus' men," Claudius said. "I'll deal with him. Why isn't he here? I told you to let him come in, didn't I?"

Narcissus gave the necessary order.

The Emperor stretched himself and yawned. "I want a game of dice tonight," he announced. "Get Marullus, Aemilius and Vindex for me."

"The noble Aemilius won't be able to come, Caesar," Narcissus murmured.

"Ah? Why not? He's the nicest player of the lot. I want him."

"He was executed three weeks ago, Caesar," Narcissus told him in a tactful whisper.

Claudius frowned fiercely. "One can't remember everything, can one?" he complained. "Get somebody else then. Get Favonius. He's all right, isn't he?"

"Yes, Caesar." Narcissus was by no means surprised. Two days after the execution of Messalina for conspiracy Claudius, lying down for his dinner, inquired irritably why the Empress was not present.

Meanwhile Cassius Longinus had been ushered into the presence and saluted. He still had his lean, wiry soldier's figure, but his temples were graying and there was a network of tiny wrinkles around his eyes.

"How's your gout?" Claudius asked.

"Marsus, Caesar," Narcissus whispered. "Marsus, not Longinus."

"Nonsense," Claudius said. "That's not Marsus. Marsus is a small man with a paunch."

"I mean it is Marsus who is gouty, Caesar."

"They're always trying to confuse me," Claudius complained. "You're getting old, Narcissus. How are things in Syria, Longinus?"

"They were fairly peaceful when I was there, Caesar," Cassius replied. "But that was five years ago."

Claudius sighed. "Time flies," he said. "How is it that I haven't seen you before?"

"I am not living in Rome, Caesar. My house is in Puteoli."

"Not in Rome? Why not?"

Cassius looked straight into the rheumy eyes. "My wife and I arrived in Italy just after you decreed the banishment of all Jews from Rome, Caesar. My wife is a Jewess."

The Emperor pursed his lips. "Troublesome people, Jews. Very difficult to get on with; difficult religion, too, can't eat this, that and the other thing, always keep apart. We had riots here because of some new branch of 'em, led by somebody called Chrestus or something like it, so I threw them out. And the Druids, too—old tricksters, always out to cheat people with their magic. Sent them packing, let them go and trick their own people in Gaul. Do you play dice?"

"N-no, Caesar."

"Pity. Why do you want to go back to Gaul?"

"Not to Gaul, Caesar. To Syria."

"You can't," Claudius told him. "Can't have a governor and an ex-governor there. Trouble enough as it is. Syria's bad and Judaea's worse. Riots all the time for no reason at all."

"I have no intention of going there in any official capacity, Caesar," Cassius said, "and no wish to mingle in politics in any way. And as I cannot live in Rome . . ."

"One can't be too careful about marriage," Claudius interrupted. "I should know. I've been married six times. Five or six times. How often is it, Narcissus?"

There was a crash as the guards banged their spears against their gold-rimmed shields. A tall, majestically beautiful woman came in, glittering with jewels.

Cassius did not have to look at her purple robe—a shade lighter than the Emperor's—to know who she was. The elderly man in her wake was wearing the toga of a senator. "I know him," Cassius

241

thought, but he got no further. Instead he found himself watching, with a kind of grim fascination, the meeting of husband and wife.

Claudius seemed to shrink. The wide folds of his mantle wobbled around him. He smiled, but it was no more than a baring of very bad teeth, and there was a flicker of fear in his eyes before he forced them to be cold and expressionless.

The Empress Agrippina approached with unhurried bad temper, a woman of forty but with features, complexion and figure few younger women could rival. "You asked for me," she said. "I hope it's important. I have a great many things to do."

"It's about your son," Claudius said. "What can be more important to a mother?"

"*Our* son," the Empress corrected coldly.

Claudius tittered behind his hand. "As you wish," he said. "I'm well aware I adopted him. You must admit I do everything to please you. There are some who regard it as weakness. Perhaps it is. Nevertheless there are certain limits."

She turned away from him and looked about. "Out," she said and the slaves and under-secretaries scampered off as if they had been whipped.

Cassius looked at the Emperor.

"Family matter," Claudius said quite amiably. "Better go. See that you get rid of your gout."

Cassius bowed and withdrew. Passing through the door, flanked by two Praetorian Guards he could hear the Empress say: "Now then, what is it this time?" and glancing back he saw her staring at her husband with ugly expectancy.

*　　*　　*

The huge anteroom seemed to be even fuller than before, although some people had left; the common-looking fellow all dressed in gold cloth in clear daylight, for instance—Vatinius one of the ushers had called him; and the haughty architect or whatever he was, with his bundle of plans.

Should he leave also? Technically at least, there was some doubt whether his audience had been terminated. In any case, he could take the point of view, if he wished to, that there had been an interruption. Besides, the Emperor himself might have him recalled when his wife had finished with him. There was little likelihood of it, but if it happened and he had left the palace, he would never get an audience again. Bah, it didn't matter. Claudius had given some sort of an answer in the negative.

Yet Cassius decided to stay for a while at least. The reason had little or nothing to do with his arguments for and against; some wraith of a thought was winging through his mind, too nebulous to be recognized and yet compelling.

After a while, Narcissus came out, with the elderly senator, and proclaimed the end of audiences for the day. The anteroom, filled with dashed hopes, became unbearable and Cassius moved toward the door when he saw the senator looking at him with a puzzled smile.

Suddenly he knew that it was Seneca. Seneca, who had been his father's legal adviser; who had withdrawn quickly and cautiously when things began to become dangerous. But that was in another era, and since then the promising young lawyer had become the foremost philosopher of Rome, a multi-millionaire, the lover of one of Caligula's sisters, an exile and, after his recall, a senator and the private tutor of Agrippina's son.

Seneca came straight up to him. "General Longinus' son," he said. "No doubt about it. It's been . . . let me see . . . twenty-five, twenty-eight years, but I never forget a face when it's worth while."

"I didn't recognize you in there," Cassius replied with a slight motion of his head. "Until just now, when you looked at me."

The senator smiled. "In a thunderstorm we must think of our safety first. Besides, I've become an old man—no, I'm not asking to be contradicted. Where are you living these days?"

"In Puteoli."

"Wise man. *Beatus ille qui procul negotiis.* Funny that Horace, of all people, should have said that since he never bothered about business affairs at all! Now if I had said it . . . but never mind. When are you returning home?"

"Today," Cassius replied dryly. "I was trying to get the Emperor's permission to return to Syria, but he wouldn't give it. I was temporarily governor there years ago and he thinks or somebody thinks that my presence might be unwelcome."

Seneca shook his head. "Puteoli," he said, "one of the loveliest places in the world—and he wants to go back to the provinces. I know there is riffraff everywhere, but I prefer the Roman kind. Ah well—we must talk about this and many other things, and we shall. As a favor to me—postpone your journey until tomorrow and dine with me tonight. My house is south of the Palatine Hill, very near the Carinae. Anyone will tell your slaves the way. You accept? Excellent."

CHAPTER TWENTY-FIVE

ACTE's FAVORITE WALK was across the garden, past the huts of old Mucius and his son and upward through the orange groves until she reached the old wall, mossy and topped by the statue of the god Terminus with his pointed head, the symbol of a strange and unknown realm. Beyond that wall there were more orange groves, groups of palm trees and, at a far distance, the gleam of yellow Numidian marble, of which the neighboring villa was built. The wall was fairly high, but she had found a way to climb it, with the help of half a dozen rough stones. Half-way up was a niche that gave a good foothold and then she could drag herself up and sit astride the wall. From there the view was unforgettable, especially in the late afternoon when the sun was shining full on the upper story of the yellow marble villa. There was a ring of cyprus trees around it and behind it was the deep-blue sea, dotted with the white and rusty-red sails of fishing vessels.

Here one could sit and think and dream.

Life was sleepy in Puteoli, but she did not mind that very much. She could not go to the college where Senator Ausonius' girls went, because there they had to learn hymns in honor of Diana and Vesta and Ceres and adore their statues. When mother explained she had asked: "Why not? None of the girls take it seriously. They laugh about it, Flavia says. And Ausonia says only ignorant and stupid people still believe in these gods and everyone else knows that they are only sym . . . sym . . ."

"Symbols," mother said. "That makes it worse, really. It is bad enough to pray to idols, things made of brass and silver. But it is worse to go through an act of worship in a spirit of mockery. God forbid that you should do such a thing."

Mother was sometimes a little old-fashioned, Flavia said. Ausonia called it "oriental"; they both meant more or less the same thing. But there was one standard of which one could be sure.

"Do you think Saul would not like it either?"

"That I know for certain, darling."

Sitting on the high wall, Acte pondered about where Saul might be. She had seen him again in Antioch, when he and Bar Naba returned in triumph from their journey, after an absence of several years. They had been on Cyprus and won over the governor and his household and people all over the island. Then they had gone to Perga and to Galatia and Lystra, where Saul cured a lame man in the name of the Lord and the silly people there promptly wanted to worship him as a god, and Bar Naba too; but then their enemies rose and Saul was stoned and left for dead in a ditch. He had suffered terribly before that and afterward. Once he had fallen ill with the burning illness that befell people in marshy countries, Lukas said. Once he had been flogged and that also might easily have cost him his life, Lukas said. All that made him look so much older. He had a lot of white hair, not only on the temples, like father, but all round his head, except on top where he didn't have any hair at all. But father said it was a great triumph, much greater than the triumph of a victorious general, entering Rome on a gilded chariot and acclaimed by all the people.

"Why do you think so, father?" she asked.

"When a general is granted a triumph, he leaves behind him many dead, both of the enemy and of his own troops. But Paul left behind him many who are now much more alive than ever before, people who have in them the seed of eternal life."

They all called him Paul now, except mother, who somehow went on calling him Saul as before, but then, mother was a little old-fashioned— Flavia was right about that, if about nothing else. It was always, "A girl mustn't do this and a girl mustn't do that" with her. One could never admit that to Flavia, of course, but one could admit it to oneself, if only a little. She would probably not approve of a girl climbing a wall.

But where was Saul—Paul—now? He had been in Jerusalem when the *Minerva* left for Italy, with father, mother and herself on board, just after Abigail died, dear Abigail. Mother had cried her eyes out and she had done a good deal of crying herself. Iucunda and Virena and Aglae were all very nice, but there was no one like Abigail and never would be, although she had been far more old-fashioned than mother.

Once Bar Naba had written that Paul had gone on a journey again; this time without him, to some place called—Thessalonica, was it? Anyway it was in Macedonia, wherever that was. And from there he had gone to Athens, which was in Greece, everybody knew *that*. Also, he had been declared an apostle, just like Petrus whom mother still called Cephas.

But all that was a long time ago and he might be anywhere now. He might even be dead.

Acte wriggled a little on the wall. He was *not* dead, he could not be. He was not like other people. When he came back from his first journey she had asked him something she had been wanting to ask him ever since . . . that day. They were alone for a few minutes, there was a big reception and both father and mother were receiving other guests at the door. She must have been twelve or thirteen.

"Do you remember when I came into your room, the day when you were chosen for the journey?"

"Yes, Acte."

"You were asleep, but you weren't." It was a silly thing to say, but then she had been very young at the time.

"Yes, Acte."

"You looked so happy and far away."

"I was both."

"Were you in Heaven?"

"Yes, Acte."

Just like that. And he did not mean it in a sym . . . symbolic way as other people would. He had gone to Heaven and come back.

"Is that why you were so sad when you woke up—I mean, when you came back? I mean, were you sad because you had to come back?"

"Yes, Acte. But you must never tell anybody else."

"I won't. Of course I won't. They wouldn't understand. Except mother, perhaps. And father. And Bar Naba. And Lukas. And little old Agabus."

"That is right," he said, "but you must not tell them either."

So she hadn't. But he could not be dead. He was much too alive for that, more alive than anybody else. If only he'd come to Puteoli one day. He could tell Flavia and Ausonia a few things that would make them feel less superior.

Two small, green lizards were chasing each other playfully across the mossy stones. Acte kept quite still to avoid frightening them, but felt a little cramped after a while and swung her legs around. Her movement was a little too vehement; she lost her balance and had to grip the god Terminus quickly not to fall off. She managed, but only just and she giggled a little at the thought that she might have fallen into a strange garden.

"So you are alive," said a cheerful voice.

She was so startled that she had to clutch old Terminus again.

A boy was standing down there on the lawn, arms akimbo, and laughing up to her. A boy, or perhaps a young man, with a round, handsome face and absolutely horrible red hair.

"Of course I'm alive," she said, haughtily. "Why shouldn't I be?"

"You kept so still," he said, still laughing. "I thought you were a statue—one of those painted ones that look really human. Polydorus makes them and Coriander of Syracuse."

"I'm neither a statue nor am I painted," she declared. "And now I must go."

"No, don't," he said hastily. "Please, don't. You are such a lovely

247

sight up there. You are a nymph, of course, a dryad. It's very lucky for a man to meet a dryad—unless she vanishes at once. Then it's terribly unlucky. Don't you know that?"

"No. And I don't believe in nymphs."

"That's possible," the boy said. "After all, there are men who don't believe in mankind, so why shouldn't a dryad disbelieve in nymphs?"

"I think you think that's witty," Acte said. "Perhaps it is," she added when she saw his face fall a little. Nymphs were supposed to be pretty, so he meant well with his nonsense, and it wouldn't be right to hurt his feelings. He was wearing a yellow tunic and his sandals were gilded. He did look nice, despite his red hair.

"I don't care about being witty," the boy said. "No real poet should. Wit is something for those who want to amuse the masses, and most of them are slaves."

Acte's eyes were wide now. "Are you a real poet?" she asked incredulously.

"So they tell me," the boy said modestly. "But I shall be a poet with a crooked neck if I go on talking up to you like this. Wait." He came up to the wall and began to climb it.

"Be careful," she warned. "Some of those stones . . . there you are. I told you so."

The young poet had lost his foothold and was holding on with his hands alone, his knuckles white with the effort. "Don't worry," he said, panting, "I'll get there." He did, too, by sheer tenacity, and sat beside her.

"You are very strong," Acte said. "I thought poets were frail men, living on starlight and flowers and a little fruit."

"I'm strong enough," he said contentedly, "both by nature and by training. I'm good at wrestling and with the sword and I can drive a chariot better than most."

"You are rather satisfied with yourself, aren't you?" Old Abigail had told her that sometimes and, unwittingly, she imitated Abigail's severe frown.

"In some ways I am." He made it a statement of fact, not an admission. "But what I've told you so far are little things."

"Not for one so young," she said. "I think you're younger than I am. I'm seventeen and a little over."

"I'm seventeen too. When I was nine I commanded the second squadron of boys at the Secular Games."

"I don't know what that means, but it sounds very grand."

"Last year," he said, "I made a great oration in honor of Rhodes in front of the entire . . . in front of many people. Everybody said I spoke like a trained orator. Well, I am."

"All this and a poet as well," Acte said, shaking her head. "I think you're boasting."

He frowned. "How dare you think such a thing. All I've told you so far is nothing, except the poetry. Art is the one thing worth living for, I know that in my heart and no one can dissuade me from it. Art. All art. I've tried sculpture and painting, too—and singing. Seneca says I have too many talents, but that is his way of putting it. How can one have too much of what is divine?"

"Seneca," Acte repeated. "Is he a relative of the author and philosopher?"

"As close as I am to myself," he replied, appeased by the eagerness of her question.

"What? You know him? My father does, too."

"Everybody does. Seneca is my teacher. I rather like him, except when he talks about Seneca. He usually does, though," he added, wrinkling his short nose. "He's as vain as a peacock."

"Your teacher," she said admiringly. "Your parents must be wonderful people, to let you have him as a teacher."

"They are—in a way."

"Perhaps they are a little old-fashioned, sometimes," she suggested. "Or one of them is."

He threw back his head. "I don't think that accusation has ever been made before," he said with a short laugh. "Great gods, I'd like to see mother's face if someone called her old-fashioned. Mother!" He was laughing uproariously now, but somehow she could not chime in. There was something mirthless about it, mirthless and . . . bitter. She remembered that Flavia sometimes complained about her mother. "She's so elegant, she's got to be everywhere

where elegant people are, in Baiae for the season, in Rome for the games, always with the right people at the right places. So we see very little of her."

"Do you mean, your mother doesn't care enough about you?" she asked simply.

He stared at her. "On the contrary, little nymph, very much on the contrary. She cares so much that it hurts. You don't know her, do you? That means you don't know who I am either! How amusing!"

"I don't even know your name," she said. "All I do know is that you're living at the golden villa. . . ."

"That's a pretty word," he said. "The golden villa. The golden house. Perhaps I'll compose a poem on that theme." All bitterness was gone and his eyes were warm and friendly. I don't know your name either," he said. "What does it matter? To me you are the nymph of this grove. You probably live in a cherry tree. Your eyes are like cherries."

"You and your nymphs," she said. "I'm Acte. My father is Cassius Longinus and I was born in Damascus."

"I was born in Antium," he said. "My father was Gnaeus Domitius Ahenobarbus. He's dead. My name is Lucius." He looked at her intently, as if to see whether this meant anything to her.

She clapped her hands together. "Ahenobarbus," she said, "Red-Iron-Beard. Your father must have had red hair too!"

"He had and so had his father and grandfather. There's a story about it. An ancestor of mine was on his way to Rome, when two strangers appeared to him and asked him to go to the Senate and tell about a great Roman victory of which the senators knew nothing. My ancestor was impressed by the appearance of the strangers, but he hesitated. After all, they might be telling him a lie and he would make himself ridiculous by passing it on. But the two strangers stretched out their hands and touched his cheeks. 'This may prove to you who we are,' they said, both at the same time, and went their way. When my ancestor came to a small river he saw his reflection in the water; his black beard had turned a flaming red. Ever since we have been called the Ahenobarbi, and we've all had red hair and red beards."

"Never mind," Acte comforted him. "You look very nice with red hair. I . . . I didn't think so at the beginning, but now I do."

He smiled, preening himself a little. After a while he asked: "You don't know anything about my family, do you?"

"No. Why? Was your father a famous general or statesman or something? I wouldn't know too much about that. We only came to Italy four years ago—no, it's almost five now, I think. My grandfather was a general, father says."

"We're quits then," he said with half-concealed amusement. "I don't know about your grandfather either. But I do know something about his granddaughter."

"What do you mean?"

"She is a girl so lovely that it's hard to believe her to be human. Even now I can't quite believe it. I shall need proof."

"Proof?"

"Certainly. Don't you know that a nymph will never consent to be kissed by a mortal?"

Acte blushed violently. "I must go now," she said. He made a move to stop her, but she was too quick for him. Wrenching herself free she slid off the wall. Her foot found the niche it knew so well and she jumped and landed and stood triumphantly, looking up at Lucius over her shoulder.

"Now I know you're a nymph," he shouted.

Tossing her head she fled toward home, but once more she could hear his voice, suddenly plaintive, saying: "You'll come back, won't you?" before she dived, swift-footed, into the thick of the orange groves.

*　　*　　*

She did not go anywhere near the old wall the next day, but her thoughts were climbing it and sitting on it, brooding over the witty answers she should have given.

She did not tell her mother, or Jucunda or Virena or anyone. This was her secret and it must remain her secret.

She would have loved asking mother many questions—whether

she knew a family called Domitius Ahenobarbus; whether she thought the story about the changed beard could be true; any question that centered about Lucius and what he had said. But there would certainly have been questions in return and then her secret would be out and she might even be forbidden to go to the old wall again. She did not really want to go to the old wall; but she did not like to be forbidden.

Flavia, of course, would have lied her way out. "Avoiding the truth in an intelligent manner," she called it. "There are situations when one's got to do that," she said. "And don't tell me you never did, Acte."

"I did it once, years ago, in Antioch. I dropped a vase, and it broke on the stone floor. Mother asked me whether I had done it and I said I hadn't. Then a slave was to be punished for what I'd done and it was awful to confess the lie and still more awful not to. In the end, I did tell mother and I had to go into father's study and tell him. He was terribly serious about it, much more so than about the vase being broken. He said we belong to the Truth in person and that lying was deserting the Truth, and I had to go to the slave who had been unjustly accused and bow before him and ask his forgiveness, and the slave howled and it was all quite horrid and just not worth it. Much later mother told me that she had known all the time that I lied."

Flavia laughed. "The only thing that matters is not to be found out. You were clumsy about it, Acte, I bet you were. You probably went all red in the face or looked solemn or disinterested in an exaggerated way and then they knew, of course. They'd never find out about me, or about Ausonia."

"Not even if you knew a slave would be whipped for it?"

"Of course not," Flavia said. "Slaves aren't people."

"But we mustn't lie. It's against our Faith." And she tried to tell Flavia and Ausonia about Paul and about the Anointed One, but the two girls looked down their noses and Ausonia said, with a little sniff, "We've heard all about that and it's just a Jewish superstition and that's why your parents can't settle down in Rome, father says, and he's a senator and knows what's going on."

Senator Quintus Ausonius was a sour man with a big paunch; his head was bald and pointed, almost like that of the god Terminus on the old wall. Father did not like him much, she could feel that, although he never said so, but he admitted that all Jewish people had been banished from Rome a few years ago. "The Emperor was badly advised," he said. Mother said nothing at all.

On the second day after the meeting with Lucius, Acte told herself that it was silly not to go to her favorite place in the garden, just because a boy with red hair might be in the neighborhood. So she crossed the garden, passed the huts of old Mucius and his son, and went up through the orange groves. She climbed the old wall as usual and sat down on it.

The golden villa looked strangely distant. Heat shimmered above the roof like a mirage.

She sat motionless, like a painted statue. Nothing happened.

*　　*　　*

He was there the next day. She had not been sitting on the wall for more than a few minutes when he emerged from a cluster of trees, crossed the lawn and climbed up to her. "I *am* glad you're back," he said. "I made a poem about you."

"About me? You're joking. You know nothing about me—well, almost nothing."

"Enough to realize that all nature bows and curtsies at your approach; that all flowers long for the touch of your little feet and are ready to give up their frail lives for the favor of being held just once in your dainty fingers—are you glad I am here? Tell me, honestly."

"I . . . I was here yesterday," she said, wondering whether Flavia would call it "avoiding the truth intelligently."

In any case, he seemed to be happy about her answer. He had a trick of raising his round chin when he was pleased.

"*Now* I will read my poem to you," he said, producing a small sheet of parchment from inside his tunic.

She listened, wide-eyed, to smooth verses about a young dryad, ruling all the land around the most wonderful bay in the world

253

by her beauty, but secretly unhappy, because everyone worshiped but no one loved her, and yearning for a lover to share her power. In the end the lover came, a young poet, and with her embrace she conveyed to him the gift of being immortal, as she herself was. But a jealous god, in love with the dryad, set limits to her gift and thus not the poet but only his poetry became immortal. The dryad wept when she found that her lover would have to die, but he accepted his fate with deep joy, as through his art he would be able to tell mankind for all time about the beauty of his beloved.

"But that is lovely," Acte said when he had ended. "You really are a poet." Her voice was a little shaky and suddenly he saw that there were tears in her eyes.

"This is higher praise than I deserve," he said.

"It's so sad," she said. "How can she be happy for a moment, knowing that he will die and she must go on and on."

"I thought of that." He nodded. "And I toyed with the idea that she might ask the jealous god to take her own immortality away from her so that she could share her lover's fate. But I doubt whether any nymph would do that. . . ."

"I don't know," Acte said, shivering a little. "I don't know. Oh, look—you've dropped the poem."

The small piece of parchment was sailing down, slowly. As she was leaning forward, trying in vain to catch it, she heard him say anxiously: "Don't fall," and felt his arms around her waist. Turning, startled, she saw his face very close above hers.

"Dear nymph," he said in a low, eager voice, "I love you. Give me immortality."

CHAPTER TWENTY-SIX

SENECA'S HOUSE, on the slopes of the Palatine Hill, was by far the most beautiful Cassius had ever seen, and he said so, as they went through rooms and halls, each vying with the other for loveliness and exquisite workmanship of decoration and furniture. "It really is quite a pretty house," the philosopher agreed. "And do you know that I manage to run it with no more than two hundred and fifty slaves? Nowadays people seem to believe that four hundred are the absolute minimum for a well-run town house. Despite Pythagoras I have never put much faith in numbers, nor in any of the strange fads based upon them. Of all deceptive things, numbers and figures are the worst. This is my study."

They passed through a small room, almost devoid of furniture or ornament. There was only a simple desk, a shelf with a few book-rolls on it and a single chair with no cushion. "This is all I need," Seneca said, smiling. "Here I can concentrate. Besides it is easier to write about wealth or luxury when one has retreated some distance from it; and it's impossible to write about poverty on a table of the rarest citrus wood, adorned with a Myrrhenian vase."

"I wonder which of you is the pretender?" Cassius said, with a twinkle to take the sting out of his question. "The Stoic or the millionaire."

"My enemies say: both," Seneca replied cheerfully, "I say: neither. To be a philosopher one must taste everything. How could I write about Consolation, as I have, if I'd never known suffering?"

"You have, then?"

"My dear fellow, I have been in exile for eight years. Eight years on Corsica! Ye gods, what an island! What people! I'd feel sure that the Furies whispered, 'Corsica' into the Emperor's ear, if I didn't know who the fury was who did."

"Messalina, wasn't it?"

"Yes, Rome's most virtuous lady—so virtuous that in the end she could not bear having a lover without getting married to him, with fine disregard for the fact that she was still married to the Emperor. Homer was right about the gods blinding the mortal whom they wish to destroy. Claudius is a patient, a very patient man, but he, too, has a boiling point."

"I don't think he was in a very good mood when I saw him," Cassius remarked. "And I remember that he mentioned the word 'limits' just before the Empress—er—had the room cleared for action."

Seneca laughed. "You are quick enough," he said. "I'll tell you more about it at dinner."

"What? In company?"

"We're by ourselves, friend. I hope you won't mind!"

"On the contrary, I am delighted. But I imagined that you had dozens of guests every day."

"I have, as a rule, and it's a great bore, often enough."

"It is bound to be—when one is superior in intelligence to everyone of them."

Seneca laughed again. "They must have a fine school of flattery in Syria. One of your predecessors, Lucius Vitellius, was the best flatterer I ever met. Do you know that he always carried one of Messalina's shoes with him wherever he went? He had it with him even in the Senate. But how quickly he lost it when the Emperor had her killed! He died only last year, did you know? No, no, it was a natural death, from a heart attack. His son Aulus is in Rome and the Emperor often invites him to his gambling parties. He has all his father's faults but none of his virtues."

They were entering the triclinium now. It was a very small room, but as they lay down on the silk cushions, Cassius admired the tortoise-shell paneling around the walls.

"I use it for my ideal parties." Seneca smiled. "As you see I cannot place more than nine people here. The ideal party consists of at least three, but never more than nine people. Never less than the Graces, never more than the Muses. Today is an exception, but a very welcome one." He gave a sign to four slaves in dark blue tunics and dinner began.

"To be frank," Seneca went on, spearing little titbits from his first plate, "I canceled a dinner for twenty-two, partly because this gives us an opportunity to talk about old times and new; partly for an entirely different reason."

Cassius looked at his host questioningly.

"I've touched on it," Seneca said, smiling, "when I mentioned our Emperor's boiling point. We had a somewhat stormy meeting, as you may have gathered, and I had no wish to be questioned by guests. So I'm ill, you see, and must stay in bed after having been bled, which, incidentally, is an excellent remedy for certain illnesses, including life itself, in certain circumstances."

"Seneca! You don't intend . . ."

"No, friend. On the contrary, I've never found life more interesting, although I am in my sixtieth year—or almost. But I do think that the eternal law has arranged nothing better than this— that it has provided but one entrance into life, but many exits. I am always free to escape. Thus no man need be unhappy, except through his own fault. Live, if you're content; if you're dissatisfied, you are free to return whence you came."

"I disagree with you," Cassius said, "fundamentally. You would be right only if your life were your own. But it isn't, and you cannot tell me with any certainty whence you came or where you would return."

"There are many who will say that my possessions are my own only as long as the Emperor does not see fit to decide otherwise," Seneca replied, lifting his crystal goblet and appraising the color of the wine. "But no one so far has told me that my life is not my own."

"It has been given you on trust by your Maker," Cassius said. "To fling it away would be an act of contempt and of rebellion."

"My maker," Seneca repeated with a quizzical lift of his eyebrows. "Who is he? I thought my parents and ancestors were to blame for my existence."

"The flower might have said that about the butterfly," Cassius replied, "the grass about the dew, the loaf of bread about the field of wheat; yet when a man receives a letter from the Emperor, he will not confuse the sender with the messenger."

"What you are trying to tell me," Seneca said indulgently, "is that I am confusing the author with the agent, I suppose. But who is the author or maker? Jupiter? Venus? Cybele? Isis? Things have come to such a pass in Rome, you must ask a man politely what his favorite belief is, just as you'll ask him whether he prefers Italian wine or Greek. Which reminds me. . . ." He again made a sign to the slaves and they promptly changed the goblets and filled the fresh ones from another decanter, a beautiful thing made of gold-veined silver in the form of an eagle.

"This is wine from my own vineyards on the slopes of Mount Vesuvius," Seneca said. "You like it? Good. But you did not answer my question."

"I don't believe in gods," Cassius said, "but in one God."

Seneca nodded. "You've been in Judaea a long time. Some men pick up that Jewish belief. And the Jews made quite a number of converts here, too, before the Emperor banished them. Ah well— why not, if it suits your feelings, or perhaps your temperament."

"I know a man," Cassius said, "who once told me that we can recognize the divine only as through a glass, darkly. God must be perfect, but the mirror called man will not reflect Him as He is. God—and call Him the God of the Jews, if you like as they alone have had no other beside Him through the ages—God is reality, not symbol; the Source of all virtues, not the personification of one of them."

"You have become a Jew, then." Seneca had his goblet refilled.

"I am not circumcised," Cassius replied, "but I believe in the same God they do. And in the Son of God, the Christ."

"Yes, yes, I know." Seneca nodded. "I mean, I know about this Son of God of yours. He was killed, wasn't he? No, don't tell me, let me tell you instead. He was crucified when poor old Pilatus was Procurator of Judaea—he's dead too, died in exile, somewhere in Gaul. I'm told the followers of the Christ believe that he came back from the dead and that he was seen by many people and spoke to them, too."

"You know all that?" Cassius looked at his host, surprised.

"I hear a good many things," Seneca told him amiably.

"But you don't believe it, do you?"

"I see no reason to disbelieve it," Seneca replied calmly. "From what I hear, some of the witnesses are or were quite reliable men and not the hysterical kind. Which proves to me only one thing."

"What?"

"That the man wasn't dead, of course. Oh, I made my inquiries,

258

my dear fellow. He died after three hours, they say. But there are records of men crucified who died only after several days. He was an extraordinary man, no doubt. Maybe he feigned death or he deliberately went into a trance. That's a state very closely resembling death. I've seen several men capable of doing that, one was an Indian, the other came from Egypt. So they took him off the cross and buried him and his followers freed him."

"Very plausible," Cassius said in a strange voice. "But that is not what happened. You see, before he was taken off the cross, a man pierced his heart. With a spear."

"How do you know that?"

"Because I was that man," Cassius said. His hands were trembling. There was a pause.

"There goes a good theory," Seneca said at last, trying hard to keep his tone light, but not too light. "Extraordinary how one dislikes the destruction of thought by a fact, isn't it? But after what you told me about your beliefs, this must be a very painful subject to you. Let's change it."

"I could tell you more. . . ."

"No doubt," Seneca interposed gently, "but let me tell you instead how I know about that . . . strange man. My brother Gallio wrote to me that he had met one of his disciples, under rather unusual circumstances, a man called Paul who hailed from the same town as the great Athenodorus—from Tarsus. Ah, that interests you, I see."

"Paul of Tarsus," Cassius murmured, "my great friend. I wish he were here. He could tell you so much better. . . ."

"He must be a man of great erudition and eloquence," Seneca said. "And the quaint thing is that he met my brother in a way quite similar to that by which this Christ of yours met Pilatus. Gallio was his judge. No, don't be afraid, nothing happened to your friend. Gallio is not Pilatus. In fact, no mortal can be more gracious to a friend than Gallio is to every man. Everybody loves him, of course, but no one loves him enough. But you haven't come here to hear me sing the praises of my own brother. . . ."

"On the contrary, I am glad to see how warmly you feel about him," Cassius said. He seemed to have regained control of himself. "So often in the rarefied atmosphere of intellectualism neither feelings nor love have an easy life."

"Intellectual search *is* love," Seneca reminded him.

"True," Cassius admitted, "but it is not the highest form, and only too often tends to become the master when it should be the servant."

"I think I can agree with that," the philosopher said. "And I think I know what you are driving at. To some extent I owe that to Athenodorus. 'Know this,' he says, 'you will not have freed yourself of all your passions until you do not ask anything of God that you cannot ask in public.' Or: 'Every man's conscience is his God'; or 'Live with your fellow men as if God saw you; and speak to God as if men heard you.'"

"You do believe in conscience, then?"

"I believe in an unseen observer, yes," Seneca said, "in a holy spirit watching and recording. That is as far as I will go. But it's strange that your friend Paul should come from the same town as my old teacher."

"You didn't tell me about the trial."

"Didn't I? Try some of these roast quail, friend, even Vitellius swore that one couldn't get anything better in Rome. We've both forgotten to eat—another proof of that rarified atmosphere you mentioned. Yes, the trial. It was in Corinth. Your friend Paul must be a fascinating but spiky sort of man. My brother—I think I forgot to tell you that he is Proconsul of Greece—had known about him before he came to Corinth, because Paul had been in Athens before that and there had been reports about him. I needn't tell the former Governor of Syria that this kind of thing is inevitable—particularly when a man makes speeches before large assemblies, including one at the Areopagus itself."

"Paul in Athens," Cassius murmured. "Paul on the steps of the Acropolis, in the shadow of the Erechtheion, on the Agora. I wish I had been there."

"He was a failure," Seneca said. "Yes, a failure, although he started off with a perfectly charming idea and a sly one at that. You know they have an altar 'To the Unknown God' in Athens, which is both charming and sly. Charming, because it is so courteous toward a divine stranger—sly, because it was built to make sure that the Athenians wouldn't be smitten by the wrath of some unknown deity who found itself templeless in the teeming city. Paul fully understood that, and promptly set out to make use of it, by proclaiming that he knew all about that Unknown God and would tell them what he knew."

Cassius nodded. With a slow smile he said: "I saw him just before he went on board ship on the first of what must since have been many journeys, and he said: 'I know I shall have to be all things to all people.' I didn't understand the meaning of that at the time, but I think I'm beginning to understand now. It's not just charming and sly. He is *right*. Before you can lift a body you must catch hold of it; and the same applies to the soul."

Seneca took a sip of wine. "He told them all about his universal god," he went on, "and they listened with much interest. Mind you, they would have listened with as much interest had he told them about his experiences with two-headed men in some country beyond India. I know my Athenians. However, as soon as Paul mentioned the resurrection from the dead—of your Christ—they very politely excused themselves and left, all except a few people. Here the report of our agent ended. Apparently the man was now satisfied that the learned man from Tarsus had no political significance. Very reasonable of him. Soon afterwards Paul appeared in Corinth. And there the trouble started."

"How?"

"At first he worked perfectly peacefully as a tentmaker, in partnership with another Jew, one Aquila or something like it, a refugee from Rome, thanks to that extraordinary edict of our glorious ruler. But he also spoke or preached in the synagogue and there seem to have been mighty disputes, with some accepting his teaching and others opposing it. In the end Paul left in a huff and took the ruler of the synagogue with him, a man called Crispus."

"How can you remember all these details?" Cassius asked in sincere admiration.

"That Maker you mentioned has given me a very good memory."

261

Seneca smiled. "I started out as a lawyer, as you will remember, which meant that I had thoroughly trained my memory. The training was perfected when I became a member of the imperial court. As a lawyer a slip of memory could bring about the death of my client; as a courtier it could only too easily bring about my own. Even so, I occasionally make a small mistake. Only the other day my very gifted young nephew Lucanus accused me of having appropriated two lines of one of his poems. Besides, I always read my brother's letters at least two or three times. And finally: I became interested in this Paul—more so, perhaps than my brother. You'll soon see why. Any more of the sweetmeats? No? Then let's have some fruit. You should try my Persian apples."

"You were telling me about the ruler of the synagogue . . ."

"Crispus, yes. Paul won him over completely so the others had to choose a new ruler and did. His name was Sosthenes and he and his friends decided to take action. They attacked Paul in his workshop and had him dragged to the Agora where Gallio held his tribunal. Their accusation was that Paul persuaded people to worship God in a way contrary to the law, a juridical point no doubt of great weight among Jews, but entirely lost on Gallio who dismissed the evidence immediately as irrelevant. The accuser howled with fury, Paul's friends howled back, some of the mob that is always present joined in and there was quite a little riot in which a number of people were injured, worst of all the chief accuser, Sosthenes. Gallio wrote: 'As I had told them to settle the matter among themselves, I did not let my soldiers interfere. After all they only did what I had asked them to do, though they did it in a somewhat surprising manner.' "

"Did he speak to Paul afterwards?"

"No, but he heard him speak and he told me, 'This is the only man against whom I would not advise you to speak in the Forum. I confess to you that the Proconsul of Greece was sorely tempted to resign and follow that little Jewish orator as one more of his disciples. I fled just in time.' "

"To flee from happiness is one of the sorry privileges of man,"

Cassius said. "But now I understand why you became interested in Paul."

"There is another reason," Seneca told him. "Gallio had him watched after this little incident. He was curious. He wanted to know more about him, without exposing himself to his powers of persuasion, I suppose. He says the man is not just an excellent orator, he is a new kind of general, priest, organizer and scholar, all rolled into one rather small man. He had not come to settle down in Corinth, but to found a community or church, as he calls it. And he must have done so in at least half a dozen other towns *and* countries. Delegates came from Macedonia to see him. Letters came from and went to Derbe, Lystra, Beroea and other places in Asia Minor. In short the man is setting up a world-wide organization for a purely religious purpose. At least, Gallio could not discover anything at all political about it. He stayed on a few more months, then he left for Ephesus."

"And Sosthenes and his people? Did they leave him in peace?"

Seneca laughed. "Ask rather whether he left them in peace. He didn't, you know. When he left for Ephesus, he took Sosthenes with him—as his disciple."

Cassius joined in his host's merriment. But then he said: "I'm grateful to you for telling me about my great friend's exploits. Unlike your brother I hope you will meet Paul and cross swords with him, though not necessarily in the Forum. He was called into the service of Christ in a way quite unique; and only now I begin to see the tremendous importance of it."

"That I know nothing about," Seneca replied. "Rome has seen so many cults; she absorbs them all and still remains Rome. You, too, have never ceased to be a Roman, or you wouldn't have consented to work under old Marsus. You did very well, from what little I've heard."

"I tried. Being married to a Jewess has helped me to understand the position in Judaea where all procurators used to run into trouble. I nominated one who didn't—Tiberius Alexander, the nephew of the Jewish philosopher Philo in Alexandria."

"Philo is another man who interests me greatly," Seneca said. "Perhaps you should have persuaded him to assume the post instead of his nephew. You remember what Plato said about philosophers being the only ones in whose hands the state would be safe."

"Do you agree with him?" Cassius asked.

"I agree with Plato about many issues," Seneca answered noncommittally. "But I don't think your views had much in agreement with those of your successor in Syria, had they?"

"Ummidus Quadratus," Cassius said hotly, "is a butcher. And so is—or was—*his* Procurator of Judaea, Cumanus."

"There have been some pretty bad riots." Seneca nodded. "The choice of these men was a bad one. But what can one expect, with a fool on the throne."

Cassius looked instinctively at the four slaves present. None of their faces conveyed the least expression.

"You needn't worry, friend," Seneca said. "They're deaf-mutes. Their former master had them mutilated and I bought them fairly cheaply when he died."

"So that's why you use signs when giving your orders," Cassius said. And he thought: "If Paul were here, he would at once study sign-language, to be able to talk to them about Christ."

"Yes. This room has heard many things, friend."

"I am not a deaf-mute," Cassius said.

Seneca smiled at him. "You are not in favor with the Emperor—nor is he in favor with you. You served him well, but he never gave you so much as a word of thanks, merely because of your friendship with poor Marsus. The man Claudius sent out as your successor upset all your work. You are married to a Jewess, and Claudius has banished the Jews from Rome. Besides—forgive me for mentioning it—you are not strong enough to be dangerous to me."

"Summed up admirably," Cassius said. "And—forgive *me* for mentioning it—I think I know now why you asked me to have dinner with you tonight. You didn't wish to talk to people who would ask you certain questions about what happened at the palace, but you didn't wish to be alone, for some reason, and you could talk to me about anything without restraint, for all the reasons you just gave me."

"Quite correct," Seneca said, "except that you should add that I like talking to you. You have changed a good deal from the impetuous, erratic young man you were in the old days. Who would have thought that you could become seriously interested in a branch of the Jewish religion? Yet, as I said before, you have remained a Roman and therefore you will be glad to hear that we are on the verge of a new age."

"I know that," Cassius said gravely.

But Seneca shook his head. "The new age will not be brought about by your Christ or your Paul, not if he goes on traveling around and founding churches for the rest of his life. It will be brought about, as it should be, by a new ruler."

"The Emperor is an old man," Cassius said thoughtfully. "Old that is, beyond his years. He's sixty-four or so, isn't he? But his son Britannicus is little more than a child. . . ."

"His son," Seneca repeated slowly. "Yes, yes—that is what the little quarrel, whose beginning you witnessed, was about. His son."

The entire atmosphere had changed. The room was dark with intrigue and unspoken thoughts.

"Britannicus," Seneca resumed, "is the son of Messalina, as you know. He's quite a nice boy, certainly the only thing of value she ever produced. I owe her my involuntary sojourn on Corsica, as you know. I was a friend, a great friend, I might say, of Julia, the youngest sister of Agrippina, and Julia was ambitious and incautious, a mixture usually fatal to the owner. Messalina felt—rightly or wrongly—that Julia was threatening her position, so she made the necessary accusations and ruined her . . . and me. When Messalina had come to the inevitable end the Emperor swore he would never marry again. Being a fool he broke his oath. And being the greatest of all fools, he married Agrippina."

"The Empress is a beautiful woman."

"A tigress," Seneca said, "is a very beautiful animal. By the heavens, the woman is Caligula's sister! What do you expect?

Not only did Claudius break his oath, he also had to change the law of Rome to enable him to marry his own niece. Did I say that Julia was ambitious? Her ambition was as nothing in comparison with that of the tigress. And the tigress, too, has a son from a previous marriage. She adores him. Nothing is good enough for him. He must have the best of educations. So she manages to get Claudius to recall me from Corsica."

"I see."

"You don't, friend. Not yet. Not even I myself see the whole picture, though I can see at least part of it fairly clearly, and I can guess at other parts. I talked to the boy and, to my surprise, found him absolutely delightful. He is highly intelligent and most versatile in his talents. Above all, he has a generous, noble nature. I told Agrippina that I accepted the task with joy and would do my best for him. When I mentioned a course in philosophy, she cut me short: 'An Emperor has no need of philosophy.'"

Cassius whistled through his teeth.

"I'm afraid," Seneca went on grimly, "she wanted me to be her son's teacher mainly because my name, despite years in exile, still meant something to the public. Mere ostentation, one would think, and you may remember what Cicero said about women: that they put value only on two things, conservation and ostentation."

"Cicero had his cynical moments," Cassius said, "but he was not really a cynic."

"Whatever he was, he certainly didn't know Agrippina," Seneca said. "Never in all my life have I encountered such ambition. She has been living in a world of conspiracy all her life, but she has always managed to survive—at the expense of others. She conspired with Lepidus against her brother. Lepidus was executed, but she escaped with a few years of exile. She survived two husbands and waxed rich on their estates. As soon as Messalina fell, she decided to marry the Emperor. For that she needed the support of Claudius' closest adviser. She couldn't very well bribe Pallas—the man is head of the treasury and as such has enriched himself beyond belief. So she began an affair with him—the sister of a former emperor, the daughter of the great Germanicus, and a freedman! And Pallas

266

softened up Claudius, if it's possible to further soften up an already jelly-like substance."

"And ever since . . ."

"Ever since she has been the real ruler of Rome and the Empire. She has eliminated everyone who ever spoke against her. She managed to get her creature, Afranius Burrus, made Prefect of the Praetorian Guards. She practically forced Claudius to have the Senate give her the title of Augusta, and like another Livia, she is working not only on the conservation, but also the extension and perpetuation of her power. This can be done only through her own flesh and blood. Therefore she has been doing everything to undermine the position of Britannicus and to better that of her own son."

"And the Emperor just looks on?"

"He is a tired man and he hates scenes. Agrippina saw to it that her son was given the command of a squadron at the Secular Games, where he outshone Britannicus, who was no more than a little boy. She persuaded Claudius to let her son make speeches on certain public occasions. . . ."

"With your gracious help, I suppose," Cassius inquired.

"Well, yes, I did have a hand, once or twice, in the forming of ideas, the sequence of thoughts and in the right presentation, but the boy did very well, also. Then came Agrippina's masterpiece. She was worried about her husband's health. The affairs of state were such a heavy burden for him and though she tried hard to take some of it on her own shoulders as a conscientious wife should, she was only too well aware of a mere woman's lack of strength. Lack of strength in Agrippina! So she suggested that he should adopt her son, Lucius Domitius. The most primitive of traps, as you see, but apparently not too primitive for the fool on the throne. He agreed and young Lucius Domitius was accepted into the gens Claudia, new name and all."

"I knew about that," Cassius said. "But what I cannot understand is how they could let the young man marry the Emperor's daughter. After all, she was now his sister by adoption."

"A little thing like that wouldn't disturb Agrippina," Seneca said. "But she saw that it might endanger her son's legal position, so she persuaded Claudius to have his own daughter adopted too—by another gens."

"And little Britannicus has no allies?" Cassius asked.

"Narcissus is for him—but Narcissus is not likely to live long and he knows it. The boy himself is beginning to see what is going on and that is creating a rather difficult situation and has actually led to the—er—bit of trouble whose beginning you witnessed."

"Ah, has it? Yes, I remember the Emperor saying that it concerned the Augusta's son and that she corrected him—'our son.' But what was it all about? Or should I not ask that question?"

"If I hadn't wanted to tell you, I shouldn't have led up to it," Seneca said amiably. "It appears that when little Britannicus met his stepbrother a couple of weeks ago, he addressed him rather pointedly as 'Domitius.' The young man was so incensed at this obvious hint that Britannicus would not recognize him as a real member of the Claudian family that he ran to the Emperor to complain. Claudius happened to be rather ill-tempered—it was just before the midday meal and he is usually ill-tempered when he is hungry. So he would not listen to the complaint and in his rage the young man seems to have made an allusion, or maybe even more than an allusion to the effect that many people doubted whether Britannicus was the Emperor's son at all, and then ran away to complain to his mother as well."

"Phew."

"I was with Agrippina at the time," Seneca continued, "and we both agreed that something had to be done at once. So we sent the boy away from the city to one of her less known villas in the South, where he was safe. Then we just sat back and waited. Claudius always takes a few days to make up his mind about anything. When finally he sent for her and me, we knew that the moment had come. The tigress made a magnificent entrance. . . ."

"She certainly did."

". . . but as soon as we were alone, except for the inevitable Narcissus and the guards, she became all loving wife and mother. She was full of regret for the unbecoming and disrespectful way her son had behaved toward his imperial father. She had punished

268

him by banishing him from Rome and he wouldn't be allowed to come back until his father called for him! But surely he must understand also that the young man had been greatly provoked by Britannicus who was becoming more and more difficult lately and who started the whole matter by his unseemly address. Her son, after all was no longer Lucius Domitius, but Tiberius Claudius Nero Drusus Germanicus. He had behaved badly, yes, but only because his pride was hurt, the pride of belonging to the Claudian family! Oh, she was most impressive. I had given her all the arguments, of course. Unfortunately, like most strong-minded women, she has no patience. And when Claudius went on complaining in his sullen, whining way, she shed the loving wife and mother and became the tigress again. She screamed and yelled like a fishwife. Claudius must have had an intention of rebuking me as well, as his son's teacher, but it never came to that. When Agrippina raves, no one can get a word in edgeways. In the end she just walked off, but later we heard that Claudius had said to Narcissus: 'It seems to be my fate to endure the nastiness of my wives and to have to punish them for it in the end.' "

"A bad sign for Agrippina."

"Yes, it is," Seneca said quietly. "Or rather: it would be, if she didn't know about it. Weak men like Claudius can be very dangerous once they have made up their minds. Fortunately it takes them some time to do so. And Agrippina has many ways to cope with danger. In the duel between these two my money is on her."

"You want her to win?"

"Not at all," Seneca said. "I can't stand the sight of her. But I want her son to be the next Emperor. Mark my words, friend, Tiberius Claudius Nero will become a ruler of renown. He has little or no military leanings, so he will keep the peace. He has an artistic nature, so he will patronize the arts. He is young and enthusiastic, so he will get things done."

"But the influence of his mother . . ."

"He will outgrow it, never fear. And I think—I am practically certain he will choose the right advisers. The rule of the freedmen is nearing its end."

"He will choose . . . you?" Cassius asked.

Seneca smiled. Perhaps he would have given an answer, but at that moment a slave in a richly embroidered yellow tunic entered and succeeded in getting his master's attention.

Seneca frowned. "Yes, Canio?"

"An imperial messenger, master."

Seneca rose. "You will excuse me, friend." He left the room. A few moments later he returned. "Imperial service is demanding," he said, smiling a little ruefully. "It forces me to be rude to my guest. I'm afraid I must leave at once. As for you, friend, I think you should stay in the city a little longer, say a week at least."

"I will, if that is your advice," Cassius said, rising to his feet, "although I have no idea why I should."

"I am not quite sure myself." Seneca smiled. "But there are signs and portents of all kinds and anything might happen. I can say no more."

CHAPTER TWENTY-SEVEN

THE NYMPH might not have been able to meet her poet so frequently if Naomi had not fallen ill, from the bite of a small, black spider which crawled from under a curtain in her bedroom. She soon became feverish and Aglae had to summon the physician who cut the tiny wound, sucked it rather belatedly and applied some sweet-smelling ointment. He also told her earnestly to sacrifice two black doves to Aesculapius, god of healing, a suggestion which she received noncommittally. The physician left with the admonition that the patient must remain in bed and sleep as much as possible. A drink of poppyseeds, sweetened with honey, would help.

Except for the pigeons, Naomi followed the physician's prescriptions, despite the feeling that Lukas probably would have ordered a different therapy. Sosicles was a man of standing in the medical world and the entire household of Senator Ausonius swore by him.

Lukas . . . where was he now? And Paul and Bar Naba and

270

all the friends from the golden days of Antioch!

Even Cassius missed them. Even he, the Roman, no longer really felt at home in his homeland. One evening he had said, quite suddenly: "I have become a stranger here," and then would not talk any more about the subject. Naomi knew that it was not the power he was missing—the sentries, the couriers, the audiences and all the pomp surrounding the supreme Roman official of a province. In the East they had met and come to love each other; there he had stood on the terrible hillock of the crucifixion and later at His open tomb. . . . There he had met Cephas and Judah and Saul; there Acte was born. The East drew him back, because there he had encountered God and those whom God had enlightened.

Acte, too, was bound to miss Antioch and Paul, her hero, although she would feel it less at her age. What was going on in her little head? She was so absent-minded, lately, and nervous—yes, nervous. It was not easy for her, here, either.

Naomi sighed deeply. She had never told her husband how desperately homesick she was. Homesick for the air, the sights, the very smell of the East; homesick for people who spoke her own tongue, the tongue that *He* had spoken, and for the wise, serene faces of the men who were carrying on His work. She had suffered silently. She knew, of course, that it was because of her they could not live in Rome, although Cassius never spoke of it. He, too, was hurt, and not only for her sake. "They" never had so much as a good word for all the work he had done and he was much too proud to remind them of it. When he set out for Rome, to get an audience with the Emperor and ask for permission to return to Syria, she had felt strange and unreasonable misgivings. She knew he had done so once before and had been refused by some high official of the court. Such a decision might well be reversed by the Emperor. But she feared the city. She had always feared it. They could not do anything to him. He had done no wrong. And yet she could not help feeling that he should not have gone, that he should have stayed here and gone on praying with her that God Himself would solve the problem.

Now she had to pray alone.

Then the poppy-seed drink began to make her limbs heavy and after a while she fell asleep.

*   *   *

"I love you," said the poet and "I love you," replied the nymph gravely. That was the way they had come to greet each other. Their meeting place was no longer the top of the old wall, beside the old god Terminus with the pointed head, but the garden of the golden villa, and there they lay on the lawn and, lying there, made voyages to faraway countries and underwent hair-raising adventures. The old gardener, passing by at some distance, was the chief of a band of brigands who would hold them for ransom if he caught them; the six slaves, setting up a table with wine and exquisite titbits in the shade of a cluster of trees were doing it for the Emperor and the Empress, but as soon as they had left, poet and nymph would come out of their hiding place and sit down on two small footstools and eat and drink to their hearts' content, leaving absolutely nothing for the rulers. It was all the poet's idea, of course, and he so obviously enjoyed it that the nymph fell in with it.

"Just wait," the poet said. "When the imperial couple comes and finds that everything is gone, you'll see what will happen. The Emperor will waggle his head and stammer, the way he always does when he's excited or angry; he may even burst into tears, and complain that everybody is against him; and the Empress will look around stonily and say she had known it all the time and that she was the only one who knew what to do about it, as usual."

"It's a disrespectful game, really," Acte said.

"I didn't say *which* emperor, did I?" the poet defended himself.

"You made it clear enough. Everybody knows that Emperor Claudius stammers when he's excited."

"He certainly did when I last saw him," the poet agreed.

Acte stared at him, incredulously. "What? You know him?"

"Well, yes, we have met a few times."

"My father has gone to see him."

The young man looked up quickly. "Has he? Why?"

"To ask permission for us to go back to Syria."

"Why do you need permission for that? Your father is no longer in the service of the state, is he? He's not a senator or holding some public office."

"No, but he used to. It's all very complicated. He may be refused because he was governor there."

"I wouldn't permit it, if I were the Emperor," he said firmly.

"No?" She was outraged. "Why not?"

"Because he'd take you with him," he replied. "Or better still: I'd let him go under the condition that you stay."

"But how could I? He's my father and . . ."

". . . and I'm your Emperor," he said. "Who is higher than the Emperor?"

"Only God," she said.

He laughed. "Nowadays emperors are gods as well, although I do admit that Claudius is a strange one. Perhaps some day, when he arrives on the other side, Jupiter will let him be the god of stammerers. Anyway, if I'm the Emperor, I'm god as well."

"In that case, I'm glad you're not the emperor," Acte told him emphatically.

"Why?"

"Because I couldn't love you if you regarded yourself as a god. I love you because you're human. And anyway there is only one God."

"Sh . . ." he said with mock-seriousness. "Don't let anybody hear you. He might tell the Pontifex Maximus and that worthy would let his army loose on you, priests, augurs, vestals, and they'd tear you to pieces as the hounds of Diana destroyed poor Actaeon."

"He might do that," she said, "but he couldn't make me believe differently."

"Not even if I were the Pontifex Maximus?" he asked with much severity and a little twinkle.

"Not even then," she answered, "but how glad I am you're not the Pontifex Maximus."

"I might be, one day," he said lightly.

She threw back her head, laughing. "Never," she cried, "not you;

not my poet. You're just right as you are. Stay like that—never change. Then I can always love you."

"I won't change then," he said. "I can live without a throne and without a temple to officiate in, but I cannot be without your love."

She laughed happily. But he stood before her unsmiling and she knew suddenly that he was no longer play-acting. Many a time he had embraced and kissed her, but now for the first time she laid her arms round his neck and kissed him full on the mouth. "You have me and my love," she said, and then his arms closed around her waist with a strength that almost frightened her, and his eyes shone huge and luminous, blotting out the sunlight.

* * *

Mother was much better, but still very, very sleepy and the physician came again, applied his ointment and prescribed another drink of poppyseeds. "Sleep is what she needs most."

Impossible to tell her about Lucius Domitius and . . . and everything. At some later stage he would come and pay a visit to her, he said. Things would be much better then. A secret was a secret, but when it became so very big it was like trying to hide a city under a cloak.

That night Acte dreamed that Lucius, dressed as a priest of Jupiter, told her he had become Pontifex Maximus and now he was going to make a sacrifice of her and she was very frightened, but knew that it had to be done and he put her on the altar and raised a knife to kill her. But a thunderous divine voice stopped him saying that his sacrifice was not acceptable and then asked him: "What have you done to your brother?" She woke up, bathed in perspiration. It was a stupid dream, of course. Lucius did not even have a brother. He was an only child.

* * *

She told him about the dream when they met again in the garden the next day and he laughed. "Few dreams have anything to do with real life," he said. "Or so Seneca tells me. I have a stepbrother,

274

but he is only a little boy. Last time we met he was discourteous to me and I had to complain about it. I should have boxed his ears instead, perhaps."

"A stepbrother," she repeated. "Your mother must have married again, then, after your father's death."

"Oh yes, twice." He looked at her intently. "You still don't know who I am, it seems."

"Of course I do," she protested. "You told me yourself. I did so wish to tell my mother the lovely story about your ancestor whose beard was changed to red, but I didn't, because . . . because . . ."

"And you haven't talked about us to anyone else either?"

"That would have been silly," Acte said. "They would have gone straight to mother and told her and then . . ." She broke off again. "I hate secrets," she suddenly concluded.

He nodded. "My mother loves them. I hate them, too. At least there shouldn't be any between us. I have never met anybody like you. I want you to know all about me, everything. I wondered, you know, why so far you've never wanted to come with me to the villa. . . ."

"Ah, but I told you that," she said, wide-eyed. "It's the golden villa and like . . . like a dream. I feel, if I go there, I'll wake up. It's like . . . like a hope. And then there are people there, aren't there? I don't want to see anybody but you It isn't very reasonable; it's just a feeling. Besides, you only asked me once."

"I thought you were afraid of meeting people there," he said slowly.

"Well, I am. Is . . . is your mother there?"

He laughed. "Mother is in Rome. No, there are only slaves at the villa and two old Greek freedmen who are supposed to teach me all kinds of things all day. So I usually raise an issue about which I know they are in violent disagreement and I leave them arguing their heads off. Erudite asses who think they're little replicas of Seneca. I think he's left them in charge because he wants me to see how big a man he is himself. I want you to come with me to the villa, Acte. I thought—I really did think you didn't want to go there, because you knew more about me and did not want to be talked about—though I wager most women would have come to the opposite conclusion."

"I don't understand a word you say," Acte confessed.

"Dear nymph . . . I'm glad you don't. You're the only woman I've ever known who is not an actress."

"You don't mean that," she said. "Why, your mother . . ."

"My mother is the most consummate actress of them all. Everything I know about acting I learned from her. Most people have only two or three faces. She has a hundred."

"Oh poet! What exaggerations! And you shouldn't talk like that about your own mother."

"Just listen," he said. "She is a loving mother, a stern disciplinarian, a cooing wife, a shrew and a noble patriot, she is a conscientious nurse, a courtesan and a schemer. . . ."

"Lucius! You can't . . ."

". . . an empress and a fishwife, a brave fighter and a brazen deceiver, a sweet companion and a cruel leopard and there is only one thing she loves. . . ."

"She loves you! However many terrible things you say about her, she loves you. How can she not love you!"

"The thing she loves is power," he said. "And that is why she loves me. I mean power to her, her power over everything. Don't contradict, little nymph, I know. From the moment I was born she knew that I meant power to her. . . ."

"How can she have known that!"

"I was born feet forward," he said, frowning. "That's a sign of an early death, they say, either mine or my mother's—the astrologers couldn't make up their minds. And I was born at the very moment of sunrise, so the sun touched my body before the earth did. That is an omen of great power over many."

"I never heard of such things. . . ."

"I was born of parents who hated each other from the bottom of their hearts. . . ."

"Oh, no, no, it isn't possible, you're inventing it all. . . ."

"It is true, little nymph. That horrible old monster, Tiberius, ordered my parents to marry and the one who made him do so was that still more horrible old monster, Livia, yes, Caesar Augustus' widow. My father, as I told you, died soon, and mother at once pursued her plans to gain the throne, occupied by her brother, Caesar Gaius, whom they called Caligula and many other less complimentary things. . . ."

"The Caesar . . . then your mother is . . ."

"Agrippina," he said, his musical voice resting almost voluptuously on the vowels of the name. "Daughter of the first Agrippina and of the great Germanicus, who was murdered by Tiberius and Livia; involved in the conspiracy of Lepidus, condemned to be banished to a desert island by her brother, condemned also to carry the urn with the ashes of her dead lover and fellow conspirator Lepidus, all the way from Gaul to Rome; leaving her only son in the care of two slaves, one a barber and one a dancer; returned to Rome after the assassination of her mad brother; married to Passionus; widowed again and now married to Emperor Tiberius Claudius Caesar, also called Claudius the Lame and Claudius the Stammerer . . . and ruling him, Rome and the world. Are you crying, little nymph?"

Acte was hiding her face between her hands.

"The Emperor was most gracious to me," he went on, "not because he cared for me—he didn't in the least—but because mother insisted on it; and when she insists it is extremely difficult to resist. She is a remarkable woman. So I was made a member of the Claudian family by adoption under the name of Nero Claudius Drusus Germanicus. My little stepbrother refused to address me as such and I complained—somewhat vehemently. So mother made me leave Rome and come here for a while. It's the best thing she's ever done for me. Because I met you."

"Oh, how can you say that," she whispered. "How can you! No, don't touch me. Let me go. I must never see you again."

"That," he said firmly, "I will not permit."

"Oh, but you must! How can I . . . you deceived me terribly."

"I did not," he said quietly. "I never told you anything that was not true. I simply avoided telling you all about me until now. Deliberately."

"But, why? Why!"

"At first it amused me to be no more than an unknown poet," he said. "It was like living one of the ancient stories of Homer, when the gods themselves roamed the world disguised as mere mortals."

"It amused you. . . ."

"Yes, at first. But then I realized that this was a very great, very wonderful thing that had happened to me. Can't you understand, Acte? All the young women I meet know who I am, they all know that to win me means . . . means a great deal. You didn't. You fell in love with the poet, with the real *me*. And with you I am happier than ever before in my life. It started as a story, a song, a ballad— it has become real."

"And now it has ended," she said, trying hard to banish the sob from her voice.

"It will never end," he said. "You are mine and I am yours and this is how it will be always."

Her eyes were burning with shame and tears fought back. "You still haven't told me everything, but I know anyway, now that you have said who you are. Last year there was a great feast here and in all the towns and villages, in honor of the marriage of the Emperor's adopted son, Nero, with the Emperor's young daughter, Octavia. I saw statues of them carried through the streets, with flowers all over them."

The change that came over him was so violent that she recoiled. He was deathly pale and his hands were trembling. "Octavia," he said hoarsely. "That was the worst my mother did to me. That is my curse. Octavia. A child, a whining, tear-sodden, sniveling child. A pale shadow, sired by a senile fool. I'd hate her, but how can one hate what is nothing! There was a feast here, was there? They made speeches about that marriage, I daresay. But I can tell you a few things they did not say. That we were forced into it, as part of mother's plan. That I loathed her from the first moment I set eyes

278

on her, but was powerless to prevent the accursed ceremony. There was one thing, however, about which *they* were powerless, mother and the Emperor and Pallas and Narcissus, and everybody else. They could not force me to treat Octavia as my wife, except in outward form! Believe me, I shall know how to get rid of her as soon as . . . as soon as I can."

Acte shook her head. "This is no longer my poet speaking, but another man," she whispered. "A man I am afraid of. I must go."

He stretched out his hands. "Have pity on me," he begged. "You alone are my happiness. I mean no harm to the wretched girl, I'll see to it that she finds her happiness elsewhere. But without you I will not live. Don't leave me, Acte, never leave me."

Moved despite herself she, too, stretched out her arms and he rushed to her and their embrace was fiercer than ever as suffering was added to their love. "I swear," he whispered breathlessly, "I swear by all the gods I will never let you go."

He needed her. He was lost without her. That thought to her was stronger than all the little whispering voices. All the people around him were cold, thinking only of their own advantage, even his own mother. He had a mother who was no mother and a wife who was no wife. He was a great prince and the poorest of men, and the golden villa was a golden jail. But she loved him and she alone could help him. Surely Paul would understand. And the Christ.

"As long as you need me," she said weakly, "I will stay."

Then she saw the man approaching them across the lawn.

He was tall and lean and sad-eyed and a wisp of white hair covered part of his large forehead. There was nothing either friendly or hostile about him, but something inexorable, as if he were Fate itself.

Her body stiffened and Lucius—Nero—felt it. He looked up and turned his head and his arms left her.

"Seneca," he exclaimed and she could not make out whether there was fear or anger or pleasure in his voice—perhaps something of all three.

The old man smoothed the pleats of his mantle—a travel cloak, not the toga—and smiled very courteously. "My lord, I am sorry to disturb your peace—a most delightful peace. . . ."

The young man drew himself up. "You are very welcome," he said a little stiffly. "Acte, this is Senator Annaeus Seneca, my great teacher and adviser and the wisest of all living men. Seneca, this is Acte, daughter of Cassius Longinus, a former Governor of Syria, and you are the first witness of our love."

Seneca seemed to be quite unaware both of the challenge in the young man's voice and of Acte's confusion. "What a charming coincidence," he said, smiling at her. "Your dear father had dinner with me only a few days ago. I am one of his oldest friends, you know."

"He . . . he's spoken of you many times," Acte managed to say.

Seneca bowed to her, then turned to Nero. "In anticipation of your wishes," he said, "I have given orders to have your carriage made ready, my lord. We must return to Rome as quickly as possible."

The young man's mouth curled slightly. "Have I been forgiven?" he asked, with more than a touch of irony. But Acte saw that he was tense.

Seneca was no longer smiling. "All I know," he said, "is what your august mother has ordered me to do: to travel here as fast as I could and to take you with me to Rome without a moment's delay." There was a terrible urgency about him and again Acte felt that this man was in some unknown way the messenger of Fate. Nero, too, felt it, she knew from the way his eyes held Seneca's.

"I won't go," he said, "unless Acte comes with us."

For a moment the old man looked nonplussed. Then he said: "May I speak to you alone, my lord?"

The young man's face became a mask of stone.

"By all means. But this I will tell you first: I will not budge from here unless Acte shares my carriage. I swear it. Now, do you still wish to speak to me alone?"

The messenger of destiny passed a weary hand across the large forehead with the white wisp of hair, and changed back into a benevolent old man who could take everything in his stride.

"The young lady's father is in Rome," Seneca said. "I see no reason why she should not come with us."

For a moment Acte managed to shake off the assault of contradictory emotions. "But mother," she stammered, "I . . . I can't leave her just like this . . . I . . ."

"I shall inform her myself," Seneca said, and Nero rushed to embrace him.

From that moment on things happened with a strange, dreamlike rapidity. They walked up to the villa, no longer a distant hope but a wide, yellow front of marble, with huge pillars flanking the entrance and slaves in white tunics everywhere. Seneca was giving orders right and left; two carriages came rolling up, each drawn by four horses and one laden with luggage; Seneca asked her where her parents' house was and she answered something; there was the smell of leather, and her poet's face bending over her, his eyes shining with love, the rolling of wheels. . . . The carriage halting in front of a house, her house, her parents' house, and Seneca entering it with her, her legs were numb, she could scarcely walk, there was Aglae and Iucunda, eyes as big as plates, no, the mistress could receive no one, she was asleep, no, no, definitely recovering, no danger at all, she would be up in a day or so, perhaps if the noble lord would come back then.

A dream. A mad dream, like the one in which Lucius was going to sacrifice her. He was standing beside her, fretting.

The quiet, cultured voice of the old man explaining, explaining, Dikos, the little major-domo, bowing deeply and taking orders like a lamb, dresses and things, certainly, my lord, at once, my lord. She had to slip into mother's bedroom for a moment and there she was, fast asleep, breathing regularly. . . . Dear mother, I can't help it, I must, he needs me."

The *atrium* again, the rushing of feet, luggage bundled on the second carriage, she had no idea what was packed and what wasn't, what did it matter, it was all a dream anyway, they were waving, Dikos and Aglae and the others, the wheels were rolling, whips cracking, the clattering of hooves, she was carried away.

The last she remembered was that there were no more houses and instead a long, long road, straight as an arrow and flanked by cyprus trees—and *his* eyes resting on her all the time.

CHAPTER TWENTY-EIGHT

THE DREAM went on and on. Periods of fitful sleep, interrupted by sudden halts, with raucous voices bellowing orders, exhausted horses being led away and fresh ones taking their places; the flickering flames of a smithy; food spread on a tray across their knees—she could not eat but Nero's appetite was good; a goblet of wine and another and a third, mixed with water and a little honey as if it were breakfast time—perhaps it was. . . . There was a sunrise, but had it come after the sunset or before? There was a troop of slaves galloping ahead and behind them and once she heard Nero ask indignantly why they did not wear imperial liveries, but Seneca's answer was a murmur and she did not catch it. The old man was ghostlike—he seemed to be there only when he was invoked, a disembodied but comforting voice, it did not really matter what he said—or perhaps it did, but she did not hear him.

Twice they all left the carriages—or was it three times? Walking was very difficult, they were so cramped. She remembered being stared at by people, but there was one young woman who was nice and in some strange way compassionate. Why? And once there was a fright, somebody suddenly galloping beside the carriage, an officer with a scarlet crest on his helmet, he looked like an eagle, but Seneca's voice became sharp as a whiplash and the eagle looked tame and obedient and withdrew instantly.

She was tired, dreadfully tired and it was dark, a darkness full of little lights floating by at a distance; there was a nasty, pungent odor and she asked what it was.

"That's Rome," Nero said, and he laughed. Seneca mumbled something about "Subura" and "canalization." The shadow of a gigantic gate, some men with torches . . . uniforms, helmets with a reddish glow on them. A short stop, just long enough for Seneca's voice to ring out angrily, demanding passage for a senator or something like that. And still they went on, the wheels louder than ever and the carriage jolting over cobblestones, huge shadowy statues towering over them, a slow way uphill and a stop before a large door, flanked by pillars, a group of slaves, some of them with torches.

Nero was asking something and Seneca answered: "Yes, for tonight only."

They had to help her to descend and somebody led her into the house, it was warm and pleasant and terribly elegant. "I must look a fright," she thought, fumbling with her hair, but Nero smiled at her and wished her "dreams as beautiful as a rainbow" and Seneca, too, smiled and said something and two young slave-women led her away to a bedroom more luxurious even than mother's and helped her undress and put her to bed like a baby.

*   *   *

Acte was not the only one to whom the journey and all that followed blurred into a sequence of pictures and events only partly understood. All Nero could find out from Seneca was that some moves were afoot at the palace to restore the peace between him and the Emperor and that for this reason it was necessary that he should be in Rome, but not yet back in the palace until the Empress called for him.

But in the morning there was a rumor that the Emperor had fallen ill—one of his fairly frequent stomach attacks, nothing to be alarmed about, but no doubt it would delay everything.

Nero fumed and fretted when Seneca told him that he must not leave the house: "Officially you are not yet back in Rome." But when the senator suggested that Acte should be given into her father's care, the young man burst out: "Never! He'd take her back to Puteoli at once. I have charged you with her protection. She is the woman I love. No one is going to separate us."

"It would look much better, if . . ."

"She's not to be handed over to her father."

"My lord, the air is heavy with most important issues. I do not know what they are, but I have reason to believe that the next days will decide the fate of many people and perhaps even the name of the next occupant of the throne. This is not the time to do anything that might jeopardize your position."

"Acte means everything to me, everything. . . ."

"A reason more," Seneca said, "not to expose her to danger."

"What do you mean? Why should she be in danger?"

"We all are, at this moment," Seneca said gravely. "And therefore she is, as long as she stays here. The princess Octavia, too, has her partisans."

Nero bit his lip. "Not to her father," he said between clenched teeth. "She must be where I can see her every day. I will not live without her."

For a fleeting moment Seneca thought of Cassius Longinus, of the love and the rights of a father. He himself had entered Longinus' house and taken his daughter away. True, he had hoped that the girl's mother would exercise her authority, which she did not, or rather could not. But now he really ought to call him in.

It did not take him more than a moment to banish these thoughts. Bigger issues were at stake. And he had never before seen his pupil so determined. Agrippina would have to handle the matter herself—if she could. Nevertheless the girl had to leave his house. He could afford the enmity of Cassius Longinus and his wife. He could not afford the enmity of Nero and least of all that of Agrippina.

"Very well," he said, "with your permission I shall ask my old cousin Serenus to take her into his house, for the time being. You know him. No one will suspect anything if you pay him visits. Later, at a more suitable moment, we shall think of other arrangements."

Nero thought it over. "I'll agree to that," he said, not without some reluctance, "but on the condition that he is responsible for her to me—he and you, too—and that her father is not told about her whereabouts until I give permission."

Seneca bowed. "I shall take her to Serenus myself," he said.

*　　*　　*

The message, summoning both Nero and Seneca to the palace arrived in the afternoon, verified by a seal ring which the senator recognized. "Without this," he told his pupil grimly, "I wouldn't go."

Nero shook his head. "What is all this mystery?" he asked irritably. "What is mother up to?"

"I don't know, my lord, but we shall soon see."

They found the huge palace in an uproar, with people running in all directions and stony-looking Praetorian Guards in front of many doors, including those of the Emperor's son, Britannicus, and of the two imperial princesses, Octavia and Antonia.

Massurius, master of ceremonies, was almost in hysterics. "I can't get order into anything," he wailed. "Neither the Emperor nor the Empress are approachable, they've put guards before the doors of most of the chamberlains. . . ."

"On whose orders?"

"The Prefect of the Guards."

"Burrus, then. Where is he?"

"That's just it, he isn't here; I have no idea where he has gone and there's nobody I can ask. There are hundreds of people in the Blue Anteroom waiting for news, but I can't tell them anything."

"How *is* the Emperor?"

Massurius shrugged his shoulders. "He was much better and a little worse and recovering and practically dying, all in one hour. There's General Vespasianus now—no, my lord, you can't enter there, please step back, no one is allowed there. . . ."

The sturdy general with the shrewd eyes and the mean mouth shrugged and stepped back.

"Where is Pallas?" Seneca asked in a whisper. "Where is Narcissus?"

"Narcissus is ill himself," Massurius whispered in reply. "And Pallas is in there. So is Xenophon, the physician."

"Who else?"

"Well, the Empress, of course; she has never budged from the Emperor's side since the first signs, except to confer with Xenophon. . . ."

"She has sent for the prince and for me," Seneca said. "Go and announce us."

Poor Massurius was dancing from one leg to the other. "I daren't," he said. "Strict orders have been given to admit no one."

"Here is her seal ring," Seneca said, frowning.

"I know, noble Seneca, I know, the Empress gave it to me and I dispatched the messenger, but we must wait nevertheless."

"Wait for what?" Nero asked disdainfully.

To his dismay Massurius burst into tears.

Seneca gave an embarrassed little smile. "This is really quite impossible," he said. "An imperial prince . . ." He broke off because at this moment Pallas, pale and austere, came out of the Emperor's private suite.

Pallas bowed deeply to Nero. "Welcome, my prince," he said, showing no reaction whatever to the cool nod he received as an answer. "I hope you had a good journey. Glad you are here, Seneca. If you will excuse me one moment. . . . Massurius!"

"Noble lord?"

"Send for musicians and jugglers; some of those acrobats, too."

Nero looked at Seneca as if doubting that he had heard aright. Seneca did not bat an eyelid, but Massurius gaped with surprise.

"They will perform here in this room," Pallas went on. "The Empress feels that the diversion will do the Emperor good. We shall have the doors open so that he can see from his couch."

"The Emperor is better, then," Massurius stammered.

"Obviously," Pallas said coldly. "Hurry, please."

Massurius sped off.

"The Empress has sent for the prince and for me. . . ." Seneca began.

"Yes, of course," Pallas said. "If you will come with me now. . . ."

The twelve giant guards at the door made way for them and closed ranks again as soon as they had passed.

A heavy curtain was all that separated them from the imperial bedroom.

"My prince," Pallas said gravely, "I must ask you to prepare yourself for a shock. There must be no noise, no exclamation. . . ."

Angrily Nero stepped past him into the bedroom. And stopped.

His mother stood before him, tall, erect, her eyes in the bloodless face unnaturally large, staring at him with a terrible intensity. She held one finger to her lips.

Behind her he saw the Emperor, propped up with cushions in a half-lying, half-sitting position. His jaw was hanging down, his eyes stared glassily into nothingness.

"Not a word," Agrippina's voice whispered sharply. "Not a sound."

The young man gulped.

"Control yourself," his mother told him. "If you must vomit, go next door, to the dressing room. We have trouble enough here without you. He's been dead five hours."

He controlled himself, more afraid of her than of the dead man. "By the gods," he thought, "she looks like the Medusa."

But the Medusa changed as by magic into a noble and tragic figure as Seneca entered. He said a few appropriate sentences in a low voice and she bowed her head in acknowledgment.

"The time to give in to grief will come later," she said. "At present there is work to be done."

"The Senate," Seneca said.

"Yes, but not yet. I'm waiting for Burrus to return. He ought to be back any moment. Until he is, and with his mission completed and . . . ratified, the Emperor must be alive."

"I understand. There have been contradictory rumors. . . ."

"I'm killing them," Agrippina said curtly. "That's why I ordered the jugglers to perform."

"They're outside now, my Empress," Pallas reported.

"Very good. Sit down, son. No, not there, next to . . . him. Let everybody see that you are on the best of terms with him. I'll sit on the other side. The light is too strong. Two of the three lamps there must go, there'll be light enough from the hall. Tell the musicians to play, Pallas. My . . . the Emperor loves music. How far is the distance from here to the performers?"

"Far enough," Seneca said. "Or rather: too far to see more than they should."

"You are certain? Massurius is outside, isn't he? And others?"

"Yes, my Empress."

"Very good. Let them see their fill. Have the doors opened. Draw the curtain."

They obeyed. As the doors opened harps, citharas and flutes began to play and jugglers in glittering costumes started throwing balls at each other—five of them did it beautifully and in the exact rhythm of the music, the sixth, a misshapen dwarf with his face painted half blue and half yellow, tried hard to upset them and could not. He tugged at them, pinched them, kicked them, but they always managed to pass the ball to the next man.

As seen by them and by anyone else in the hall, the Emperor's bedroom, though visible, was a dimly lit, shadowy world.

"Mount Olympus, seen through clouds," Seneca whispered.

"I wish Burrus were back," Agrippina said. "No good at all starting on the Senate before we have the Praetorian Guards."

"It certainly would help if I could tell them that the guards have made their decision," Seneca admitted. "Twelve thousand men—and the only troops available anywhere near Rome—are a very forceful argument, even for some of our more obstinate friends."

"My son will have to speak," Agrippina said, "first to the guards, then to the Senate. I want you to prepare those speeches."

"They are prepared," Seneca said quietly. "And I have them with me."

She glanced at him sharply. "How could you possibly know. . . ."

"I couldn't," he said calmly. "But a good servant must be ready for any eventuality."

He saw her smile in the semi-darkness.

"Very skillful," she said, looking at the jugglers. "Skill should always be adequately rewarded."

There was a rolling of drums as the six performers ended their act. Their place was taken by a band of Gaditan dancers, exquisitely

288

beautiful girls. They provided their own rhythm with castanets and their arms and legs were covered with gold dust.

"He *would* have liked that," Agrippina murmured and for a brief moment Seneca permitted himself to hate her.

"Let me see those speeches," the Empress ordered and Seneca gave them to her. "Short to the soldiers—long to the Senate," he explained.

Nero looked at his mother, fascinated despite the horrible proximity of the corpse. "What a performance," he thought. "Ye gods, what a performance!"

The physician Xenophon, dark and bearded, was sitting hunched up in a corner.

"I must ask him how it all happened," Nero thought.

"There is Burrus coming in," Pallas said.

Agrippina drew in her breath sharply.

The Prefect of the Praetorian Guards had to make a detour to avoid the whirling bodies of the dancers.

As soon as he entered the room Agrippina ordered: "Have the doors closed. Give out that the Emperor must rest now."

Pallas obeyed.

Afranius Burrus saluted formally, first the Empress, then Nero. He was a man of sixty, gray under the golden helmet. He looked weary and exhausted.

"Speak, man," the Empress said. She made no attempt to conceal her anxiety.

"I've got them," Burrus said, "but it's high, very."

"How much?" the Empress asked crisply.

"Fifteen thousand sesterces per man," Burrus said, "fifty thousand per officer up to the rank of first centurion; one hundred and fifty thousand for staff officers, two hundred and fifty for the sub-prefects. I've been trying to add it up ever since. It makes over one hundred and eighty million sesterces."

"One hundred eighty nine million and a half," Pallas said.

"Have we got it?" Agrippina inquired.

"You will have it tomorrow morning at the third hour," Pallas said phlegmatically.

289

Agrippina looked at Nero. "The future Emperor is well served," she said with some emphasis. "Seneca, you will want to discuss tomorrow's speeches with my son. There will be no one on the big terrace at this hour."

"I'll have fifty men posted at the entrances," Burrus said.

"Very well. Now, Seneca, in case anybody should question you about the Emperor's health: he is better, he is resting, but there will be no audiences for at least two days."

Seneca bowed. A minute later he and Nero made their way across the hall, now quite empty and out onto the big terrace. They had just reached it, when the old man stopped. "We shall go through the speeches," he said in a voice trembling with emotion, "and that will be the last time that I shall be your teacher and you my pupil. For from then on you will be my emperor and I shall be your loyal subject."

"I shall never be able to do without you," Nero said quickly. "This last hour was . . . terrible. My head is swimming. Mother was . . . I don't know what to say."

"Do not think back," Seneca said slowly. "Your life begins now. The gods have given you many gifts. Now comes the time to use them. It is in your power to give the Golden Age back to mankind. It is in your power to make an end to the silence of the laws. Remember that the sun touched your body before the earth did. Be a sun to mankind."

There was a long pause. Nero gazed across the garden. After a while he said, dreamily: "I think she killed him."

CHAPTER TWENTY-NINE

THE SENATE was in permanent session. Fleshy, bald-headed men making speeches, lean, austere old men making speeches, famous names, new names, noble faces, crafty faces. Few listeners. But a great number of little groups, whispering, with gleaming eyes and jutting chins. Standing at the entrance Seneca observed them coldly. He had seen a number of changes here but always these groups huddled together, planning and hoping, giving a nice imitation of grim and patriotic determination to regain this or that or even all the privileges of which the Caesars had stripped them. How many of them would be able to enumerate them all? He, though he had been a senator only a short time, knew them all by heart and knew, too, that certain little concessions would have to be made, and made in such a way that certain vain men would feel it was due to their personal merit.

None of the members seemed to put much value on the bulletins issued by the palace. They all expected a change, they sensed it, as indeed many people did. It was fortunate that there was not much of a Britannicus-faction. The boy was too young and Agrippina had seen to it that he was surrounded by mediocre people, or rather by people whose character would not induce them to make risky experiments. There was work to be done, but it was not too difficult, as long as the illusion was kept up that everything depended upon the men with the broad-striped togas. It would take a long time to build up a senate composed of real men.

In the mean time he himself would have to shoulder most of the great tasks, as Secretary of State, officially, as the young Emperor's mentor in reality. Pallas was a figurehead only; besides, Nero could not stand him, ever since he had found out that his relations to his mother were not—not as distant as they ought to be. Narcissus was as good as dead. Burrus had his own field of action and was a useful man in many ways. The only danger was Agrippina. Her whims could counteract anything and her power, at present, was tremendous.

Time would sort that out, time and . . . Nero. No young man will allow his mother to rule him forever. There were two issues on which Nero would soon have to show his mettle. One was Pallas; the other that young girl he was so much in love with. On both Agrippina was almost certain to oppose him. Pallas was her lover and the man who could procure any amount of millions for her when she needed them. Acte she would probably regard as a danger because she wanted to keep up the position of Octavia, both for political and for personal reasons. Octavia was a cipher, a colorless, nondescript little girl, but for some indefinable reason she evoked people's compassion. Not that she tried to do so. She did not try to do anything. But she conveyed the idea of helplessness and of a need for protection.

He would have to talk to Nero about this. But at present he had other fish to fry, large, pompous fish with broad, purple stripes on their togas.

He had done a great deal of work last night, visiting the house of Thrasea where more than a dozen senators had gathered for one of the host's parsimonious dinners. He had won a number of valuable allies whom he set to work influencing others. They were doing so now. None too soon either. Agrippina's timing was cut very fine; but then, she had had to be extremely cautious, naturally, while Claudius was still alive.

The air was heavy with pent-up emotions and the putrescence of a long-dead republicanism. The Senate always reopened that tomb when a Caesar was dead or dying, but there was little danger of another civil war. It was tedious that one had to flatter these men and be glib and smooth-tongued. But the boy was worth the trouble. A young, gifted, ardent and enthusiastic man on the throne, trained by Seneca and with Seneca standing at his right hand—that was what Rome needed, Rome and the world. That was the medicine of life.

Seneca stepped forward and at once became the center of a quickly growing group of senators, shooting questions at him from all sides.

"My friends," he said gravely, "I think we must prepare ourselves for the fact that a great change is imminent. . . ."

* * *

The chief augurs had sent in an absolutely wretched report about the dawn-sacrifice, the confounded goose they slaughtered had a malformation of the liver or some such thing. Agrippina was angry and tense. The astrologers, too, did little more than wag their heads and murmur technical formulas about Saturn being in opposition to this, that or the other.

"You have got to find me a favorable hour," she stormed at

them. "You must, do you hear? What good are you, if you can't? Calculate again if you must, but get me that hour."

After some more wagging of heads and renewed calculations the learned men decided that the best hours . . . relatively speaking, noble Augusta . . . were around noon.

Another three hours! Agrippina bit her lip and dismissed the men. She gave out the early-morning bulletin, according to which the Emperor was alive, though somewhat weak. There was one good thing about it—it gave Seneca more time for getting round those fools in the Senate. Tomorrow there would be the funeral. Claudius would have to lie in state in the Forum and Nero would have to make the oration. Seneca had been working it out all night. But first Xenophon and Antiope, her cosmetic expert, would have to get the corpse into shape. What a relief it would be when that thing was out of the house!

She had Burrus called in for final instructions.

*　　*　　*

To be on the verge of becoming an emperor was very much like being a prisoner. Nero found that wherever he went a dozen guards marched with him. There were parts of the palace where he was not allowed—the suites of Britannicus and of the imperial princesses, for instance. He could not even pay a visit to his so-called wife! Not that he wanted to, particularly, but it was a queer situation.

He had rehearsed his speeches again and again and knew them by heart, with all the postures and gestures they required. "Strong and fiery to the soldiers," Seneca said, "quiet and modest to the senators." How the old man could talk when he wanted to and how silent he could be when he didn't! One never knew how much or how little he knew. He had only tut-tutted, for instance, in response to that remark, "I think she killed him," yesterday evening, and he would not be drawn into a discussion of the subject, oh no.

So one had to get hold of Massurius, the old clown, and draw him into a corner and ask him how it all happened. He would not know the truth, of course, but he was bound to know something.

There had been a dinner, one of those quiet little dinners, the Emperor, the Empress, Senators Marullus, Favonius and Thrasea and their wives. Marullus and Favonius were supposed to play dice with the Emperor later. But why Thrasea? Neither the Emperor nor mother liked him, mother used to call him "Old Incorruptible," but she did not mean it as a compliment, she had that little snarl in her voice when she said it. Of course, if one wanted to be able to say, "Thrasea was present"—that would explain a thing or two.

At dinner, even at the first part of the dinner, the Emperor had become unwell. What was he eating? Something rather heavy, difficult to digest perhaps? Not really, just a dish of mushrooms with a magnificent sauce—Claudius loved mushrooms, everybody knew that. Behind him, on his left, as usual, was Halotus, the eunuch, the food-taster; on his right Berax, the wine-taster. Halotus tasted the mushroom dish and found it delicious. The Emperor fell to. A minute later he had a stomach cramp and was howling with pain. So they took him all doubled up to the vomitorium and he vomited beautifully. Xenophon came at once, of course, and made him lie down in the bedroom, examined him and told him and the Empress that he would soon recover and might be able to rejoin the others at dinner. But he did not. The Empress did not return either but, dutifully, remained at the side of her ailing husband. The rest of the party went on with the meal, though nobody seemed to have much appetite. Such a fine feeling of loyalty.

And that was all Massurius seemed to know, except that a little later Xenophon tried to make the Emperor vomit a second time, but apparently without much success.

The only man who ought to know more was, of course, Xenophon himself, faithful old Xenophon. One of these days one ought to talk to him. At present it was not advisable, not with all those guards trailing behind. Perhaps it would be even wiser to drop the matter altogether. There was little doubt that mother hated the stupid old guzzler. She was playing her part as the imperial widow magnificently, but she did feel relieved and she was working like Hercules for her one and only son who ought to feel

294

grateful and didn't because he knew her too well. Did she know that he knew her too well? He must be careful about that. She had hated the old man. She was relieved. But that didn't mean, necessarily, that she was responsible.

Anyway, little Britannicus who would not call him Nero, now would have to call him Caesar—like everyone else. That was something. Perhaps mother didn't do it after all. It was disturbing to think about it. It would have been a heroic action, but disturbing. Much better leave it at that.

"Soldiers! You, the most faithful and loyal of all have a right to be the first to hear the great and tragic news. . . ." Tragic, the accent was on tragic, Seneca said.

What would Acte say! He had not been able to pay her even a short visit. No one was allowed to leave the palace, even those wretched jugglers and dancers were still here, herded together in some corner of the building and watched by Burrus' men. The palace was a mousetrap.

What would Acte say? Her poet was to be the Emperor. He was to be Pontifex Maximus as well. "But I won't sacrifice you, Acte, that's where your dream went wrong. Anybody and everybody, but not you. Mother perhaps, but not you."

"Soldiers! You the most faithful and loyal of all have a right . . ."

It was raining. "The gods are weeping," they said. But scarcely for Claudius—except that now they would have to receive him into their company. Mushrooms, it seemed, were the food that could change a mere mortal into a god. Seneca would like that idea.

* * *

The rain would not stop. Agrippina decided that Nero would have to be carried to the Praetorian barracks in a litter. He ought to have been on horseback, but it was no good arriving at the camp with his tunic, mantle and caparison bespattered with mud. On the other hand, the litter might be regarded as a sign of effeminacy. It did not matter, really, considering the guards were going to get a hundred and eighty nine million sesterces.

She wondered how much Burrus would keep for himself, especially since he had never asked for anything. She decided to let him have a million and told him so. He promptly said that there was no need for that, and indeed there was not, for according to Pallas he had a great deal of money, Pallas knew it to the last denarius as usual.

"Take it nevertheless," she told him. "Why should I pay money only to people I don't care about? Take it, I say. And watch over Nero."

Massurius reported that there were several thousand people crowding around the palace gates and waiting for news about the Emperor's state of health. Should he let them know? The man was utterly incapable.

"Not a word to the rabble. Let them guess what they like."

It would be fatal if they were told before an official message had reached the Senate. Even Massurius ought to know better.

Perhaps there was something in what those star-gazers said after all. In any case, there was a report from Seneca that he was satisfied with the progress made in the Senate "about a certain issue" and that "only minor and, in his personal opinion, temporary concessions about senatorial privileges" would have to be agreed upon.

However minor they were, they certainly would be temporary. She would see to that. If only the next few hours were over. She would have gladly given another hundred million sesterces for that. She had not slept for an eon.

"Burrus!"

"Augusta?"

"I think it's time."

"Another quarter of an hour, according to your previous orders, Augusta."

"It is time, I tell you. How many men were you going to take with you as an escort?"

"Two hundred, Augusta. That leaves eight hundred for the protection of the palace."

"Take three hundred with you. No, five hundred. There are too many people outside for my liking."

*　　*　　*

All went well. It was a strange feeling to talk to more than eleven thousand soldiers, all dripping with rain. Strong and fiery. They had erected a canopy for him, so he could make the gestures as rehearsed without splashing water about. The soldiers cheered. "Nero Imperator!" There was a kind of rousing sweetness in the call. Eagles and steel and pennants and horses rearing at the shout. This was a poem and he would write it: "The Young Eagle."

He felt a little giddy when they carried him back in the litter. Nero Imperator. Nero Imperator.

At the palace mother smiled at him. He had a goblet of wine and a few morsels of food, then he was carried off again to the Senate. "Most Noble and Wise Fathers of the City and the World . . ." Quiet and modest. Twice he got stuck, but he managed to recover himself and they seemed to like him for hesitating!

Seneca was at his side, but a step below him so that he looked up to the new Emperor; he always did the right thing.

One senator—who was it?—jumped up and suggested that the Emperor had made an oration the like of which the Senate had not heard since the times of the Divine Augustus himself.

Almost two thirds of the Senate applauded and the last third fell in after that.

The same senator then proposed to confer on the Emperor the title of Father of the Fatherland; there was applause again, but not so strong as before and from Seneca came a sharp whisper. He could not hear what he said, so he bent his head in his direction and Seneca whispered: "Don't accept. Say it was not a fitting title for one so young and that so far you haven't done anything to merit it. Shake your head at me, as if I had advised you to accept and you didn't agree with me. Let the refusal come from you."

He shook his head obediently, turned away and spoke his refusal. Quiet and modest.

They applauded madly. He had done the right thing again.

When he left the Senate he was walking on air.

Outside there were no longer thousands, but hundreds of thousands of people and by now they knew and they shouted like madmen. "Nero Imperator!" "Divine Nero!" "Eternal life to the young

Emperor!" What a poem it all was. The soldiers; the Senate; and now the people.

They loved him! He hadn't done anything for them yet, but they loved him. Perhaps there really was something credible about the divinity of emperors. All this did make one feel very near the gods.

At the palace everyone bowed low.

Mother was there, in grand attire despite her widowhood; she was wearing the pearl necklace that once belonged to Cleopatra and that Augustus had given to Livia. She too bowed—only a little, but she bowed to him!

And there came the tribune of the watch, Marcellus Rufio, and stood to attention. "The password for today, Caesar."

This, more than anything that had happened before, was the proof that he was the ruler.

Profoundly moved he looked at his mother. For the first time he saw the lines of exhaustion around her eyes and mouth. She had been working incessantly for this hour. Whatever she had done, she had done for him.

He walked up to her, took her hand and kissed it. Turning to the tribune, he said in a trembling voice: "The password is: Mater optima—the best of mothers."

Agrippina smiled.

CHAPTER THIRTY

LESS THAN A WEEK later Rome had good reason to believe that the young Emperor meant every word of what he had said in his maiden speech to the Senate. His very first measure was a general reduction of taxes. There was an obstinate rumor that he had wanted to abolish taxation altogether and that his advisers had great difficulty in persuading him that so radical a measure would ruin the empire.

Inns had a busy time, as every citizen was granted a donation of four hundred sesterces. The amount of wine drunk in the Emperor's honor threatened to empty the stocks in the city and hasty new orders were given to the wine-growing provinces.

The Praetorian cohorts received, on top of their gifts, free meals. The minor concessions made to the Senate were fulfilled to the letter and even exceeded by granting impoverished members special annual subsidies. Among the most hated people were the professional, semi-professional and amateur sleuths who denounced adulteries and other misdemeanors against the old Papian law to the Praetor's office. The Emperor would not abolish a law introduced by the Divine Augustus himself, but he cut the rewards of the denouncers to a fourth.

Many people were deeply touched when they heard how he refused to sign the first death warrant put before him, until Seneca convinced him that it was his duty and he signed, exclaiming, "Would I had never learned how to write!"

What a change after the gloomy, vacillating, fumbling regime of Claudius, after the madness and cruelty of Caius Caligula and the aloof sternness and leaden atmosphere of the time of Tiberius! The Augustan Age, the Golden Age had come back.

*　　*　　*

Agrippina did not object to her son devoting a great deal of his time to things other than business of state. The more he left in her hands, the stronger her position. Soon there were many issues about which she alone made the necessary decisions.

He was having singing lessons and the most famous cithara player of Rome, Terpnos, came to see him daily. Well and good. But there were other reports she liked considerably less, and she decided to tackle them at once.

"The house of old Serenus seems to have a great attraction for you these days," she said, when they were alone in his study.

He looked up. "Yes, mother," he said curtly.

She sighed. "I hate to spoil a pleasure for you," she said, "but I'm afraid I must ask you to end this little affair. It's beneath your dignity and it's doing you harm."

"Beneath my dignity? What are you talking about, mother?"

She sighed again. "I did hope you wouldn't ask me to go into all the details, but if you insist: I mean your little affair with a girl called Acte, whom you picked up somewhere in Puteoli, or rather thought you did. There is no doubt that Seneca is behind it, as he had the girl sent to his cousin Serenus. It's probably his plan to get more influence over you through her."

"I'm afraid you are misinformed for once, mother."

"I wish I were," Agrippina said coldly.

"I met Acte before Seneca did," Nero said, with a shrug.

"Of course, of course . . ."

"Mother, I'm not a fool! I . . ."

"You are a fool. Don't you understand that an emperor is not like other men? That everything you do is talked about? That idiotic little affair of yours is all over Rome. Serenus is inundated with invitations, 'and couldn't he bring the charming lady Acte who was enjoying his hospitality?' Do you want to strengthen the group of those who are always whispering that Octavia is sadly neglected? Your reign has only started. Consolidate it before you think of adventures of that kind."

"Acte is not an adventure," Nero said. "Nothing in connection with her can be spoken of as beneath my dignity. And if you want me to be an emperor, mother, you'd better treat me as one."

"May it please the Divine Caesar," Agrippina jeered, "the people of Rome are joking that you put down the reward of the spies of the Papian law to a fourth of what it used to be, because you don't want to have to pay too much yourself for your illicit affair with a slave girl."

Nero rose, white with rage. "A slave girl? How dare anyone say such a thing about Acte!"

Agrippina shrugged. "Well, at least her father was a slave once. I know that he was temporary Governor of Syria, you don't have to inform me of that. But in his youth he sold himself as a slave to somebody. His earlobes are slit. He was made free after fighting in the arena when he won against some gladiator. You will have to get accustomed to the fact that your mother usually knows what she's talking about—Caesar."

"This was before Acte was born," Nero said. "She therefore is, at worst, the daughter of a freedman. And I'm told that to be a freedman oneself is no longer regarded as a serious drawback, dear mother. There are freedman enjoying extremely high positions in Rome. Rumors, as you say, spread quickly in the city and unless they are untrue, a certain freedman is not only the wealthiest of men but also a man with the highest possible personal associations."

The reference to Pallas was unmistakable.

Agrippina gasped. She had never received an answer like that before. "If you want to be treated as Caesar, behave like Caesar," she said icily. "That girl will leave Serenus' house at once."

"I agree," Nero said, "under the condition that she stays at the palace forthwith."

Agrippina raised her eyes to the ceiling. "Under the same roof with Octavia," she exclaimed. "You must be out of your mind!"

"Oh, stop being hypocritical about it," Nero told her disgustedly. "You know perfectly well that Octavia means nothing to me."

"She means something to Rome, though. Ye gods, let me have patience with this boy who is working out his own destruction. Will you give up that little slut or not?"

"I forbid you to insult Acte," Nero shouted. "And I shall never give her up. Never, do you hear?"

Agrippina rose, too. "The slave girl," she said in a rasping voice, "has an extremely bad influence on your manners. You are ranting like an innkeeper of the Subura. Besotted as you are with that sordid affair of yours, you have had no time to bother about things that matter. You know nothing of the many voices whispering in the dark, not only about poor, neglected little Octavia, but also about Britannicus. And it is true that for your sake I have done him a grave injustice. Your stepfather's will has not been found yet. Perhaps it will be discovered somewhere. Perhaps it will show that he did not leave the empire to you, his son only by adoption, but to his own flesh and blood. Then what . . . *Caesar*?" She came nearer. "I made you," she said slowly. "I can unmake you."

She meant it. He knew she did. She never threatened unless she was able to make good her threat. He had experienced it many a time, as a child, as a little boy and later, too.

"Very well, mother," he said wearily. "Perhaps you can do that. But there is one thing you cannot do. You cannot force me to remain where, as you say, you put me. I shall abdicate."

She made a step back. "Ridiculous," she gasped. "You wouldn't dream of it."

"I shall abdicate," he repeated. "And I shall go with Acte to Rhodus and live there, quietly, happily. I shall take Terpnos with me, I think. He'll teach me to play the cithara. I've always wanted to be able to play it and it takes years to learn."

"You . . . you don't mean a word you say. You're trying to force my hand, that's all."

He shook his head. "I know you meant what you said. But I do too. It may be strange to you, mother, you, who love only power, but Acte and Art mean more to me than the throne. I love Acte, mother. You don't know her. She wouldn't be anybody's tool, not Seneca's, or yours or anyone else's. She is the sweetest, the most innocent girl and to be with her is like walking in the Elysian Fields. I know you can't understand that, mother, but that is how it is. Will you have all the necessary documents drawn up? If you feel that Britannicus should be Caesar, have him. And be sure that I shall be quite happy. As for Acte, she'll be delighted. Our only sadness is that we have to part each day, and now that will no longer be necessary."

Speechless, Agrippina stared at him. His eyes were moist, the tone of his voice almost gentle. She began to realize that she had made a great, an almost fatal mistake. Her own position was linked up irrevocably with that of her son. At seventeen a man was capable of any kind of irresponsibility, even of throwing away a throne, for the sake of an infatuation.

"My dear boy," she said softly, "how wonderful this girl must be to be loved so much."

Nero frowned. He did not believe his ears.

"I didn't know," she went on, "I couldn't know, could I, that this was not only an . . . an infatuation, but real, very real love? Once more I can see that, of all the gods, Venus Genetrix is the strongest. You certainly have withstood the strongest of all tests. Be happy with her, then. The only thing I ask is that you do nothing rash about Octavia's position. Not at present. Later on, we shall see what can be done."

He bowed to her, but she stepped nearer and embraced him.

"I have the noblest son in the world," she said. "Who else would have been ready to give up the throne of all the world for the sake of a girl? Forget what I said about Britannicus. He could never replace you, nor can anyone else."

*　　*　　*

In the afternoon Seneca came to report to the Empress about a number of new laws to be put before the Senate, including the repeal of the Claudian law banishing the Jews from Rome.

"Who suggested that?" Agrippina asked ironically. "The Emperor himself, I wager. I believe that girl of his is half-Jewish."

When Seneca was surprised he looked a little like a flustered parrot. "The repeal," he said, "was first suggested by Thrasea. I seconded it because it should bring a great deal of commerce to Rome. Jews are hard-working people."

Agrippina gave an angry laugh. "I should be very annoyed with you, you know," she said. "I had a most disagreeable talk with the Emperor about that young woman. You brought her to Rome, didn't you? You picked her for him too, I suppose."

"In the same hour," Seneca told her, "when I met the . . . the lady in question for the first time, the Emperor declared that he would not come to Rome with me, unless she went too. In the circumstances I thought it wiser to comply. I would have informed the Divine Augusta earlier, but for the fast-moving events of the last days."

"What is she like?" Agrippina asked casually.

"Muliercula nulla," Seneca said with an indulgent smile. "A mere nothing of a girl. A sentimental attachment entirely. One never knows for sure, of course, but in this case I would be ready to wager that she will never develop any kind of political ambition."

"He'll get tired of her, I suppose," the Empress murmured. "But even if she has no ambitions, her parents will have. Look how they've been working on her about the repeal of the law against the Jews. What speed! Yes, I know you told me it was Thrasea who suggested it in the Senate. But who suggested it to Thrasea?"

"I did," Seneca admitted calmly. "What is more, it was I who suggested it to the Emperor as well. It may well be, in fact I feel sure, that the young lady's half-Jewish origin did not exactly hamper the issue. But her parents had nothing to do with it."

"Sooner or later," Agrippina said softly, "Rome will become a little impatient with so many foreigners trying to influence her affairs. . . ."

Seneca's family hailed from Spain. The challenge was a personal one. "I have reason to believe," he said with a hurt expression, "that the imperial family did not fare too badly in the past with the service of those who might be called foreigners in a wider sense. Apart from myself, there are Pallas and Narcissus who are Greeks. . . ."

Agrippina bit her lip.

"And," Seneca went on, "the man who did more than anyone else to gain the throne for the late Emperor Claudius was a Jewish ruler, Herod Agrippa."

"Nevertheless," Agrippina snapped, "Claudius banished the Jews."

"Ingratitude is rarely good policy," he replied dryly. "As for the matter we were discussing: the Lady Acte's father is a Roman and of good family."

"Caesar and Marcus Antonius came from better families than he," the Empress jeered, "and their foreign consort was the Queen of Egypt. Even so, their offspring were not recognized by Rome."

Seneca understood the need for caution. "As a historian I must concede the point, Divine Augusta, and I shall not fail to bring it to the Emperor's attention, if and when the occasion should arise."

"Very well."

"In the meantime, however, I would submit that something like the present situation was bound to develop in the life of a passionate young man who unfortunately is not compatible with his wife, and that in the circumstances a certain lack of importance about the person of his favorite may be in the nature of an advantage rather than the opposite."

"Very nicely put." Agrippina's tone was acid. "Nevertheless I don't like it. I've never seen my son so insistent about anything."

"At his age . . ."

"Yes, yes, I know. But let's get rid of the parents. Where are they?"

"Cassius Longinus is in Rome," Seneca admitted.

Agrippina's eyes narrowed. "Does he live here? With his Jewish wife? Despite the law? It isn't repealed yet, is it?"

"No, Divine Augusta. He came here alone, some weeks ago for an audience with the late Emperor."

"More and more interesting," Agrippina said coldly. "This insignificant little girl seems to have a political-minded father. I thought as much."

"The purpose of the audience," Seneca continued, unruffled, "was to be allowed to return to Syria, despite the fact that he had been temporary governor there some years ago." He smiled thinly. "The audience was interrupted by the sudden arrival of the Divine Augusta and her faithful servant Seneca."

Agrippina nodded. "I think I remember that." She raised her strong chin. "Very well. The petition is herewith granted. Let him go back to Syria. Let him go anywhere he likes, as long as he doesn't pester us here in Rome. I only wish I could make him pack up that brat of his as well. You may go."

Seneca bowed and withdrew.

Agrippina sighed. She had not recovered from the terrible strain of the last weeks. It was not enough to go through what she had to obtain the purple for her son; she must be on guard constantly to make sure that he could keep it. When the young idiot gabbled to her about his love she had been tempted, sorely, to shout at him what she had done for him. He, who wouldn't look at Octavia, who after all was a nice-looking young girl even if she was utterly dull—couldn't he grasp what it had meant to marry that stammering, limping, drooling old fool Claudius? And *stay* married to him until . . . until his death? That much at least he knew. She wondered what he would have said if she had told him more—about the nerve-destroying weeks of preparation, about that horrible old hag Locusta, who had to be got out of jail where she was sitting under suspicion of having poisoned a number of people—Locusta, with her filthy hair full of vermin, with that infamous grin that said so clearly: "I know you think I'm dirt, but you can't do without me." How one had to rack one's brains for a scheme that made it possible to avoid discovery; to be able to sprinkle a few drops of the colorless, tasteless liquid on that big mushroom in the middle, with no one looking; to make Halotus, the food-taster, taste only of the sauce. And that most terrible moment of all, when the old monster began to recover, when old Xenophon quite cheerfully announced that he would be well again in a few hours. So much planning, down to the smallest detail—who was to serve the dish, who was to attend, who were to be the guests, which guards could be relied upon—and then, in the last moment, with the deed already done, the sudden need of complete improvisation! How like Claudius, to try and spoil a thing in the very last minute simply by vomiting! She had to take Xenophon aside and transform Claudius' creature into Claudius' killer in the course of five breath-less minutes, with enormous promises, wrapped in even more enormous threats. When she told him that he had to decide at once whether he preferred a million sesterces or to be accused by her of having poisoned the Emperor, he gave in and even had the in-genious idea of trying to make his patient vomit again with the help of a goose-quill, dipped in what was left in the tiny phial. . . .

All that effort—and then she had to face threats of abdication for the sake of a pretty face.

But what a good thing that she had not given in to the urge, the dreadful urge to tell the boy. He was not only her own flesh and blood but also that of Domitius of the warped and twisted mind and there was no knowing what he would say or do.

*　　*　　*

In the afternoon one of the Emperor's secretaries came to her with a letter.

"The plans for the temple of the Divine Claudius will be worked out by Veturius, the architect. As soon as they arrive they will be put before you, for your approval. As Pontifex Maximus it is my duty to elect as Chief Priestess of the temple a lady suitable for this high rank both by station and quality. I can think of no one better suited than yourself who looked after the Divine Claudius' well-being with so much care and devotion during his lifetime and assisted him so ably to the very end."

"He knows," she thought in a flash. "Either he guesses it or he knows." She felt the stare of the secretary, the man was watching her reaction—smile, she must smile.

She smiled beautifully. "Tell the Emperor that I accept. I am very, very touched and pleased."

CHAPTER THIRTY-ONE

WHEN SENECA came home, his major-domo approached him at once.

"The noble Cassius Longinus is here, master—for the fourth time. I told him you were still out, but he said he would await your arrival."

Seneca nodded wearily. "Show him into my study. The big one, not my working room."

"Yes, master. That is where he is now, master."

"Very well."

At Seneca's entry, Cassius jumped to his feet. His face was ashen.

"Welcome," the senator said jovially. "You've come at the right moment, friend. I have news for you."

"Where is Acte?" Cassius asked bluntly. "Where is my daughter?"

"My dear friend . . ."

"You abducted her."

"What a word!"

"What other word is there for it? You turned up at my house, when you knew that I was in Rome—you had told me to stay here! My wife was ill, unconscious. You took Acte away with you without parental consent."

"I don't like either your tone or your insinuations," Seneca said. "Remember, if you please, that you are speaking to a senator and the Secretary of State. Remember also that I am an older man than you. Discourtesy will accomplish nothing."

"Where is Acte?" Cassius repeated.

"To the best of my knowledge," Seneca said stiffly, "the lady is in the house of my cousin, Serenus, a man of seventy-four and of proconsular rank. I took her there myself the very day after her arrival. Please try to control yourself! It is clear that you do not know what happened. If you did, you would know that you have every reason to be content."

"Content!"

"Yes, and more than content. Grateful. You did not think that I 'abducted her' as you put it, for any . . . selfish reasons, did you?"

"There was a young man with you, I'm told," Cassius said tonelessly. "His name was not mentioned. He had reddish hair. Was it by any chance . . ."

"He was then the Emperor's stepson. He is now the Caesar."

"That," Cassius said, "is what I feared."

"By all the gods, man, what are you made of?" Seneca exclaimed in genuine surprise. "It's the most beautiful, the most poetic love story! I told you the young man had to leave Rome for the South. I knew he was in Puteoli where you, too, have your house, but I had no idea that he had met your daughter. When I arrived there, to bring him back with me, the two were together and very much in love. So much so, that Nero flatly refused to return to Rome, unless she came with him! So quite correctly I paid a visit to your house. It was most unfortunate that your wife's illness

308

prevented me from seeing her—I sincerely hope she is better now—is she?"

"She is here," Cassius said. "As soon as she could move, she came here at once."

"Ah well, please give her my respects and tell her how very much I regret that I had to act without her consent. But what else could I do? The issues at stake were so much greater than any private fate and, besides, I can assure you that your daughter, too, had only the one wish, not to be separated from the man she loved."

"As a Roman," Cassius said gratingly, "I owe loyalty not only to the Emperor but also to the Empress."

Seneca smiled indulgently. "The Empress Octavia is little more than a child. It is an open secret that the union—if one can call it that at all—is not likely to last. Don't you see that it is quite possible that one day . . ."

"I hope I shall not live to see the day you allude to."

"You certainly won't," Seneca said, frowning, "if you go on making remarks like that and are overheard by someone less well-intentioned than I. You still do not realize the situation, friend. The Empress-Mother herself knows about it and has tried to oppose it. The Caesar not only resisted her, but threatened to abdicate rather than be separated from your daughter. Why, man, listening to you one would think we are still in the Rome of dear old Cato Censorius. Times have changed—and your attitude, if you will forgive me, is just a little absurd."

"I can ask for an audience," Cassius was thinking aloud.

"You will not be granted one," Seneca said at once. "I shall see to that. Not for the Emperor's sake, but for your sake and that of your wife."

"In that case," Cassius said, "I shall go and see Acte at Serenus' house. A father is not without rights."

Seneca nodded. "You seem to be determined to ruin yourself and your wife. She shouldn't be in Rome, you know. The Emperor—most likely on the suggestion of your daughter—is considering the repeal of the Claudian law, but technically at least it is not yet repealed. If you go to Serenus, there will be a scandal. The whole thing will be dragged into the open. How do you think the Emperor will react to that? Listen to reason and go back to Puteoli, or, better still, to Syria. I told you I had news for you, didn't I? I am empowered to inform you that your petition to return to Antioch is granted by the government."

Cassius gave a bitter smile. "I understand," he said. "Farewell, Seneca. We shall not meet again in this life."

* * *

Cassius' abode in Rome was the house of Varro, one of Vibius Marsus' freedmen, near the Esquiline Hill.

He found Naomi in her room. She looked so small, so forlorn and lost that he could not bear it and closed his eyes. She was suffering, he knew from her incessant, illogical self-reproaches, for not having guarded Acte better, for not having been conscious when they came to take her away from her. And now he had to hurt her more. "I have seen Seneca at last," he said, dully. She would break down if he told her everything; she would never be able to stand it. Slowly, haltingly he said what he had to say. His head was throbbing. His hands were clammy.

She did not cry out. She made no move. Her eyes remained dry. When he had finished she came up to him and put one arm around his shoulder. "Oh, my dear," she said, "my poor dear . . ."

He knew then that far from succumbing to her own sorrow she was fully aware of his own. They had lost a daughter, their only child. But he had lost Rome as well. The strong ties of loyalty were severed; the respect for Rome's greatness was killed; the veneration for things ancestral, gray with tradition and of noble dignity was gone. All these had been wounded in the past; now they were dead and she knew it and understood his pain, the pain beyond the loss of their child—because she loved him.

"My dear, my own," she said, "I, too, lost my country when those in power rejected our Lord."

Tears welled up in his eyes.

"Acte . . ." he said. "Naomi, what are we going to do?"

He felt her body quiver. After a while she said: "I don't know.

I must think. But this I know: you are very weary. You must lie down."

The walls were swaying softly, as white as oblivion.

He nodded. "I will."

She walked with him, but he no longer felt the closeness of her body. In his room, he let himself fall on the couch with its soft, furry rug, and lay there, his face buried in his hands. The noises of the street faded in his ears. "Oh, Lord," he thought. "Oh, Christ."

*　　*　　*

When he woke up, he saw Naomi standing at the door. She was wearing mantle and veil. He sat up with a jerk.

"Naomi! You mustn't go out. It's too dangerous."

"I am not going out, I have just returned."

He rubbed the sleep from his eyes. "You are . . . what?" He jumped to his feet. "Where have you been?"

"I've seen Acte."

He stared at her, speechless.

"I took a litter," she said, "to the house of that man Serenus. It is a very big house and there were soldiers in front of it—and a golden litter."

"An imperial visitor," Cassius said between clenched teeth.

"Yes. I waited at the street corner and he came out. He was very young, with red hair. The people in the street all clapped and he waved at them. He looked very happy. As soon as he and the soldiers had gone, I walked into the house. Acte was still in the atrium, so she saw me and they couldn't stop me. Serenus wasn't there. She led me into a big room and we talked."

Cassius looked out of the window. It was growing dark. He must have been sleeping for hours. "Go on," he said.

"She loves him," Naomi said. "She loves him as much as I loved you—then; and perhaps even more."

"Naomi!"

"Yes. My love for you grew and grew—hers fell on her like lightning. She is blind to anything else."

"She is swept off her feet by her lover's glory."

"She doesn't love the Emperor, Cassius. She loves the man. She was in love with him before she knew who he was. She can talk only of him. She lives only for the hours when they can see each other."

"And Octavia?" Cassius asked grimly. "Doesn't Acte realize . . ."

"She looks at that through his eyes. He says that marriage was forced on him and on Octavia, that neither of them was asked whether they wanted it and that it isn't a marriage anyway."

Cassius nodded. "You asked her to leave with you—to come back to us?"

Naomi smiled wanly. "There was no need. *She* said: 'Please, Mother, don't ask me to leave him. I can't. I promised him not to leave this house as it might be dangerous, but even if I hadn't promised, I just couldn't. I'd die. I wouldn't want to live, but that's not the important thing. *He* wouldn't want to live, Mother. We belong together.' And she said: 'Don't you feel like that about father?' I told her, I did. But that there was a great difference here, because our love was hallowed and made sacred by our Lord and that such love alone could be lasting happiness." She turned aside a little. Her mouth was trembling.

"She had no reply to that," Cassius said.

Naomi bit her lip. "She said, 'Who am I to expect lasting happiness at his side? All I know is that I love him and that he needs me now. I can think no further.' Then she talked again about him, how much he cared for her, there was a girl who had to taste everything she ate and drank, not only of the dish but of every piece of the dish, to make sure that it was not poisoned by an enemy. She laughed a little at that. 'I can't think of any enemy,' she said, 'but it shows how much he loves me, so I faithfully allow it be done like that.' "

"We have lost her," Cassius said. He hung his head. "And she is lost to our Lord."

"You have no right to say that."

He looked up, surprised at her vehemence.

"Neither of us has," she went on. "I was married to Boz bar

Sebulun when we met, you and I. He was an old man and I was never asked whether I wanted to marry him or not. There was no need for that. A girl had to obey. The day came when they dragged me to the Temple and there our Lord Himself sat in judgment over me and told my accusers, 'Whichever of you is free from sin shall cast the first stone at her.' And after a while He asked me: 'Woman, where are thy accusers?' They had all gone. So He said: 'Has no one condemned thee? I will not condemn thee either. Go, and do not sin again henceforward.' Have you forgotten?"

"I beg my Lord's pardon," Cassius said in a low voice.

"And later," Naomi went on, "my great friend Miriam of Migdal told me how she, too, had been forgiven. She was forgiven much because she loved much, said our Lord. And still later, in Antioch, I heard Saul say: 'We have not a High Priest who cannot have compassion on our infirmities, but one tried as we are in all things except sin.'"

"Paul," Cassius said. "I wish he were here."

"I felt the same a moment ago, when I thought of Miriam of Migdal," Naomi told him. "She is far away in Gaul, they say, with her brother Eleazar; and Saul may be anywhere. But our longing for them has a meaning. We wish they were here because they are so much nearer to our Lord than we are. Which means that we feel too far away from Him and so we are."

"What do you mean?"

"We have thought too much of ourselves and our own feelings, as a father and a mother, as a Roman—we have almost forgotten to whom we belong."

"True. That's at least one of the reasons why I wanted us to return to Antioch. Here we are cut off from the source of strength. There is no Paul, no Petrus, no Judah. . . ."

Naomi shook her head. "We shall get strength for the asking."

He looked at her. He said nothing.

"We have been accepting all the time," she went on. "Riches and honors and a life of ease. Now He has reminded us through our child that we are His servants. He atoned for us on the cross. But he also told us that we must take up our own cross, if we were

313

to follow him. Helping to pay off the debt, Saul calls it. Lukas told me that, in Antioch."

"Perhaps that is what He wants of us," he said slowly. "Perhaps that is why He has taken away my last illusions about Rome. He wants the whole man, nothing less."

"Acte will suffer," Naomi said. Her eyes were far away. "She is bound to. Perhaps I shall be allowed to carry some of it. I pray that I may be. But I feel most strongly that we should not go back to Antioch. That is what we would *like* to do. That's what I hanker for in my weakness; peace and ease and the consoling help of our friends, If we do that . . ."

". . . it would be like desertion. You're right. We've been leaning on the spiritual strength of others for too long. Now He is telling us to work. But how shall we set about it?"

"Let Him answer that, "Naomi said gravely. "Remember what He said to that young man . . . I don't think I ever knew his name . . . 'Sell all that belongs to thee, and give to the poor . . . then come and follow Me.' "

"Naomi! Do you know what you are saying?"

"I think I do. I am saying what our Lord said."

"We are no longer so very young—at least I'm not."

"He was sad, I'm told, when the young man would not do it," Naomi said simply.

"I am responsible to Him for your well-being. . . ."

She looked up to him. "And so am I, for yours. Can't we trust Him?"

"Sell the house in Puteoli," he said, "use the money and all other money to help the poor. Live with them, say, in a suburb of Naples. Tell them about Him. Win some of them for Him. . . ."

"Aglae will come with us, I think," Naomi said, "and Iucunda, perhaps, too."

"Dikas might." He nodded. "And Syrus certainly will."

"Let's leave here as soon as possible," Naomi suggested. "Can we go tomorrow?"

"No."

"The day after tomorrow, then?"

314

"Oh no. Today. At once. I'll go and get the carriage ready. By the morning we shall be far away from here."

"I didn't think I'd ever see you smile again," Naomi said.

"I feel as if I'd been given a new life," he replied. "And you're smiling too, you know."

"I think," she said in a small voice, "the moment we decided to work for Him, He began working for us, too. . . ."

BOOK FOUR

CHAPTER THIRTY-TWO

Tribune Apronius coughed, but the lean old man at the window took no notice and went on staring down at the courtyard of the praetorium, where the prisoner was sitting. What was the old man trying to do, read the little fellow's mind? If so, he hadn't a chance. The little fellow was a deep one.

Tribune Apronius coughed again and then said: "Excuse me, sir."

The old man turned. "Yes, Apronius?"

"The prisoner's dossier, sir."

"Oh, thank you. Put it down on my desk, will you? My, what a mountain of paperwork. Procurator Felix must have been much interested in the case. Did you do all this?"

"A small part of it only, sir. Some of it was done by my predecessor, Tribune Vindex, but the main part is from all over the place, sir. The little fellow . . . beg pardon, sir, the prisoner has been everywhere."

The new procurator's long, slim fingers were toying with the package. "The man's been here two years," he said. "Why didn't *my* predecessor finish the case?"

Apronius' florid face took on an oxlike expression. "That's not for me to say, sir."

"I asked you and I want an answer, tribune."

"Well, sir, the procurator said he first wanted to hear the Chiliarch Lysias about it—he said that to the accusers, sir, but the chiliarch was in Jerusalem and no order was issued to summon him to Caesarea."

"In other words, Procurator Felix *wanted* a delay. Why?"

"I don't know, sir, but he had long talks with the prisoner at his palace. Sometimes the Queen was present, too."

"The Queen?"

"His wife, sir. We had orders to address her by that title."

"I see. Well, I shall have to study these papers as fast as I can. The trial is this afternoon. No, don't go yet, tribune. I'd like to hear your own opinion of the prisoner. What kind of a man is he?"

"It's not an easy thing to say, sir. . . ."

The new procurator frowned. "You've been in charge of Intelligence here; you've had the man under observation for two solid years; you must have summed him up by now or else you don't know your job."

"He's not one of the usual types, sir."

"Is he capable of a crime of violence, for instance?"

"Everybody is, sir," Apronius replied stolidly. "But he wouldn't commit such a crime with his hands. He might, easily, with his mind."

"That's better." The procurator nodded. "Inciting people to violence, is that it?"

"No, sir. Yes, sir. He'd incite people to violence against *himself*."

"Interesting. Why?"

"Because he's so sure of what he says, sir. He won't give in. He's quite cocky about that, sir, I've often seen him talk them off their feet. Come in all puffed up and sure of themselves, and when he had finished with them they'd slink off, like whipped dogs—*or* they'd sort of skip away as if he'd made little children out of them and promised them a big cake. That last kind would always come back for more."

"What does he talk to them about?"

"Religion, sir. Made a positive synagogue out of the praetorium, sometimes."

"Procurator Felix didn't try to stop that?"

"No, sir. The prisoner is in custodia militaris, sir, so he's entitled to see his friends whenever he likes. . . ."

"Of course. He's got quarters in town?"

"Not exactly, sir. He lives in barrack eleven at the back of the palace. Some of the men go to see him frequently, men of different units; officers, too, like Tribune Theophilus."

"Any signs of undermining the morale of the men? I'd ask Tribune Theophilus that directly, but he's on leave, as you know. What's the prisoner in for? Preaching sedition? Freedom for Judaea, that kind of thing?"

"Not exactly, sir. All religion again. The men don't seem to be any the worse, sir."

"I see. Have *you* listened to him sometimes, Apronius?"

"N-no, sir."

"Ah? Why not? Come on, man, tell me!"

"Well, sir . . . he's a very persuasive little fellow. I don't want him to . . . I don't want to be influenced, sir. He gets you, sort of playfully, and before you know where you are, you're in the net. Centurions Florus and Ateius—he got them, and they both had to give up their girls, sir; at least Florus had to."

The procurator gave a wintry smile. "Really. And why only he and not Ateius as well?"

"Ateius married his girl, sir. *That* was all right."

"And I take it you don't want to give up yours and you don't want to marry her either, is that it? Never mind, you don't have to answer that question."

"Thank you, sir."

"You may go now, tribune."

Apronius saluted and marched off, visibly relieved.

"An ox," Festus thought, "a fairly shrewd ox, but an ox." It was just like Felix to have such a man as his Intelligence officer. He'd either have that type or one of those effeminate young tribunes with the mind of a petulant woman. Having his wife addressed as Queen! Little Drusilla was a princess by birth, true enough, her father was King Herod Agrippa the First; she'd been a queen of sorts, too, when she married the ruler of Emesa, Azizus. But Felix had got her away from that petty monarch with the help of some unsavory emissary who managed to convince her that Felix was destined for greatness in the empire. It flattered her, to be the wife of a Roman, of course. And it flattered Felix to have a wife of royal birth, naturally. What else could one expect from a freedman?

Felix and his brother Pallas—thirty years ago they had stood on the slave block, their feet whitened with chalk and a shield with a number on it round their necks. Scum.

Festus sighed. He had been happy enough in his retirement in Tusculum, but one could not very well say no to the Emperor, not when he was obviously trying to do what should have been done a long time ago: to clean the Augean stable by getting rid of the clique of freedmen who were ruling the empire. There were some people—usually quite trustworthy people—who were convinced that young Nero no longer had clean hands himself, and one had to admit that the circumstances of young Britannicus' death could be interpreted in a rather nasty way. Some people even doubted that Agrippina had committed suicide because she saw that her conspiracy against her son had failed. The people of Rome seemed to regard it as a kind of privilege to indulge in such stories and even people of good families sometimes joined the rabble in that respect.

Certain it was that Nero had ousted Narcissus and Pallas, those master criminals, who between them had stolen fifty or sixty millions of the taxpayers' money; and now Felix, too, had followed his brother into oblivion, he and his "queen," and at long last the Procurator of Judaea was not an upstart, but Marcus Porcius Festus, a descendant of the same great family that gave Marcus Porcius Cato to Rome.

Rumors or no rumors, when the Emperor was bent on cleaning up the administration of his provinces, Marcus Porcius Festus could not afford to refuse office.

And the very first issue to be solved was the case of that prisoner, that grizzled little man sitting out there in the courtyard and dictating a letter to some scribe, as if he were in command of the praetorium.

One would have thought that the Jews had more important matters to discuss with a new procurator. A short while before Felix received the order to return to Rome at once, there had been a riot in Caesarea, Jews versus Greeks, as usual, about the law of equality and Felix had quelled it in his own way: first he let the Sebastene cohort attack a Jewish demonstration and kill a great number; then he permitted his troops—most of them Syrian Greeks—to pillage the homes of wealthy Jews all over the city until the richest of them "talked" him into calling the men off. Felix being Felix there was little doubt that talking in this case meant talking figures.

Naturally, the tension between Jews and Greeks still prevailed and that was why Festus had decided to pay a formal visit to Jerusalem immediately after his arrival in Caesarea. He stayed there for a week. He received the High Priest Ismael ben Phabi, newly appointed not by Rome, but by young King Herod Agrippa the Second; he received authorities galore, both ecclesiastic and civic. And all they would talk of was that prisoner!

The prisoner should be summoned to Jerusalem. He should be tried in Jerusalem. The Procurator Felix had delayed his case simply out of spite. The new procurator was reputedly a man of great justice. He would grant them that favor, the one and only favor they were asking for.

They overdid it a little. Festus had no previous experience with the mentality and the methods of the Temple set, but he believed certain simple rules to be applicable to most men and one of them was: "When somebody tries to get you to do something in a great hurry, the chances are that he does not want you to have time to think it over."

Festus replied that he would have to think it over. Next day the Intelligence Section reported that several detachments of Temple guards had left Jerusalem and taken up positions at two villages commanding the main road between Jerusalem and Caesarea. This could mean an ambush against that formidable prisoner in case he was escorted to Jerusalem; it could also mean an ambush against the procurator, in case he refused to comply with the wishes of the Temple.

The following day another deputation was sent to him and Festus, a shade cooler, told them that he would return to Caesarea as soon as possible; and as the prisoner Saulus or Paulus was in custody there, he would also be tried there. But as the High Priest and the heads of other important bodies seemed to take such a great interest in the case, they should come with him. . . .

"There you can bring your charges against the man," he said benevolently. "And please tell the High Priest he has no need to worry about his safety on the way. I shall take a strong escort with me and he will ride at my side."

To his astonishment his offer was accepted. The only condition the High Priest made was that the trial should take place immediately as he could not be away from Jerusalem for long. That seemed reasonable enough and Festus agreed.

Why was that man so important to them? He tried to find out from the High Priest on the journey and was rewarded with a stream of religious arguments punctuated with so much gesticulation that he had trouble keeping his horse quiet. But if this was solely a religious issue, why had Felix kept the man a prisoner? Had he thought he could make use of him in some way?

For a moment or two Festus thought of having the man called into his office. But that would not be the proper thing to do, just before the trial. Besides, if that man Phabi or one of his learned men came to hear of it, there might be talk of collusion. Much better to try and get some sort of a picture from that colossal monument of Roman Intelligence, the prisoner's dossier.

Sighing, Marcus Porcius Festus settled himself in his chair and began to read.

Confirmation on the part of the civic authorities of the city of Tarsus that Paulus (Saulus) as son of the Roman citizen Gilead ben Simeon was a Roman citizen by birth. Ah well, that explained a good many things. Even slipshod Felix couldn't afford to treat the matter lightly, in the circumstances. There were quite a number of legal consequences. The man was still subject to the High Priest's jurisdiction because he was a Jew, but only in religious matters and even that probably only if the crime was committed in Judaea—he would have to inquire about that point. Next document.

Copy of a report of Intelligence Section XII (Judaea), a summary, describing Saul of Tarsus as a member of the Pharisee sect, erudite, pupil of the teacher Gamaliel (see reports filed under Pharisee

324

Leaders, volume III), connection with ruling High Priest Caiphas not very intimate—that was twenty-five years ago, perfectly absurd —another copy from the same period, wait a minute, though, now the man was in command of the Temple guards, no, a detachment of Temple guards, sent to Damascus for the purpose of making a number of arrests. Seemed to have become intimate with the High Priest, to be given a task like that. There was a remark, scribbled in a corner: "seems to have been connected with the death by stoning of a certain Stephanus, Rabbi, for the execution of which Caiphas was deposed by H. E. the Governor of Syria, L. Vitellius. No direct evidence. Saul no longer resident of Jerusalem, new abode unknown. V." That wasn't Vitellius' signature, of course, but some Intelligence officer's. "V." . . . probably that fellow Vindex whom Apronius mentioned. Death by stoning, eh? But no direct evidence. And Apronius said—for what it was worth—that the man might well incite people to violence, but to violence *against himself*. A good remark, but on what was it based?

"Report LXXII of Intelligence Section XX (Syria, HQ) to Intelligence Section XXII (Judaea, HQ): The man Saul (Paulus) of Tarsus was resident here at the time of Vibius Marsus. Together with a certain Bar Naba (Barnabas) of Cyprus, Lucius of Cyrene, Manahen (related to Herod family) and Niger overseer of a Jewish sect, usually called Nazarenes. Assemblies in the Epiphania district (Singon Street). No disturbances reported. According to some reports Nazarene leaders sometimes capable of magical feats. This checked by us. Evidence of several cases of magical cures, nothing else, therefore paragraph relating to crime of Hatred Against Mankind does not seem to be relevant."

Not illogical. But magic. Bah . . . whatever next?

"Government Office, Paphos, Cyprus. The learned Saul of Tarsus paid a short visit to our island in the fifth year of the reign of Emperor Claudius. (*Signed*) P. Sergius Paulus, Governor."

Terse. Sounded as if Felix had tried to obtain information and the governor had snubbed him a bit, either because he liked Saul or because he did not like Felix. Perhaps both.

A treatise about Jewish sects. Pharisees, Sadducees, Essenes, one couldn't possibly read all that stuff.

A treatise about the relations of Roman procurators with the reigning High Priests from the time of Marcus Antonius to the reign of Emperor Caius. Might be instructive to read that one, but not now.

A report from a city in Lycaonia, which was it? Lystra, never heard of it. It mentioned that a certain Paul had caused a minor disturbance in Iconium, where some people tried to stone him, and added that "some people from Iconium and Pisidian Antioch" had assaulted the man and beaten him, in Lystra. He then went to Derbe, shadowed, by the agent who apparently wanted to find out whether there was any political reason for the incident.

From Derbe the man had the audacity to return to Lystra, Iconium and Pisidian Antioch. "He preached there again and held assemblies, as if he had been welcomed instead of being stoned. And all that just to talk about some god and the son of that god and some such matters."

Festus nodded. Good report. When a man showed unusual courage it was always worth while making a note of it, whatever his aims seemed to be. And Apronius seemed to be right about Paul's capacity for inflicting trouble on himself rather than making it for others.

Another note from the agent in Lystra. "The man Saul, also called Paul, has been back for a while. It is clear now that his activities concern only a Jewish sect, people calling themselves Christians, but called Nazarenes by the other Jews. I took part in some of their assemblies, posing as a potential adherent. The sect does not appear to have political aims of any kind." The report, like the earlier one, had gone to the headquarters of the Fifth Legion, stationed in camp at the Isaurian frontier. Copy was forwarded to Intelligence Section XX(Syria, HQ) and from there to Caesarea.

Report from Troas: ". . . no more than the founder or agent of a small religious sect without importance."

Report from Philippi, from Intelligence Section VI B(Macedonia): "The inquiry asked for was made. According to police authorities the man Paulus of Tarsus was arrested here, together with one Silas, nine years ago, on the charge of disturbing the peace and recommending customs impossible for Roman citizens to admit or observe. Decurion Glabrio imposed a sentence of thirty-nine strokes (rods only) on both men and ordered their transfer to the town jail. The case is unusual because an earthquake destroyed part of the prison that night and the prisoners could have escaped but chose not to do so. Subprefect T. Patulus, still in charge of town administration, sends his respects and submits that in case the said Paulus and Silas should intend to bring a charge for infringement of the Lex Valeria, such charge should be dismissed on the grounds of being made too late. Decurion Glabrio died from a stroke four years ago. Subprefect Patulus himself ordered the immediate liberation of the two prisoners when the case was put before him in the morning. When informed, belatedly, that the prisoners were Roman citizens, he went to the jail in person, accompanied by the officials A. Turbio and Q. Arcanius and tendered his apologies to the prisoners, thereby fulfilling the request of the same. No other request was made by the prisoners in regard to an infringement of the Lex Valeria."

Festus chuckled. Apronius' "little fellow" had got himself into trouble again, but he certainly knew how to stand on his dignity. He should have told that decurion about his citizenship, though. Probably was shouted down by the good Philippians and the decurion acted on impulse. The most wretched figure in the whole affair was Patulus. When the procurator of another province made an inquiry, the man became terrified that it might mean a claim against him and his administration and that was all he was concerned about.

Report from Thessalonica, police authorities there via Intelligence Section VI B(Macedonia): "The man Paulus of Tarsus known here as a textile worker and the ringleader of small disturbances. Accusations brought in against him, the Jew Jason, owner of a textile factory, and others for opposing the decrees of the Emperor and talk of a king of the name of Jesus. The accused Paulus fled by night. Jason, known as a respectable citizen, was allowed bail. The charges against all the accused were proved groundless and the case dismissed."

A letter to the Procurator of Judaea from Annaeus Gallio, Proconsul, Governor of Achaia, and ye gods, what a letter! Pages and pages of it, all very chatty. Annaeus . . . must be one of Seneca's relatives, brother or cousin, Iberian by birth then. Ah well, such are the times. Seemed to be quite a nice man, though. Sense of humor. Chatty, yes, but he had something to say all the same.

Festus grinned wryly over the story of the trial before Gallio. All very easy for him. The Jews in Achaia were a minority and did not seem to be very popular. Things here were different. Gallio did not have to cope with a high priest and his lawyers and above all, he didn't have to consider the influence these people had at court. No procurator of Judaea had had an easy time. Valerius Gratus, Pilatus, Marcellus, Cuspius Fadus, Cumanus and Felix . . . a whole chain of defeats and costly defeats at that, the end of careers, trials in Rome, exile. . . .

Judaea was not a safe post. Achaia was.

But then the letter began to fascinate him. So Gallio, too, felt the influence of the "little fellow" and in fact his manner of escaping from it was not very dissimilar from that of the worthy Apronius. Perhaps Gallio, too, didn't want to have to give up a girl or two? And what was this about deputations arriving from Thessalonica and Philippi? From Galatia, too. Why, the man Paul was founding communities wherever he went, he remained in touch with them, he built up something, but what, in the name of all the gods and beasts, what?

Some kind of religious realm, apparently, to be ruled by that mysterious King Jesus. This letter was a much more illuminating document than all the police reports, which gave only the facts as seen from their own bull-necked perspective. And nothing could be more misleading than facts—especially when incomplete.

The man Paul was organizing a chain of communities as he went along, from place to place, from province to province. But Gallio, like the others, insisted that he could find nothing illegal in his activities. The more one knew about that man, the more enigmatic he seemed to become.

"There is another thing, my dear Felix, that I rather like about the man. As the head organizer of so many communities, congregations or whatever you may call them, he is bound to have fairly large sums of money passing through his hands. At least, I have never encountered any man in such a position where this was not the case; and all of them, without exception, paid themselves good salaries and expenses from these moneys. But Paul earns his living as a skilled worker. He left here in the last year of Emperor Claudius' reign and has not come back so far, but his community, I am told, is flourishing—if one may use such a word to describe the life of these earnest people. They are not gloomy like some of my Stoic friends and some of the more orthodox Jews, too, but they seem to shun all the most exciting activities, the bacchanalian processions, the festivals of Aphrodite and the games in the circus. Talking of the games, we had a real fight here between eleven jailbirds and two panthers and got rid of all the jailbirds for the loss of only one of the panthers. . . ."

Festus dropped the letter. Money. That might have been Felix' object in keeping Paul here. It probably was. He thought he had got hold of the head—and of course at the same time the chief treasurer—of a large religious organization. He wanted ransom. He wasn't Pallas' brother for nothing. If this was so, then Felix, like most men chiefly interested in money, had little understanding of human nature in general and that of this man Paul in special.

Festus smiled. He had never spoken to the man, only looked at him from a distance, asked Apronius a few questions and studied the dossier, or rather part of it—but now a picture began to form, carefully put together from many little things, like a mosaic of the kind so much in fashion lately. Just as well to read through to the end. He had another hour or so before he must change, put on the regalia and sit in judgment over the man whose travels seemed to be as laborious and adventurous as those of Ulysses himself. A Jewish Ulysses, that's what he was.

The next report came from Ephesus. Here the man seemed to have stayed more than two years. Surely there must have been some trouble there as well. That man would always cause trouble.

Sure enough, here it was. And what a riot! For a long time things seemed to have gone smoothly enough, his influence expanding steadily. According to a couple of reports from agents to Intelligence Section XV(Lydia), received by Caesarea via Antioch there had been a number of magical cures. Magic again! But this time names were mentioned, and addresses, a case of leprosy here, another of lifelong blindness there, and people were trying to get possession of handkerchiefs and working aprons that Paul had worn and these things, too, had cured people.

Magic. On the other hand, this Paul seemed to insist that no one else was allowed to exercise such powers, or, as one agent put it, they could be used only in the name of that king of his and only by him. And here was the first police report.

"Copy of report by Sebasthaeus Munda, Chief of City Police, Ephesus, to Marcus Sestorius Pansa, Prefect (to Intelligence Section XV(Lydia); To the Most Venerable Theodoulios, Head Priest of the Grand Temple of Diana; to Artemisios Nikaios, Head of the Guild of Gold and Silversmiths.

"At the instigation of the weaver and tentmaker Paul of Tarsus and a number of his co-religionists (Nazarenes), viz. Timotheos, Erastus, Aquila and others, a demonstration has taken place in the fruit-market. Several hundred people built a pyre of books about occult rituals, textbooks of the magic art and the paraphernalia appertaining thereto. The pyre was set afire. A number of statues of various gods and goddesses, but mainly those of the goddess Diana, were thrown on the burning pyre. The value of the objects burned is estimated at fifty thousand silver pieces. The demonstrators sang in praise of the god of the Nazarenes. Inquiries made by agents showed that most of the demonstrators had gone to see the said Paul who asked them to confess their sins to him, maintaining that he had been given the power to take these sins from them in the name of his god Jesus."

There was another report by the police chief to the same authorities that Paul and his collaborators or co-religionists had spread the word far and wide and apparently quite systematically that gods made by the hands of men were no gods at all.

Festus whistled softly. The relations between the police authorities and the guild of gold- and silversmiths seemed to be pretty intimate. To send a copy of such a report to the good pontifex of the temple of Diana was a natural thing to do, but to pass it on to that fellow Artemisios Nikaios was asking for trouble. Most likely Sebasthaeus Munda was in the pay of the powerful guild, and it was both brazen and stupid of him to mention the extra copy to his friends instead of treating the matter with a little discretion.

But what a lot of damage this could do to the guild! As for the books on secret arts, magician Paul definitely seemed to wish to exclude all competition. Did he take money for his cures? Nothing was said about that, so probably he didn't. Had he done so the police might have taken action.

Felix, of course, would not have drawn those conclusions.

The very next report showed the reaction of the guild, a reaction amounting almost to a revolt. A mass assembly, inflammatory speeches, violent threats, thousands of voices chanting the ancient slogan of the most famous temple in the world, save that of the Capitoline Jupiter: "Great is Diana of Ephesus!" The whole thing would have resulted in a mass riot and bloodshed, but for the timely intervention of one Curio, the town clerk, a Roman of course; who else could keep a cool head on his shoulders, with all the oriental rabble shouting and yelling around him. What did he say: "We have court days, we have a proconsul; let the two parties go to law." That was the Roman way. The report ended tersely: "The instigator of it all, Paul of Tarsus, left Ephesus forthwith and has not been seen here again."

All very well, but what about the community he founded? A community large enough to threaten the income of a substantial part of the home industry? As for that lawsuit the guild intended to launch, it was perfectly hopeless. No one could force a man to buy a statue of Diana if he didn't want to. Curio knew that quite well, of course, he only suggested a lawsuit to stop the riot.

By now the man from Tarsus had been put on the General List, the list of those whose comings and goings were to be checked by the Roman authorities. There were the monotonous, but often helpful reports of police headquarters, just one sheet of parchment, but revealing all the places the man had passed through. The department in Antioch seemed to have made a good job in collecting them all.

Several places in Macedonia; some more in eastern Greece. One report mentioned the names of no less than seven companions, his general staff, most likely.

Troas again. "Stayed here one week." Assos. Mytilene. Miletus. Arrival by ship on Cos. On Rhodos. Patara. Phoenice. Tyre.

Ulysses was a stay-at-home in comparison.

Jerusalem. The last phase was approaching. A short letter from T. Claudius Lysias—ye gods, what a name!—to the governor. Who was he? "Commander in charge"—that meant that the legate himself was absent at the time and the first chiliarch had taken over. Quite obviously a man who had come up from the ranks, original name Lysias, the "Claudius" was added when he became a Roman citizen.

"T. Claudius Lysias, to His Excellency, Antonius Felix, Procurator, Greetings: This man was seized by the Jews and was on the point of being killed by them, when I came on them with troops and rescued him, having learned that he was a Roman. As I wished to know what charge they had preferred against him, I took him to their Sanhedrin. I found him accused on matters of their Law, but not of any crime deserving of death or imprisonment. And when I was told of an ambush which they had prepared for him, I sent him to you, directing his accusers also to state their case before you. Farewell."

Proper report. Proper action, too. Roman or not, the man was a good officer. No sign, of course, of Felix recommending him for promotion.

And Paul had managed to get himself into trouble again, as usual. What was it this time? The files of the trial under Felix would show. It was inconceivable that Felix had done nothing at all, if only because the Jewish leaders must have seen to it that there was no delay. But here was one more letter, this time from Intelligence Section XXII(Judaea, Fortress of Antonia, Jerusalem).

"Regarding prisoner Paulus of Tarsus, see General List. Known as spreading a new Jewish cult in other provinces. Caution advisable, as attempts on his life may be made by members of the orthodox cult. A relative of the prisoner informed us about a conspiracy of forty men who have vowed to kill the man. As figures in such reports are often unreliable, the escort of the prisoner was chosen as follows: two hundred men of the second cohort; seventy cavalry. The escort on foot is to go as far as Antipatris and then will return to quarters. Start: midnight.

"We have been able to ascertain that the prisoner is not identical with the Egyptian (name unknown) who started the revolt of four thousand men and escaped when Your Excellency defeated him. It is known that the Egyptian did not speak Greek, a language Paulus speaks fluently and with little accent, except for the typical Cilician burr. (*Signed*) F. Cerinus, Trib."

Busybody, Festus thought. Must show how careful they were about the escort. Tried to ingratiate himself with Felix, by reminding him of his precious victory against that agitator.

Now the documents of the trial, two years ago. "Before His Excellency Antonius Felix, Procurator of Judaea, appeared for the prosecution the High Priest Ananias. . . . The chief priests," et cetera, et cetera . . . "the learned lawyer Tertullus . . ." A freedman, obviously, with *that* name. "The accused, Paulus(Saul) of Tarsus was his own counsel." Well, that man Tertullus had better be good to be a match for the accused.

The opening speech of Tertullus, complete. "Whereas we live in much peace through you and whereas many reforms are in progress through your foresight . . ." By the knees of Venus, that to Felix when the land was swarming with assassins, no road safe, and extortion rampant! Slimy rascal. "We found this man a pest and a promoter of seditions . . . tried to desecrate the Temple. . . ."

If that was true, it was serious. But the accused denied it. Said he had come to distribute alms in Jerusalem and offer sacrifice.

Said . . . said what? "What they found wrong in me was that I shouted out as I stood among them: It is about the resurrection of the dead that I am being judged by you this day."

Then the procurator: "I shall need the testimony of the Chiliarch Lysias. Case adjourned. The prisoner remains in custody here."

Deliberate delay. Lysias had given him his report, a very clear, concise report. But Paul's statement about having come to Jerusalem to distribute alms might be the reason why Felix wanted to keep him here. Money. A man who came to Jerusalem to distribute alms was a man who had money. And that must have also been the impression that the shrewd ox Apronius had. "It's not for me to say, sir."

Festus closed the dossier. "What on earth," he thought, "does the man mean by 'the resurrection of the dead'?"

The man who emerged from the pages of the dossier was anything but a fool. He knew exactly what he wanted and how to get what he wanted. They could beat him, throw him in jail, chase him away—he went on with his activities undaunted and apparently uncompromisingly. He was an organizer. He was a man who could and did arouse enmity wherever he went—but who also won over sufficient numbers to send deputations to him in whatever faraway country he happened to be. His influence was felt for years after he had gone away. Whole communities went on living according to the precepts he had laid down for them, not in his own name, but in that of some mysterious figure called Jesus. And these precepts did not seem easy to assail. Time and again the accusations brought against him had failed to make much of an impression on the judges and more often than not the accusers resorted to violence— a good sign that they had come off second best in mere argument.

There was no evidence that he used violence himself. Beaten, he would return to the place and start afresh. And his influence on people—even cultured people like Gallio—was amazing.

He was not out for money for himself either. That was evident from the fact that he worked with his hands wherever he stayed for more than a few days.

But how could he combine all this with wild nonsense like talk about the "resurrection of the dead?"

Some religious squabble, some metaphysical daydreaming of the kind that would perhaps matter to that Phabi man and his Temple crowd, but nothing that could be weighed and judged by a Roman court. The same situation as before Gallio's judgment seat, then— and the same result? Festus sighed. It was not quite that easy. *If* the issue proved to be purely a religious one, how could one refuse the High Priest's request to have the prisoner sent to Jerusalem, to be tried there by an ecclesiastic court? It was simple enough to say no. But that probably meant another of those Jewish complaints in Rome—not exactly a good beginning for a new procurator.

Festus began to feel something very like hatred against Felix with whom he was linked, inextricably, by the chains of Paul. One could take the point of view, of course, that Rome was best served by delivering the prisoner to the High Priest, the religious Jew to his religious authority. The man had caused a good many disturbances in various provinces; surely, Rome had nothing to gain by letting him loose again to win more adherents for his peculiar creed, to wreck more home industries and have himself maltreated a few more times. Let the High Priest have him and be done with the whole matter. Except—somebody might get up in the Senate and ask why a Roman official had given up a Roman citizen to a non-Roman authority . . .

Festus groaned. All this was possible only because these were degenerate times. Never, never ought Roman citizenship have been granted to anybody outside Italy.

He rose heavily and stalked out of the room. Time to get dressed for the trial.

CHAPTER THIRTY-THREE

THE PRISONER, squatting on the sand of the praetorium court had no anxiety about his attire. He was wearing an old brown robe which some years ago had been brown and yellow, and an even older brown kerchief perched on the back of his head. As the forepart of his skull was bald his forehead looked enormous. The remaining black strands of black in his beard were fighting a losing battle against the waves of gray and silvery white, and his face was heavily wrinkled.

The prisoner was in a rare good humor, and when a surly centurion allowed a middle-aged, good-looking man to enter the courtyard he jumped up, beaming and they embraced.

"This is a great joy," Paul said. "I began to think you wouldn't be back in time."

"I was in Nazareth when I heard about the new procurator having gone to Jerusalem," Lukas told him, "and I thought at once that some people we know would use the occasion to put your case before him, in their own fashion. So I hastened back as fast as I could to be with you. Just as well I did . . . I saw Aristarchus on the way to the praetorium and he told me the trial is today."

Paul nodded. "You really have become a historian, my Lukas. You have to be where things are happening." When Lukas looked hurt, he laughed heartily and patted him on the back. "As sensitive as ever," he said. "Don't you think I know you are a good friend? Now tell me about Galilee. . . ."

Lukas ruffled his light brown hair, cascading from under his traveling cap. "How can you think of Galilee?" he protested. "They may call you any moment. . . ."

"They won't," Paul said. "The trial will be here in the court-yard."

"But aren't you worried? Aristarchus says he has seen the Temple people, High Priest, chief priests, lawyers and all, in a huddle under the colonnades outside; he says they're looking triumphant and absolutely sure of themselves. And he says the new governor is supposed to be a very severe man of the old kind and that he was with them for days and days in Jerusalem—and they even traveled here together."

Paul nodded. "They have been waiting a long time for this."

"But . . . but what are they going to do to you?"

"Nothing much."

"How do you know?"

"Our Lord told me."

Lukas looked at him sharply. "When?"

"Oh, a long time ago. I never told you, but I will now so that you may stop worrying. Two years ago when I was arrested in Jerusalem, the Roman commander led me to the Sanhedrin to find out more about the case and I told them all that I had a perfectly good conscience before God. An old man ordered those beside me to strike me on the mouth. . . ."

"And you thundered at him that God would strike him and you called him a whitewashed wall. He was the High Priest Ananias."

"I didn't know that then," Paul said. With a little shiver he added: "God knew. And He made me speak the words of condemnation. Ananias was assassinated."

"I've written down everything you told me at the time," Lukas said. "There were both Sadducees and Pharisee rabbis present and you insisted that you were accused because you proclaimed the resurrection of the dead, in which Pharisees believe and Sadducees don't and thus you set them at each other's throats . . ."

Paul smiled. "I was almost torn to pieces between the two factions and the Roman commander ordered his soldiers into the hall to rescue me from friend and foe alike."

"I don't think it made the case clearer to him," Lukas said dryly.

"I was taken back to the barracks of the praetorium in the Antonia fortress," Paul went on, "the very place where our Lord had suffered the scourging. . . ."

"You spent the night there," Lukas interposed quickly. "Was it that night that our Lord . . ."

"He stood at my side and said, 'Be steadfast; for just as thou hast borne witness to Me in Jerusalem, bear witness in Rome also.' "

Lukas hastily took tablet and stylus from his belt and began to make notes.

"So I know I shall get to Rome sooner or later," Paul concluded. "Which means that they can't kill me now."

"They'll try to get you extradited," Lukas warned. "And once they have you back in Jerusalem they'll certainly have you killed."

Paul nodded tranquilly. "That means I won't be extradited."

"The Roman procurator is a new man, he has no experience with the people here; and he will want to ingratiate himself with them. They all do, at least at the beginning."

"What does it matter?" Paul gave a cheerful shrug. "All I know is: I shall get to Rome."

"Cephas is there," Lukas said. "I heard that in Galilee."

Paul smiled. He said nothing.

"You . . . fought with him at the Great Council in Antioch," Lukas said rather timidly, "and I wondered . . . I wondered . . ."

"I love him as much as I love Paul," Paul said slowly. "Many a time our Lord has spoken to me through Cephas—that once He spoke to Cephas through me. And mind you . . . Cephas went wrong not in his teaching but in what he did, and from that no man is secure. Have you written about the Council in Antioch?"

"No."

"It is well," Paul said. "I have done so myself. And I am longing to see Cephas again. You gave me the happiest news when you told me that he is in Rome. The very heart of the empire is where he ought to be. That is what has been drawing me there too, even before our Lord told me that such was His will. Different as we are, my brother Cephas and I, I know that we are very near each other in Christ. What else did you hear in Galilee?"

"The Apostle Judah is in Persia and . . . and. . . . I met the mother of our Lord. . . ."

After a while Paul said: "Tell me more."

"If I am to be a historian," Luke said, "I must go back to the beginnings. That is why I went to Nazareth, and Bethlehem and Caphernaum. She is in Nazareth, with Jochanaan and his mother, and I was allowed to see her, on several days though not for very long at a time. Not because of her age. She is like the earth—old and venerable and yet young and fresh at the same time. Not because of her frailty. She is so light, one feels she might be carried away by the wind and yet her strength is such that she could live on with her soul pierced by a sword. I could not stay long because in her presence I was overwhelmed."

Lukas passed a trembling hand over his forehead. "What a great thing it is to be a human being, when one of us could conceive and carry and give birth to the Lord! Not in mythology, not in legend, but in history! She was right to exclaim as she did, 'Henceforth all generations shall call me blessed!' "

Paul nodded dreamily. "You wrote it all down, son?"

"Yes. Yes."

"It is well," Paul said again. "That is how it is about the Way. For each of us it begins in a different manner and all of us it leads to the same goal, unless we fall by the wayside or turn our backs, and walk in the opposite direction. You have written down faithfully how the Lord struck down his servant Saul on the road to Damascus. Now yours is the task of writing what will be the true beginning to many: how the Lord lifted up His handmaid and exalted her. It happened to a daughter of Israel; but it is meet and just that a Greek should write the story. A Greek . . ." He broke off.

Three soldiers came out of the guardroom in full armor and marched up to him.

Paul saw that one was carrying manacles and a chain in his left hand. "I'm getting my jewels back, I believe," he said merrily. But Lukas blanched and bit his lip.

As the soldiers were putting Paul in chains, two servants, escorted by four more soldiers, carried a gilded chair to the center of the courtyard and set it down.

From the guardroom came the staccato bark of Roman commands and a troop of twenty soldiers came marching out, led by a centurion. They took their position behind and on both sides of the judgment chair.

The centurion at the gate leading to the colonnades bellowed an order. The gate clanked open and the procession of the accusers entered. Two learned scribes, two chief priests, the High Priest Ismael ben Phabi, his secretary, four more scribes, with a dozen lawyers and secretaries bringing up the rear. All of them stopped in front of the empty chair.

Ismael ben Phabi was a stout little man with a straggly gray beard and a perpetual frown between bushy gray eyebrows. He stood with his feet fairly wide apart and firmly planted in the sand like a fighting bull in the arena; there was a kind of bellicose dignity about him. There could not be the slightest doubt that he had seen the prisoner, but he took no notice of him. Most of the men of his retinue stared at Paul with unconcealed hatred and several of the lawyers began to shout insults, but stopped at once when the centurion barked an order and the soldiers raised their spears and let the shafts crash against the metal-plating of their shields.

A moment later the procurator appeared in the courtyard. He wore no armor. His toga showed the thin purple stripe of a knight. His heavy face betrayed no emotion. As he settled down in the chair, six lictors in scarlet tunics took up their positions on his right and left. The fasces on their shoulders contained both rods and axes, indicating that the judge had full powers.

Apart from the lictors, the procurator's suite consisted only of two military tribunes, two legal advisers, both of them civilians, and two recording clerks.

From afar came the cry, long-drawn and whining, of the slave in charge of the sundial.

"The eleventh hour," Festus thought, half closing his eyes. "Only three hours until sunset. Just as well it can't run on longer than that; but we'll never get through in three hours."

Every one of the lawyers of the Temple was carrying bundles of papers. They had had more than two years to prepare their case. The High Priest himself would probably leave tomorrow, but there was nothing to stop him from putting one of his chief priests in charge and leaving him here with all these lawyer fellows.

The droning voice of the clerk, announcing the case, announcing the persons here for the prosecution, announcing the name of the defendant who at his request would undertake his own defense; announcing that the accusers would now put forth the formal accusation and the evidence supporting it.

Then, all of a sudden, pandamonium broke out, with most of the lawyers and at least half of the priests present shouting at the same time.

Festus could not understand more than a few occasional words, most of them shrilling from the lips of a turbaned scribe who combined a height of six feet with a piercing falsetto voice.

"Pestilential . . . seditious . . . ringleader . . ."

The procurator gave a casual look at the recording clerks. The poor men were trying desperately hard to follow but it was easy to see that they were bound to fail. He frowned. But before he could give an order, Ismael ben Phabi raised his right arm and the noise stopped abruptly.

The High Priest called up one of the lawyers and the man began to complain, passionately and with eloquent gestures that the accused was a rebel against the Jewish Law.

Festus, observing him shrewdly, decided that the man was absolutely sincere.

When he had finished the High Priest gave another lawyer a nod, an elderly man who began by confirming everything the previous speaker had said, but beyond that accused the prisoner of having incited others to the same crimes he was constantly committing himself and of glorying in such incitements. With flashing eyes and an admonitory finger wagging at the prisoner the man assured the procurator that in thirty years of practice he had never come across a more flagrant case of sedition. He, too, gave an impression of sincerity and almost seemed to regret that he had to say such harsh things about a co-religionist.

Ismael ben Phabi sent his third man into the battle who added the crime of "violation of the Temple" to the other accusations. The violation seemed to consist in Paul taking a Gentile with him to hallowed ground where Gentiles were not allowed, and the lawyer quoted at length from the various edicts of Roman Caesars, granting to Jews rights and privileges in connection with their way of worship. Apparently there was some slight doubt whether or not the Gentile who accompanied Paul had actually entered the forbidden court—Festus observed that sharply—and there was no proof for the motive he insinuated: hatred against the Temple and all things sacred.

The fourth lawyer added a long story about the prisoner's seditious activities in Jewish communities outside of Jerusalem and even outside of Judaea itself, which had led to bloodshed, grave

341

disturbances of public safety and a general lowering of the reputation of Jewish minorities in various provinces of the empire.

The fifth lawyer seemed to resent most that Paul had feloniously affirmed a certain man to be alive, when in reality he was dead. The man's name was something like Jesha or Yeshua—he was probably identical with the mysterious Jesus whose name turned up several times in the dossier.

Then the High Priest himself spoke. He had full understanding of the problem by which His Excellency the Procurator found himself burdened in this sad case. Most of the accusations were based upon the Jewish Law and fell under the jurisdiction of the Temple authorities. His predecessor in office, the High Priest Ananias, had explained this to the former procurator, but His Excellency Antonius Felix, for reasons difficult to grasp, had insisted on keeping the prisoner here in Caesarea. The official motivation for such procedure, as given by him at the time was that further evidence was required from the Roman officer who had made the arrest. But that officer had never been called to Caesarea and had been transferred to Germany a year and a half ago. Perhaps the former procurator needed time to check up on potential crimes committed by the prisoner against Roman law? He, Ismael ben Phabi, did not know. However, he and his colleagues did not insist on His Excellency, the present procurator, trying the case; indeed, they felt convinced that this case should be tried by the Jewish authorities in Jerusalem. The prisoner, though a native of Tarsus, had resided in Jerusalem a long time and some of his worst misdeeds had been committed there. He submitted therefore with all courtesy that the prisoner should be delivered to the Jewish authorities here and now, or, if the procurator preferred, sent to Jerusalem under escort to be handed over to the Temple authorities there on arrival. There had been many delays and he felt sure that His Excellency would agree with him that the case must be brought to an end.

Festus shifted in his chair. "First," he said dryly, "I will hear what the prisoner has to answer to the accusations made against him."

Paul, looking absurdly small between two raw-boned guards, spoke a single sentence. "Neither against the Law of the Jews, nor against the Temple, nor against Caesar have I committed any offense."

A howl went up from lawyers and priests alike, fists were shaken in the prisoner's face; one of the lawyers, dancing with rage, tried to make himself understood by the procurator but could not be heard above the din. The High Priest alone remained disdainfully quiet.

Festus waited patiently until the storm subsided. The idea of some sort of a compromise dawned upon him, a compromise that would perhaps placate these enraged people and yet make it possible for him to avert the worst, if he found it necessary. It was not a very good compromise, but he was glad to have found it. The prisoner was, unfortunately, a Roman citizen. He had to put the matter before him.

Festus leaned forward. "Are you willing," he asked affably, "to go up to Jerusalem and be tried there before me on these charges?"

Jerusalem. The praetorium. The Lithostrotos. The same place where Christ was tried. Take up your cross and follow Me.

For one wild moment Paul almost gave his assent. But then he hesitated. The Lord had appeared to him that night in the praetorium barracks, and had given him his orders. He had to do as he was told. He looked at the procurator and saw the worry and anxiety behind the smooth façade, the same weakness that had cost the Lord's life. Another small man, troubled about his own position, trying to save his own skin. And if he was troubled here in Caesarea, where Rome's position was far more powerful, how would it be in Jerusalem, where the High Priest was on his own grounds? There would be a hundred voices yelling for Paul's death for every single voice here.

Paul decided that he was not going to make it easy for Festus. "I am standing at the tribunal of Caesar," he said. "There I ought to be tried. To Jews I have done no wrong, as you yourself know very well. For if I am guilty, if I have done anything wrong or committed a crime deserving death I do not refuse to die. But if there is no ground to their charges against me, *no one can give me up to them.*" His eyes bored into those of the procurator.

Festus looked down. The corners of his mouth drooped a little, not unlike that of an old lady who feels that she can't please anyone.

In a flash, Paul knew that he could expect no further help from this man. Before his own conscience he was totally innocent. He had done only what Christ had told him to do. Christ, whose authority had superseded that of the Sanhedrin. Only Rome could find fault with him now, and only Rome could decide whether or not he had violated Roman law.

And Christ had told him to go to Rome. He must go to Rome.

Suddenly, with preternatural clarity he saw himself standing at his father's side before the big, fleshy decurion who inscribed his name on the register of Roman citizens as "The Little One," Paulus. As was usual, the decurion had made a little speech, telling the new citizen what an honor had been bestowed upon him, and at the end of the speech he said: "And if ever you get into trouble and the magistrate or judge does not give you full justice, you have the right to appeal to Caesar himself and, lo and behold, to Caesar you will go. Remember that, my boy, remember that." And his father smiling, a little embarrassed at the thought that his son should ever get himself into trouble.

All that came to him in an instant. It was not a thing to be done lightly. Anything could happen in Rome. Even hardened criminals would hesitate before asking for this last, this desperate and dangerous remedy. But the idea of forcing his enemies to shoot him like an arrow into the very heart of the empire illuminated his mind.

The lawyers started shouting and yelling again, some at him, some at Festus.

Paul stepped forward, so suddenly that the two guards to whom he was chained were caught off balance and stumbled a little. In a voice as strident as a trumpet, Paul cried: "I appeal to Caesar!"

There was a hush.

Festus sat up with a jerk. With his finger he beckoned to one of the civilian advisers behind him. The man approached. A few whispered remarks went back and forth. Then Festus turned to Paul, and spoke the formula required by law: "You have appealed to Caesar? To Caesar you shall go!"

He rose, and at that sign of finality the centurion on guard rapped out an order. Paul was marched off to the barracks by his guards.

Lukas, his mind awhirl, closed his writing tablet and shoved it back into his belt. He saw the High Priest follow Paul's departure with the eyes of an angry bull whose victim has jumped over the fence. Half a dozen of his retinue were talking to him, but he did not pay attention. Then the procurator walked up to him and Lukas could see him make a polite gesture of regret. The two men bowed to each other, the procurator with an apologetic smile, the High Priest with a forced one.

Festus walked away, and now that his back was turned on the Temple crowd, Lukas could see the expression of immense relief on his heavy face. The soldiers and the lictors followed him, rods and axes unused. Three men escorted the High Priest and his retinue to the gate, let them out and closed the gate behind them.

"I should leave, too," Lukas thought. But he could not tear himself away. As his excitement ebbed he began to see the golden thread of Providence enmeshing human affairs. Christ wanted Paul to go to Rome. So, despite all human traps and schemes and machinations, Paul was going to Rome.

Two slaves appeared and removed the gilded chair of judgment, no longer a thing of awe, but almost an object of ridicule. Things were the servants of men and no servant could be greater than his master. Three times only Paul had raised his voice and after the third time the judge was his judge no longer.

"History is where Paul is," Lukas thought. "And what is more: Christ is where Paul is."

There and then he decided to go to Rome with him.

CHAPTER THIRTY-FOUR

THE ARRIVAL of a grain ship from Egypt was always an event in Puteoli. People knew about it at once: no other kind of ship was allowed to fly its flag from the masthead when sailing into port. Bread was coming, dear bread. Few asked why Italy's own fertile soil no longer produced it as it had in the past. The past was far away and one had become accustomed to the fact that a few hundred very rich men owned most of the country and were not interested in growing wheat or barley. For a long time Sicily had been Rome's granary, but now it was Egypt.

The arrival of the *Castor and Pollux* was a minor sensation. She was early. Between the Calends of October and the Ides of March all major navigation ceased in the Mediterranean and the Ides of March had only just gone by.

"She is early because she is late," a know-all in a dirty tunic told the bystanders. "She must have left Egypt so late that she could not complete the voyage and spent the stormy months in winter quarters near by, in Leptis, maybe, or Thapsus or Melita."

The prefect of the port went on board with some of his men and the captain handed him the list of passengers and freight.

"There's an additional list," the captain told him, producing it. "Centurion M. Julius of the Augustan Cohort, with twelve soldiers, in charge of a transport of criminals, most of them for the games in Rome. Came on board in the port of Valetta."

"How many jailbirds?"

"Twenty-two—and one state prisoner, a Roman citizen and his two slaves. Made it quite clear to me that he wasn't a criminal, but merely remanded in custody. Didn't prevent him from being on very friendly terms with the criminals."

The prefect raised his brows. "Who is he?"

"A Jew from Tarsus. Called Paulus. Seems to be the head of some Jewish sect. The centurion took him ashore in Syracuse and he made a two hours' speech to some of his co-religionists there. Came together in no time, those people."

"I'll see that centurion now," the prefect said.

The captain gave the order and a few moments later the officer came into the captain's cabin.

"What is this I hear about one of your prisoners being allowed to make speeches ashore, centurion?" the prefect asked sharply.

Centurion Julius was a wiry little man, growing gray after twenty-odd years of service. The prefect was a big, lumbering man with white, well-manicured hands. There was not much love lost between the regular army and the port police in charge of Customs and Excise.

"Not speeches," Centurion Julius said dryly. "Only one speech. Don't know of any law against it, prefect."

The prefect flushed angrily. "You are in charge of those rascals. You ought to know that they mustn't be allowed . . ."

"Excuse me, prefect," Julius interrupted, "I *do* know the regulations *and* when to make an exception. In case you're interested: I heard two other speeches of the prisoner you're referring to. . . ."

"There you are," the prefect snapped. "Perfectly incredible."

Centurion Julius nodded. "Maybe," he said. "I really don't know about that. Way over my head, they were. One was before His Excellency the Procurator of Judaea, Marcus Porcius Festus and the High Priest of Judaea. . . ."

"What?"

"And the other, a few days later, before his excellency again and King Herod Agrippa the Second and his sister, Queen Berenice. At the Herodion, sir, the palace in Caesarea. All theology, sir. Most interesting. The King said he could almost be persuaded to accept what the prisoner said."

"I see," said the prefect. "Ah well, I suppose you know what you're doing. Where's the man going?"

"Praetorian barracks, sir. I have a letter from his excellency regarding him, to Prefect Burrus."

The prefect of the port seemed to shrink. "All right, all right," he said hastily. "I seem to have spoken out of turn."

But Centurion Julius had warmed up to his theme. "You don't know the best of it yet, prefect. He's a man who combines three things, none of which I encountered before in my life, and, believe me, I've seen a good many things. I thought I'd seen the lot."

"What do you mean?"

"The man's one of those prophets," Centurion Julius said earnestly. "Now, don't laugh. I don't mean those chicken-bowel inspectors who tell you what you want to hear, when you give 'em what you'll be missing before the next payday. I mean a man who'll tell you that your ship will founder and that you and all the people on board will be saved and then that's what happens."

"He did that, did he?"

"That's one of the things he did. We were on the *Memnon*, sir, went on board in Myra. . . ."

"I thought you came from Caesarea?"

"That's right, sir. But there was no ship for Italy there, so we had to sail in a nutshell of a thing from Adrumythium to Myra, where we caught the *Memnon*. Got into a bad storm, lasted two weeks and they had to girdle the ship, have a cable lashed around the gunwale . . ."

"It was an Euroclydon," the captain chimed in. "The master of the *Memnon* told me all about it in Valetta. Bad luck."

"That it was," the centurion agreed. "But I'll bet you the master didn't tell you that he could still have his ship, if he had done what my prisoner told him to do: stay at the last anchoring place, Fair Havens Bay near Thalassa, and winter *there*. But the captain would have none of it and I thought at the time that he should know what he was talking about, more so than my prisoner, so I didn't object, and we sailed straight into that Euroclydon wind."

"The *Memnon* lost," the prefect said, pursing his lips. "That'll be a hard blow on Senator Rubrius. He only owns sixteen other ships. Big ship she was, though; must have been over two hundred people on board."

"Two hundred and seventy-six," the centurion told him, "including me, my men, my criminals and my prisoner with his two slaves."

"And all hands were saved, you say?"

"Just as my prisoner predicted, sir."

"And the captain and the crew of the *Memnon* are still in Valetta?" the prefect inquired.

"I couldn't take all those men on board," the master of the *Castor and Pollux* defended himself. "I'm full of wheat to the gunwales *and* this officer forced me to take him and his crowd. I'm responsible for my ship and . . ."

"All right, no one's blaming you," the prefect said shortly.

"If you ask me, sir," the centurion said, "neither the master nor the crew of the *Memnon* are worth preferential treatment. The crew tried to get away with the lifeboat, when we were on the rocks, and they would have succeeded if my prisoner had not heard them and told me. So I ordered my men to cut the boat's cables and just as well I did. We would all have been lost, if those cowards had left us."

"That prisoner of yours!" the prefect said, half admiring, half ironically. "He seems to be a paragon of all virtues. Can't think why he's a prisoner at all."

"Quite right, sir," the centurion agreed. "That's exactly what I asked myself a couple of times. He's a prophet and he's mighty lucky to others, sir—that's the second thing I never met before, a man who brings luck to others. My decurion was all for killing the prisoners when the ship was wrecked, but I wouldn't have it. I didn't want that man killed for anything and what with the darkness and the men all worked up it might easily have happened. Besides, he had said we'd get away safely and I sort of believed him by then. Didn't lose a single man. And one more thing, the third . . . you can't harm him. He's . . . he's protected by his god, I think."

"That's strange language, from an army officer," the prefect said, frowning.

The centurion shrugged. "Work it out for yourself, sir," he said phlegmatically. "That first evening on the island—Melita—we were sitting together and my prisoner had collected some wood for a fire. There were a lot of people all around us quite friendly, cattle-herders, most of them, and chatting away like anything. All of a sudden they shriek, and I see a snake hanging on the hand of my prisoner, fairly long, yellow thing. . . ."

"A viper," the captain interposed. "There used to be quite a lot of them on Melita, but they're pretty rare now."

"I didn't know what sort of a snake it was," the centurion went on, "but the herders knew and they said my prisoner must be a murderer because the snake attacked him."

"Strange logic," the prefect said.

"Not really," Julius explained. "You see, they thought, here is a man who has managed to escape from a shipwreck and at once the gods send a snake to kill him, so he must be a guilty man who is not allowed to escape just punishment. That's how they explained it to me later. They were all waiting for the bitten man to swell up and get convulsions and die, but all he did was to shake the beast off so it fell into the fire. I *think* he closed his eyes for a moment or two and prayed, but I'm not sure. In any case, nothing happened to him. So the islanders decided he must be a god himself and he had a lot of trouble explaining to them that he wasn't, but that he was, as he called it, a servant of the one true God. Well, they took us all to their headman who looked after us well enough. His father was ill. My prisoner went to see him, put his hands on his head—and the man was cured. Fever gone, chills gone, everything."

The prefect shook his head. He said nothing.

"Terrible thing to do," the centurion went on. "For now they sent us every single person on the whole confounded island who was ill. They came in carts, they came on asses, they came on stretchers, masses of them."

"What did he do?" the prefect inquired. "Hide?"

"He cured them all," the centurion said gleefully. "And if I hadn't seen it myself, I wouldn't believe it. I shall have to report to Prefect Burrus that there isn't a single case of illness on Melita. At least, there wasn't when we left."

"That," the prefect said, "is about as much as I can take in one swallow."

"If you want to meet him yourself, sir. . . ." Julius suggested.

"No, thanks," the prefect replied. "He gives me the shivers. You get him to Rome safely."

"And that," the captain said, "will be quite a task, I think." He was standing at the entrance of the cabin, looking ashore. "There seem to be a few hundred friends of his here, all waving at him and some shouting his name."

"Same as in Syracuse," Juluis said, unruffled. "We landed in Rhegium after that and he had friends there, too. What's more, they knew he was on board when we came into port and now these people seem to know it too. Looks like news travels quicker by land than by sea, doesn't it?"

"All the gods in Hades," the prefect swore. "Now we shall have all the cripples and the diseased flocking around that man. They'll come from Neapolis and a dozen other places and we'll have an epidemic here. Get that magician or prophet or whatever he is away as fast as you can, man, or I shall get in trouble."

Julius shook his head. "Can't leave at once. Got to report to headquarters here. But don't worry, sir. I told you my prisoner cures people, he doesn't make them ill."

The prefect was still uneasy. "Don't know what to do with those jailbirds of yours either," he grumbled. "The city jails are full and so is my little prison here in port."

"No problem at all," Julius told him cheerfully. "I'll let my decurion march them off to Rome, at once, with my men. There'll be no escape on the way. He's a sharp one. I'll stay with my prisoner." He grinned. "He won't run away either," he added. "He *wants* to go to Rome. Told me so. Anything else, sir?"

"No," the prefect said. "Do what you like. But if there's trouble, I'll . . . I'll . . ."

"That's all right, sir," Julius said gravely. He raised his hand in a somewhat perfunctory salute and ambled away.

On deck, Paul was waiting for permission to go ashore. The way was still barred by four of the port-prefects men.

The Decurion Scaurus and his men were lining up the convicts. Four of them managed to pass by close to Paul and to touch his coat. Frowning, Scaurus saw that he was whispering something to them and making a magical sign over them. No good trying to interfere with him, he thought, not with the centurion's pet wizard.

Ashore, the group of people near the long, low Customs' shed was shouting again for "Paul," and "Paul, the Apostle," and Paul tried in vain to discover a face he knew. He beckoned his "slaves" to join him. "Can you see anyone we know?" he asked. "My eyes are worse again."

"No," Aristarchus of Thessalonica said, but Lukas shouted excitedly. "Yes! Yes! At least I think I can . . . it's Cassius Longinus, but he's disguised as a plebeian and he looks much older. There's his wife, too, I think . . . yes, it is she." He began to wave enthusiastically.

Paul smiled. "Can you see little Acte, too?" he asked.

"Not yet, but surely she can't be far."

Centurion Julius went up to the decurion and began to give him instructions.

The port-prefect appeared and waved to his soldiers. "Permission to land," he barked.

A few minutes later he and the captain saw Paul and his two companions step ashore. The little man raised his right hand and instead of the usual salute, drew first a vertical and then a horizontal line in the air. At that sight all the people awaiting him knelt down and bowed their heads. Then they rose and pressed around him like children whose father had come home after a long journey.

"That's how it was in Syracuse," the captain said. "*And* in Rhegium."

"A prisoner," the port-prefect said. "Great Jupiter, what's Rome coming to, these days."

CHAPTER THIRTY-FIVE

NOTHING SEEMED to surprise Paul. That the man he had last known as the governor of a great province was now living in a small room of a tenement house in a poor district; that both he and his wife with a few faithful freedmen and freedwomen were working for the Way only; that they had completely retired from the circle of people they were accustomed to—all that he took in stride as if it were a perfectly natural development.

Only when they told him about Acte he closed his eyes and the sharp lines around his mouth became deeper still. For a long time he said nothing and the pain he was sharing with them made them feel very close to him, closer than ever before.

They were alone at the time—everybody else was busy preparing the Agape, the love-meal, they would have together in a small hall belonging to a member of the little community.

"It happened over six years ago," Cassius said, unable to bear the silence any longer, "and we've heard very little since then. Our only link with Rome is Linus. . . ."

"Linus?" Paul asked in a low voice.

"He's been sent here by Cephas," Naomi explained. "By Petrus, I mean. He has come three times so far, to give us the Lord's Supper."

"Linus," Cassius added, "is a friend of Senator Pudens and of the Lady Pomponia Graecina, the wife of General Aulus Plautius; they both belong to us and through them we hear about Acte from time to time."

"She is still with . . . Caesar," Naomi said tonelessly.

"She is living in the palace," Cassius added stonily. "But she is no longer happy."

Paul's thoughts seemed far away. His eyes were still closed.

"He is falling asleep," Cassius thought. He quickly dismissed the shadow of disappointment rising in his heart. Paul was an old man now. He had only just landed, after what must have been a terrible voyage of many months; and wherever he showed himself, people would come to him with their burdens for him to share them. He had been fond of Acte in the old days, or had seemed to be. One never really knew what was going on in his mind. But in any case, after so many years, after thirteen years, Acte could scarcely be more to him than the memory of a pretty child who put a paper crown on her little head because she was "an anointed one". . . .

But then Cassius saw Naomi staring at Paul with such intensity that he gave a start. What did she expect, what could she expect from the poor old man, hunched up in his chair, frail, almost wizened?

Paul opened his eyes. He smiled. Suddenly, miraculously, he looked twenty years younger. "Say no more about her," he said with an almost motherly gentleness. "God is patient. Be patient, too."

Before he could prevent it, Naomi seized his hand and kissed it.

Cassius chewed his lip, grudging himself the warmth of a sudden emotion, so ready to trust the little old man implicitly, even beyond the words he had spoken.

Over Naomi's head Paul smiled at him. "Why do you worry? What do you fear? You have been working for God all these years—do you think He will let you outdo Him in generosity?"

"I . . . I've done very little," Cassius said, frowning at the thought that his words might be taken for false modesty. "I have lost people through clumsiness, through temper, through indifference. . . . I've missed opportunities . . . I wanted to establish a new center in Neapolis, but couldn't. . . . I wanted . . ."

"What does it matter what you wanted?" Paul interrupted. "What matters is the will of the Lord. Only the effort is ours; the success is His. You've always been a great one for wanting to *do* things and do them your own way."

"He's been working hard," Naomi pleaded.

Paul looked from one to the other, beaming. "Of course he has," he said, "but he's so ambitious that he has too little joy in him, and how can you spread the tidings of joy unless joy is in yourself? The Way itself is joy."

"We have seen much suffering," Cassius said. "I thought I knew life in all its aspects and forms. I wasn't always Governor of Syria. But only during these last years have I discovered how terribly people suffer. . . ."

"I know," Paul said quietly. "I have spent many days in prison and often looked death in the face. Five times I was given forty strokes of the lash and spared only the last; three times I was beaten with rods; once I was stoned; I've been shipwrecked more than once, I've been in danger from floods and from robbers, in danger from my own people and from the Gentiles; there is danger in cities, in the wilderness, in the sea, among false brethren! So often I was hungry, thirsty, sleepless, cold, naked and to all this is added the burden I carry with me every day, the anxious care for the churches, so many of them dotted all around the sea, beacons

354

of light to greet the Lord when He comes again as come He will. We have the grace of suffering with Christ, not merely believing in Him. Shall we complain? Why, how could we hope to share His glory, if we refuse to share His suffering?"

After a while he added, dreamily: "The whole of nature groans in a common travail all the while. And nature, in turn, will be set free from the tyranny of corruption, to share in the glorious freedom of God's sons."

Cassius sat bolt upright, a soldier being briefed by a great commander.

But Naomi, in a flash, saw the veil lifted from a mystery of whose very existence she had been only dimly aware, and with that lifting of the veil everything was changed. The universe was no longer an orderly thing which those who studied it would understand if only they went on studying and searching long enough. It was a tremendous thing in the process of being made. Creation was not an act of the past; it was going on and on towards a goal of indescribable greatness and beauty. The men of knowledge, the men of science would try to solve what she had seen and would never be able to do so because all measures were forever changing. Nothing was fixed but the will of God, and the God-Man walking on earth, her judge and everyone's, her saviour and everyone's, was the expression of the will of God. . . .

She stretched out her hands. In a trembling voice she said: "If only you could stay with us a while."

*　　*　　*

He stayed for one week. Centurion Julius just grinned and shrugged his shoulders. "No need to hurry too much. *They* won't be in much of a hurry to judge your case either. Would have been a different thing, if my jailbirds had still been with us, but they'll be in Rome now anyway. I shall have to be present whenever you make a speech, though. Better for both of us. That way I can report that you didn't try to rouse people to rebellion or any other nonsense of that kind. I know you don't, but it's better if I can say that I've heard everything."

Within that week the little community almost doubled.

Paul treated each as if he were the only person who mattered, he shared his interests and listened eagerly to his conversation, only to lead him in the end, with gentle irresistibility, in Paul's own direction. At the beginning of a meeting the little man in his shabby brown robe gave the impression of being unimportant; in the end he dominated it. And when he broke the Bread and lifted up the Chalice he was a High Priest of royal lineage. The quick, nervous gestures were gone, instead, his movements were of a quiet majesty, and the wizened old man, sharp-featured and almost bald, looked noble and beautiful.

"There are moments," Naomi said to Lukas, "when he seems to be already in his risen body."

Lukas nodded. "Aristarchus and I traveled with him as his slaves," he said. "It was the only way for us to be allowed on the same ship. As a Roman citizen, he had the right to take two slaves with him even as a prisoner, so slaves we became. And many a time we both felt that this was really our true status towards him. He really has 'put on Christ' as he calls it. He is so near our Lord, I could envy him, if . . . if . . ."

"If you could," Naomi said, smiling.

"You are right," Lukas told her. "When I see something perfect, I may wish to be more like it, but not to be it myself. For if that wish were fulfilled, my love and admiration for it would cease."

"I am worried about his health," Naomi said. "His eyes . . ."

"They have never been strong, not since his first journey. That's why he has to dictate most of his letters. Sometimes he will add a sentence or two, in very large letters."

"He never gets enough sleep, Lukas. I don't think he has slept as much as three hours a night since he came. It's . . . it's not human."

"The source of his love is not human," Lukas answered. "And I know he has never forgotten that he is a Jew."

Naomi raised her head. "What do you mean?"

"He mentions it again and again," Lukas said. "And I think nothing has moved him so much as our Lord's outcry: 'Jerusalem,

Jerusalem, still murdering the prophets, and stoning the messengers that are sent to thee, how often have I been ready to gather thy children together, as a hen gathers her brood under her wings, and thou didst refuse it.' I think he wants to atone for that, for the whole of his people. There is no other people so gifted and capable of spreading the Way among the nations, none so persuasive and eager in its dealings. So he is doing, almost single-handed, what they all ought to do. Mind you, I cannot tell you for sure whether this is what he feels," he added quickly. "It's just a thought I had, and I'd never dare ask him about it."

Naomi's eyes were moist. "If it is so, it's a secret between him and our Lord," she said.

"One of the secrets," he replied.

She nodded. "It must be very terrible to . . . come back and go on living here," she said.

He looked at her, surprised. "You know, then?"

"I felt it."

* * *

In the morning of the eighth day after the landing in Puteoli the last stage of Paul's journey to Rome began. Even Centurion Julius could delay no longer.

Paul cut the farewell short. At his request Cassius and Naomi did not accompany him, as they wanted to, at least for a few miles up the dusty road to Capua. They saw him leave, from the doorway of the tenement house, brown, small and a little bent, a figure few would have given a second glance, if it had not been for his chains, and the centurion walking beside him. Lukas and Aristarchus, as his slaves, followed at some distance.

"A prisoner going to his trial," Cassius said. "An old man tramping along the road—that's what people see. Yet there goes the greatest conqueror in the world of today."

"There goes Israel," Naomi said, "proclaiming the Messiah to the Gentiles, as the Prophet Isaiah foretold, centuries ago."

* * *

The nearer they came to Rome, the more quiet and monosyllabic

Paul seemed to become. For hours he said nothing at all. He was pale and his feet dragged.

"It'll soon be over now," the centurion said amiably. "It's been a long way, I know, for a man of your age."

Paul seemed to wake up just in time to give the friendly man a courteous smile. Then he fell back into what seemed to be a brooding silence.

Lukas, who had been his shadow for so long, recognized the signs without seeing his face, from his manner of walking, and he stepped out more briskly to diminish the distance between them, in case Paul should faint, as he sometimes did when the soul, engaged in a battle of its own, could no longer sufficiently vitalize the body.

They were passing the forty-fourth milestone, behind the Forum Appii. Before them, as it had for days, the Via Appia stretched into what seemed to be an infinite distance. Rome was still much too far away to be seen, hidden, beyond the horizon, by the heights of Velitrae, the Alban hills and a long stretch of the Campagna.

But to Paul Rome was near. He could feel its heartbeat, its rhythm, he sensed its breath. There before him was the terrible city, the high citadel of human power, ruled by all the demons of vice. He could not think of Petrus and Linus who had been fighting inside the monster for years, nor of the many to whom he had given greetings in his long letter from Caesarea, a few years ago. Rome itself was upon him, its claws ready to strike.

With every step he drew nearer the monster.

"Lord," he thought, "I am old and weak and as nothing without Thee." He thought in Hebrew, as he would in moments of black night.

The answer was instantaneous.

Before him, at the forty-third milestone a group of people was waiting. A dozen, no, more, twenty or thirty. Now they began to move forward, hesitantly at first, then faster.

Centurion Julius frowned. But soon he saw that these people, men and women, young and old, far from meaning harm, were beaming with joy. "More friends of yours, I suppose." He grinned. "I never saw a man with so many."

A moment later they were all around them and Paul found himself embraced by his old friends from Corinth, Aquila and his wife Priscilla and by the two sons of Simon of Cyrene, Alexander and Rufinus, who told him that their mother, too, was awaiting him at the city gate.

Paul's lips were trembling. "Praise be to God," was all he could say.

There would be another delegation waiting for him at the Three Taverns, they told him, elders and deacons and with them Linus, to give him the greetings of Petrus.

Two young men brought a donkey along for him.

"God forbid," he said, "that I should ride into Rome as our Lord rode into Jerusalem, on an ass's colt. We shall all walk together."

He marched on with such vigor that the centurion shook his head and turned to Lukas. "What is he made of?" he murmured.

Lukas smiled. "Body and soul, like all of us. But the soul is in command."

CHAPTER THIRTY-SIX

AFRANIUS BURRUS, Prefect of the Praetorian Guards needed less than ten minutes to deal with the case before him.

Centurion Julius delivered the commitment papers, the procurator's personal letter and his own short report.

The prefect scanned them. "The appeal was made before judgment was given," he said. "Who is here for the accusers? No one yet? Ah well, in that case we'd better wait." He scribbled a line on the top document in front of him. "Custodia militaris," he said, passing on the papers to the officer sitting beside him. He looked up, an elderly man whose uniform seemed to be a little too big for him. "I'm afraid I cannot rid you of your chains," he told Paul affably, "at least not yet. But you will be allowed to rent an apartment or house for yourself, at your own expense. A soldier will be on guard there, but you'll be chained to him only when you leave the house. You may receive visits or make them. You will not be allowed to work for gain and you must abstain from public speaking. That is all."

Outside of the prefect's office Julius said, grinning: "Now you're right back where you were in Caesarea. This may take months or it may take years."

"I wanted to come to Rome," Paul replied. "And I am in Rome."

The community found a house for him in the eleventh district, not far from the little island in the Tiber. Fortunately it was a one-story house and not an apartment in one of the many six-story tenement houses full of noise and often the residence of people of doubtful repute. Lukas and Aristarchus, too, found quarters in the neighborhood.

On the third day after his arrival Paul sent for a number of Jewish leaders and was told that they had not heard anything about him and his case, either by letter or by messenger.

He raised his hands. "It is because I hope as Israel hopes that I wear these chains." He invited them to come, as many of them as possible, so that he could speak to them about the Way, and they accepted politely. "We ask for nothing better than to hear what your opinions are." But one gnarled old man said stiffly: "All we know of this sect of yours is that it is opposed everywhere."

The meeting took place. It began at dawn. Ever since the edict of Claudius had been revoked, early in Nero's reign—and no one really knew why—Jews had been streaming back to the capital of the world. There were at least twenty perhaps as many as twenty-five thousand of them here and there were synagogues in every district, but particularly on the outskirts of the city. At least thirty learned rabbis were present and the "gerusiarchs" and even some of the "Fathers" of many synagogues.

What happened was what had happened so many times before, in Damascus and Jerusalem, in Lystra and Derbe and in Corinth. This Paul was teaching an authority superseding, no, surpassing that of Moses. He was setting up a Messiah who had died the shameful death on the gibbet. They quoted texts at Paul and at each other. They agreed and disagreed and fought each other in little groups. Some left in a huff. Some pleaded, entreated, argued and shouted.

Paul tried hard to keep his patience. He knew that it was not easy for them and he knew why. He could hear himself in many of the arguments used against him, young Saul fighting for all he was worth against Rabbi Stephanos, eyes flashing, arms flailing.

But at sunset they rose to go, still disagreeing with him and with each other.

Paul, too, rose. "Well did the Holy Spirit speak through Isaias the prophet to our fathers: 'Go to this people and tell them: You will listen and listen, but for you there is no understanding; you will watch and watch, but for you there is no perceiving. The heart of this people has become dull, their ears are slow to listen, and they keep their eyes shut, so that they may never see with those eyes, or hear with those ears, or understand with that heart, and turn back to me, and win healing from me.'"

There was a terrible finality in expression and gesture as he added: "Take notice, then, that this message of salvation has been sent by God to the Gentiles, and they, at least, will listen to it."

He watched them depart, still arguing.

Turning back with a sigh, Paul saw three lonely figures still sitting in the room. He was so weary that for a moment he did not recollect the name of any of them.

The oldest, a man at least seventy years of age, said in a quiet, apologetic voice: "Brother Saul, suffer us to stay a little longer. We would like to hear more. . . ."

All weariness was gone.

*   *   *

The little house in the eleventh district saw many visitors. The simple people came in daytime, those in high positions mostly at night, like Senator Pudens.

"We have to be careful," the senator explained. "There is a stupid old law against what is called 'enemies of mankind' which encompasses all kinds of things, including magical ceremonies and foreign superstitions. The interpretation of the law is left to the magistrate in office and as there are many absurd rumors about the Way, there are some who regard it as a Jewish superstition. Poor Pomponia Graecina—she comes from Britain and is the wife of General Aulus Plautius—"

"I have heard of her."

"She would have been jailed, if the court had not decided to let her husband as pater familias try her himself. He did, in front of all his household and solemnly acquitted her."

"She denied Christ?"

"Not she. But she denied superstition, Jewish or otherwise."

"They can't imprison me." Paul smiled, shaking his chains.

But he soon found that there was something spectral and eerie about the atmosphere in Rome. It centered around the Palatine Hill.

"What do you expect," the senator said, with a shrug, but then broke off and looked significantly toward the adjacent room, where a guard was sitting, polishing his armor.

"You needn't worry about Tuscus," Paul said. "I baptized him this morning."

The senator grinned cheerfully. "Seems to be a dangerous business to guard you. Tuscus, eh? And how many others, I wonder."

"Some," Paul replied noncommittally.

"Undermining the Praetorian Guards! I hope you get them all and then people could sleep quietly at night. Petrus himself baptized me. He's gone north for a while. How different you are, you and he! Like fire and water."

"Both are needed," Paul said.

"He is very worried about the Emperor," Pudens told him. "He knows there are still a few decent men left who have some influence with Nero—Burrus, for instance, and, to some extent, Seneca, but he says: 'What can you expect from a man who murdered first his brother and then his mother?'"

"It is true, then?"

"Oh yes, it is true," Pudens said in a low voice. "We were told that Britannicus died of an epileptic fit. What really happened was that he was poisoned. I thought at first that it was Agrippina's work—after all, she had done exactly the same thing to her husband. But this time she was innocent and rather horrified to see how quickly her son had learned her own methods. Nero got the poison from Locusta, you know, the same woman whose services Agrippina employed when she did away with Claudius."

"And is it true that his mother conspired against him?"

"It was true at a time, I think, although Burrus says there was not much evidence. But she certainly wanted to rule, one way or the other. There was nothing she wouldn't do to be in power and to remain in power, nothing. She . . . there are things I cannot even get past my lips. She was a monster. Nero planned her death with the most elaborate care. . . ."

"She was on board a ship that foundered, I heard."

"It did not sink by accident, and she knew it as soon as it happened. So she told one of her ladies-in-waiting who was, like her, in the water, to shout for help in her name. The unfortunate woman did and was clubbed over the head by the oarsmen. That way Agrippina escaped. She was a good swimmer and very strong. The man in charge of her death, Admiral Anicetus, then sent killers to her villa. Later we were told that she had committed suicide because she knew that the conspiracy against her son had failed. Seneca should have invented a better story than that."

"Seneca! Do you really believe he had a hand in this?"

"He probably hadn't. But as Nero's First Minister he had to cover up what happened. That was four years ago; but now we may well be headed for another crisis."

"What do you mean?"

"Octavia," Pudens whispered. "There are strong rumors that Nero will divorce her. He's madly in love, everybody knows that."

Paul's face was dark. "With whom?"

"With Poppaea Sabina, the wife of his best friend, Otho. It's been going on for a long time. Some say that she instigated the murder of Agrippina, because she wants the throne herself and Agrippina seemed to be a far more powerful obstacle than poor little Octavia. She is working on him incessantly and with great skill."

"But her husband?"

"Otho? He has been promoted to Governor of Lusitania. That's far away in the west, even beyond Spain."

"The Emperor will give in to her, then?"

Senator Pudens raised his brows. "He would have done so long ago, if he didn't fear the consequences. Burrus told him point-blank: 'You can divorce Octavia, if you give her back her dowry.' And when Nero asked what he meant, Burrus said: 'The empire.'"

"A courageous man," Paul said.

"He and his guards are the men who would have to deal with the consequences Nero fears," Pudens said. "After all, Octavia was the late Emperor's daughter and Nero was his son only by adoption." The senator sighed. "That is what first made me go and hear Petrus speak," he said. "Rome is as rotten as her gods; a man desires to commit adultery so he prays to Venus for success. I was longing for decency. Little did I know that I would find so much more than that."

"I wonder if you ever heard of a woman called Acte, at court," Paul asked casually.

The senator gave him a look of surprise. "You know about her? Pomponia Graecina seems to think that she is one of us."

"What makes her think so?" Paul asked calmly.

"She says, it's known that Acte never takes part in any of the orgies at the palace, and she has heard, I don't know from whom, that Acte has read your great letter to the Roman community. She is supposed to have quoted from it to somebody. Nero was in love with her for a time, but that's been over for years."

"But she is still living at the palace."

"Where could she go, poor creature? There is one rather curious thing about her: she has no enemies; at least none that I know of. And Pomponia says it has always been like that."

"Surely the Empress . . ."

"Octavia never minded her and now the two women are friends. It takes courage, these days, to be known as a friend of Octavia.

Most people at court take pains not to encounter her at all, except at official functions. But no one speaks against Acte. It's said that Nero regards her as lucky to him, that he believes nothing can happen to him as long as she is in the palace. Yet he never goes to see her."

* * *

The news of Burrus' death reached Paul by way of one of his guards. The man was quite dejected. "We all liked him," he said. "When the centurion was a brute or a young tribune too snooty, a man could always get his rights from the prefect."

"How did he die?" Paul asked.

"Something wrong with his throat. The Emperor—he was so worried, he sent him his own physician, but that didn't help; fact is, the prefect got worse. Don't know anything much about the new man."

"Who is he?"

"Ofonius Tigellinus. Not a regular. Decurion says he'd been banished by Emperor Claudius for something and went to Greece, where he sold fish. Then he came back to Italy and bred horses in Apulia. Don't know whether it's the fish or the horses that make him the right man to be our prefect."

* * *

A few months later Rome heard officially that the Emperor was divorcing Octavia for unfaithfulness. The people soon knew that the charge was trumped up; that Octavia's servants had professed her innocence even under torture. The "evidence" put before the court was ludicrous. Nevertheless, she was declared guilty and banished to the Campania, where the country house of the late Prefect Burrus was put at her disposal. Burrus had left it to the Emperor in his will.

Demonstrations took place as the young ex-Empress left the city. They multiplied when Nero married Poppaea Sabina.

Riots occurred. Statues of the beautiful woman were thrown off their pedestals and mutilated.

Ofonius Tigellinus, the new Prefect of the Praetorian Guards, quelled the riots and, strongly supported by the new Empress, suggested a series of drastic measures to be taken. Thoroughly frightened, Nero agreed.

Another trumped-up charge accused Octavia of conspiracy. She was banished to the island of Pandataria. A few days after her arrival she was given the order to commit suicide. When she refused, soldiers bound, opened the veins in her arms and legs and threw her into a hot bath where she suffocated.

"They cut off her head and sent it to the palace," Pudens told Paul. "Nero refused to look at it, but Poppaea did, gleefully. And the Senate! The Senate . . ." Pudens was shaking with indignation. "There was a meeting today," he went on. "I knew about the agenda and excused myself for reasons of health. The Senate was asked to and did vote presents to all the gods in gratitude for the death of a dangerous enemy of the state. Octavia!"

Paul remained silent.

"Your case may take years now," Pudens went on. "Tigellinus has no time for anything but conspiracies. He smells them out, he hunts them down and when there aren't any he invents them. As long as he can report conspiracies he knows that his position is safe."

When the senator had gone, Paul tried in vain to concentrate on the letter he had started dictating before dusk to Aristarchus, addressed to the community of Ephesus. He did not want to have Aristarchus called back to him at so late an hour, only to tell him that his thoughts would not come. Once more the terrible vision of Rome as a seven-headed monster was before his eyes, a monster like the Lernaean hydra of Greek lore, whose heads grew again when they were cut off. The head Tiberius had been cut off and Caligula grew. Caligula was cut off and Claudius grew instead; now it was Nero.

Would he live to see the end of the monster and the glorious return of the Lord?

"How long, oh Lord," he prayed.

The thought came to him on silent wings that the Church, too, was growing all the time under the eyes of the Risen One who was sitting at the right hand of God, above the heavens, high above all princedoms and powers and virtues and dominations and every name that was known, not in the world only, but in the world to come. And God had put everything under His dominion, and made Him the Head to which the whole Church was joined, so that the Church was His Body, the completion of Him who everywhere and in all things was complete.

There was no need to write this down now. He would never forget it. Tomorrow he would dictate it to Aristarchus.

The guard was entering, large, lumbering Corax, a new one. He was grinning sheepishly. "Lady to see you," he announced.

Paul frowned. "It is late . . ." he began.

"Great lady," the guard said. "Came in a litter with palace markings."

Behind the man's broad back a woman's voice said diffidently: "May I come in, please?"

Corax stepped aside.

The woman, standing in the door threw back her veil. "I'm afraid you won't recognize me," she said sadly. "I'm Acte."

CHAPTER THIRTY-SEVEN

PAUL GAZED at her silently. Acte. She had been a child when he saw her last, in Antioch. Now she was a woman of twenty-six or seven. She belonged to Christ when he saw her last. Now she belonged to Nero. He rose slowly. She did not move.

"Come nearer," he said.

She approached. By the light of the battered old pewter oil-lamp he could see that lines were already beginning to form around her eyes and the corners of her mouth.

"Why have you come to see me?" he asked, not unkindly. "And how did you find me?"

The second question was easier to answer. "One of the guards told me," she said. "A man called Fabricius."

Paul nodded. He had baptized Fabricius four months ago. "How did he come to mention me?"

"He . . . he saw me crying. So he told me he knew a man who could bring comfort to people who suffered. He is a Christian."

"And have you come to be comforted?" he asked.

"I have come to ask for your help. There is someone who needs it above all others."

"You?"

"The Emperor."

Paul did not bat an eyelash. "Is he aware of it?" he asked.

Acte took a deep breath. "He feels it . . . there are moments when he feels it, I know that."

"Does he know that you are here?"

"No."

"Does he know anything about me?"

"I don't think so."

Paul shook his head.

"I know it sounds foolish," she said hastily. "Perhaps it is, too. But it's the only chance. I . . . I took a great risk coming here. He doesn't allow me to leave the palace at any time. He . . . he believes that I am . . . that he is safe only when I am in the palace." She looked aside, embarrassed. "It is the only thing that remains," she added tonelessly.

"He is in danger only through his own actions," Paul said gravely.

"His actions . . . the ones you mean . . . are born of fear. Tiberius was murdered. Caligula was murdered. Claudius was murdered. He had no part in these deeds, but he knows that many people want him to die too. 'I must strike first,' he said to me once. 'Or else I am lost.' He still believes that and there are people who skillfully play on his feelings. Oh, if only you knew . . ."

"What?"

"He was good and noble, when I met him first," she said, "although he had seen nothing but evil and baseness all around him. There was a day, just after he became Emperor, when he was ready to abdicate and retire to Rhodus. . . ."

"With Octavia?" Paul asked harshly.

She hung her head. "No. With me. We meant everything to each other—at that time. His mother would not let him abdicate. She needed him on the throne. She wanted to rule through him. She had been ruling him all his life, chiding him, jeering at him, twisting his mind and soul. How often I've seen him suffer; how often I had to . . . make him human again, after she had left him and he sat there, black and brooding. I . . . I tried to be a good influence in his life, I wanted . . ." she broke off.

There was a pause.

"Never mind what I wanted," Acte went on. "I haven't come to talk about myself. I do not matter. He does. You do not know him; no one knows him as I do. To those around him he is only the one who can give them honors, rank, wealth . . . or exile and death. To the people he is the one to talk about, the great object of gossip; they whisper and giggle and turn up their eyes; and all they want to talk about is evil. They wallow in it, they taste it with all their senses and yet sit in judgment. The good he does they take for granted. He was a good ruler, in the first years of his reign, but they flatter him and flatter him, they tell him that he is a god, that every order of his is good and right because it is he who gives it. . . ."

Paul had listened intently. Now he asked: "Why do you think that I could be of help to him?"

"Because you are so near to the Lord."

"You still acknowledge our Lord?"

"Yes," she whispered.

"But you acted against His law."

"And I was punished. I am still being punished and shall be as long as I live."

"You know that?"

"That is why I said I do not matter. I have become powerless. The people who count with him now are Tigellinus, Petronius and his set and . . . she; the Empress. I am no more than an amulet, a talisman he keeps in the palace as some people will keep a 'lucky' feather or stone in their cupboards."

"That is then what you are to Nero," Paul said. "But what are you to Christ?"

She said nothing.

"You have followed a man not your husband," he went on. "The love of that man meant more to you than our Lord. You broke His law, you caused offense to Him who gave His Life for you; you caused pain and anguish to those who gave you your earthly life. Is your punishment just or unjust?"

"It is just," Acte said, her voice scarcely audible.

"Your punishment, you say, will last a lifetime; and well it may. But can you wish it to last beyond that? Can you want to be separated from our Lord forever? Or are you ready to repent and make your peace with Him?"

"I cannot repent my love."

"That," Paul said, "is not demanded of you. You came here, not for your sake but for Nero's sake; not to regain dominion over his body, but to ask for help in the struggle for his soul. Don't you see that your punishment is the remedy for your own soul, purifying it of what was wrong in your love, but not destroying that which is good?"

Outside, in the narrow corridor, the guard peered into the room. In the praetorium they told all kinds of stories about the old Jewish prisoner, and a strange one he was. There was the lady now, on her knees before him and he was making a weird gesture over her head and murmuring spells. She was crying.

Corax withdrew, before the old man could see him, and cautiously fingered the little piece of leather into which the priests of the Epona temple back home in Lutetia had inserted three hairs of the tail of one of the goddess' horses.

CHAPTER THIRTY-EIGHT

WHEN A CENTURION and six men came to fetch him early in the morning, Paul thought that the hour of his trial had arrived and that he would have to face Prefect Tigellinus or, more likely, one of his subordinates. But after a while he saw that they were not taking the way to the Praetorian camp; instead, they were approaching the Palatine Hill and at once Acte's visit to him, now more than two months ago, leaped back into his mind. Her last words to him were "Will you talk to Caesar?" And he replied: "I am his prisoner, awaiting the sentence of his court. He will know where to find me."

Could it be that she had really managed to persuade Nero to give him a hearing? He decided that she might have succeeded in arousing the ruler's curiosity. If so, anything was possible. One word displeasing to Nero's vanity, and the instant consequence was lifelong exile to a desert island or even death. Roman law, so strictly administered in the provinces, was a hollow mockery in Rome itself. Acte, of course, had never thought of such a possibility. Yes, they were leading him to the palace. Little had he thought, that day in Caesarea, when he appealed to Caesar, that he would really stand before Caesar himself! But then, there was little likelihood that his case would be discussed or even mentioned—unless he did so himself. He decided not to do so, and to say instead what he had to say—if the Emperor would let him. Then he prayed.

Through the gate, across the main court, another gate, stairs, and stairs again, statues, carpets and guards and an anteroom then another and a third. In the third he was allowed to sit down and was grateful for it, after the long walk. A number of people were assembled here: a worried-looking, elderly man, clutching a number of leatherbags, a jeweler probably, asked to put his wares before the Emperor; a matron with her two daughters, little more than children, but dressed up and painted to look like exotic birds, an old Egyptian with a face as wrinkled as a mummy's, on his lap a small ivory chest; and a dozen athletically built young men in the care of a *lanista,* the trainer of a school of fighters for the arena.

No one said a word. There was nothing the anteroom had not seen before. A little old Jew in chains, guarded by an officer and four men was no more of a sensation than the band of jugglers or the Persian trainer with a couple of tame leopards waiting in the adjacent room. The only thing that interested anyone was whether he would be allowed in the presence today or whether, like most of them, he would have to come back tomorrow.

When, after the better part of an hour, a richly dressed official appeared and pointed to Paul with a gold-tipped ebony stick no one dared so much as a whisper.

Led by the official the guards marched Paul along corridors that seemed endless, till they suddenly halted before a small door on the left. The official beat against it with his stick and it opened.

Again an anteroom, filled with slaves in the imperial livery.

Paul realized then that he had been led through the palace by way of passages used only by slaves. The audience was to be unofficial.

The man with the ebony stick vanished behind a heavy curtain at one end of the room and reappeared a few moments later. Pointing to Paul he said: "You may enter alone."

But as Paul walked towards the curtain, the official barred his way with the stick. "You will not speak to Caesar before he addresses you. You will not ask Caesar a question. You will not leave Caesar's presence before Caesar gives you permission. You will address Caesar simply as 'Divinity'. Enter . . . *now!*"

The stick was withdrawn, the heavy folds of the curtain were lifted slightly.

Paul walked on. He found himself in a large, oblong room. Floor and walls were of yellow marble. There was no furniture at all except for a narrow table in the middle, at which a tall, slender Numidian in a white tunic was standing with his back to Paul, kneading a large, pinkish mass.

A melodious, somewhat affected voice said: "Enough, Jubal, enough, you're killing me. Help me up."

The Numidian, grinning, pulled up the pinkish mass very gently —it was a human body, it was the body of a man, a man, stark naked, soft, babyish, pot-bellied, a round face with the beginnings of a double chin, a woman's mouth, full-lipped and too near the nose, reddish hair, set in curls down the forehead, the face Paul had seen on coins long before he had set foot on Italian soil, but fatter and less dignified.

The Lord of the Empire looked at Paul and giggled. "Epaphroditus is a fool," he said. "Isn't he, Jubal? This little man can't be dangerous. Why, you could tear him apart with two fingers. Don't be frightened, old man, he won't do it unless I tell him to but he could, you know; he's very strong. Used to be a fairly good gladiator, not exactly first class, but fairly good, now don't protest, Jubal, you know quite well that you couldn't match Spiculus or Barbatio or Myrillus, not at your best. On the other hand, I wouldn't like any of them to give me a massage."

"I also am a gladiator, Caesar," Paul said.

"Of the mind you mean, eh?"

"The mind and the spirit, yes, Caesar."

"The spirit." Nero frowned a little. "Spirit. Spirits. Spirits frighten me sometimes. Do you know a remedy against dark dreams? That's where I meet them and I cannot give orders to my dreams and be obeyed. I talked to Menes about it—he's my new physician, an Egyptian, the Greeks are all charlatans—but even he could only recommend silly things: I must have my last meal earlier, I mustn't eat this, that or the other in the evening. You're a Jew and the Jews know a good many things. You may do my arms now, Jubal, but gently. I don't want to sweat. There's no time for a bath again, they'll come to dress me any moment now."

"Our actions are recorded in our soul," Paul said. "In a dream memories are released sometimes and we are reminded of things we would like to forget. All of us have done wrong, at times, and our conscience . . ."

"Dreams, dreams . . . the world of shadows is a world of dreams," Nero said. "There's a poem in this, I think. I shall tell Lucan to work on it. The theme is not big enough for me."

"You are right to direct your mind to the big issues, Caesar," Paul said. "Not to the land of dreams, but to the great reality of life to come, the life compared to which life on earth is no more than that of childhood. Life after death."

"You believe in that?" Nero was interested. "Surely you contradict the philosophers . . . the right arm now, Jubal . . . and then we'd be back in the shadow world again."

"No, Caesar. This life on earth is the shadow world. The real life is one of absolute happiness for those who follow the Way."

"The Way, the Way, I must have heard that before. Oh yes, of course, Acte mentioned it sometimes. But tell me . . . in this other life of yours, shall I be Caesar?"

"What you will be there God alone can decide," Paul said. "He is the Judge. All we know is that some of those who are the first here will be the last there and some of the last here will be the first in Heaven."

Nero stared at him. "You are very frank, little Jew."

"What good would I be to you if I weren't?" Paul replied quietly. "Of those who say only what you wish them to say you have enough."

"I don't like people saying disagreeable things," Nero said sulkily. "I never liked Thersites and I always think Ulysses was quite right for punishing him the way he did."

"Thersites," Paul said, "was his own messenger, or rather that of his own envy. I am the messenger of Jesus who is the Christ and I have come to bring you the Truth."

Nero blinked at him. "What do you expect me to do for you in exchange?" he asked. "Give you your freedom?"

"No, Caesar. The Truth is not a matter for sale or barter. I am a prisoner. But there is no imprisoning the Word of God."

"The legs now, Jubal. What is that truth of yours, little Jew?"

"That God has redeemed the world from sin by the life, the death and the resurrection of His only-begotten Son."

"I am worshiped as a god," Nero said.

Paul stared at him, hard. "And do you believe in your own godhead, Caesar?"

Nero looked down, blinking rapidly.

"Sometimes I do. When I give birth to a poem . . . when I sing. . . ."

"What you feel then is that you are nearer God," Paul said patiently. "Such is the purpose of art. But . . ."

"Art," Nero exclaimed. "That is the only thing worth living for. I cannot tell you how bored I am with politics and affairs of state. They always want me to do this and that and the other thing, they work me to death. . . . See? Here they're coming to dress me for still another state function. Let me go, Jubal."

The room was suddenly swarming with slaves of both sexes.

"The sandals with the amethyst buttons," Nero ordered. "The tunic with the silver palm embroidery. Go away, Attys, I don't want any of those belts. Where is Ismene with the mirror?"

"Here I am, Divinity."

The beautiful girl had the most difficult job—to hold and move the four-foot sheet of polished silver in such a way that Nero could always see himself. Lynx-eyed, she watched every movement of her master. He was nearsighted—Ismene knew the exact distance from which he could still see clearly. He was nervous and shifty—Ismene seemed to divine a split second before in which direction he would turn next.

"Very little make-up," Nero ordered. "I have to go out into daylight."

"The new poems of Lucanus," the chief lector announced.

"Decidedly not," Nero said. "I'd rather—go away. You go on, little Jew. Tell me more about this god of yours and of his son."

The vestiplicae came forward with the great mantle of purple silk. The two freedwomen in charge of the jewel box knelt before the Emperor with a tray full of rings and bracelets and another with a selection of necklaces. The precious stones sparkled like fire.

"Jesus of Nazareth was born, not in a palace, but in a stable," Paul said. "Yet at the mention of His name every knee will bow. He was and is and will be the Truth incarnate. Heaven and earth will pass away but His words will not pass away."

"The rubies," Nero said, "not the emeralds." He was looking with satisfaction at his reflection in Ismene's mirror.

The great moment came for the vestiplicae. With a movement as graceful as that of dancers they let the purple mantle fly up and settle in just the right folds on the Emperor's shoulders.

Nero turned right and left before the mirror. "It is well done," he said graciously and as all the slaves knelt down he walked away to the adjacent room whose curtains opened before him as by magic. For a moment a whole series of rooms became visible: those more distant were filled with a glittering mass of robes and uniforms. The court was awaiting the Lord of the Empire.

Like a swarm of birds the slaves withdrew.

Paul was alone. "Lord," he prayed in Hebrew. "Lord, Lord, I offer up to thee my weakness and humiliation."

A hand touched his arm, a brown, sinewy hand.

"He's no god," Jubal muttered disdainfully. *"I* know. When I touch him just a little hard he squeals like an old woman. Is it true what you said about another life when we're dead?"

"Yes, Jubal."

The ex-gladiator rubbed his cheek. "We're all told to call him Divinity," he said. "Epaphroditus told you too, I'm sure. He can be very nasty if you don't call him that. You never said anything but 'Caesar.' You've got courage. *He* hasn't got any. I know. I trust a man who's got courage. Can I come and see you and will you tell me more about it?"

CHAPTER THIRTY-NINE

THE YOUNG TRIBUNE in the judgment chair looked at the documents in the case. After a while he said: "You have been here almost three years. The late Prefect Burrus remarks that your accusers were not represented at the time of your arrival." He looked up. "They don't seem to have turned up even yet," he drawled.

The prisoner said nothing.

"Surely they've had ample time. . . ." The tribune buried his nose in the documents again. Report of the Procurator of Judaea, document in a shocking state, but the text still legible and decidedly favorable in the usual cautious way; these old fogeys never seemed to come to a definite statement. Report of the officer in charge of transporting the prisoner: favorable again. As for the "res" itself, quite impossible to make head or tail of it. A matter for Jews, not for a Roman court. If the procurator of that province couldn't decide it, who could? One could send the man back to where he came from, of course. Endless documents to be signed, request to the shipping authorities, guards for the prisoner, expenses, signature of the prefect, quite a nuisance. Besides, old Festus was no longer there; was no longer anywhere, in fact. He had died and there was a new man there, Albinus. *He* wouldn't be grateful to be burdened with another old case of his predecessor; might write an irate letter to the prefect, what's the right of appeal coming to if a case that has gone to Caesar comes back undecided. Quite right, too.

The tribune thought of an adjournment. Discuss the case with a few older colleagues, was it or was it not a crime to belong to a Jewish sect not conforming in some points with the beliefs of the Jewish ecclesiastic authorities in Jerusalem. They'd laugh at him. What did it matter to Rome? What mattered was to get through this and a few hundred more cases of appeal. The prefect had said so, emphatically. Approach him in person? The tribune shuddered at the idea. Tigellinus had no time for nonsense.

He made up his mind. "In the name of the Divine Emperor," he began, and at once the pens of the recording clerks went into motion. As soon as the formula of acquittal was pronounced, the guard next to the prisoner struck off the chains. He had worn them for almost five years. Now he was free to go wherever he liked.

*   *   *

Six weeks later the tribune was ordered to appear before the prefect.

"We seem to have a prisoner called Paul of Tarsus here," Tigellinus said. "Subprefect Maximus tells me he's one of your cases. I have received an order from the Divine Emperor in regard to him."

The tribune gulped. He felt like fainting.

"The Lady Acte seems to have put in a word for him," Tigellinus went on. "The Emperor wants the man acquitted. See to it at once."

"Y-yes, sir," the tribune croaked.

"What's the matter with you, man, are you ill?"

"N-no, sir."

"Then get out."

The tribune stumbled out of the office.

CHAPTER FORTY

IN THE MIDDLE of July of the year sixty-four, according to Christian reckoning, catastrophe befell Rome.

A fire broke out in the vicinity of the Circus Maximus, among the many wooden sheds there. It jumped over to the shops, the stables and warehouses. There had been no rain for weeks and all wood was dried out. The fire raced up the Via Nova to the Forum and along the Via Triumphalis to the Caelian Hill and the Subura, with its tens of thousands of lightly built houses.

Every attempt to stop it failed. The fire brigade seemed to be utterly inefficient, headless, planless and incredibly slow.

When men were seen throwing torches into houses, the rumor went that the slaves had revolted. But in many places the men with the torches were recognized as soldiers out of uniform—or so people said.

Messengers hurried to the Emperor who, with the whole court, was in Antium, and Nero at once returned to Rome with Tigellinus and other high officials. He inspected and directed, he was the Father of all Romans, he promised help, food, new houses. But the people did not listen and soon it was known that the Emperor had spent hours composing a special hymn dealing with the destruction of Troy, that he intended to sing it in sight of the burning city—that he had done so, applauded by the court. People remembered that he had often complained about the bad odors of the poor districts, especially in summer; that he had spoken of building a new capital of the empire to be called Neronia or Neropolis. They began to put two and two together. Riots occurred, small revolts, ruthlessly curbed by the Praetorian Guards.

And the fire went on burning, although now everyone could see that those in power were trying to stop it. Tigellinus had hundreds of houses torn down around the Esquiline Hill alone to stop the flames from spreading farther.

After seven days the fire subsided. Of the fourteen districts of Rome no more than four remained intact, including the Trans-Tiber. The number of people who burned to death, were murdered or died from lack of food and water could never be counted.

The administration did its utmost to master the situation. Huge transports of wheat were commanded from Egypt, fruit from Sicily, cattle from Apulia. But the palace soon became aware of the fact that all these efforts did not suffice. The people were in a nasty mood. The riots increased and huge demonstrations took place, with agitators all over the city screaming against the Senate, against Tigellinus and . . . the Emperor himself.

The throne was in danger.

A scapegoat was needed and found. The idea of arson, at first hushed up and suppressed wherever it turned up, was now encouraged and even proclaimed. At last the criminals had been found, not individuals, but a whole sect of enemies of mankind, bent on the destruction of the empire, the followers of a criminal, executed long ago and called after him: Christians.

The hunt was on.

*　　*　　*

They died in the arena, mangled by lions, tigers, leopards and bears. They died as living torches in the newly reopened imperial gardens; they were torn to pieces in the streets and tortured to death at festivities in the palace. They died in overcrowded jails from want of air and of disease.

They died, but they would not revoke their Faith. And many died singing.

People began to ask themselves what kind of faith this could be that made people adhere to it in the face of the most horrible death, when they could have saved themselves by denying it? What would they themselves do in such a situation? Would they be ready to die for Jupiter or Venus? For Apollo or Mars, for Diana, Leto, Vulcan, Mercury or the great Cybele?

And these children, dying in the arena, torn to pieces by Molossian dogs, could they have set Rome on fire?

There was much whispering going on.

But the hunt continued. The secret police tried hard to find the "ringleaders" of the sect, especially a certain Petrus, also called Cephas, of whom it was said that he never left Rome for one single day during the persecutions. Some people said that, giving in at last to the entreaties of his disciples, he had left the city, only to return a few hours later when he had had a vision of Christ going to Rome to be crucified there for a second time.

Slowly the hunt spread to the provinces.

*   *   *

Nero was building. The new imperial palace was to be called The Golden House. "I don't know what made me think of that name," he said, "but it's been in my mind a long time."

Petronius murmured something about "divine inspiration." A few months later Nero forced him to commit suicide and confiscated his estate, worth many millions, which in turn served to pay some of the costs of the divine inspiration.

The same thing happened to Seneca whose immense fortune, over three hundred million sesterces, the Emperor badly needed.

Tigellinus proved to be a pastmaster in the art of discovering conspiracies of wealthy people.

The Empress was expecting a child. But she was incautious enough to chide Nero when he burst into her suite late at night, drunk after an orgy with horse-trainers, stable boys and the women to match. Nero kicked her in the abdomen and she died the same night from internal haemorrhage.

The Emperor had her embalmed, in the Egyptian style.

There was only one thing that could console him now: he would travel to Greece, with an enormous retinue, and appear on the stage in all the cities and towns of the very country of art. He would compete with the best for the palm, as a singer, a poet and a charioteer.

He left Rome in the charge of his trusted friend Helius, a freedman of a character very similar to that of his imperial master.

*　　*　　*

Acte remained in Rome, in the Golden House. She had seen the man she loved disintegrate into a monster, surpassing even Caligula in his cruelty and folly. When the persecution of the Christians began, she had asked for an audience, with him alone.

Nero granted it. When she appeared before him he said: "I know everything you want to tell me and I do not wish to hear it. Instead, you listen to me: there are grave reasons of state for what is going on. I have no intention of interfering. I will hear no pleadings for mercy for anyone. It is a capital crime to belong to a certain sect. Some people have drawn my attention to you as a potential member . . . be quiet, I say. I have told them never to mention that again and not to take any notice if anyone else should mention it . . . *including yourself.* Now go. Go!"

She soon discovered that people at court had come to regard her as just a little deranged. Everyone was polite and somewhat embarrassed in her presence.

Occasionally she was able to send out a warning, when she heard of any particular region of Rome that was to be raided by the Praetorian Guards.

In spring Helius succeeded at last in arresting Petrus, and had him crucified, like his Master, but with his head downward. It was said that Petrus himself asked for that, "as he was not worthy to die in the same fashion as Christ."

Acte received the news from one of the four guards she knew to be Christians. The man's name was Tuscus.

A few weeks later Tuscus was on watch at the palace again and Acte could see from the way he looked at her that he had more news.

She approached until she was near enough to hear him whisper: "Friend of yours is to die tomorrow morning. Man called Paul of Tarsus."

Her body became rigid. "It can't be," she whispered back. "He left Rome long ago; years ago."

"He's been back for some time. Arrested in Asia, in Troas, brought back here. Better turn round, noble lady, people mustn't see us talk."

She obeyed. From behind her back the whisper went on, inexorably. "Only found out myself last week. Couldn't let you know earlier. He was tried. Helius himself was in charge of the court. Condemned to death by the sword."

Paul . . . Paul . . .

The whispering voice started again: "Friend of mine saw him in jail. One of us. Paul gave him some messages. One for you."

"For . . . me . . . ?"

"It's about your parents, noble lady. They're safe."

She was trembling like a leaf.

"They're in Antioch," the voice went on. "Paul sent them there. Your father is one of the elders there, helping the bishop. Nothing has happened to our people in Syria so far."

"Paul saved them," she whispered. "Oh, Tuscus, I must see him. . . . I must see him once more, before he goes to our Lord."

"Can't take you where he is, noble lady."

"I'll give you every jewel I have, every piece of gold, for the jailer and his people. . . ."

"Impossible, my lady. He's been taken to the Tullianum. They let them down there with a rope and drag them up with a hook. Many common criminals in it, too. Won't let you near the place."

Sobs racked her body.

The voice came again. "Tell you what I'll do, lady. They'll lead him away tomorrow morning at dawn. Can't kill him within the city, it's against the law for a citizen who's had a regular trial. They'll have to go to the third milestone. If you'll be at the Porta Trigemina . . . no, better still, at the corner where the Ostian Way starts. They'll pass there and if—someone coming. Better go, my lady."

"The Lord bless you for what you've done for me," Acte

whispered. Then she walked away slowly, her head erect. Only when she reached her own rooms did she break down.

*   *   *

She had to leave the palace in a litter and with one of her maids. Any other way would have caused gossip among the officials at the gate. Even so she might have to think of something to tell them.

She could not think of anything. But no one questioned her and the centurion on watch gave her a courteous salute. She was veiled and he probably took her for the mistress of some official, returning home instead of leaving.

"Porta Trigemina," she told the slaves.

It was still dark, but the sky began to clear as they approached the city gate.

"Stop here," she ordered. "And wait for me."

The four men put the litter down and she stepped out. She had not walked more than half a dozen steps when the maid came running after her.

"I didn't tell you to come," Acte said.

"Oh, but my lady, you can't walk alone, it isn't fitting."

Acte looked at the young face. Myra was not a Christian and had been with her only a few months. "I'll take you with me," she said, "if you promise to forget everything you see or hear."

"I promise, my lady."

They walked on.

When they reached the corner where the Ostian Way started, Acte stopped. The sky was red, as red as blood, and she shuddered, drawing her cloak closer around her shoulders.

But the red paled and became gold. The air was full of bird calls; the birds themselves remained invisible in the heavy morning mist. The meadow on the left looked as if it were steaming.

After a while Acte could hear footsteps and the clanking of armor. They were coming. She lifted her veil.

Six soldiers. Two lictors. The prisoner. More soldiers.

She could not move. All strength was drained from her.

But when Paul's eyes fell on her, she raised her hands. "Sha-ul," she cried. It was what she had called him when she was a child.

He stopped, and the lictors to whom he was chained stopped as well.

The centurion in charge turned his head. "Make it short," he said curtly.

Paul's face was radiant. "I have fought a good fight," he said. "I have finished my course. I have kept the Faith. To die is gain."

Acte fell on her knees and he made the sign of the cross over her. Then he walked on.

Rising, Acte saw the little troop turn left and march across the meadow and into a golden mist that engulfed them.

Slowly she began to walk back.

A shy voice beside her said: "My lady . . ."

She gave no answer. She walked on.

"My lady, I won't be able to keep my promise."

Acte stopped and looked at the girl.

Myra's face was stained with tears. "I shall never forget it as long as I live," she whispered. "How can he go to die with such joy?"

"He goes to Christ."

"Won't you tell me more about it, my lady?"

Acte closed her eyes. "He has given me work to do," she thought. She said, "I will tell you. . . ."